...s *of Coin and Spice*

*Winner of the 2008 Mythopoeic Award
for Adult Literature for* The Orphan's Tales *Duology*

"A fairy-tale-lover's wildest dream come true. Cleverly examining and reconstructing the conventions of the fairy tale, especially the traditional roles of men and women. Valente has created a thought-provoking storytelling tour de force."
—*Publishers Weekly*

"Extraordinary... no summary can do justice to the bedazzling intricacies on bountiful display here." —*Kirkus Reviews* (starred review)

"A lovely, epical, awe-inspiring piece of work." —*Booklist*

"In Catherynne M. Valente's imaginary realms, stories splinter and reflect, causing the sweetest sensation of vertigo for the reader.... Flashes of wry humor balance Valente's lush imaginings.... It's the postmodern version of the never-ending story." —*Los Angeles Times*

"A masterpiece of imagery and sensual detail while evoking an entire world through the medium of mythmaking. As with its predecessor, this *Arabian Nights*–like fantasy belongs in every library." —*Library Journal* (starred review)

"For fans of smart, surrealistic fairy tales steeped in *Arabian Nights* lore and the gnarled fables of Hans Christian Andersen. The overall effect is intoxicating." —*Entertainment Weekly*

D1016131

"Abundantly imaginative, gorgeously written, and stunningly and intricately framed . . . Valente's imagination is prodigious, and she weaves lovely new patterns with existing mythological threads, and she finds gorgeous new fabric as well. And all knitted together with poetic prose . . . should be looked for on next year's award short lists." —*Locus*

"Valente's language is lovely, her imagery evocative, and she can make even the ugliest and strangest things seem briefly luminescent. I loved it." —*Fantasy & Science Fiction*

PRAISE FOR

## The Orphan's Tales: In the Night Garden

*Winner of the James Tiptree Jr. Award*
*Short-listed for the World Fantasy Award*
*Named One of Kirkus Reviews Top 10 SF Books of 2006*
*Selected for the 2007 New York Public Library Books for the Teen Age List*

"A work of beautifully relayed, interlinked fairy tales."
—*Kirkus Reviews* (starred review)

"There is an entire mythology in this book, in which the themes of familiar fairy tales are picked apart and rearranged into a new and wonderful whole. . . . A wonderful interpretation of what fairy tales ought to be. The illustrations by Michael Kaluta constitute an excellent supplement." —*Booklist* (starred review)

"A fabulous, recursive *Arabian Nights*–style narrative . . . lush, hallucinogenic." —*Publishers Weekly*

"Lyrical, witchy . . . mixes feminist grit with pixie dust."
—*Entertainment Weekly*

"Valente's lyrical prose and masterful storytelling brings to life a fabulous world, solidifies Valente's place at the forefront of imaginative storytelling, and belongs in libraries of all sizes." —*Library Journal*

"Valente weaves an intricate, exquisite web.... While the obvious comparison is to *One Thousand and One Nights*, the spirit and artistry of these tales may be even closer to those of Angela Carter. These are fairy tales that bite and bleed." —*Washington Post Book World*

"Written with poetic imagination and tremendous skill ... Valente, like her nameless orphan in the garden, is a captivating storyteller."
—*Contra Costa Times*

"What Valente has accomplished in this book is far more than a collection of stories; she has sown the seeds of an entire mythos all her own. The blooms in her night garden dazzle and bewitch, and are wondrous fair." —SFRevu.com

"Catherynne M. Valente uses this inventive basis to weave in and out of tales that are part nouveau mythology and part fairy tale, interflowing in a river of dreams. Her use of language is often quite beautiful, and the basic elements with which she works are further enhanced by knavish twists of standard fantasy archetypes.... The spellbinding descriptive almost forces readers to continue just a few pages more, the stories can be appreciated equally by children and adults, and both good and evil are vividly defined in the mind's eye.... The overall effect is to make reading *In the Night Garden* as close to a genuinely magical experience as it's possible to get, and elevates the work above most other contemporary fantasy. One day in the not too distant future, it could easily come to be regarded as a literary classic. Savvy school librarians should add it to their lists right now. Cover to cover, this is an astonishing work which reinterprets and redefines the modern classic fairy tale." —SFSite.com

"I really, really enjoyed this book; it was a pleasure to read, from start to finish, and the end note of the volume . . . was unexpectedly moving." —*Fantasy & Science Fiction*

"Valente's prose is creative and sophisticated; her imagery is intricate and arresting. Any lover of well-written fantasy will find much to enjoy about Valente's book." —*Green Man Review*

"[A] jaunt into fantastic fiction that is *epic* in the truest sense of the word. *The Orphan's Tales* is the poet, short-fiction writer, and novelist maximizing her entire skill set in an offering that caters to the sensibilities of the fan of all forms. Catherynne M. Valente is a *storyteller*." —Fantasybookspot.com

"A fine patchwork of tales, quilted in diverse colours and textures. Refreshingly original in both style and form, *In the Night Garden* should delight lovers of myth and folklore."
—Juliet Marillier, author of the Sevenwaters trilogy

"Catherynne Valente weaves layer upon layer of marvels in her debut novel. *In the Night Garden* is a treat for all who love puzzle stories and the mystical language of tale spinners."
—Carol Berg, author of *Daughter of Ancients*

"Fabulous tale spinning in the tradition of story cycles such as *The Arabian Nights*. Lyrical, wildly imaginative and slyly humorous, Valente's prose possesses an irrepressible spirit."
—K. J. Bishop, author of *The Etched City*

"Astonishing work! Valente's endless invention and mythic range are breathtaking. It's as if she's gone night-wandering, and plucked a hundred cultures out of the air to deliver their stories to us."
—Ellen Kushner, host of public radio's *Sound & Spirit*; author of *Thomas the Rhymer*

Also by
# CATHERYNNE M. VALENTE

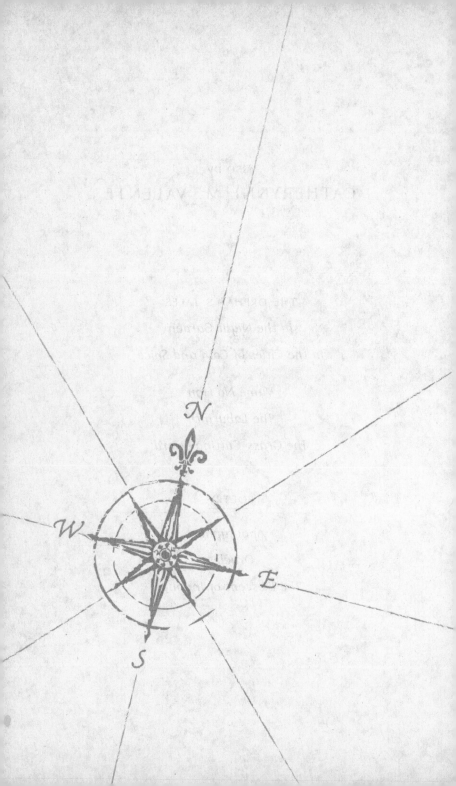

# PALIMPSEST

## CATHERYNNE M. VALENTE

BANTAM BOOKS

PALIMPSEST

A Bantam Spectra Book / March 2009

Published by Bantam Dell
A Division of Random House, Inc.
New York, New York

Book design by Sarah Smith

Library of Congress Cataloging-in-Publication Data
Valente, Catherynne M., 1979–
Palimpsest / Catherynne Valente.
p. cm.
ISBN 978-0-553-38576-2 (pbk.)
1. Locksmiths—Fiction.  2. Bookbinders—Fiction.  3. Girls—Fiction.
4. Beekeepers—Fiction.  I. Title.

PS3622.A4258P36 2009
813'.6—dc22
2008035650

Printed in the United States of America
Published simultaneously in Canada

www.bantamdell.com

BVG   10 9 8 7 6 5 4 3

Look, how the floor of heaven
Is thick inlaid with patines of bright gold:
There's not the smallest orb which thou behold'st
But in his motion like an angel sings,
Still quiring to the young-eyed cherubins;
Such harmony is in immortal souls;
But, whilst this muddy vesture of decay
Doth grossly close it in, we cannot hear it.

—WILLIAM SHAKESPEARE
*The Merchant of Venice*

For Dmitri,
the map by which
I found this place

# FRONTISPIECE:

## The Cradle of Becoming and Unbecoming

# 16th and Hieratica

**ON THE CORNER OF 16TH STREET AND HIERATICA** a factory sings and sighs. Look: its thin spires flash green, and spit long loops of white flame into the night. Casimira owns this place, as did her father and her grandmother and probably her most distant progenitor. It is pleasant to imagine them, curling and uncurling their proboscis-fingers against machines of stick and bone. There has always been a Casimira, except when, occasionally, there is a Casimir.

Workers carry their lunches in clamshells. They wear extraordi-nary uniforms: white and green scales laid one over the other, clinging obscenely to the skin, glittering in the spirelight. They wear nothing else; every wrinkle and curve is visible. They dance into the factory, their serpentine bodies writhing a shift change, undulating under the punch clock with its cheerful metronomic chime. Their eyes are piscine, third eyelid half-drawn in drowsy pleasure as they side step and gambol and spin to the rhythm of the machines.

And what do they make in this factory? Why, the vermin of Palimpsest. There is a machine for stamping cockroaches with glis-tening green carapaces, their maker's mark hidden cleverly under the left wing. There is a machine for shaping and pounding rats, soft gray fur stiff and shining when they are first released. There is another mold for squirrels, one for chipmunks and one for plain mice. There is a centrifuge for spiders, a lizard-pour, a delicate and ancient machine which turns out flies and mosquitoes by turn, so exquisite, so perfect that they seem to be made of nothing but copper wire, spun sugar, and light. There is a printing press for graffiti which spits out effervescent letters in scarlet, black, angry yellows, and the trademark green of Casimira. They fly from the high windows and flatten themselves against walls, trestles, train cars.

When the shift horn sounds at the factory, the long antler-trumpet passed down to Casimira by the one uncle in her line who defied tradition and became a humble hunter, setting the whole clan to a vociferous but well-fed consternation, a wave of life wafts from the service exit: moles and beetles and starlings and bats, ants and worms and moths and mantises. Each gleaming with its last coat of sealant, each quivering with near-invisible devices which whisper into their atavistic minds that their mistress loves them, that she thinks of them always, and longs to hold them to her breast.

In her office, Casimira closes her eyes and listens to the teeming masses as they whisper back to their mother. At the end of each day they tell her all they have learned of living.

It is necessary work. No family has been so often formally thanked by the city as hers.

———

On the other side of the street: a fortune-teller's shop. Palm fronds cross before the door. Inside are four red chairs with four lustral basins before them, filled with ink, swirling and black. Orlande lumbers in, a woman wrapped in ragged fox fur. Her head amid heaps of scarves is that of a frog, mottled green and bulbous-eyed. A licking pink tongue keeps its place in her wide mouth. Her webbed hands are full of cups: a swill of tea afloat with yellow leaves. She spills not a drop, and the tea is sweet, sweeter than anything.

She does not see individual clients.

Thus it is that four strangers sit in the red chairs, strip off their socks, plunge their feet into the ink-baths, and hold hands under an amphibian stare. This is the first act of anyone entering Palimpsest: Orlande will take your coats, sit you down, and make you family. She will fold you four together like Quartos. She will draw you each a card—look, for you it is the Broken Ship reversed, which signifies Perversion, a Long Journey without Enlightenment, Gout—and tie your hands together with red yarn. Wherever you go in Palimpsest, you are bound to these strangers who happened onto Orlande's salon just when you did, and you will go nowhere, eat no capon or dormouse, drink no oversweet port that they do not also taste, and they will visit no whore that you do not also feel beneath you, and until that ink washes from your feet—which, given that Orlande is a creature of the marsh and no stranger to mud, will be some time—you cannot breathe but that they breathe also.

———

There are four of them there now. Shall we peer in? Shall we disrupt their private sacraments? Are you and I such unrepentant voyeurs? I think we must be, else why have we come so close to the door of cassia, the windows of cracked glass? Let us peer; let us disrupt. It is our nature.

A girl with blue hair slumps slack against her chair. Her listless hand is tied to the wrist of a man with thinning blond hair. His unkept fingernails are thoroughly stained with violet-black ink, his attention sharp, his gaze fixed on Orlande, who is for him a miracle, a revelation—for her he is another customer and she will forget him easy and quick. Another woman, too, is there. A wimple of vague dark hair hangs over her shoulders; a bee sting blooms on her cheek like a kiss. Her fingers are entwined with a young, skinny thing, a bundle of keys at his belt, his trousers gray, workmanlike. He tries to catch the woman's gaze—but he will fail. She is not for you, poor boy!

They are so young, young and sleepy and unknowing—unknowable, if you want to know the truth. Orlande's muddy ink seeps up through the soles of their feet and the girl with blue hair yawns, a frank and unchecked gesture, like a newborn swaddled in her crèche.

# ONE

# SIC TRANSIT TOKYO

Sei pressed her cheek against the cold glass; strips of black mountains tore by under lantern-blue clouds beyond her wide window. She knew a man was watching her—the way men on trains always watched her. The train car rocked gently from side to side, hushing its charges like a worried mother. She chewed on the ends of her dark blue hair. A stupid childhood habit, but Sei couldn't let it go. She let the wet curl fall back against her bare shoulder blades. She stroked the glass with her fingertips, shifted her hips against the white of the carriage—she was always moved to do this on the long-distance trains which crisscrossed the islands like corset stays. They were so pale and pure and unfathomably fast, like iridescent snakes hissing down to the sea. The Shinkansen was always pristine, always perfect, its aim always true.

Sei's skin prickled as the man's eyes slid over her back. She felt their cold black weight, shifting her shoulders to bear up under it. He would be watching the small of her back now, where her silver-black shirt fell away into a mess of carefully arranged silk ropes and tin chains. He would watch her angles under the strings, the crease of her legs beneath an immodest skirt, her lips moving against the glass. The little wet fog of her breath. She could almost tell what he looked like without turn-ing her head: good black suit, a little too small, clutching his briefcase like a talisman, probably a little gray at the temples, no rings on his hands. They all looked like that.

Sei turned, her blue hair brushing her hipbones. Good black suit, a little too small, clutched briefcase, freckles of gray in the hair. No rings. He did not seem startled or doubled over with desire as they sometimes were. He was calm, his answering smile measured and almost sweet, like a photograph of a soldier lost in a long-ago war. Coolly, without taking his dark eyes from hers, he turned over his left palm and rested it on the creamy brown edge of his briefcase.

His hand was covered in a mark she first thought horrible—it snaked and snarled, black and swollen, where fortune-teller's lines ought to have been. Like a spider it sent long web-spokes out from a circle in the center, shooting towards the pads of his fingers and burrowing into the tiny webbing of skin between them. She took a step forward, balancing expertly as the car sped on, and stared. It was something like a little map, drawn there by an inartful and savage hand. She could make out minuscule lettering along the inky corridors: street names she could hardly read. There seemed even to be an arcane compass near his thumb. As she leaned in, the man shut his fist.

"Sato Kenji," he said, his voice neither high nor low, but cul-tured, clipped, quiet.

"Amaya Sei."

He quirked an eyebrow briefly, slightly, in such a way that no one afterwards might be able to safely accuse him of having done it. Sei knew the look. Names are meaningless, plosives and breath, but those who liked the slope of her waist often made much of hers, which denoted purity, clarity—as though it had any more in the way of depth than others. They wondered, all of them, if she really was pure, as pure as her name announced her to be, all white banners and hymeneal grace.

She balanced one hand—many-ringed—on her hip and jerked her head in the manner of a fox snuffling the air for roasting things. "What's wrong with your hand?"

"Nothing." Kenji smiled in his long-ago way again. She quirked her own eyebrow, also blue, and delicately pierced with a frosted ring. He gestured for her to sit down and, though she knew better, they sat together for a moment, her body held tense and tight, ready to run, to cry out if need be. Their thighs touched—a gesture of intimacy she had never allowed herself with another passenger.

"I think you like trains rather too much, Sei." The older man smelled of sandalwood and the peculiar *thin* scent of clean train cars.

"I'm not sure how that's any of your business."

"It isn't, of course. I like them, too. I own a car, I have no need to ride the Shinkansen back and forth from Tokyo to Kyoto like some kind of Bedouin. It's an expensive habit. But love is love, and love is compulsion. I must, and I do."

He gently tapped the brass clasp on his briefcase and drew out a slender book, bound in black, its title embossed in silver:

A HISTORY OF TRAIN TRAVEL ON THE JAPANESE ISLES,
by Sato Kenji

Sei ran her hand over the cover as she had done the window glass. Her skin felt hot, too small for her bones. He opened the book—the pages were thick and expensive, so that the stamp of the press had almost made little valleys of the kanji, the cream-colored paper rising slightly above the ink. Kenji took her hand in his. His fingernails were very clean. He read to her with the low, vibratory tones of shared obsession.

*A folktale current in Hokkaido just after the war and passed from conductor to conductor held that the floor of heaven is laced with silver train tracks, and the third rail is solid pearl. The trains that ran along them were fabulous even by the standards of the Shinkansen of today: carriages containing whole pine forests hung with golden lanterns, carriages full of rice terraces, carriages lined in red silk where the meal service brought soup, rice-balls, and a neat lump of opium with persimmon tea poured over it in the most delicate of cups. These trains sped past each other, utterly silent, carrying each a complement of ghosts who clutched the branches like leather handholds, and plucked the green rice to eat raw, and fell back insensate into the laps of women whose faces were painted red from brow to chin. They never stop, never slow, and only with great courage and grace could a spirit slowly progress from car to car, all the way to the conductor's cabin, where all accounts cease, and no man knows what lies therein.*

*In Hokkaido, where the snow and ice are so white and pure that they glow blue, it is said that only the highest engineers of Japan Railways know the layout of the railroads on the floor of heaven. They say that those exalted engineers are working, slowly, generation by generation, to lay the tracks on earth so that they mirror exactly the tracks in heaven. When this is done, those marvelous carriages will fall from the sky, and we may know on earth, without paying the terrible fare of death, the gaze of the red women, the light of the forest lanterns, and the taste of persimmon tea.*

Sato Kenji looked up from his book and into Sei's eyes. She knew her face was flushed and red—she did not care. Her hands shook, her legs ached. She could not harness her breath. She did not need these trains for simple transport either, but longed for them, the cold rush of their passing as she stood on the wind-whipped platform, the slink of doors sliding closed behind her as the train accepted her as its own. That ache had begun long before Kenji had come on board. She felt their hands touching, their train-haunted hands. She took his book from his easy grip and held it to her, her heart beating against it, as if to read it through bone and flesh and leather, directly, needfully, ventricle pressed to page. A kind of knowledge passed between them—she would not return it, and he would not ask for it back.

Instead—and later she would wonder why she did it, why such a thing would have occurred to her, and will never be able to say—she took Sato Kenji by their linked hands and led him to the rickety, shivering place between the carriage cars, where the wind keened and crooned through the cracks in the grating and the white walls gave way to chrome. She kissed the gray of his hair. The space between them was thick, crackling, and though she told herself that it was unwise, a reckless thing, she moved through that wild, manic air and into him, his mouth, his skin.

He buried his face in her neck and, as though she weighed nothing, hefted her up against the carriage door, her blue hair flattening against the glass. Sei let out a small cry, like the whistle of an engine, and ground against him, shifting to let him enter her, his breath warm and even against her collarbone. His palm was pressed against her back, the black mark hot there, a sear, a brand. Sei clutched his book against his back and shut her eyes, feeling the train jerk and jolt against her. She felt enormous, cracked open, as though she had taken all of the great train into herself, as though the shuddering, scholarly thrusts of Sato Kenji were the loving gestures of her beloved Shinkansen, only guided by the man with the briefcase, guided up and out of him, guided into her, guided across the silver tracks of heaven.

# TWO

## CITIES OF THE BEES

There is a place on the interstate where the last black fingernails of Los Angeles fall away and the whole of the San Joaquin valley spreads out below the mountains, impossibly golden, checkered in green and wheat and strawberry fields and orange groves and infinitely long rows of radishes, where the land is shriven of all the sins of palm-bound, artifice-mad Southern California.

November knew that place, knew it so well that her bare foot on the gas pedal throbbed as it approached, as her little green car, heavy with produce, crested the last rise in the tangled highways of the Grapevine, and the light began to change, gratefully, from raw, livid brume to a gold like the blood of saints. Her throat caught as the great, soft fields unfolded below her, yawning, stretching all the way to San Francisco and further still, to the redwoods and Oregon, all the way up.

She had often imagined, as a girl, when her mother drove back and forth between the two great cities of the west, that I-5 went on simply forever, past Canada to the North Pole, where the center divider would be wrapped up in ice and the bridges cut out of arctic stone. Even now, charting the coast in her own right, she sometimes thought of ignoring the off-ramps and speeding up and up, to the cold stars and fox-haunted glaciers. But in the end, it was always the city of St. Francis that stopped her, and the rest of the world was lost behind a curtain of fog and gnarled red trees.

She could never escape the feeling of strange Spanish holiness that California bestowed—the cities named for saints, angels, benediction. The capital itself a sacrament. Like communion wafers she tasted the places on her tongue, the red roof tiles blood-vivid. Her own blood bisected the state, her mother, retired, warming her bones against the southern sea, her father, dead ten years, buried in the wet northern moss.

They met in the south, on a dock far out in the frothing turquoise Pacific, her young mother in rolled-up olive overalls with a great long knife in her hands, slaughtering a small blue shark she had caught by accident, trying for salmon. She was bloody to her elbows, her clothes a ruin, arterial spray across her cheek. Her father tied his little sailboat to the pier and she looked up at him over a carcass of silver and scarlet. They had both laughed.

Long before he died, November's father was gone, up north, away from his wife and the sea. They could not bear each other, in the end, and perhaps a thing begun in blood and death and salt must end that way. They could not live with less than three mountain ranges to separate them. And between them they strung their daughter, and like a shining black bead counting out refutations of love, she slowly slid back and forth, back and forth. Finally, she had settled on her father's country, and left the loud blues and golds of the south, unable to bear them herself.

She did not live in San Francisco, of course. She could not afford it. But she was drawn to it, rising up from the bay like the star of the sea, resting in a shell, all blue veils and promises of absolution. And at night it was a mass of light at the end of all those bridges, all those highways, looking east with huge black eyes.

November kept her father's grave in Benicia, holding tenuously to the town's boldly proclaimed blessings, and with the grave she tended sixteen hexagonal beehives. She had named all the queens. She kept for them pristine and intricate gardens to flavor their feet, and the honey in turn, and it was this golden science that occupied the small and guarded territory of her interior, even as she traveled the long, slow road out of the desert, her trunk full of sleeping yucca bulbs and infant jacarandas, their roots bound up in earth and linen. Even as she found herself turning from the last scrap of highway and into the interminable column of cars creeping across the great iron mass of the Bay Bridge.

*How we are willing to wait*, she thought, *like a line of penitent adulterers at a white altar, to be allowed into the city.* How we gather at this dull gray gate, knowing that the golden one is a lie. It is only there for show. The faithful know that God lives nowhere near gold. The tourists gawk at the orange cathedral, while the wise gather here, in the low and long, waiting patiently to hand over their coins and be permitted, for a moment, to look upon, but not touch, the mass of jewels and offerings in which San Francisco wallows.

November drove slowly in, and the water below her was black. She sought out Chinatown reflexively, found a shop cashiered by a spectacled biology student which sold star anise and scallions. She loved Chinatown at three in the morning— the reds and greens were muted, shadowed into black by the gaps between streetlamps. It was secret, lonely; every pink neon character seemed brave against the dark.

It took skill, a mapmaker's skill, to find an open restaurant that would not turn a lone woman away, sure that her cup of coffee and wonton soup are hardly worth the effort of clearing a table. But on that night of all nights, November needed only a half an hour's cartomancy before she found one, and the starchy benevolence of a plate full of steaming soup dumplings, braised pork, and peppered oysters.

The booth was hard, cracked vinyl the color of a Chevrolet interior left in the sun for twenty years. A television mounted in the ceiling corner flashed the news from Beijing without subtitles. Thus, her attention wandered and fell on a young woman in the next booth over sipping soup, her bright blue eyes belying Chinese features. The two women watched each other for a space, the only customers in an empty café, until finally, the other woman placed one delicate finger against her iris and deftly slid the contact lens aside like a curtain, quirking a smile as the wrinkled lens showed black beneath.

When November tries to remember this night a year from now, she will think the woman's name was Xiaohui. She will be almost sure she can remember the ring of the name, falling into her ear like a little copper bell. She will remember that they shared dumplings, and that the woman was a Berkeley student, a historian who knew the names of every one of Mohammed's grandchildren, and could recite the drifting census data of the ancient city of Karakorum, where the Khans raised tents of scarlet.

November had only her bees. They suddenly seemed paltry to her, poor and needy.

"Tell me about the cities of the bees," Xiaohui said, her head cupped in one hand. "Tell me how big around the queen's belly is. Tell me what their honey tastes like."

November laughed, and the owner's wife scowled over a tray of tomorrow's cookies.

"I gave them orchids this year," November said shyly, "orchids and belladonna and poppies. You can only alter honey a little, really—it tastes like itself, and only faintly of anything else, as though it remembers, with difficulty, white and purple petals, thick greenery, woody stems. Last year I kept them to a patch of red lilies and lavender. I like . . . I like to use brightly colored flowers, even though I suppose it doesn't make any difference."

Xiaohui arched her eyebrows, and November blushed. She reached into her purse, drew out a small jar with a lily stamped on the lid, and passed it over the plastic table like a spy relinquishing her secrets. The blue-eyed woman dipped her thumb into the murky honey and licked it quickly from her skin, closing her eyes, pressing her lips together, so as not to lose a drop. She took November's hand in hers as she tasted, lacing their fingers.

The fortune cookies came, not wrapped in cellophane but fresh from the oven, sitting greasily on the check. They cracked into them, and Xiaohui nodded in the direction of the owner's wife.

"My mother makes them every day," she whispered. "She writes nonsense-fortunes, whatever she is thinking about when she's baking: *The fog is too thick today! Jiangxi Province had proper mist.*

*I am allergic to milk,* that sort of thing. People think she's crazy, but they buy the cookies by the dozen."

"What do you think?"

Xiaohui shrugged. "She's my mother. Jiangxi Province *did* have nicer weather."

November glanced down at the scrap of white paper in her hand. It read:

*Is not my daughter sweet?*

But she was not, November found, when she kissed her outside the restaurant, under the washed-out constellations. She tasted like flour, flour and salt. Their breasts pressed tight together between two fog-dewed overcoats, the ache of it half-painful and half-pleasant. Xiaohui took her to a little apartment above a grocery store, and they fell together just inside the doorframe, awkwardly, like great beasts too eager for niceties. She bit November's lower lip, and there was blood between them then.

"You need me," said Xiaohui breathlessly, pulling November over her, sliding hands under her belt to claw and knead. "You need me."

"Don't you mean 'I need you'?" whispered November in the girl's ear.

"No," she sighed, arching her back, tipping her chin up, making herself easy to kiss, easy to fall into, easy to devour. "You'll see. You'll see."

————

As Xiaohui drifted to sleep, one arm thrown over her now black and honest eyes, the other lying open and soft on her thin student's sheets, November stared up into the dark, awake. This was not such a new thing in her ordered world—relationships required such vigilance, such attention. You had to hold them together by force of will, and other people took up so much space, demanded so much time. It was exhausting. This was better, the occasional excursion into Chinatown, into the city of St. Francis, who after all watched over wild and wayward animals. This was better, but she slept fitfully afterward.

November stroked the inside of Xiaohui's thigh gently, a mark there, terribly stark, like a tattoo: a spidery network of blue-black lines, intersecting each other, intersecting her pores, turning at sharp angles, rounding out into clear and unbroken skin. It looked like her veins had darkened and hardened, organized themselves into something more than veins, determined to escape the borders of their mistress's flesh. In her sleep, Xiaohui murmured against her lover's neck, something about the grain yields of the farms in fourteenth-century Avignon.

"It looks like a streetmap," November whispered, pressing her hand tenderly against it, so that Xiaohui's pale skin seemed whole and unbroken.

# THE DREAMLIFE
# OF LOCK AND KEY

There was nothing in Oleg's apartment that was not locked away, safer than treasure, safer than a heart. Even the thin light from a tall and dusty lamp, tinged brown at the edges like an old apple, was bound and locked, a key turned, bolts slung firm. It could not leave this room, it would shine only here, for Oleg, and only for him.

Oleg was a locksmith. He had always thought the term overwrought, implying that he spent his days torturously pouring molten brass into molds banging out locks on some infernal anvil. It implied a burlier, more archaic man than he. Anyway, most of his public business was in keys, not locks. His private business was collection.

Keys did not really fascinate him, though he collected them as well, matching them carefully, not to the lock that was made for them, modern to modern, brass to brass, keycard to slot, as a common locksmith might, but to the ones he felt they yearned for, deep in their pressed metal hearts. He possessed a rusted iron key with an ornate lion's grimace at its head, slung alongside a gleaming hotel's card-slot lock, its red and green lights dead. He had laid an everyday steel housekey against the rarest of locks, real gold, with lilies raised up on its surface, a complex system of bolts and tumblers concealed within. Only Oleg had heard their cries for each other. Only Oleg knew their silent grief that they could not join.

He remembered Novgorod only vaguely, where he was born, where he had been a boy, briefly. It did not seem to Oleg that he could have been a boy long. Surely he would remember more of it, if it had been an important time. He had only images, as though he had once gone on vacation there—snapshots, post-cards, souvenirs. He was born, properly, when they left, wafting like tea-steam through Vienna, Naples, and into New York. They had gone silently from those places, trying hard not to disturb the air. In his memory he searched for a single word his mother might have said to him on the trains and ships between the two mismatched slabs of his life. He could only summon her cold white hands and the aquamarine that hung from her neck on a golden chain, clear and hard, swinging back and forth to the rhythm of the train. Snapshots. Souvenirs.

Yet Novgorod hung in his heart, an alien thing, hidden as a key. He could recall dimly the quicksilver bleed of the Volkhov River, pale cupolas under the snow like great garlic bulbs. But those churches were all nameless to him—he could not pluck the saints who owned them from his forgetful heart, and for this sin he did guilty penance among his locks. Everything was white and gray in that Novgorod-of-the-mind, even the violinists on Orlovskaya Street, men without blood, playing fiddles of ash. This white pendulum swung within him, even as he bent with his tools to locks more beautiful and complicated than memory.

He lived in New York, but the New York of Oleg Sadakov was not the New York of others, and he alone ministered this secret place, stamped onto the back of the city like a maker's mark. He crept and crawled through it, listening, for Oleg could listen very well, better than rabbits or horses or safe-crackers.

The trouble was, New York was famous. Oleg had even seen it in Novgorod—a city so often photographed, filmed, recorded that there was truly no one who did not know its name, its outline, the shape of its body. So many books had been written about it, so many people had loved it and lived in it until their clothes smelled of its musk, so many had eaten its food and drunk its water and extolled its virtues like a gospel of the new world, that it had, with infinitesimal slowness, ceased to be, melted into vapor and dust. What rose now on the island of Manhattan was no more than the silver-white echo of all those millions of words expended on its vanity, the afterimage of all those endless photographs and movies which broadcast it to anyone who might live ignorant of its majesty. A monster, a fairy-tale mirror, glittering but false, a doppelgänger, a golem with *New York City* engraved roughly on its forehead.

No one had noticed.

Oleg retreated from the broad limbs of this new metropolitan giant and saw only the locks. He let people into places both secret and obvious, places they owned and places where they trespassed, into lovers' hallways and grocers' shops, into hotel rooms and abandoned buildings. Oleg did not care. He only wanted to touch the locks and find the keys for whom they wept. He saw nothing but the infinite city of locks, turning and

winding through and around and behind the monochrome be-
hemoth, and when the hours were very late, he often felt as
though he could look through one lock and see all the others
lined up behind it, opening up into forever, into a hundred
thousand houses, into the Hudson, into the Atlantic. He could
almost see the whitecaps breaking.

———

Oleg had only once confessed to another soul that he knew the
secret of what had happened to New York. He felt foolish
about it later, but he could not help it—her name was
Lyudmila. It was not his fault that that simple thing instilled so
much trust in him, so much instinctive, automatic familiarity.
Lyudmila had locked herself out of her tall, narrow house,
where her cats mewled in panicked sopranos from within.

"That was my sister's name," he said softly as he put his eye
to the lock in her brownstone, his lashes falling just inside the
old metal.

The woman spoke to him hopefully in Russian. This occasionally happened, and he dreaded it. He could speak no more
than a few words now, those snow-slushed consonants and
swallowed vowels having receded into the same icy mist as
Novgorod. He stopped her, blushed, admitted his forgetful-
ness. She only smiled, her hands white and cold, her blond hair
swept heavily to one side of her face, spilling over the collar of
her blue coat.

"It's all right," she said. "Remembering is very hard work.
Not everyone is built for it. I asked if your sister lives in the
city?"

Oleg shook his head, opening his tool casket. "She drowned, in the Volkhov, before I was born. She was wearing a red dress and black stockings—it was a cold day. My mother was pregnant with me, she closed her eyes for only a minute, to rest, and she always said she heard the splash in her bones before she heard it in her ears."

"I'm sorry," said Lyudmila, pulling up her collar as if to stave off icy waters a continent and a half away.

"These things happen," he sighed, and the lock released its grip on the house with a loud click. Oleg felt as if his heart echoed with that click, unbuckled with it, bled out over the threshold of the door. His forehead was warm, his chest ached. It was only his third lock of the day, his service hardly even begun. He looked up at Lyudmila, the Lyudmila who was not his sister, who wore a topaz ring and had terribly long eyelashes.

"Invite me in, Mila," he said, the boldness of the lock in him.

She looked alarmed for a moment but nodded slowly and ushered him into her small kitchen. As though it was his own house (and truthfully, as he had done in many houses that were not his before he had discovered a virtuous use for his passion), Oleg spread butter and salmon roe onto thick bread, sliced salted fish, filled two glasses with cold wine. Lyudmila let him, reclining placidly on her chair. She opened her mouth to speak several times, but instead simply watched him move, watched his hands on the bread, the fish.

They ate without conversation, and Lyudmila seemed to burn in the middle of the pale blue room like a little sun. She finally removed her coat after they had eaten, and Oleg saw a thing like a spider on her neck, black and blazing, a mark sending up tendrils along her jaw, which her long hair had hidden, brachiating lines like streets and alleys, so vivid and dark they seemed to pulse with her heartbeat.

"It's a birthmark, or something like that." She laughed shortly. "Or would be, if I had been born last year."

"I don't mind it," he said softly.

"I've never been to Novgorod. I was born in Odessa. It is so warm there, so warm and the buildings are so white. When I remember it, I only remember the whiteness. And the seabirds. I am cold here all the time. Sometimes I wake up and I think I can still smell the Black Sea. How lucky you are, that you remember so little."

Oleg moved his hand over hers—it must have been the turn of the lock, how easily it had come open in his hands, how flushed he had been with success, with its little sigh of relief that only he could hear. Only that could explain how he could dredge up courage to touch her like that, so soon, without permission. His blood beat too high, too fast. He was a shy man, he spoke little, after his mother's habit. But he heard the key in her, weeping old, rusty tears.

"It's usually harder than this," she said quietly, looking down at their joined hands.

"What is?"

Lyudmila shut her eyes and her mouth together, pressing lids and lips tightly, as though to keep her whole self inside.

"To touch a person . . . to sleep with a person . . . is to become a pioneer," she whispered then, "a frontiersman at the edge of their private world, the strange, incomprehensible world of their interior, filled with customs you could never imitate, a language which sounds like your own but is really totally foreign, knowable only to them. I have been so many times to countries like that. I have learned how to make coffee in all their ways, how to share food, how to comfort, how to dance in the native ways. It is harder, usually, to find a person who wants to walk the streets of me, to taste the teas of my country, to . . . immigrate, you could say. Especially . . . well." She gestured at her painted throat.

Oleg touched her neck, the black lines there, hot and moving slightly with her pulse.

"I think I would like your country," he said shyly. He said nothing of his own, too full of the dead and the locked.

He took her into his arms, holding her golden head to his chest—how cold she was! Her skin was frost-dry, and he thought he could hear seabirds inside her, flapping at the freezing joints of her shoulders.

Lyudmila, who was not his sister, lay her arms around Oleg's neck like a child. He could not bear to breathe, but he kissed her blighted jaw.

"I'm married," she said simply, casually, an announcement of no more importance than her address or height. She did not move from him.

"It doesn't matter," he said huskily, his voice sliding from him like the skin peeled from a black fruit. He took a long breath and whispered into her hair, "This is not a real place. Didn't you know? Didn't you guess? Everyone looked at it and looked at it, never blinking, working so hard at remembering, taking pictures and writing novels, and never stopping, even for a moment, and when you look at a thing like that, you kill it, like the ant and the magnifying glass. There is no Manhattan left. We float in the black, and see the Empire State Building where there is nothing but void. What does it matter what we do in a place like that? Who we marry? If we lie?"

Lyudmila kissed him then, and in her mouth was the void, and in his throat was the void, and in the dark of dead Manhattan he lifted her up against the pantry door, and the jars of jam rattled within, raspberry against currant against plum.

---

When he returned home, his own lock relieved and welcoming, his sister was sitting in the kitchen with her hands clasped in her lap, staring at him with great dark eyes. He tried not to look at her.

"I missed you, Olezhka," said the dead mouth of the other Lyudmila, her red dress far too small now, the weeds of the Volkhov still throttling her neck.

## FOUR

# THE BOOKBINDER'S WIFE

The pads of Ludovico's fingers were scored with paper cuts like lines of longitude and latitude. They had long since gone the murky gold color of expensive glue, the kind one can be absolutely certain has its source in rendered beast—perhaps, if one is fortunate and paid a great deal of money, one as interesting as a camel or lynx. Ludo used those murky, malevolent glues almost to exclusion—he was interested in them, in tools, in origins. He liked to think that he bound his books with the sinew of a Chinese tiger. He liked to think that while he slept, the endless spines stretched and growled, licking the typesetting with wide, rough tongues.

Ludovico's wife did not hear the prowling of the feline volumes in the dark. Lucia slept soundly, the form of her like a little hillock in his bed, her green nightgown barely rising, barely falling, part of the landscape of his house, so embedded in the soil of him that he often expected a flower to sprout from her shoulders, or wind up between their lips when they shared their morning kiss, as simple and necessary as a cup of coffee. Ludovico considered himself a contemplative man and held such thoughts as proof. The flowers that grew lightless in his skull were many and pale.

Lucia was not Catholic, rather, a hybrid: half atheist and half classicist. This had once given him pause, in the days when he, a good Roman boy, visited St. Peter's and Trajan's market with equal and untroubled reverence. She scorned the flat coin of his St. Isidore's medal, hanging faithful and constant against his chest—*what kind of man is beholden to a saint no one remembers? He's not even Italian!* And though he loved her he could not explain that St. Isidore, though in no official capacity did he serve men of Ludovico's persuasion, seemed to him the great saint of books, haloed in bumblebees who demanded at least two full columns devoted to their sociology in the saint's *Etymologiae,* that massive compendium of medieval knowledge, the first encyclopedia, possessing the whole world between its boards.

When Lucia descended into such contrary moods, Ludo simply kissed the place where her soft black hair faded into the skin of her temple, and recited to her Isidore's thoughts on the contrary nature of the chimera. For that was Lucia—his chimera, his composite beast, his snarling, biting, kissing thing.

But how intricate and sweet were the figures she inscribed in the margins of his books! What sort of bookbinder could he have been without her, her infinite variation, her obsessive knowledge of ink? She did not hear the tiger-books, but she smelled the trees of India and the terror of cuttlefish in her finger bowls full of black and violet and brown, no less vivid than oil paint. Together, they rarely needed to speak as he cut the pages and wrapped the boards in coppery silk, as he set the type in their ancient printing press: a truculent old dragon in the corner of the kitchen where they had had the stove removed to make room for it. It ate paper and excreted books, and

Ludovico loved it, while Lucia, hands on her hips, shamed it into yet another year of groaning, protesting service.

Their happiness was the kind which is fashioned of the comfortable disorder of sauvignon bottles and coffee cups in the sink, paperback thrillers with split spines on the nightstand, bathrobes hung haphazard on high-backed, brocade-seated chairs, shutters left open all night, and the hallway ever in need of new paint.

In the second winter of their marriage, when Ludo drove up to visit his brothers in Umbria and left his wife alone, Lucia had been possessed by the vexatious and serpent-tailed temper of the chimera that was only ever leashed, grumbling, within her. She burned all the furniture in that hall: the telephone table and four Japanese paper lamps, a year's worth of ignored mail, and a reading chair Ludovico had especially loved. Without eating or sleeping for days upon nights, she covered the bare, vaguely yellowish walls with the entire text of the *Etymologiae*, in a tiny, wild script he had never seen her use before and would never see again. When he returned she was curled up on the floor of the hall like an exhausted fox, sleeping among the words of St. Isidore.

Ludo wept when he saw it, falling to his knees beside her. From then on he visited St. Peter's no longer, but held his own, silent mass in the empty, illuminated hall, kissing the Spaniard's words like rosary beads. He forgave her the chair, of course, and she forgave him his saint, having satisfied herself of Isidore's sanctity with her own suffering.

Thus they lived, intractable, silent beasts, yet adored of each other. He brought her slivers of marble from the streets in the place of the flowers other women might love, and these she held against her cheek until they warmed like flesh. She brought him strange and foreign glues in pots like witch's unguents, and they understood each other. Until it was that he set to the task of binding a new book for a miniscule specialty press in Florence.

The book had a great many strange and ugly illustrations, he suspected done by the author himself, a Japanese gentleman, a practice of which Ludovico did not at all approve. Bookbinding, however, is a luxury trade, and he could not afford to pick and choose projects. Papers and silks and boards crowded the house—though none touched the precious hallway, which remained bare as a pauper's cupboard.

Having nothing to do with the commission, Lucia amused herself in the city, and Ludo saw little of her. He imagined, when she let the door close softly in the morning, a golden paw and emerald tail disappearing out of the door in place of her sleek black heels and the flick of a crisp, cream-colored dress. This made him smile, and the sun of many days passed through his thinning blond hair.

He did not notice it, therefore, until she was ministering to the printing press, ink smudged onto her cheek like a crow's errant feather. Her back was to him, so that he saw the hollow of her knee. At first his gaze slid over it easily—what part of Lucia did not have ink splattered over it in the casual and elaborate patterns of any novitiate to a printing press's mysteries? But it drew his eyes back to it, a pulse of thin, livid lines, like an impossibly complicated bruise, an arcane brand. It was bounded by cherubs blowing winds at her calves, like old maps, and a serpent humped near the south end of the grid—for it was a grid, a crooked, broken grid, angling over her skin, intersections and alleys and monuments labeled in the same miniature script that covered their hallway. He could not read the names, but he was sure they would be in Latin, Lucia's clear and lucid favored tongue, and the only appropriate dialect for mapmaking, as well Ludovico knew.

"What happened to your leg?" he asked gently.

Lucia twisted to look over her shoulder, her waist crinkling, and extended her leg like a statue of Daphne in mid-tree. "Oh." She sighed. "That. I don't know. I went to the doctor, so you needn't worry, I'm fine. It's ugly, but, well, benign, I guess, is the word." She put down a plate and crossed the kitchen to kiss his temple sweetly. "Maybe the books have taken a liking to me and have begun to dare kisses."

"I've never printed a book like that."

"Well, I can't tell you what it is. I don't know. Pretend your wild chimera-wife got a tattoo and don't think about it."

But he could not stop thinking about it, and the Japanese book receded from his care like water tossed from a window. He began, instead, to sketch the patterns of the grid on his wife's leg in the margins of the errata copies, invading neat lines about the essential nature of trains and their conductors with serpents and winds. When Lucia dressed to go out in the evening, he begged her to stay, to crook her knee for him, to let him touch the stain, the grid, the map.

She acquiesced, and lay on her stomach so that he could examine her like a manuscript in desperate need of restoration. She pressed her face into the pillow; he pressed his lips to her skin, tasting the rough, salty roads printed there by whatever invisible press had hunted and leapt upon Lucia in the dark. Ludo closed his eyes against them, let his eyelashes shudder over their routes and byways. His tongue was a letter press on her, stamping out his desire. She tried to turn over, but he stopped her, unable to bear the disappearance of the knee-map. He kissed the backs of her thighs and slid his hands under her stomach, whispering her name with all the reverence of abandoned Catholicism, pressing his cheek to the side of her long neck, which he had always thought slightly too long for comfortable human proportion. He held her hair aside in one hand as he entered her, and she shut her eyes, silent, pliable as pages. He willed her to cry out, pushing harder, to hurt her, even, if she would only say his name, or moan, anything. But she did not, and he could not make her.

As they moved in an old and practiced pattern, his fingers found her knee again and felt the streets of some unnamable city tremble under his hand.

# Hieratica Street

**THEY DREAM AGAINST WARM BREASTS** and empty beds of the four black pools in Orlande's house. They stare straight ahead into her pink and gray-speckled mouth, and the red thread sweeps tight against their wrists. On four laps the frog-oracle lays four cards, but they do not look down, not yet.

But we may, we who peer. We who disturb.

On her bare knees sits the Flayed Horse, signifying Sacrifice in Vain, Loveless Pursuit, Fecundity Unlooked-For. Her blue hair brushes the hard, creased edges of the old card.

On his threadbare lap balances the Three of Tenements, predicting Auditory Hallucination, Cirrhosis, a Man Turned Away from Salvation. He fondles his keys, and the sound of it seems, to our eyes at least, to soothe him.

On her denim-shrouded thighs lies the Unhappy Rook, suggesting Grief without Name, Symmetry of Experience, an Empty Larder. She alone takes up the card, holds it to her cheek, covering the bee sting there with the plain, stark image of a broken chess piece.

On his linen trousers rests the Archipelago, foretelling a Plague of Eels, Loveless Pursuit, a Dark-Haired Woman with Two Fingers Missing. His ink-stained fingers dig into the meat of his palms.

They lace their hands together instinctively as she ties the yarn—all their many fingers tenuous and needful, blindly groping. Before their eyes Orlande's great green head floats, rimmed in silver, like an icon. The frog-woman shows them a small card, red words printed neatly on yellow paper:

*Go. You have been Quartered.*

The knots slacken, fall away. The four of them walk out, across the frond-threshold, into the night which smells of sassafras and rum, and onto broad, cinnamon-colored Hieratica Street. They stumble into the cane-strewn night, their feet filthy, their heads swimming with the winds of a not-too-distant sea.

This is the part I like best. When they are so new. Newborn colts are not so innocent.

The frog pushes them out of her shop like a mother urging her children toward the coach on their first day of school: *Never fear, my darlings! All these horrors are yours to survive!*

Is it an accident of the clock that the four of them wheel dazed onto the thoroughfare at the same moment that a wave of crickets come hopping from the factory, bowing a complex binary minuet on their platinum legs? Or perhaps merely poetic? Casimira presses vermin beneath her porcelain and chitin molds, Orlande presses them beneath red yarn, and out they go into the city together, new and raw and empty as a saucepan. It is an admirable symmetry.

The four of them stand in a street cross-hatched with desiccated lily leaves, as though they did not know that one may be crushed there, staring dumbly at each other, a herd of idiot gazelles. They have not let go of each other's hands; they cannot bear it: *not yet, not yet!* Their feet, benumbed, are overrun by crickets with glass wings.

There are obvious things to say, but none of the four of them can find a voice buried in their ribs. Will you stand there forever? Will you become a piece of statuary on which children will swing and clover will grow?

No—here is a gilded cart drawn by twin herons, their long black legs rustling the street-leaves. Out of the green-curtained window the head of a third heron, spectacularly turquoise, extends, eyes narrowed to avian slits.

"Out of the way! I shall trample you thoroughly, see if I won't!"

The cart-herons squawk harshly and swing wildly around the quartet, galloping onto 16th Street with long, graceless strides. Eight hands shake free of each other; the men clutch their elbows in nervous agitation. The girl with blue hair stares at them with dark eyes.

"Which way to the trains?" she whispers to her comrades. Wrong question, child! You mean to say: *Where am I? Who are all of you? What has happened to us?* But no one ever asks after sensible things. The others shake their heads—they cannot help her. And so she runs in the direction that seems best, turning as sharply as the herons onto a brightly glowing avenue that shears off from Hieratica like a broken branch.

———

Abandoned, the others scatter like ashes. The road stretches before and beyond, lit by streetlamps with swollen pumpkin-globes, and the gutters run with a sudden, utter rain.

# PART I:

Incipit Liber de Naturis Bestiarum

# ONE

# THE FLAYED HORSE

Sei woke with the grassy, half-rotten smell of ryokan-tatami in her nose and her face streaked with tears. She immediately tried to go back to sleep, to catch the herons, fading already, but alas—sleep lost is sleep lost. She felt a weight on her wrists, like the memory of heavy bracelets. Her second thought was to find Sato Kenji, to shake him and bite his mouth and ask him if he had written a book about the city, too, if she could press it against the other, which lay still in her backpack, cold and black. When would he fly north again to Tokyo on their sleek white serpent? Tomorrow? Never? In what car might he wait for her? Useless, she decided, to ask.

She dressed without thinking about it much, took two rice-balls—one stuffed with salted plum, one with salmon—and Sato Kenji's little book with her, and fled the milling, noisy hostel into the city. Kyoto was designed on the pattern of a Go board, by imaginative and impish urban planners who surely drank a great deal. As she progressed from square to square, staring vacantly at the thick cypress bark rooftops and leering Fu dogs, Sei felt strange, floating. She was a smooth white disc, clapped on all sides by slippery black pieces, reflecting the sky, helpless, with the Shinkansen on one hand and the endless pavilions of Kyoto on the other.

She chose the Silver Pavilion out of all the temples. It had been her mother's favorite, and so, like an inheritance, was hers. It was shaded in autumn leaves so bright the trees seemed to bleed. The persimmons were so golden they hurt her eyes, and the sun stabbed at her through the blazing fruit. She had a terrible dry taste in her mouth, as though she had drunk too much, though she had had nothing but water since Tokyo.

The temple grounds were deserted. She settled onto the grass a ways off from the great silver temple. She watched it, how dark and mottled its silver leaf was, centuries of tarnish which the monks, in their inscrutable perambulations, had never polished, settling on the holiness of obscured metal. It looked like the crouched and looming house of a succubus from one of her mother's books. She almost expected some yellow-eyed monster with wings of patchworked sin to snap open the door and screech some infernal koan at her. Yet Sei liked the mossy, irritable temple, which seemed honest, unflappable, like an old, hunchbacked elephant.

She opened Kenji's book on her lap and flipped through the pages. She did not want to read this book from start to finish, or rather, she thought perhaps it did not want her to. Instead she practiced the art of bibliomancy, trusting the book to show her what it wanted her to know.

*In Osaka, I heard a very strange account of the antique initiation rituals of conductors. I was told by a retired man who was adamant I not reveal his name that before the war, when new conductors were assigned their first train, they were brought on board on a very cold winter's night when the train was stopped and no one lingered in the cars. The senior engineers gathered tightly in the conductor's cabin. They put the earnest young man's hands onto the control console and anointed them with viscous oil from the engine before pulling loose several wires and tying them into knots around the man's fingers. He was then told the se-cret name of the train, which he could reveal to no one. They cut into the third finger of his left hand, mingling his blood with the oil, which was then returned to circulation in the engine. In this way the train be-came the beloved of the conductor, and the man who told me this story said that it felt very much like a grave wedding service.*

Sei's hands throbbed, feeling the open, oil-spattered wires beneath her own hands, a phantom console alive beneath her. The wind picked up and rustled her blue hair, blowing it over her cheeks. She might have remained in such a pose until the sun slid away below the tin rooftops, her hands frozen over the book, had a young woman not sat down next to her without warning, still dressed in her school uniform, her hair hanging in a long, loose braid. Sei started and scowled, but she uttered nothing, as manners demanded.

"It's funny," the young student said casually, in the authori-tative, overeager tone of a local girl speaking to a tourist, her accent unmistakably Kyoto. She turned to Sei, her face open and attentive as a cat's. "The Golden Pavilion is the famous one, but it only ever looked yellow to me. It's ugly, just kind of garish. All that gold, and it just looks like yellow paint. But the Silver Pavilion . . . nobody cares, it's not a big tourist draw, and if you didn't know, you might not even think it was silver—the tarnish is so thick it matches the cypress bark on the roof. Doesn't it look sad and run down? But it seems *real* to me, and the Golden Pavilion seems . . . well, it's belligerent, thinking it's so beautiful. Arrogant old bitch."

Sei blinked.

"My name is Yumiko," the girl said helpfully.

Sei frowned further. "I haven't been to the Golden Pavilion yet," she said, handing over her grudging answer like bus fare. Yumiko shook her dark head.

"If you do, you'll see what I mean."

Yumiko was silent then. She stared at Sei for a long while before grinning, wiping her palms on a blue plaid skirt, and extending her tongue slowly, as far as it could reach, nearly grazing the tip of her delicate chin. Sei gaped; blood rushed to her cheeks. She saw it there, on the red flesh of the girl's tongue, whipped with wind: Kenji's mark, the grid of lines, the map, blazing blue-bright.

"What *is* that?" she cried, leaping up from the grass. The black book tumbled to the ground. "Tell me!"

Yumiko closed her mouth with a gentle little sound. "Don't you know?" she said, her brow creased as a page.

"No, of course not, how could I?"

The girl stood, her braid slipping entirely loose, and stood very close, so close they might have kissed. She reached for Sei's blouse and began to slide the buttons from their stitched eyelets. Sei pushed her away, but Yumiko smiled.

"Please," she murmured.

Yumiko opened the crisp black shirt like a theater's curtains. There, on Sei's skin, were the strange dark lines, snaking across her sternum, arcing slightly onto the curve of her breasts. It seemed as though a great insect had attached itself to her, to suckle and grow.

Yumiko did not step away. She cradled Sei's face in her manicured hand and leaned back, stretching, a smug, satisfied cat.

"I would like to be a novice here," she said airily. "I would like to live in the temple and drink bamboo tea every day, and eat only seven grains of rice until I was thinner than the Buddha and twice as beautiful. I would leave clean water for the sacred cats and sweep the rushes and the red leaves aside in the fall. I would smell the sake breweries in the winter, and eat one persimmon a year, on the Emperor's birthday. Every morning and every evening, I would cut a square from one of my kimonos and with it I would polish the walls until the tarnish fell away like an old woman's hair, until it gleamed like water. After a year I would be naked and polish the walls with my own hair, and under my body it would look like a house hollowed out of the moon."

Sei stared.

"What happened to me?" she whispered. "Who are you?"

"What happens to any of us? Novices all."

"That's not an answer! How did you know? Just walking up to a stranger in a temple, how did you know I had that thing on me?"

"It's not a thing, you know. It's . . . like a ticket. And once you've bought your ticket, and been to the circus, ridden the little red train, then you can sort of see other people who've done it, too. They . . . walk a certain way. Smell a certain way. Their whole body becomes like an accent. And you always recognize your own accent. I recognized you."

Sei's cheeks burned. She looked at the grass, and then at the sky. She didn't want to ask, like some stupid club girl begging for drugs, or a child begging for the candy she just knows will make her life complete.

"How do I get back there?"

Yumiko looked at her sideways, puzzled, as though Sei should know this, as though she had asked how to count to ten—*basic stuff, kid! Who brought you up?* But Yumiko sidled close and lowered her voice until it was no more than a dragonfly's cough. She let her lips brush Sei's ear. "Come with me. Peregrine and 125th is on my tongue. I'll meet you there. We'll take the subway to the end of the world!"

She kissed her then, and the Silver Pavilion glowed dully behind them. Yumiko slid her hand under Sei's skirt and pressed her fingers against her urgently, furtively—there was no one around them, but the sun was frosty and white on them, and they were so bare. Sei opened her legs to allow the girl's hand inside her and shut her eyes against the warm air, the red leaves, the silver temple. She could not draw breath for the taste of sassafras and rum in Yumiko's mouth, the sharpness of her small white teeth. Sei felt herself flip over—white to black, disappearing into the board, lost.

# 125th and Peregrine

# 125th and Peregrine

**SEI DREAMS AGAINST HER TATAMI** that night of an intersection garlanded with black flags fastened to string with clothespins of mother-of-pearl. On the north corner: a cartographer's studio. Pots of ink hide in every crevice, parchment spreads out over dozens of tables. A Casimira pigeon perches in a baleen cage and trills out the hours faithfully. Its droppings are pure squid-ink, and a little tin trough collects them dutifully. Imogen and Philomena have run this place since the last cartographer went mad and began eating telegraph tape like pasta. Philomena with her silver compass draws the maps, her exactitude radiant and unerring, while Imogen illuminates them with exquisite miniatures, dancing in the spaces between streets. They each wear dozens of watches on their forearms.

This is the second stop, after the amphibian salon, of Palimpsest's visitors, and especially of her immigrants, for whom the two women are especial patrons. Everyone needs a map, and Philomena supplies them: subway maps and street maps and historical maps and topographical maps, false maps and correct-to-the-minute maps and maps of cities far from this one. Look—for this lost child she has made a folding pamphlet that shows the famous sights: the factory, the churches, the salon, the memorial. Follow it, girl, and you will be safe!

Each morning, Philomena places her latest map on the windowsill like a fresh pie. Slowly, as it cools, it opens along its own creases, its corners like wings, and takes halting flight, flapping over the city with susurring strokes. It folds itself, origami-exact, in midair: it has papery eyes, inky feathers, vellum claws.

It stares down the long avenues, searching for mice. This is the life cycle of Palimpsest fauna.

Yumiko leans against the door post, holding her arms out like a sister who had never hoped to see her dear one again. She is not wearing her schoolgirl's dress any longer, but a red scrap that clings to her waist like a spool of yarn pulled tighter than breathing. With a local girl's surety she guides Sei inside—a little scalloped bell chimes, and Imogen looks up from her parchments with a stern face, her black hair soft around a neck just slightly too long for a woman to wear in company.

"The trains," Sei murmurs. "I need a map of the trains. A . . . schedule."

Imogen produces a tiny booklet, hardly larger than her hand, with a design on the cover like an infinite tangle of wires compacted into a disc. Yumiko pays her with a fingernail cut quickly and fed to the pigeon. The cartographer smiles, and when she does, her face breaks open, smooths and unfolds into a heartbreaking beauty.

Her map clutched to her breast, Sei runs out into the street, her hair streaming behind her like a smokestack's exhalation. She looks desperately around her, her breath quick and hoarse.

She finds it on the south corner: lit globes, covered with thick wrought-iron serpents which break the light, of a subway entrance. Trains barrel along at the bottom of the stairs every fifteen minutes. On the glass platform below stands Adalgiso the Apostle-Fingered, playing his viola with six fingers on each hand. He is bald, with a felt hat that does not sit quite right on his head. Beside him is Assia, the Nymph of the Phonograph. She is singing tenor, her smoke-throated voice pressing long kisses against his strings. His playing is so quick and lovely that the trains stop to listen, inclining on the rails and opening their doors to catch the glissandos spilling from him. His instrument case lies open at his feet, and each passenger who takes the Marginalia Line brings his fee—single pearls, dropped one by one into the leather case until it overflows like a pitcher of milk. In the corners of the station, cockroaches with fiber-optic wings scrape the tiles with their feet, and their scraping keeps the beat for the player and his singer.

Sei dashes down the steps into darkness and the metallic smell of the subterranean palaces of transportation before Yumiko can catch her. She stops short before the viola player and his tenor, and their eyes meet like magnets clicking together over the vibrating strings of his instrument.

———

Miles away, on a street planked in cedar, a beekeeper cries out—her vision has gone dark, and all she can smell is the wet blackness of the underground.

# TWO

# THE UNHAPPY ROOK

*Things which are gone in the morning: sleep, darkness, grief, the moon. Women. Dreams.*

November sat cross-legged in her bedroom, a bare, white place she would never have thought to compare to her stacked hives but which nevertheless was cousin to them, those sixteen calm, angular spaces.

On her lap was a wide blank book with rough-chewed edges, which she would never have thought to compare to her fingers, her thrice-dyed, badly cut hair, her chapped lips, but which nevertheless was sister to these things: the woman, the raw flesh, the small white room. She was possessed of a self as bare as the month her parents met, the month of her own name, a core fashioned from stark wood and a prescience of snow.

In the book she had written, hesitantly. Her handwriting had been long ago corrupted: the vagaries of overzealous typing and an adolescent passion for calligraphy. What remained was a ruin of pens pressed too deeply and sweeping capitals too uncertain to be majestic. She had sketched out the morning list without thinking, desperate to list her morning bed, empty as a coffee cup, used up, dry, to fold it into a kind of column that made sense of the depression where once Xiaohui lay, which was still warm with her.

The keeping of lists was for November an exercise kin to the repeating of a rosary. She considered it neither obsessive nor compulsive, but a ritual, an essential ordering of the world into tall, thin jars containing perfect nouns. Enough nouns connected one to the other create a verb, and verbs had created everything, had skittered across the face of the void like pebbles across a frozen pond. She had not yet created a verb herself, but the cherry-wood cabinet in the hall contained book after book, jar after jar, vessel upon vessel, all brown as branches, and she had faith.

And so she did not think that she was lonely, or as her mother would have said, drawn up into herself like an old turtle, simply that she was absorbed in a greater task than the wrangling of humans and the collecting of large houses or automobiles. She moved in long lines between her books, along her lists like ranked soldiers, administrating, shaping, carving with her quick, corruptible hands.

November tasted the ink of her pen lightly. Acorns and copper. Ash.

She had dreamed heavily and the dream clung to her still—November had always been a prodigy of dreams. Her father, a librarian, had made her write them down, and perhaps this had been the beginning of the slim brown books which now numbered so very many. She dreamed in color, more than color, in shades of gold and scarlet impossible in the waking world. She dreamed in languages she did and did not know, she dreamed strange and wonderful faces, narratives of recursive complexity, and her recall was meticulous, detailed, perfect as a list.

There had been such a smell in the place of her dream, of sassafras and the sea, bay leaves and dandelion seeds blowing wild, of coffee plants, of sweat. The smell burned into her; she had striven after it in the way of dreams until she could hear the starry surf on a bright shore.

*The following things are essential to a city*, she wrote. She crossed out *essential* and wrote *necessary* above it in compressed script. She did not erase or begin again—mistakes were as essential to the noun-stacks, the combs of names, as industry to a city. They showed that the stack was not arbitrary, that some words had been excised in favor of others, that choices had been made, casualties counted.

*Industry*, she wrote below it. *Commerce. Transportation, construction, tenements. Habitation. Suburbs. Circuses. Exhibitions of Force and Fervor. Religion. Ritual.*

*Darkness, grief, the moon. Women. Dreams.*

———

The skin of her cheek recalled pressing against the legs of the lost Xiaohui. November mourned, as much as she could ever mourn those gone in the morning, in her kitchen, at a red table, with a white cup full of milky coffee. She held her palm against her face—she was not sorry the historian had gone, but her body wept. She stared into her coffee, sitting in a thin blue dress that tangled in her calves. She often felt that she chased the ideal cup of coffee in her mind from table to table, the rich, thick, creamy coffee, spicy, bittersweet, that betrayed no hint of thinness or chemical flavoring, nothing less than total, fathomless devotion to the state of being itself. Every morning she pulled a delicate cup from its brass hook and filled it, hoping that it would be dark and deep and secret as a forest, and each morning it cooled too fast, had too much milk, stained the cup, made her nervous.

She wore copper rings that turned her fingers green, and tapped them idly against her cup. Her book of lists lay closed on the table, and she considered briefly a roll of the attributes of the grail-coffee which did not fill her cups, but could not, in the end, decide it had sufficient worth. The bees would be no help; they would tumble over each other like golden babies and thrum wordlessly on the subjects of queens and sex and pollen-gluey feet.

November, like a queen in a story, with black hair and a long story ahead of her, was possessed of a beautiful mirror that had belonged to her mother. Its frame was oily iron, figured in broken fleur-de-lis and curling leaves. She kept it near the door of her little house, for it was only when she meant to go into the world that she cared how the world might see her.

Her face showed faithfully on that morning, ringed with baroque foliage: a messy knot of hair, a mild brown gaze—and a black mark like a slap on her cheek, an explosion of lines and angles like the work of a furious spider or a drunken architect, brachiating from a point near her ear up towards the corner of her right eye and down towards the crease of her lip, long, undulating lines like the banks of a black river. She put her hand against it, shaking—rubbed at it, but it remained, a mark like the one on Xiaohui's vanished thigh, hot, as though only just branded there.

*Things that are left in the morning: memory, thought, snow. Light. Work. Disease. Dreams.*

November returned to the Chinatown café and the soupy peppered oysters, the greasy, soft fortune cookies, but Xiaohui was not there. She briefly considered becoming a hermit, a nun, a bee-abbess. She was halfway there already, really. She could not hide her face as Xiaohui had hidden her leg, and the toll-taker at the crux of the gloomy gray bridge had stared so long that the cars behind her had blared indignation. But the wizened woman at the café counter, Xiaohui's mother, her wrinkled hands clamped up in rings so old their metals had gone black, did not stare. She looked up at November through blue-white hair and allowed the smallest smile, as if in broad, universal pity, the way Mary smiles when she is the star of the sea. November blushed—what she had done blazed as plain as a pregnancy. She offered no excuse, and the crone said nothing. She shrugged a little, as if to say: *That's what you get for sleeping with strange women.*

Slumped into her plates, November swallowed the happy steam of onions, shrimp paste, plum sauce. She sat separated by two tables from her lone fellow patron—a young man with glasses and a glossy willow-colored button-down shirt. He ate deftly and she thought his hands had a woman's grace, or a bee-keeper's. He was reading a book with a black cover and embossed silver characters. When he reached up to turn the onionskin page, November saw that his forefinger was black from nail to palm, wound around with those broken, swerving lines, haphazardly, as if drawn with a terrible, shaking pen.

He would look up eventually, he had to. She was patient—nothing she could say would cry out in the same shrill pitch as her ruined face. Her blood beat like a bruise blossoming, and she willed him to see her, to abandon his book and raise up his eyes. While she waited for him, her folded cookie arrived, and she unfolded it with great care. She could hear so much blood in her ears, more blood and thicker than she could have had in her. On the thin slip of sugared paper she read:

*I am sorry. My daughter is also careless.*

As if a bell had rung in his ear, the man in willow-green looked up—and smiled, beatifically, light opening across his face like a window flung open at noon. His dark eyes flashed recognition, and in two quick strides he reached her table, casting a green shadow. He took her face in his hands and kissed her mouth hard, clumsily, a disaster of teeth and skin.

# 212th, Vituperation, Seraphim, and Alphabet

**IN THE CENTER OF THE ROUNDABOUT** sits the Memorial. It is tall and thin, a baroque spire sheltering a single black figure—a gagged child with the corded, elastic legs of an ostrich, fashioned from linked hoops of iron. Through the gaps in her knees you can see the weeds with their flame-tipped flowers. She sits in the grass, her arms thrown out in supplication. Bronze and titanium chariots click by in endless circles, drawn on tracks in the street, ticking as they pass like shining clocks. Between her knock-knees is a plaque of white stone, blank as a cheek. Once, on this spot, one thousand and twelve hearts stopped without a gasp. An army wrangled without screams, without sound. In the center of the roundabout, the ostrich-girl died unweeping while her father had his long throat slashed with an ivory bayonet. The great post-war sculptor Lydia Weckweet, who is responsible for so many of the small and lovely renderings that grin or frown at innumerable corners and cornices in the city, remembered her little face, made still and hard and old by death, and so too remembers all of Palimpsest who pass by her on their way to night-fast and the stockades.

---

November stumbles across the tracks, tripping on their glittering rails, blind, the smell of train-catacombs in her nose, the smell of things that crawl, but also things that race and never cease. She falls into the arms of the iron ostrich-wastrel, hanging on her bolted neck, shuddering as the traffic clatters around her in an endless circuit, like breath, like blood. Under her hands she feels the heft and shape of strange great scissors with wet handles, but her fingers are empty. Under her mouth she tastes a bitter woman with nails in her tongue, but she is alone. The beekeeper hunches in the half-circle of the orphan's outflung hands, rocking on her heels, her fists pressed up against her eyes.

A soft thing falls onto her feet. The feel of it is familiar. The infinitesimal motion, the golden weight. She hears, through the din of the sensations that pit her hands against her eyes, a dim, welcome thrum, a hum like a heartbeat, and November laughs amid the wheeling cars and far-sung indignant squawks of drivers she cannot see. She seeks out the little weight and scoops it into her palm—and in that action she can also feel herself diving from a long boat, and also gripping a woman by her hair, such hair, shining and bristling as she knows the tiny creature in her grip to be, though she still sees nothing but black, but endless tunnels, but shadows angular and impenetrable.

She brings the bee to her lips; its wings hush against her. Slowly, as if to prove the deliberateness of its small deed, the creature presses its stinger into November's mouth, pauses for a moment on the tip of her tongue, stiff against the taut flesh of it, and then eases into her, piercing her tongue deftly and perishing in a paroxysm of venom and religious ecstasy.

In answer to her cry, a second bee arrives, and a third, floating at her fingertips like hopeful wedding bands, golden and bright. November's vision clears as the bee-venom forks through the meat of her tongue, and the underground recedes, claws at the periphery, rings her sight like the iris of an old movie camera. She takes in the Memorial, the blank plaque, the night sky waving with palm fronds, the streetside's tangled red manzanita branches. The carriages are flashes of scarlet or silver, curtained, small worlds she cannot enter. But the bees tip her fingers, and there are ten now; they skip away and return, buzzing encouragingly, and she knows when a creature beckons her if she knows anything at all.

She steps off the Memorial. There are bees at her feet, now, too. The carriages part to let her by, and November feels, somewhere far off, tears on cheeks that are and are not hers.

———

Down the mahogany alleys of Seraphim Street the bees lead her, now hundreds in number, a buzzing triumphal march at her back. Clothes shops line the spotless, polished road. In the window of one is a dress in the latest style: startlingly blue, sweeping up to the shoulders of a golden manikin. It cuts away to reveal a glittering belly; the join is fastened with a cluster of tiny cerulean eyes that blink lazily, in succession. The whites are diamonds, the pupils ebony. The skirt winds down in deep, rigid creases that tumble out of the window in a carefully arranged train, hemmed in crow feathers. The shopkeeper, Aloysius, keeps a pale green Casimira grasshopper on a beaded leash. It rubs its legs together while he works in a heap of black quills, sewing an identical trio of gowns like the one in the window for triplet girls who demanded them in violet, not blue.

At night, he ties the leash to his bedpost and the little thing lies next to his broad, lined face, clicking a binary lullaby into the old man's beard. He dreams of endless bodies all in a row, naked, unclothed and beautiful.

———

The bees spiral through the door of this shop, which has no bell, for this is a far place and such things are as old-fashioned as egg creams, and dive as one into the expanse of a lavender suit with a high cravat fashioned from a glossy green banana leaf and pinned by a clutch of pear-seeds. Its cuffs are wide and black, its chest crossed by a complex and voluminous sash of plantain leaves. The bees fill it utterly, pouring feet from its trousers and a solemn, thronging, buzzing head from its neck. The head totters and rights itself, pitting eyes and half a mouth into its sphere. Aloysius, mouth full of bone needles, wobbles on his stool and gapes; his grasshopper dances rapturously on its lead.

"Please," he spits, "I don't want any of *that* here. Immigrants are to keep to the secondhand stores, don't you know!"

The bee-manikin gnashes its ersatz teeth at the wizened tailor, and he cringes. November starts to apologize, but the lavender suit clasps her up in its arms so quickly it defeats the words in her mouth. It embraces her like a brother, and she can feel countless tiny bodies wriggle against her. She leans her head on its shoulder, not a queen but a mate, a maid, a whore in the kingdom of the bees, luring the workers from that singular distended belly and all its promise of gold. The manikin swoons.

"Where am I?" she whispers: finally, that first and last and most obvious of questions. Aloysius wrinkles his red and pockmarked nose in distaste.

"I will *not*," he hisses to the bees. "How unutterably *boring*. She's new as a *wound*. I don't have to." He spits at her, gripping the thick upper edge of his paisley cummerbund with veiny knuckles. The saliva explodes against her in a shower of glass beads.

The bees roar, but November holds up what she hopes is an imperious hand, trusting desperately in their love, in her place within the long and splendid list of things which bees adore: the queen, roses, hyacinth, comb, air, apple trees, jelly, the color red, herself, herself, keeper and mistress and bride in virginal white.

They freeze, fall silent, stare expectantly at her through the empty, bee-swarmed gaps in the hive-head tilting atop its crisp cravat. November puts her hands on the tailor's face, holding up his cheeks, withered as a wasp's nest. Her gaze is solemn and wide, her hold on him tender.

"Don't try that nonsense with me, girl. I've had more women than you've ever met."

But she says nothing. *This is just a dream, really,* she thinks, *and in dreams nothing is forbidden.*

"Sleeves," she sighs, and her voice is thick with poison and warmth. "Skirts, inseams, legs. Collars, cuffs, belts, bustles." She strokes his thick white hair and presses her face to his. "These are things that have touched a thousand bodies in place of your hands, in place of your kisses and your worship. These are the things that have stroked their bellies and their throats and lay alongside them in the dark."

The bee-golem grins blackly and gives a shuffling leap of delight. Victorious, they pull at the peacock feathers of the dress in the window. Aloysius just watches November, and she can feel his judgment: her hair is too coarse, striped dull, washed-out violet against dyed black. Her eyes don't match the dress either, mottled gray-green. But he wants to obey, whether her or the bees she cannot tell, and soon enough her pale, soft belly shows through deep blue cloth, her body moves beneath the silk proxy-hands of Aloysius and a regiment of bees sweeps up her hair, smooths her scalp with their loving feet.

November walks out onto Seraphim Street; her lavender-draped escort takes her arm. A few errant creatures buzz lazily behind her. They sing silently, a long and intricate song, simply to tell their queen, their mother, simply to tell Casimira that they are coming to her, coming, O Mother, O Mistress, and oh, what a thing they have brought!

# THREE

# THE THREE OF TENEMENTS

The tea at Oleg's table was bitter and red. He could not quite remember buying it, but was sure he had, of course he had, sometime. Hibiscus something. Blood orange. He didn't know. He emptied two pills from an equally orange bottle into his hand and washed them down with the phantom tea. It tasted like dead skins shriveled up to bright husks.

"Olezhka," his sister said. Water spilled out of her mouth, just a trickle. When he was a boy, it had been a torrent. Now it was just a tear. "Your tea is already cold."

He did not answer her, but shook out two more pills and rubbed a rough-stubbled cheek with one hand. He had dreamed in the night, dreamed until sweat fled from him and soaked the sheets. It had been so vivid—no, not vivid, *livid*, like a bruise. There had been the taste of sugarcane, and a girl with blue hair, and there had been something like a great iron bird . . .

"You smell like copper keys, brother. And perfume. I don't wear perfume."

"Would you rather hear that her name was Lyudmila, or that it was not?" he said softly.

The woman in the red child's dress combed a long brown

weed from her hair, embarrassed, but not for herself—she was forever without and beyond shame. Only embarrassed for him, who could still taste the blond woman's mouth in his.

"Mila, I'm still a man, I still have blood in me."

Her wide blue eyes regarded him, absent of guile or cruelty. She had never been cruel—she called herself his pet, his poor old cat, but she did not beg for milk or tear his curtains. She sat at his table, waited for him to come home from school, and then from work, and the years ground against each other like gears.

"I am not angry. When have I ever been angry? Drink your tea."

He drank, and grimaced. No honey in the house—he always forgot something at the market.

"Do you think a ghost should be angry?" she asked, her wet mouth sopping her words. "I can try, if you think I ought to be. I think I remember 'angry'—it was yellow, wasn't it? Like custard."

Oleg caught her gaze, as a fish catches a barb in its mouth—it must have known such a thing was inevitable. But he smiled. The dyed lace on her collar was twisted up around her neck, and her face was open and sweet, her broad cheeks, her dripping hair.

"I love you, Mila."

She nodded absently. "Yellow, right?"

"Yes, it was yellow."

———

When he climbed out of the bath, she was gone. It was like that. He'd grown accustomed to her comings and goings, as one becomes accustomed to a wayward wife or, indeed, a cat only partially belonging to the places she sleeps. When he was seven he had awoken from some nameless child's dream-terror to see her sitting on his ashen footboard, knees drawn up to her chin, her dress seeping a wet crescent onto the edges of his blankets.

"That's *my* bed," she had said, and crawled in next to him, sodden and sniffling and cold. She had put her arms around his neck and fallen asleep that way, her face buried behind his ear. In the morning, his father had been furious that he'd wet the bed, and though he knew he hadn't, he could not argue with the soaked, wadded sheets.

And so it had gone. She was not entirely his sister, nor really his friend. She did not do any of the things he had thought ghosts might do: steal his breath, demand sweets from the cupboard, send him on dangerous quests through the forests. She did not drive him mad. She did not plead for stories of the living. She did not, beyond dripping the Volkhov all over his bed, destroy his things or get him in trouble. He counted himself lucky to have got such a polite ghost. She also knew she was a ghost, or at least that she was dead, and Oleg felt that this was a lucky thing as well, for he would not have liked to tell her about it, about that day on the river, and how his mother cried so loud he heard it deep in her belly, and how he cried too.

Once, when he was fourteen and a brown-eyed girl in his class had made fun of his accent, when he had beat his pillow with his skinny arms and wept the sour, oily tears of that year, Lyudmila had crawled under the covers again, her dress already too short to be decent when faced with such activity, and put her arms around him, her mouth so close to his ear that afterward he would have to hop up and down like a swimmer to get the water out.

"In the land of the dead," she rasped, weeds tangling up her tongue, "a boy who was run over by a black automobile fell in love with the Princess of Cholera, who had a very bright yellow dress and yellow hair and shiny yellow shoes. The boy chased after her down all the streets of the dead, past the storefronts and the millineries, past the paper mills and the municipal parks. But the princess would not stop running, for cholera is swift as anything. Finally, he caught her in the stillborn slums, where those who have not got anything of life to make a house out of dwell. And she said to him: 'I will never love you, for you are not one of my people.' So the boy painted his face white and gray, and wore a yellow rainslicker for her sake, and bled from his mouth for her love. But still she would not look at him with sweetness, and so he was made to go to the city well and draw up the fouled water so that he might forget her, and himself, and all things save the hospice where such unfortunates sleep who cannot find peace even behind the doors of the world." She kissed his cheek, and ever after he would feel the mark. "So you see? It will all come out right."

"I don't really see. That's a terrible story."

"But he wasn't her *family*. There can be no real love between strangers. I love you, and that is enough."

But he had loved the brown-eyed girl anyway, though he never touched her, even once. Lyudmila said that this was the way of the world, but he turned his back to her in their thin little bed, and she had not been able to stop him, being as she was and not other than that.

He told no one of her except the doctor who dispensed the pills which did nothing to banish her, and she promised that she had not told her friends about him either. She seemed to grow up more or less as he did, even though she should have been older. Still, she had not chased off his girlfriends or even scowled at the occasional boyfriend or thrown jealous fits on the fire escape. She just sat on the footboard as she always had, and if there was no one in his bed and he could not sleep, she would slip in beside him and he would wake up with wrinkled fingers and drenched pillows.

"I love you, Mila," he said to the empty room. He did not ask where she went; it seemed like bad manners, and folk who have lived together as long as Oleg and Lyudmila rely on manners.

———

"You have something on your tummy," she said as he was brushing his teeth after what could hardly have been called breakfast—still he could not stand the taste of stale red tea on his teeth. She sat pertly on the sink, where she could daintily spit out her water rather than letting it run down her chin.

He looked down—beneath the slight fur there was something. He pulled up the skin of his stomach. Around his navel, brachiating out like a compass rose, were long, spindly black lines, crooked and aimless. He could almost make out writing above them, but it hurt his eyes to peer so close at something upside down. It was the mark that the other Lyudmila had had on her neck—he might pretend he had spilled ink or something, but he recognized it— had he not tasted it, kissed it?

"Maybe you shouldn't be kissing strange girls," she said archly. "You could catch something."

He rubbed at it a little—it stayed, of course. He hadn't really thought it would come off. Like Mila, he supposed, he was stuck with it. He shrugged. It didn't much matter. A man who has learned to live with a ghost can live with a scar.

"Mila," he said, drawing a tired breath, "drop dead."

She smirked, and spat into the sink. He followed suit.

———

It was nine days later. Afterward, he would count on his fingers to arrive at the number, sure he was right, within one or two. He'd been called uptown in the stiff kind of cold that growls at engines and whips them cruelly. A young man stamped his feet outside a tall brownstone, blowing into his slender fingers and tugging at a knit cap. Oleg's breath puffed in the air as he knelt to his work.

Lock-outs: the small, sweet, reliable lost souls who made up the bulk of his business with their forgetful habits and careless keys. He felt fatherly about them, even when it was a septuagenarian in his bathrobe and a cold pipe. Poor kittens, locked into the world.

Oleg looked into the lock, looking deep, as was his habit, looking as he looked into his sister's eyes, through the imagined telescoping locks of his interior estates, into the kid's kitchen door just past the threshold, and the chipped white bedroom door, and out of the brownstone into the next, all the way to Brooklyn and still further, to the foaming Atlantic nosing at the strand. He listened as to a seashell, for the lock to cry out its secret grief. It wept; he comforted.

"Thanks for getting here so fast," the young man said, shoving his hands into his black jacket pockets. He was tall and narrow, dark Spanish eyes, the opposite of soft, generous Lyudmila with her great blond mane.

"My shop isn't far." Oleg shrugged. "And we can't have you turning stray and pawing at neighbors' doors for fish."

The young man snorted laughter. They talked in the way one checks one's watch on the train platform or blows on one's fingers: something to do, a way to keep warm. The boy's name was Gabriel. He was an architecture student. He built great miserly things that held locks gingerly, fiercely.

The door popped gratefully open and Gabriel gave a yelp of relief not unlike a puppy seeing his master come home, miraculously, from the frightening world. His black jacket flopped open and Oleg could see, snaking up over his collarbone, a fine mark, as if painted by a calligrapher, black and spindled, branching out as if searching for new flesh to conquer.

Oleg leapt up. He grabbed the man's shirt before he could stop himself, but Gabriel did not protest, nor even seem surprised. He just smiled, an affable, lopsided smile utterly unlike the ghastly, knowing glances to which Oleg had all his life been subject.

"Go ahead," the boy whispered. "It's okay."

And so Oleg, his hands shaking and wind-reddened, unbuttoned the crisp workday shirt and spread it open, the mark there, livid, alive, darker than dreams.

"Do you know what it is?" Oleg said softly.

Gabriel bent his head to catch the locksmith's stare and lifted his chin with two brown fingers.

"Don't you?"

"No, I . . . it was there—"

"When you woke up? Yeah."

"Tell me, please."

"I can do better."

And the architect kissed him, very gently, the way a widow kisses the feet of a statue. His tongue tasted of orange candy. Oleg thought he ought to have been startled, affronted, even, but twenty years in the school of his sister had permanently excised the *ought* from him. He stiffened, unsure, and the strangeness of an unshaven cheek against his own habitually haggard skin struck him, an oddly innocent thing, more naked even than Lyudmila's scented face. His hand was still on Gabriel's chest, and he thought, though such a thing could not be, not really, that the black lines beneath his palm burned.

Oleg sighed into the circuit of the architect's arms, imagining Gabriel as a great house, elbows unfolding in perfect angles to take him in, to cover him in rafters and drywall, to keep the rain from his head and the cold from his bones. They stood thus as the air thinned in a sudden certainty of snow to come, and kissed a second time on the doorstep before the boy led him in, through the kitchen door just past the threshold, through the chipped white bedroom door, through the tall, thin brownstone, and still further.

―――――

When Gabriel entered him, Oleg thought he might break into pieces with the pain of it, but he did not, of course. He opened, his insides unfolding to allow another human within him. He whimpered at the bare walls, trying not to seem unprepared for the strength of it. But Gabriel smoothed his hair and kissed the back of his neck and whispered:

"It's ok, it's ok, Oleg. I need you so much. You have no idea."

# 413th and Zarzaparrilla

# 413th and Zarzaparrilla

**ZARZAPARRILLA STREET IS PAVED** with old coats. Layer after layer of fine corduroy and felt and wool the colors of coffee and ink. Those having business here must navigate with pole and gondola, ever so gently thrusting aside the sleeves and lapels and weedy ties, fluttering like seaweed, lurching as though some unlunar tide compelled them. The gondolas are rimmed in balsam and velvet, and they are silent through the depthless street. Great curving pairs of scissors are provided in case of sudden disaster, tucked neatly beneath the pilot's seat.

All along the cloth-canal are minuscule houses, barely large enough for a man to stand straight beneath the rafters. They are houses of shame, and try their best to make themselves small. Every so often the wind, fragrant with juniper and blackberry wine brewing in a great pearl vat somewhere far within the corkscrewing streets, blows a door open, and a great eye, blue or brown or yellow as cholera, will peer out from the jamb. The wind, sensitive to their natures, shuts the doors again as soon as it may.

This is the banking district of Palimpsest, and you must keep a respectful silence. Within the hunched houses a great and holy counting occurs, and even the sun does not wish to interrupt. It has been years since the sky has seen one of the beggars who dwell in the houses, who, once housed, could not bear to be parted from those precious walls, those beatific chimneys, who grew and grew until they filled the places wholly, and could not even be cut from their parlors with gondolier's scissors. But the clouds judge that they do not cry out in their sleep, and so must be learned in some school of happiness.

Almudena, Mendicant-Queen! The smallest house must surely be hers, most debased, most humble. Her scissors broke here, and she begged each splinter of her house from the great and tall. What creature was it gave her that tiled roof? That oak porch? But it is her mumbling you hear beneath the great green streetlamps with their globes of gold. They say it is her long tail that seeks the street edge in warm weather, sunning its scales on the curb.

Take her what coins you have, she will bite them to know their worth and count them into her memory, which is finite and bounded as her own bones. A rib counts for a hundred, vertebrae twenty-five each, cartilage for decimal places, her liver for units of one million, and neither you nor I will ever see her priceless heart. Without calculating machine, Almudena uses the map of her flesh to recall deposits, withdrawals, points of interest. She cannot, of course, forget her own joints, the mathematics of her own little pancreas, and her lungs cannot be robbed of their accounts. If we were to cut her open, who knows if we would find blood—at night the gondoliers swear you can hear coins rolling through her ventricles, notes folded into cranes fluttering at the ends of her hair, trying to lift her house free of Zarzaparrilla Street and bear her past all dreams of lucre.

———

Gabriel poles through the jackets, his face bright and wind-whipped—but the wind here is warm, it carries with it red flowers and the sea. Oleg peers over the edge, through the spaces between the coat-waves. He is bent double over the side of the gondola, his vision blurred as though with sudden pain, his hands cold—he feels mold beneath them, mold and metal. He tastes snail flesh in his mouth, and his head throbs with the doubled, trebled, quartered actions of each of his hands, each of his eyes. He shakes it and brass dust falls from his hair, the dust of a thousand keys grinding.

"What's at the bottom?" Oleg asks thickly, almost catching a noseful of brass buttons.

"I don't know. Can't swim, myself. Train tracks? Morlocks? Alligators, definitely."

Oleg sits back, rubs his head like an old man trying to remember his glasses.

"Why did you bring me here?" he says, staring off into the slamming doors and blinking eyes of the low houses. His gondolier—his? Probably not his, not really, not his own—turns, his haphazard black hair stung with moonlight.

"It's where I've got, Oleg. Only place I could take you. That's how it works. You sort of . . . lease your skin to this place. This is the part you saw on my chest, so this is where we end up, though I had to hustle to meet you here. And it's a big favor, Oleg. Now I have to wait till tomorrow night to find out what neighborhood you've got on you."

"What if you sleep with someone . . . new? Without the mark. Where do you go?" Where did Lyudmila go?

Gabriel shrugs and poles through a knot of tweed. "I don't know. I've never been with anyone new. It's a waste of time. Nowhere, maybe. I don't like to think about it."

Gabriel pulls open his shirt, not very different than the one they'd left crumpled in a heap on an old cedar dresser—and the mark is there again, deeper if anything, like sword-slashes, like a flaying. Oleg follows a long brown finger toward the most savage of the black lines, and yes, just above it, in the tiniest possible script, scrawled by a moth or a hummingbird: *Zarzaparrilla Street*. Crossed by 413th, 415th, and 417th at severe, acute angles, nothing like the soothingly regular grid of New York.

"Besides," Gabriel laughs, "immigrants never have any money, you know. This is the best place to get some. I guess you could say we're commuting." He poles through the coats, enormous bronze scissors stuck through his belt, which he draws now and again to slice through an impassable blue tangle of recalcitrant suits. His voice softens, quiets. "Most of them . . . most of *us* never figure it out. Bad dream, they think, or good one. Funny rash, never really goes away, but Doc says it's fine, nothing to worry about. Why dwell on it? But some people, they just can't let it go." He stares at the teetering houses with their enormous eyes blinking out of the windows. "Some people drink themselves out of school trying to find it again, trolling through bars where the shadows are so greasy they leave trails on the walls, just to find a way in, a way through. Some people forget too that you're supposed to stop sleeping, you're supposed to have a life in the sun."

"Is it always dark here?"

Gabriel sniffs, wipes his eyes with the cuff of his coat. He seems so young, young and tired and needful. "No, no, 'course not," he says. "We just never come here in the daytime."

Oleg looks over the rim of the boat again. There are flower garlands strung there, calla lilies, he thinks, and bluebells. They sag into the clothed street; their smell is old, a remnant, a relic.

"But it *is* a dream, after all," he says to the woolen tide. "Nothing matters in a dream. It's just . . . crazy things, over and over until you wake up."

There is a long and somehow ugly silence. "Sure," Gabriel says, "just a dream," but his eyes are hollow, shallow, low and dim. "What else?"

Oleg trails his hand in the street. He is good at the ephemeral, at ghosts, at dreams. At veiled things and at the untouchable. If it's a dream, he will be all right; these are places he can know. If he can bring up a ghost, he can find his way to waking in this place.

Gabriel pulls the gondola into a little dock and lashes it to the pole. He smiles, but it is breezy and thin.

"Time to punch the clock," he says.

They enter a great cathedral-like building of deep blue glass from buttress to cornice. A few others straggle in after them, and Oleg follows Gabriel's lead as they receive aprons from an absurdly tall and silent man with glossily spotted giraffe legs, along with fine shirts, rouge for their cheeks, cologne. They pass through a long hallway lined with portraits of maître d's with proud aquiline noses. Before them dozens of tables spread out with ruby-colored tablecloths and pearl candelabras—it is a restaurant, vast and bustling.

"Don't look at them," Gabriel whispers as he takes a tray of slim goblets filled with hot strawberry wine.

"At who?" Oleg struggles under the weight of his own burden: globes of white butter clattering in little dishes of hollowed-out diamonds, square loaves of moist, spiced bread. *Pressed into service as a waiter*, he thinks. *Wonderful.*

"The patrons," Gabriel hisses. "It's the law, here. You can never look them in the eye. Keep your head bent, like you're praying. There shouldn't be any need to speak, and anyway they aren't allowed to talk to you unless they call you 'Novitiate.'"

"How do I take their orders if I can't speak?"

"There's only one dish here. Just put the plates down and go back to the kitchen for more. Get through the night—you'll be paid, and it's better to have money here than not to."

And so they work. After the wine and bread come snails in flaming brandy with thin little slices of banana sizzling in their shells, followed by great bone platters piled up with obscene slabs of meat, ruby-bright steaks that slide over the rims of the plates, crusted in broiled white-brown skin: *albino elephant,* Oleg hears ten, twenty dinners breathe in ecstasy. The meat is crowned with tumbling cascades of pomegranate seeds, drenched in honey-amber wine. The smell of it is so rich and sweet it nearly knocks Oleg back—his stomach clenches, but they will not allow him to eat.

"Novitiate!" cries a woman with three rings on her right hand and a coiling bracelet of silver and agate on her left that winds around all her fingers and up her arm. Oleg is careful not to look at her. His feet ache from the pilgrimages to the kitchen, and he does not want to talk to her. Her fingernails are wet with pomegranate juice.

"How long have you lived in Palimpsest, Novitiate?" she asks haughtily.

"I..."

"Speak up!"

"I think this is my second night, if I understand everything."

She claps her hands and squeals, a high sound like a broken chime. "I *thought* so! Your gait is *quite* gauche. An *immigrant!* How charming! Tell us, boy, is it true that you can't see yellow or blue? That you feast in the rubbish heaps after we've all gone to our beds and our teawine? That you all get here by..." She leans down to catch his eye, to get him in trouble, but he averts his gaze in time, and sees only her long red hair brushing her wineglass, still streaked with strawberry. "Well, by rutting like filthy old cows? What do you eat? You *must* tell us all your foul rites!"

Oleg fixes his eyes on his shoes. His face burns with a shame he did not know, until this moment, he possessed. He has not heard the word *immigrant* flung like that since he was a boy—of course, he is an immigrant. There and here. The strange woman with her hooting, triumphal laughs and her gingery perfume makes him want to run, and also to stay and grind her glass into her face.

Slowly, with a deliberateness he savors, and will savor still in the morning, he raises his head and stares at her directly, her clear, spangle-painted eyes, her cheeks with tiny jewels embedded in the skin which is just beginning to show wrinkles, laugh lines, without bitterness or malice. Silence crashes through the hall and explodes at his feet.

"I'm sure," Oleg says evenly, "it's all true. Every word. Want to come to the rubbish heaps with me? We can *rut* under the moon and see where you end up."

The woman's violet mouth opens slightly, perhaps in shock, perhaps in pleasure at being confronted at last with real live immigrant manners. The giraffe-legged maître d' surges up behind him and cuffs his ear with one enormous, manicured hand. He seizes Oleg's arm, and without a word hauls him from the glassy cobalt hall and deposits him unceremoniously onto Zarzaparrilla Street.

Gabriel strolls out a few minutes later—sweet boy, good boy, loyal compatriot.

"I told you," is all he says, as he pulls the gondola's lead free of the dock and pushes them out into the street of coats again. He is cold, as though Oleg transgressed against him personally, embarrassed him, made him a fool.

"But it's a dream," Oleg insists. "It was fun. We won't even remember it in the morning."

"You don't know anything, Oleg," sighs Gabriel, and they do not speak while the wind picks up through the last, late stars and light begins, lemony and cool in the east.

"Give me the scissors?" Oleg says finally, smiling as brave and bright as he has ever learned to do. But Gabriel has turned away; his gaze is over the sweet, small rooftops, down alleys Oleg does not know. He is gone: softly, subtly, irrevocably. He doesn't turn to look, or graze fingers as he hands over blades longer than his legs. Oleg stands, nearly toppling them, and holds his architect—not his, not really—and whispers against his neck his best apology:

"I want to tell you a story. It's short, I promise. And it's about love. See, in the land of the dead, a boy who was run over by a black car fell in love with the Princess of Cholera, who had a very bright yellow dress and yellow hair and shiny yellow shoes..."

But Gabriel is not listening, and his back is stiff beneath his coat. Oleg sadly takes up the bronze scissors and knifes through the flowing street below the boat. Dismayed threads pop free of shoulder seams; buttons fly. Below he sees nothing but more sleeves and brume, but he is both a swimmer and a maker of keys, and he knows how to fit himself into gaps too small for others. He cannot stay in the wreck of Gabriel's disapproval, and the night is almost done. Oleg holds his breath and dives blade-first: he falls and falls, so far.

———

In a train station, a woman with blue hair is suddenly dizzy; on a street of cedar, a beekeeper in a long dress sneezes as her nose fills with wool.

———

There is a river flowing beneath the street of coats, a river the color of milk. It is slow and thick, rolling in long, lugubrious currents of cream and curdle. There is a flannel sky over it, and a long brick tunnel overgrown with golden moss and flabby, half-translucent mushrooms, slick and silver, like the flesh of oysters. It has fallen through in places, and Oleg has fallen through the places.

He walks along the bank, a crumbling, ornate rill carved with lamenting faces whose tears feed the river. Their mouths contort, their eyes plead, and they pass by unmarked beneath his feet. He limps, and this disturbs him, for in dreams does not one fall painlessly, like a sigh?

There is a bench, one of those that seem, wherever they are, that they ought to have been in Paris, with a view of the Seine. There is a woman sitting there in a long dress, watching the mushrooms flutter. As he draws closer, the dress becomes deeply blue, spattered with silver stars. It is formal; it has a bustle like the base of a cupola. Her hair is wild and loose, though, mouse-colored, very like his own, and strung through with snow, though no flakes fall underground. She turns to face him and he groans; the mushrooms recoil.

"I missed you, Olezhka," says his sister, and holds out her long arms.

# FOUR

# THE ARCHIPELAGO

Lucia was gone.

Ludovico sat naked in his hall, cross-legged, as if to be shriven. The *Etymologiae* flowed up the walls around him: Lucia's breadcrumbs, all raven-devoured, and he the child left behind in the wood. He touched them, the tiny grooves in the paint, places where she had been, where her fingers had moved. If he closed his eyes he could dwell in the circuit of air that had once held her, he could hold his breath and be inside her again, within the close and burning borders of her—she stood here, washed her hair in this sink, wrote upon this wall, ate roasted chicken at this table. There was no place he could enter where she had not also been, her echoes hanging in the air like pages hung to dry. No place that did not suppurate in her absence, which was not ringed with the light of her old selves, like film burned with a cigarette.

He could smell her leonine scent in their bed, and would still, even weeks after she had slept there. He could not bear to sleep where she had, to ruin the imperceptible outline of her body, which was surely now only a fevered hope and a lie of unwashed linens. Her laugh, harsh and cruel and short, hung like garlands of blackened roses by the long, thin windows. He had hardly eaten but to put his teeth to the bones she had left on a chipped plate in the kitchen, to fit his mouth to a dead thing she had once worried.

Ludo pressed his cheek to the wall, and the letters warmed beneath him like her shoulders in winter: *Cum leones dormierint, vigilant oculi; cum ambulant, cauda sua cooperiunt vestigial sua, ne eos venator inveniat*... the words bent the corner sharply, winding on past the telephone table with its slender green lamp. *When lions sleep, their eyes are ever watchful, and when they walk, they obliterate their tracks with their tails so that the hunter may not find them*...

Ludo dug his nails into *leones*, into *ambulant*, as if to unearth from them her face, her stride, her long golden tail brushing paw prints from the scrub-dust.

They had always been beasts, curled and snarling in their cave, intractable, invidious. Of course they had, chimera and saint—but hadn't they made their monstrous contract, hadn't they eaten youths together and made a lair of these five rooms? Hadn't he seen her face in some shield years past and been rooted to this floor, his stone arms pinning her to him? Where could she even dream of going that he would not already be there, knowing her as he did, knowing her best, knowing her nature, her origins?

He looked at the apocalypse of the Japanese book: spread over the floor, hundreds of linen pages, silver paint, black silks. He screamed at them: impassive, inelegant illustrations, trains like limp snakes. She would have done better, they would have been yawning leviathans under her pen, chewing through the belly of the earth. The ceiling swallowed his cry with genteel embarrassment. His deadline was long past, the contract given to another binder in Parma. He did not care, he had let it go. And this was left in place of his wife: pages, paint, silk. He pissed on them, he spat, he tore them, he ate them, he threw them from his window. There seemed to be no end to their number—it was an infinite beast, one surely known to whatever podium occupied his beloved Spaniard in the libraries of the dead. Ludo laughed in the dark and began to scrawl on the wall, near the baseboard, where he would not crowd Lucia's hand:

18.c.1. *In the remote west are creatures whose body is that of a great book with a spine of wood and glues the matter of which is like unto the blood of a man. In rage does the beast snap its covers and gnash its chapters one against the other, and should a man attempt to make end to such a one, it will spew forth the substance of its life in the form of pages without end, and he shall be overwhelmed entirely by the copious waste of the brute, and thus does the beast ransom itself from death . . .*

He stopped, having no further joke to share with the ghost of her.

Seven sewn covers empty of pages stacked themselves into a rough Ionian column to bear up his coffee; spilled glue from the sinew of an ox had hardened into caramel below the defunct radiator. Four hundred and twelve pages had swallowed up the couch, the one Lucia had bought in Ostia because it was precisely the color of a pecan shell, on which she had slept naked and alone for three nights so as to drink up all that billowing color into her impossible skin. The ruin of the Japanese book covered his floor like a wrought carpet, and his steps sounded loudly, too loudly, on their leaves.

Ludo lay over them, the couch soft and flaccid beneath him now, no longer smelling of Lucia or the sea, or that summer on the beach when she wore only yellow, and she had not yet frowned in his presence, not even once. He put his face into the pages and breathed the desiccated smell of long-dry ink, sifting through it with archaeological patience, searching for the vanished weight of his wife's knees pressing little cups into the fabric.

By the time the moon slid out of the sky like a button in a dress, Ludo had fallen asleep, curled in the lap of his book monster, an illuminated dining car stuck to his cheek.

————

"Have you seen her?"

The sentence, its mere shape in his mouth like an old, flattened fig, exhausted him. He had stamped it with his tongue like a press, copy after copy, into the hands of everyone he met, all of their friends with tortoise-shell glasses and buckled shoes, briefcases with embossed mottos, pens tapped against teeth, frosted lips pursed, napes pinched, Chianti in fat-bellied glasses at a dozen cafés where he tasted nothing of the cakes or coffees set before him. He and Lucia had not been good friends, the two of them curled up like turtles into the shape of the other. They had rarely sought out the people they had known before the advent of their walled world, their untouchable quiet.

The woman across from him now was a university acquaintance, quite far down the list of Lucia's folk. He was reasonably certain her name had been, presumably still was, Nerezza, something stiff and severe like that. Lucia collected severe and baroque humans like a grotesque kind of zookeeper. Nerezza's flecked eyes were small and narrow; she looked angry even when she laughed.

"Why do you assume she has left you? There might have been an accident; you could call the police." She measured out her voice through her lips like an iron flattening a sleeve.

*Lions are watchful even when they sleep,* he thought. "Because I know her! She *meant* to leave. She was always . . . a woman of intent."

Nerezza laughed like a cough. "Yes, she was. How funny that we talk about her already like she is dead. Well. I could say that I've seen her, but I don't think that would be of much use to you."

Ludo waited, trying to be patient with her, to see what Lucia had loved in her, even in this to touch his wife. His palms sweated through the knees of his trousers. Such an ugly thing, the ever-leaking body. Nerezza scowled.

"Tell me, Ludovico," she said, drawing deeply on her thin little cigarette. "Have you had any dreams lately? Bad ones, crazy ones, like the kind you have in a hospital, when they won't let you out and you can't see your family."

"Of course. My wife has left me. I have terrible dreams, when I sleep at all."

"That's not what I mean. How about a rash? Like hives, but it doesn't itch. Black. Like a tattoo."

"Yes, yes, on my back. I don't care about that. She had it on her knee. She said it was nothing. Communicable nothing, I guess."

Nerezza rolled her eyes, stubbed out her cigarette. Ludovico loathed smoking. He had tried to explain to Lucia once that it contorted the humors, it was hot and dry and would burn out the delicate phlegmatic *apparati* and leave her breathing fire. He had been earnest; she had kissed him with her mouth full of smoke, and his lungs had trembled, blazing, parched.

Nerezza rolled up the sleeve of her violet dress. There were lines on her forearm, Lucia's lines, his lines. How dare she? How dare she bear on her body that last thing which had passed from his wife to him? But no cherubs winged at the edges of Nerezza's streets. There was an oblong track in the center of the snaking avenues, like the Hippodrome seen from an impossible distance. On her flesh the mark was horrible to him, bare, violent, as though she had torn into herself with jagged glass—torn into him, into Lucia, taken their secret disease, their private travail.

"Now," she said quietly, laying her arm on the table between them like a meal, like meat. "It is possible for me to say that I have seen Lucia. It is also possible that I know where she is now, that I am certain she is safe and well. It is even possible that I touched her face not three days past, and that we have passed men like a whiskey flask between us. These things I have to give you, but they are also lies, for I have not seen Lucia in the waking world, nor do I know where she is while we speak here, at this place, drinking this coffee, eating this crème caramel. It is for you to decide if you will take these things from me."

Ludo closed his eyes. She talked like Lucia, dreamily, darkly, pregnant with meaning he sometimes thought pretended. The sun pressed its hands upon his face and he burned. "I will take them, Nerezza. Tell me where she is so that I can bring her home."

"Ludovico, poor soul, Lucia will never come home. She won't, and she doesn't want to. I think—and it has been a long while since I knew either of you well—but I think it would be better if you told yourself she was dead, and believed it, and became a widower."

Nerezza allowed a small smile, though it fit her face poorly. It was an encouraging smile, even motherly. *Go along and play, little boy,* it said. *We are so busy; it is such work to be grown up.*

Ludo grimaced. "If the world contained within it enough black to mourn her, perhaps I could. As things are, I am what I am, and she is what she is, and we are neither of us dead."

She took his hand gingerly, the gesture of a sleek-legged rider approaching a great beast she intends to master. He was surprised to find no sugar lump in her palm. If Lucia was a chimera, heaving her great lion's body from couch to floor to bed, Nerezza was an eel, dark and snapping, too slippery to touch, however fiercely she might be held. He recalled his *Etymologiae*: that the eel is born in mud, and eats earth, that the mud of the Ganges gives birth to giant eels, black and worm-blind, gargantuan, holy. Perhaps it was her and her inscrutable tribe of which Isidore spoke, sliding up out of the great ashy river with water beading on their breasts.

He gripped her hand suddenly and she disentangled herself with a deft motion, practiced at escape.

———

Her apartment was not far from the café, but they did not stumble into it in the manner of lust-addled lovers. They walked, slowly and without ardor, hand in hand, into her house, where four long windows let in the diffident afternoon sun.

Her rooms were as severe as the angles of her own bones. There was a black chaise, a glass cabinet. She poured him a resinous yellow wine he did not like. He felt his eel—not his, surely!—circle him and was feebled by her. Nerezza settled her weight on his lap—she was heavier than she looked, as though her bones were made of iron. She moved her violet skirt aside—such an expensive thing, thick as a book cover, and her legs like pages.

"I am a path to her," she said, her black eyes piercing and undeniable. Ludo had followed with a monk's faith. He opened his mouth against her neck like a wolf, as though he could tear her open that way and find Lucia hiding, or waiting, inside. She moved her legs around him, sliding, squeezing things that would not let him free, so tight that his knuckles were pressed against them as he fumbled with his belt and kissed her again, deeply, with a crawling feeling of loss—Lucia would not like this. Or she would not care. Which did he want? Ludovico scratched her back brutally with his free hand, hoping that his marks would show as dark and dire as the maps on their flesh, the map she had no right to, yet bore.

Nerezza would not open her mouth no matter how he moved in her. She was wild-eyed, seething, but breathed serenely through her aquiline nose, her black eyes clamped on him like a bite. She was narrow within and without, and the press of her all around him threatened to force his soul out through the top of his head. He screamed into her—he could not help it. He screamed into the dark, into the empty house, into the compact interior world of Nerezza, the eel-hearted, the great and solemn beast who did not cry out in her shuddering, but bit his cheek savagely and held it hissing in her canines as he came like glass breaking.

Parimutuel Circle

# Parimutuel Circle

THE LANES OF PARIMUTUEL CURVE in long, lazy arcs, so as to take in their circuit the whole of the Troposphere. The city shakes three times when the races ring the great baleen-railed track, when a hundred hooves send up sprays of black pearls, when the spectators as one throw back their heads and scream out the substance of their ecstatic wills. There is a dome, for rain in Palimpsest is like an eager lover: ever-present and zealous, steaming with ardor. Under the dome, chocolate silk sweeps down from a frame of kaleidoscopic glass, each bar blown in as many colors as a church window. Enormous orange lamps hang like miniature suns, banded up in black chains. And the track, the track of pearls, wheels in its grand circle, ever on. The stands are rarely empty: slavering, pilgrim-fervent, the crowd leans forward as one great, spangled body to see the poor beasts run.

Traugott's voice, a copper pan shaken in the wind, sings up from the stalls. He is a breeder of snails and dwells in a house of three stories. In his youth he covered each of the floors in rich soils of black and red, leaves of gold and green, grains brown and sweet, violet petals as thick as a pat of butter. In his middle age, birch and fig saplings sprouted through the kitchen tile; hedges ring the furniture. His great *petit-gris* slowly move from parlor to wash-closet, gorging themselves in paroxysms of helicicial rapture. They mate in the chimney, sing softly the hymns of snails on the windowsills when the moon blanches the verdant paint to black.

And when the days of races approach, he takes the roundest and sweetest of them into his bedchamber, and on a brocaded bed so great it spans the floor entire, so soft he cannot bear to sleep upon it, he lays them down like children. There Traugott instructs his beloveds in an ascetic discipline, a consecrated fast, for the stomachs of men cannot bear very much of what the stomachs of snails contain. He leads them in prayer to the high Helix on her throne of soil, her opalescent flesh bound with sweet grasses, her eyestalks quivering with compassion, with mercy. So Traugott quivers as his jewels perish in purgation and starvation, so Traugott weeps for them as he polishes their shells and packs them into a green valise.

And with his bright case, Traugott stalks the stalls, his beard dyed to match the favored mounts of the day—today it is a spectral scarlet, and children reach out to touch the light of his long hairs, soft as a maid's. He holds up his broad hands, full of little golden sacks—snails brim the edges, iridescent, the size of a dainty fist. He slurps one slowly, with pleasure, with grief. The taste of them like buttered brandywine, like sugared goosefat, melts on his tortured tongue. Seeing the bobbing of his ruddy, guilty throat, a dozen spectators clamor for his service.

———

Nerezza wears a wide black hat festooned with long, pale swan-feathers tipped in onyx and obsidian. The whole affair is pinned with the lacquered pelvis of a lynx. It shadows her face like an eclipse and she licks the meat from her snail shell with precise delicacy, flicking the shriveled body into her narrow mouth. She stares down at the track from their high box, garlanded with leather reins, and raises a pair of silver opera glasses, trembling, to her face.

"It will start soon," she says.

"What will?" Ludovico sits straight as a soldier. His left hand itches—there is nothing there, but he feels his flesh blazing, crawling with bees, while his right droops with the weight of a cold porcelain hand. He can hear the roaring of trains and the small voice of a viola in the dark. He is arrested by these things which he can feel but are not with him, not present in the stadium. But the scent of the steaming snail cuts through their shadows, and a murmur passes through the waiting audience. They hold their breath as one.

"The night races, Ludo."

"You promised me Lucia, not horses."

"She is here. I have not seen her yet. But I am watchful." She proffers the glasses.

*When lions sleep, their eyes are ever-watchful*, he thinks. He takes the lenses, looks down to the track and its improbable gravel—there are horses there, yes, stamping their hooves and snorting, but they are monstrosities of leather hung over a clanking, clattering framework. Bronze ribs show through tears in the brown skin, creased and stained like an old map case. Their eyes are gaping holes that show occasional flames: whatever engine drives them spits out its heart in sparks and blue jets. They are thin; constricted chests tucked up like starving whippets, spindled legs never approaching equine proportion, concluding in bronze spikes that pierce the pearls of the racing ground. Their manes are braided backward into their tails, one massive leather cord proceeding from head to haunch in a sweeping arc.

"They are so beautiful," Nerezza breathes. "I know the woman who makes them—she lives in Silverfish, on the outskirts, on an estate that would beggar Naples. She has a scar on the small of her back, shaped like a liver. A colt bit her when she was young."

"This is a dream," Ludo sighs. He is not patient. "A dream, and I shall wake up sticky."

She gives him a withering look, and several of the outlandishly dressed folk near them—one hoists a parasol of sleeping gray lizards—recoil as though he has uttered a vulgar curse. He is saved in his shame by the sounding of a long, low horn, something like those Swiss leviathans Lucia had loved. The leather horses explode from their dock—the crowd throws back their sparkling heads as one and screams. Nerezza's own cry is high and piquant and terrible, and the horses screech their response, like the death of a thousand owls. Their mechanical gait is awkward and jerky, their spikes driving into the track, but the speed is undeniable, and it is over before Ludo can think it a dream again, the one with a red handprint on its rump streaming ahead in the last stretch.

But no one applauds; their approval is silence, and it is total. Nerezza exhales slowly, shakily, as she did when she climbed from him and fell asleep on the carpet like an exhausted cat.

The next racers line up, but they are not horses. They are men, and women, too, their legs contorted into animal limbs—leopard, gazelle, lion, lizard, horse, and ostrich. They stand upright, most of them, on two exotic legs and stare miserably into the stands, their glares like accusations.

"Who are they?" Ludo asked.

"Veterans," Nerezza sniffed. "This is a charity race. Pay no attention, the box seats are not supposed to deign to watch."

The horn sounds like the death of a great whale and Ludo obediently turns away, pretends to be reading the newspaper of his neighbor, a thing more like a broadside than *La Repubblica*; he admires the letter-pressing, the decorated corners, reads idly about the paramours of a woman whose name means nothing to him, philippics on immigration and quarantine. *The Dvorniki have been spotted on the south side of Zarzaparrilla—this publication would like to take the opportunity to thank them for their difficult and vital work.* The paper smells faintly but distinctly of vinegar. Nerezza laces her black-gloved hand through his; he stiffens, but supposes resignedly that this is within the sphere of licit behavior, given that her inner thighs must still be bruised by his thumbs. She wears a ring over the glove on her middle finger, a tourmaline beetle with bulbous copper eyes. He keeps his gaze firmly on it, and cannot be sure he does not see its antennae waver. Her grip tightens on him, her finger-pads recalling thumbscrews. The beetle ring bites into his knuckle.

And he follows her eyes, eel-inscrutable, down the stands from their scarlet and leather box. Two women sit far below them: a blond creature with a green scarf, her hair like water pouring over an emerald riding uniform. Her gloved hand clasps the fingers of another woman, with coarse heaps of dark hair fastened with bronze compasses, graphite-nubs extending gracefully from their claws. She wears a calfskin dress, the exact color of her flesh. It is Lucia, of course it is Lucia, and her face is nakedly happy, a happiness it seems almost obscene to witness.

Ludovico calls out to his wife, and she turns slightly, but surely she cannot hear him over the cannonade of hooves and foot-pads below them, the sudden rain of pearls. She screams with the rest; the blond woman shuts her eyes in the convulsion of her cry.

"Does this help you?" Nerezza says. "To see her, that she is here, that she belongs somewhere, that she is happy, that she has a lover, that she knows how to behave in the society? Does it fill up the place in you where she lived?"

Ludo screeches her name over the din, but Nerezza holds him, pins him, her beetle ring, her gloved hand. She is too far away, his Lucia, his chimera, snapping her tail in the dust to hide her tracks.

"She can't hear you. If you fling yourself over the balcony you will only bleed on the couple below us and break your bones on their chairs. Ludo, I brought you to see her, I didn't say you could touch her, that you could bring her back. You are a cut-rate Orpheus, and she has already vanished behind you on the stone stair—you did not even feel her go."

"I don't understand! Lucia! *Lucia!*"

"She is blessed, Ludo. Perhaps she will touch a higher grace still, a grace we scream to enter but cannot even approach. That I cannot approach. We can only watch her, who may be permitted to see the silver cup but cannot touch it, can never drink."

Ludo weeps openly; tears drip from his chin like rain from a roof. Nerezza leans into him, covering them both with the brim of her hat. She licks the tears from his face.

Far below, Lucia throws back her shining head and laughs.

# PART II:

## The Gate of Horn

# ONE

# WEEPHOLES

S ei had never been comfortable in the presence of books. Their natural state was to be shut, closed, to grin pagily from shelves, laughing at her, promising so much and delivering such meanness, such thinness. They displayed only men and women with dead eyes and rituals of living she could not understand. When closed, books gave impressions of perfection. They did not need her.

Sei's mother had once sat with her in a room with a grass floor and windows of paper. Sei had been very small. She had not yet ridden a train. In that room she had felt as though she were secretly inside a book, walled up in paper, sewn up with grass along her spine. Her mother's hair was so long and flat it glittered like a hard stone seen through seven inches of water. Usagi was named for the rabbit in the moon, and Sei thought in those days that her mother hid a silver hammer in her yellow *yukata* with orange cranes on the sleeves, just out of her sight, and mashed rice and sugar in a great pearly barrel while Sei slept. She tried to stay up and catch her at it, but the mother of Sei was clever and quick.

"Imagine a book at the bottom of a lake," Usagi had said, pinching Sei's toes through her *tabi*-socks. "Fish read it. They wriggle into the spaces between the pages and eat up the words like rice. But the Sei-fish, who was very plump and blue and not like the other fish, could not fit in between the pages, and so was very hungry, and swam around the book eight times. Then the Sei-fish came to her mother, and the Usagi-fish said:

"'My daughter, why do you weep?'

"'Because I cannot read the book at the bottom of the lake, which all the other fish love,' said the Sei-fish.

"'Don't cry, my child, for I have read this book and I will feed you all the things inside it, one by one, so that you will not be hungry and fill the lake with your tears.'"

Sei twisted around, bunching up her persimmon-colored holiday *obi*. She put a small hand on her mother's face.

"But Usagi-fish, should I not someday read for myself?"

"It is not necessary, my little squash-flower, for I can read it, and I will always be here."

Thus books had always been slavish footmen in her mother's maddening court, sullen things that would not admit her. She learned her kanji and her katakana with a bent and proper head, but she did not read for pleasure, neither fiction nor histories nor philosophy. Other fish might own books, might love them, might know their secrets.

And so it was that Sei had been kept pure for this book, its true bride, untouched by other narratives, naïve of the wiles of any previous structures, voices, imagery.

Imagine a girl at the bottom of a lake, living among the fish. This girl was not more innocent of the ways of books than Sei. Sei felt as though this book had been written for her and only for her, as though Sato Kenji had opened her mouth like a doctor and looked within her heart for the substance of his book, and written only what he saw there. She was a nun in service of it, virginal and blank, desperate to become devoted; she had saved herself for this, stored her love within her so that this book, which could not possibly have been written for any purpose but to crawl inside her and dwell there like a holy thing, so that this book would not be ashamed of her profligacy.

And Yumiko was touching it, thinking Sei still asleep. Sei crept out of the *ryokan* bed and peered around Yumiko's naked waist to read along with her.

*There is a story told in Aomori Province concerning the patronage of trains. The Kami of the Wind and the Kami of Engines struggled over who would bless the trains of Japan, who would earn the right to enfold them into their long arms. By this time the folk of Japan were closed up into trains for hours upon hours each day, and in the cities of the Kami there was a great consternation as to who should receive the numerous silent prayers for punctuality, for speed, for unmolested progress. The Kami of Wind stood upon a platform of orange clouds and argued that the trains belonged to him, for their great speed sent up such currents of air, and the high platforms of the Shinkansen entered into his territory, and he shook them daily with his breath. The Kami of Engines, not very beloved among her kin, stood upon a dais of crushed automobiles and sewing machines drenched in old oil. Through her greasy hair she glowered and said that any machine which churned fuel and ate kilometers was hers and hers alone to adore.*

*The debate continued so long that the attending Kami fell into a deep sleep, for public debates are more tiresome than either the participants or the audience care to admit. While their assembled family slept, the Kami*

*of Wind stole onto his opponent's dais with the intention of destroying*
*her and assuming the trains for himself without contest. He drew a great*
*breath to push through her heart, but as the breath was drawn into its*
*fullest, the Kami of Engines stepped into his arms and kissed him, pulling*
*him into her with great violence, so great that the whole of his breath was*
*spent into her. But the air rushing through the heart of the Kami of*
*Engines only fed the fires within her, sending them high into heaven, and*
*she consumed him utterly, and thus the trains worship with the song of*
*their passing the Kami of Engines with her long, oily hair.*

It was terribly difficult for Sei to watch Yumiko read the
book. To see her lay her thumb in the spine and let the soft cover
fall over it. Sei winced, bit her lip, crushed within her the desire
to snatch it back. Yumiko had gotten miso on the corner of a
page. *You're ruining it!* the heart of Sei cried out. But was it not fair?
Had she not allowed this girl's mouth on her throat, her hands
within her body? Did she not know the secret things of Yumiko:
that her deepest skin tasted of the sea? That her cries were high
and breathy, like a child's hiccups? Did Sei not owe some few of
her own secret things in exchange for this knowledge?

She chewed the inside of her cheek. *No,* she thought. *Yumiko*
*has other lovers, but I have no other books.* Yumiko marked her place
and looked up.

"And he was your first?" she asked archly. "The man who
wrote this?"

Sei blinked. "Not my first, of course not. I'm twenty, not
twelve."

"No, not your first lover. When you dreamed of the fortune-
teller, was it after this man?"

"Yes."

"And then me."

"It's not like I went looking for you."

"Do you think I'm calling you a whore?"

Sei picked at the threads of the futon. Women were difficult; she had always found them so. They were like hoary old fish, keeping to the lake bottom, harder to catch than men, harder to keep. And they just looked at you with those armored piscine eyes that showed nothing at all until you turned away out of shame at some act for which you could not begin to answer.

Yumiko pushed *A History of Train Travel* firmly back across the tatami. Sei grabbed it gratefully, held it to her chest to warm again with her skin against it. Yumiko shook her head.

"I want to take you somewhere tonight, Sei, will you come?"

Of course she would. Kyoto was a great red basin, and she fell toward its center, toward Yumiko in her blue plaid skirt, toward her mouth and her dreamy, abrupt way of speaking. Toward that other place that Yumiko knew, the place on the other side of night, the place whose trains were wholly without end.

"In the meantime," Yumiko said cheerfully, "want to see a whole lot of wasted money?"

———

And so they went into the city, through the high garden walls and narrow streets, toward the phoenix-heart of Kyoto.

Yumiko was right, the Golden Pavilion was ugly. It squatted on the water like a fat yellow raccoon about to paw for fish. The pond was utterly still, reflecting the thing back at itself without a ripple. Sei could not quite convince herself the building was gold, though she knew it was: her grandmother had given over her jewelry to the leafing of the pavilion after it burned all those years ago. It just seemed yellow now, just paint. She wanted to touch it, even so, to feel her grandmother's necklaces again, bouncing against an old, soft breast.

It had burned in the fifties, the whole thing. A monk had been obsessed with it, had loved it, and had set it on fire one cold night. He had wanted to burn with it, but the smoke was not enough, and he outlived the object of his adoration. When they learned about him in school, Sei thought that she understood him, the need to be rid of a thing, and also to scream with it and in it and breathe it until you choke. Koi moved hugely through the little lake surrounding the temple, improbably moveable stones.

————

Once, she had made the mistake of asking her mother where she was born.

Usagi had put a butterfly comb into her daughter's hair and said: "I was born in a train station, my little orchid-stem. Your grandmother was too big to travel, but she longed to see the cherry blossoms at Tsukayama Park, where she was a girl, before the war, before she married and danced south to Kyoto with ribbons in her hair."

"How can you be born in a train station? There aren't any doctors," sensible little Sei had said.

"Did you know, in stations that are very deep underground, there are things called weepholes, little holes in the walls to let wetness out? Water trickles out of them and it looks as if the station is crying, crying for all those souls that pass through it and do not stay. In the station where I was born, the weepholes had been made into little kabuki faces with great eyes that really wept, all that water, rolling down their cheeks.

"'Push harder,' said the weepholes to your grandmother.

"'Lie below us, and we will watch over you,' they cried, and their mouths were very tragic, the way mask mouths so often are.

"'Your child is a girl,' they said when it was over, and though some of them were disappointed, most of them seemed pleased and wept tears of joy.

"'She is like a small rabbit, kicking her big red feet,' they said, and so I was called Usagi, and lived to become your Usagi-Mother. On Grandparents Day, I return to the station to wipe away the tears of my midwives."

"I wish I had been born in a train station," Sei had sighed.

"Perhaps when you have a baby, you will long to see cherry blossoms," Usagi had answered, and tickled her under the chin.

Sei's mother had been better than a book. She had been stranger, both more closed and more open. Even when she was a child she suspected her mother was mad—a little mad, in a charming way, that made her say funny things in funny ways, not horribly mad, like the women on television who tore their hair. But whenever her mother read from the book at the bottom of the lake, the stories were impossible and sad, and Sei knew they were not true. But she could not help remembering them, and taking them into herself like food and water, and when she learned of the wicked monk who burned up the Golden Pavilion in the holocaust of his own desire, it sounded rich and odd, like a story her mother would have told her, and she had thought of the weepholes that presided over her mother's birth, and the beautiful trains that must have borne witness to such a thing.

*What is happening to me in this old, old city? I cannot stop chasing my thoughts around, around and around. Where am I going, O Monk, O Mother, O Rabbit in the Moon?*

————

The place Yumiko wanted to take her was called the Floor of Heaven. A small plaque above the door announced as much in quiet *hiragana* like the fall of sudden rain. Yumiko held her hand tightly, still wearing her school uniform.

"Why do you wear that fucking thing?" Sei asked. "You're not in school anymore."

Yumiko giggled, put her hand over her mouth, and then stopped abruptly, utterly serious. "I enjoy the archetype," she said. "It's our greatest export, you know, this skirt, these shoes. It's like being a *kami*. I *embody*."

Yumiko knocked at the door, and when it opened reluctantly, stuck out her tongue with the catlike pleasure she had shown when she had done the same for Sei. The man in the door-shadow looked quizzically at Sei. She unbuttoned her blouse with calm fingers. He grunted acquiescence.

Inside, there was soft music, koto and guitar played together, and long copper-colored couches. There were tables and drinks of exotic colors, as in any club Sei had ever seen—black wood and a green vial on it; graceful fingers tented against the belly of a glass full of pink froth. The room was sparsely populated, patrons in clusters like grapes, no one dancing, no one laughing.

There were, as there would be, maps on the walls, of London, Paris, Buenos Aires. Low whispers floated above the drinks.

"Tell me," Yumiko said, pressing her cheek to Sei's on the empty dance floor. "Do you want to go back?"

"To Tokyo?"

"No."

"Oh. *There*."

"It has a name."

Sei found that she had trouble saying it: a foreign word, and she balked at the admission that she knew the name of an impossible place, even to Yumiko, who presumably did not think it impossible at all.

Sei thought of the trains, how perfect and white, how swift. The man playing the viola, how his hair had fallen over his face like a mourning veil and the train cars, ah, the train cars had opened for him, their doors like rapturous arms!

"It wasn't a dream."

"No. Better than a dream."

"Yes, I want to go." Sei clenched her fists against the desire for it, for those trains, trains that would nod sagely at everything in Kenji's book, saying: *yes, that is what we are*. She thought of Tokyo, waiting for her in the north like a crocodile, languid, vicious. What waited for her? Her tempered glass booth at Shinjuku Station, the endless tickets for everyone but her, her Japan Rail uniform with its crisp lapels? It was nothing, all nothing, because it was not *there*, not those trains, not that place.

Yumiko put her thumb against Sei's lower lip as though marking her place in the book of her. "That's what we all want, Sei. Hardly anyone even comes as far as this place, where we can find each other, like drawn to like. Where it is so easy to find a street which ends in that city. They built the Floor of Heaven about twelve years ago, when there were enough of us in Kyoto to need it, to long for it."

"Who's *they*?"

"I don't know, really. Big money, from up north. I don't really know about the higher-ups, the important people here who figure out how to be important in Palimpsest. I'm just a tourist, you know? But the club makes things so much simpler. You'll see."

Sei looked around the room—hardly a couple did not embrace, and hardly a couple's eyes met. They grasped each other shaking like invalids, impassive and fanatical. Sei's eyes watered. She thought she understood it, the anatomy of what Yumiko offered her—she could guess at its musculature, the number of its bones. *It's like a virus. This is more like a hospital than a nightclub, really. The Southern Prefectural Home for Invalids, with an open bar.*

Sei moved away from Yumiko across the floor and extended her arms like wings. She moved as best she could, as best she knew how, as she had moved in a hundred rooms livelier and harder than this in Tokyo. She circled her hips, she held her belly and tipped her toes. She shut her eyes and hoped herself beautiful enough to deserve what any one of these could give her: a way in, a way through. Her black dress, shimmering like depthless water, snapped and flared.

Yumiko caught her in a long turn, her breath quick, blowing out little strands of hair from her face.

"You don't have to do that," Yumiko said solemnly. "No one dances anymore. It's a waste of time. We've cut it all down to the barest necessary interactions. It's better that way. They won't say no, not ever. You don't have to dance for them."

"I want to. I want to." Sei laced her fingers into Yumiko's pink-nailed hands. "Don't you want to have fun, to feel alive here, too?"

Yumiko blinked, and she looked suddenly very tired.

"I just want to stay there, Sei," she sighed. "It's so hard to come back."

"Then stay."

"I don't know how! No one knows. We just know how to get there for a little while, how to see little parts of it. How to dream a thing that is better than a dream."

Yumiko drew her toward a table. Two tall, thin glasses glittered on the wood. One had a golden drink in it, the other a creamy, pale blue one. There was a man there, not so old as Kenji, with a poppy in his lapel. The petals were black in the low light.

"I won't promise," Yumiko whispered, pulling Sei's hand under her skirt to rest on the soft flesh of her hip, "that they will all be as pretty as me, or as easy to charm as him. Most of them will not have a book written just for you in their pockets. But this is how you do it: through the body and into the world. You fuck; you travel. That sounds crude, and you know, it usually is. It's usually ugly, and fat, and sweaty, and lonely. Luckily, it's also usually quick. But afterwards . . . we find a place where we belong."

The man, who was well on the way to fat, his neck bulging out of a black suit, his hair greasily combed over, put his hand over Sei's. He was nodding along with Yumiko; tears flowed down his round cheeks. With his other finger he pulled his ear-lobe aside so that she could see the map there, glowering, calling. Sei leaned in to examine it, but Yumiko shook her head.

"If you want to continue on the train, and not . . . come with me . . . you have to be more careful. You only get to go to the place they've got on their skin, so you need to practice some good old-fashioned cartography and map a route."

Together they auditioned men and women, lifting sleeves and hats and skirts to peer at maps so tiny they made Sei's head throb. Yumiko seemed to know what she was looking for, but all the same it was not until nearly two in the morning that she found a nervous, skinny man with scarred cheeks and a scraggly mustache whose hip was scrawled over with a dense map Yumiko seemed to like, but Sei thought looked much like the rest.

"That's the next station on the line. You should have clear passage from where you started—it should work out, one way or the other." Yumiko smiled gently, like a mother coaxing her child onto a frightening carnival ride. "It's quick," she said. "Be quick," she implored the scarred man.

But Sei thought only of the trains, hurtling through her. She gave a wan smile and leaned into her schoolgirl briefly.

*"The source of all suffering is desire,"* Sei recited.

"Yes," Yumiko breathed fervently. *"Yes, it is."*

Sei let herself fall into the man's nameless arms. His kisses were not spare or elegant, like Sato Kenji's, or sweet and fluttering, like Yumiko's, or bruising and angry like the three lovers before them. His were soft and overripe, a pear fallen in the rain. His tongue was flat and round. He pulled at her white coat and the black dress beneath it, stroking her bare back. He drew her into an alcove near the bathroom, and she felt that this was unnecessarily tawdry, needlessly crude—why could they not all be like Yumiko, who had arranged her legs over her shoulders like flowers and sank into her with a lightness like water?

The man lifted her against the wall; he was small in her, small and urgent and hard, a little bullet aimed at the center of her, and he buried his face in the mark between her breasts, his teeth bared against her in the dark.

Sei thought of the trains, and the shadows hid her face as the scarred man jerked and shook inside her.

It was quick.

# Colophon Station

**COLOPHON STATION IS THE CENTRAL** transit terminal for the trains of Palimpsest. The stately prewar cinquefoils show the evening sky, deeper than gold and warmer than blue. The great ambulatory is lined with pillars of plum trees trained to support the long, ochre-tiled roof, blossoming grasping branches twisting the doves into living capitals. Within, eleven pyrite staircases spiral down to the grand floor, a marble expanse in which the old wheel of Palimpsest is laid out in rosewood, the face of the circular city when it was small and unassuming, a walled place, home only to a few celery farmers and astronomers. Great lancet arches lead further into the earth, labeled with stern roman capitals: *Points East, Points North, Points Far, Points Near.* In the center of the rosewood wheel the Verdigris Fountain splashes and trickles: a woman bound up in railroad ties, her arms flung upward in ecstasy, water streaming from her palms, her hair spread out as in a many-armed corona. Green age encrusts her, her eyes worn smooth by water, her nose half-gone. Yet still she watches over travelers, Our Lady of Safe Transfer, Star of the Underground.

The ceiling of Colophon Station is unpainted, for it was the desire of the architect, whose name was long ago buried under a black quoin, that passersby become aware in the most piquant way that they have passed underground. Therefore the roof of Colophon is planted over with flame-colored ginger flowers, whose thick golden roots reach down thirstily into the interior, and any traveler may look up and see only earth and straining roots, and the wonderful smell of it penetrates the skin for days afterward.

Miruna dwells within a column of glass. She sleeps there, when she sleeps, standing upright like a horse. A young bellhop with a shining cap who loves her with all his valise-hung heart brings her a lavish meal once a day: six roasted finches and grapes so plump and purple it pains the eye to look on them. He is too awed to speak to her, but he brings her songbirds and watches her eat in a rapture of adulation.

Miruna faces the Lady so that her heart may always be elevated by her work. She wears a wimple of simple flax over her white hair and a diadem fashioned from—impossibly precious!—a railroad tie that fell from the Fountain decades past. She is thankful that it was during her tenure that it fell, so that she could bend her own hands to it and shape it to her own head. She is the abbess of the terminal, and her gaze bestows luck wherever it falls. A great bronze horn curls from the top of the column in a long spiral to end at her mouth in a dish very like the mouth of a trumpet. She closes her eyes in paradisiacal servitude and holds the light of the Lady, the light of the train lamps, in her breast as she speaks her psalm, her voice low and kindly as a mother:

*Arrivals, Track 3: Marginalia, Stylus, and Sgraffito Lines. Sgraffito departs for Silverfish at Eight of the Clock. Thank you and Good Evening.*

———

Sei dashes under the *Points North* lintel. She has no ticket; her heart rattles a cup against her ribs in protest. There is a screaming in her ears, a throttling of voices, thousands crying out at once, the sound of horses galloping. She shoves aside the stirring feelings of strange others within her—they are eating, all of them, and her stomach seems to fill with foreign things, her lips hum with hot goblets. Someone is smoking near one of the members of her quartet, but not tobacco, something sweeter and darker, like dry figskins. She growls within herself at them, and they recede, quivering. She prepares to leap the turnstile—she will not be turned away; she knows her mark. There is only one place she longs for in this faceted city.

Poor child—you will not see the rest! There are wonders above ground, too . . . ah, but she will not listen. They never do. They want only their very private toys and candies, and will not share.

The long brass bars part for her, smoothly, with a gentle whistle. She laughs shrilly and runs faster, her feet bare against the marble, slipping around the corner and onto the platform.

Sei cannot hear the viola anymore—that was far from here, she supposes, that small old station with no fountains. Instead she can hear a faint harpsichord, and she glimpses a young woman hunched over a painted instrument far down the track, her hair flying as she compels it to groan for her. The trains do not like the music, or have scented something they like better: they hurtle past the harpsichordist towards Sei, shying away from the music in the same elephantine manner they leaned into the viola player. As they slide to a rest at her side, the doors before her open—but the doors before the other commuters and travelers and wide-eyed children with amber lollipops in their fists remain immutably shut. The car is black within, lightless, soundless, but she is not afraid, any more than she was once afraid of the room of grass and her mother's open arms, her torn kimono, her eyes that wept so easily, so often. Usagi had been no less black inside.

Sei leaps into the train, and the doors of the car close happily behind her: the long silver beast careens forward into the tunnel, leaving the folk on the platform shaking their heads and ruefully winding their watches.

———

The rumble of the meeting of carriage and track sounds hard and happy in the marrow of the girl called Sei. She stands in the dark, hands groping up for leather straps she does not find. There is the sound of a thick match striking; Sei blinks in the soft and sudden light of a red lantern. The carriage rocks from side to side, gently, as though trying to sing her to sleep. But she will not let herself sleep; if she sleeps, she will wake, and she could not bear that.

The walls are draped in red silk. A few vague forms hunch at scattered tables—the sound of soup slurping echoes. A tall woman stands a little space away. She is wearing a black kimono with a jade-colored lining, but it is beltless; her small breasts show, and her slender legs. Her long face is painted red from brow to chin, and it is starkly angular, curiously stretched just slightly past human proportion. Her lips etch a hard black line; her hair folds back and back like the wrapping of a present. She approaches, her red eyelids downcast, and in her naked hands she cradles a teacup. The tea, too, is red, and smells of cinnamon. The woman opens her dark mouth and inserts her thumb and forefinger—she pulls a small lump of opium from beneath her tongue and places it into the cup like a lump of sugar. She sets the tea on a table with a complete and elaborate Western setting glistening on it, and strides swiftly forward, enveloping Sei in her arms and unpinning her hair so that it unfolds around them like a cut accordion. Into her ear the woman whispers:

"We are so glad you have come. Please take our food from us and also our drink. Please take our doors and open them, please find our cars beautiful. If it is not too much to ask we would wish to be dear to you, but we are patient and undemanding."

She pulls away and there is a smear of red paint on Sei's cheek. Sei shakes her head slightly, her mouth open and wondering.

"But you ... you know I have only tonight here, that I am ... nocturnal, ephemeral."

The red woman nods. "We are confident you will find your way to us no matter where you wake in the city. To believe otherwise would be to believe a carriage can exist without her train. You are our own thing, our squash-blossom, our orchid-stem. We are the leaves of you, you must look at us and call us green, call us gold."

Sei sits at the table and closes her fingers around the alien utensils. The woman sits opposite her, closing her kimono over her nakedness, her scarlet face beaming.

"Who are you?" Sei asks.

"I am the Third Rail."

Sei laughs hollowly, her voice echoing metallic in the car, disturbing the diners. "You don't look like it. Or feel like it."

The Third Rail demurs, her excitement crackling at the tips of her hair. "I wanted a body, and the components of a body were available to me. But I run beneath you, silent and fatal and huge, and I love you, Amaya Sei. For you I have put on this red flesh and poured their red tea, for you alone."

And Sei notices for the first time that other crimson women walk the car, tending to the hunched figures. Other women have folded up their hair, donned a mask, and painted their mouths into a black line. Other women pull opium from their mouths. But none are naked under their kimono but the one who called herself the Third Rail, none show their flesh to the drinkers of their tea. The others wear four layers of robes and wide belts of stiff silk.

Sei covers her eyes with one hand. She would like to think this is true, that a train could really love her back this way. But she knows better. "Why should you love me, Rail? I'm nobody. I'm a ticket-taker for Japan Rail. I live alone. I go to work. I eat rice-balls. I'm not special, I'm not anyone."

The Third Rail twirls a finger in her own cooling tea. "We need you. That is what love is, we think. Needing. Taking."

"What for?"

The Third Rail shifts in her chair like a child who fears that permission for ice cream is about to be revoked. "Can you not just love us as we are without silly questions?" she pleads. "We have waited so long for you. We do not want to spoil everything with long interrogations. It is a small thing, so very small. We will be so good to you, we will give you such nice things. We promise."

"You sound like my mother."

"She can come too, if that will please you."

Sei laughs hollowly. "She can't. She's dead. Tickets from the underworld are so expensive, you know?"

"We are sorry. Are we expected to be sorry?"

"You don't have to be. It was a long time ago." Sei does not want to think about Usagi, not here. This is her own thing, her mother cannot have it. "She killed herself," Sei says shortly, and even the Third Rail seems to understand that the topic is shut.

"Will you come with me, Sei? Please say yes."

Sei looks into her tea, bloody and bright. She shuts her eyes and drinks it down, the spice of it puckering her cheeks. She feels the opium ball knock against her teeth but does not swallow it.

"Yes," she says finally, setting down her cup. "I need you, too."

She takes the hand of the Third Rail, and the woman's fingers laced in hers are white and hot.

# TWO

# PROTOCOLS

*Things that begin and end in grief: marriage, harvest, childbirth.*
*Journeys away from home. Journeys toward home. Surgeries. Love.*
*Weeping.*

November pulled herself into a gray corner and clutched her notebook. She found the man in the willow-green shirt's apartment unutterably lonely: only the corner she pressed up into spoke to her of living souls. She wriggled into the empty space there, a pale square in the dust-shabby paint: the ghost of a previous tenant, the restless shade of a vanished bookshelf. She huddled into its borders, knees drawn up against her nakedness. She pressed her cheek against the cold wall, her blackened, burning cheek. A tear slipped between her face and the plaster.

The young man slept still. The willow-green shirt slept, too, forgotten in the small kitchen. His books were propped up on cement blocks; there was a thin lithoid television, a pair of brown shoes. November drew further into the corner. She missed the bees, her own bees and the dream-bees. She worried for her hives like a mother—spending the night in the city is reckless behavior for the mistress of so many.

"I'm not going to hurt you," he said, muffled in powder-colored sheets. "You could have stayed in bed. It's warmer."

"I'm not good at that."

He emerged from linen, a blur of haphazard black hair and sleep-flattened cheeks. He groped for his glasses. "You're not good at staying in bed?"

"At any of it. At other people. At mornings." She closed her lips against the forming list. They were for her notebooks, not for speaking, not for *saying*. Air could ruin them, take them apart, make them meaningless. They were fragile, like honeybees. Like cobwebs. November sniffed and wiped at her face. Men were difficult, she had always found them so. Hoary old birds on the bough, staring with sharp mouths. They chewed and chewed at you until there was nothing of interest left.

He watched her, propped on one elbow; he had watched her even when he had pulled her onto him, watched her in the calculating way of owls watching a hinge-jawed vole—*will she run? Will she scream? What will she taste like? How many others like her are hidden in the grass?*

"You're so new," he had breathed into her collarbone, his thumbs under her breasts, fingers splayed out against her back. "So new."

She had watched him, too. Distantly, from a great height, from far off. She had moved mechanically, keeping her mouth bitten shut. She hadn't come; she hadn't wanted to. She hadn't wanted him particularly, he had no blue eyes, no lineages in his heart, prophet to caliph to teacher's assistant. He had not even told her his name, so eager was he to touch her face, to trace the streets there. So eager to return to this gray smear of a house, to the mattress on the floor, lonely of box spring or frame. And his long, tapered finger, so wound with blackness, sliding in and out of her, as though the whole city could fuck her, just like that.

He had told her about that place, told her its name, told her how to get there, pulled her close with the promise of a city she remembered in small bursts, like novae, a dream that was not a dream.

That was enough, she would suffer his body in hers for that. And she believed him, she believed because of Xiaohui, who had told her nothing but wedged her open, and all these others, now, all these others could enter where Xiaohui had forgotten to close her when she went.

"Living alone," November whispered, "is a skill, like running long distance or programming old computers. You have to know parameters, protocols. You have to learn them so well that they become like a language: to have music always so that the silence doesn't overwhelm you, to perform your work exquisitely well so that your time is filled. You have to allow yourself to open up until you are the exact size of the place you live, no more, or else you get restless. No less, or else you drown. There are rules; there are ways of being and not being. This sort of thing," she gestured imprecisely at the room, the bed, him, "is forbidden. It expands or contracts me, I'm not sure which, beyond the . . . set limits. I'm not good at that, either. Expanding, contracting."

Her companion uttered a small noise between a sharp sigh and a soft laugh.

"You don't have to be, you know," he said with a sliding sadness. "This has been going on for some time. There are patterns to us now." He moved his hand on the sheets as if to reach out to her. "Rules. Protocols. You don't even have to talk to me, if you don't want to. People worked this out a long time ago. It used to be awkward, when you wanted the *entrance* and not the person. The invitation, not the plus-one. It varies a little from place to place—it's pretty formal here, like a transaction. If," he looked down at his fingernails, "if you'd wanted me for myself, you would have turned the stone on that ring you wear on your middle left finger inward. If you wanted it to be more than once, you would have turned your pinky ring in. There are codes like that. If you wanted a feast, elaborate sex, if you wanted to make a ritual of it, you would have worn green shoes. I didn't expect you to be here in the morning, with no ribbons in your hair and all your rings turned out. And two buttons, not three, undone on your dress. That means strictly business, altogether. But you're new, so I guess I should have figured you didn't know the ropes."

"How long have you had it? Has your finger been like that? Have you been . . ."

He drank from a glass of water left on a makeshift night-stand—a pile of thick hardbacks. "Traveling? Passing over? Expatriating? About five years, I think. It's hard to pinpoint, because hardly anyone remembers the first night. One dream is just a dream, you don't give it a thought. It's only the second one that sticks, and if you're lucky, your second lover has been at it long enough to have figured out a thing or two."

November swallowed. "How many of . . . *us* . . . are there?"

He looked at her very seriously, tilting his gaze over his glasses. "Not as many as you'd think. But enough. We're secretive about it, you know? It's *precious*, like a pearl at the bottom of the sea. There are no magazine ads, no decadent clubs, in this country anyway, no websites. We keep it contained. If a site goes up, the rest of us take it down, one way or another. You gotta be strictly *low-tech*. Analog. Fly low—an old-fashioned underground, get it? Sometimes I think I spend half my time crawling the web for . . . well, we call them *errata*. Hasn't been one that's stayed up longer than twenty-four hours in years. It's . . . hard. Holy work is always hard. We keep to ourselves on this side, to protect it. Sacred places, you owe them something. We owe it. You wouldn't want just *anybody*—"

"So only the *right* people get to go? People who are rich enough or pretty enough?" November said bitterly.

The young man clenched his jaw and released it slowly.

"Sweetheart, imagine someone who's a big man over here. The head of a corporation, or, hell, the president of a country. Imagine that in the sorts of places those men go to cheat on their perfect little wives, one of them picks up a little virus— hey, it doesn't hurt his health, really, and he can cover up the black mark for press meetings. But imagine that he's smart enough to figure out what's happening to him when he goes to sleep, which, given his Ivy League pedigree, he probably is. Imagine what happens when a man like that finds a city of impossible, untapped wealth, a nearly limitless labor force, power that isn't magic, not really, but close enough that he could dazzle the world, become a wizard-king with his amazing machines." The young man crossed his arms.

"Now you tell me how long you think it would be before troops started forming lines at brothels. How long before there are boots in every street in Palimpsest? Sacred places, November.

You *owe* them something. You stand between them and the rest of the world, or else the world gets its ugly, stupid way."

November reeled back, chastened. She could not bear the thought of a man like that in Orlande's shop, his feet filthy with ink. She did not want to know it could happen.

"But Xiaohui—"

He barked laughter like a sea lion. "Xiaohui? Oh, god. You poor kid." He got up and padded over to her, sitting against the wall without noticing the absent bookshelf, his naked limbs tossed casually about like toys.

"Xiaohui's . . . sort of an evangelist. There's a few of us like her. We try to keep them contained, too. They don't get invited to parties, generally. She's a big girl, bigger on the inside than on the outside, you know, and she can't bear the thought of being alone in that place. She takes anyone she finds, even blanks like you. It's . . . well, some people would call it immoral. She never cared. I spent my junior year chasing her errata through these obscure little knitting magazines."

"Have you and she . . . ?"

The young man blinked. "She's my sister. You knew that, didn't you? I mean, it's our mother's shop, there's hardly anyone but you who eats there without blood ties."

November chewed her lip vigorously, as though she meant to devour herself voice-first. She glanced up at him gravely, for there were not so very many blithe expressions granted to her grim and earnest face.

"But have you?"

He seemed to grow sudden wrinkles, his eyes creased with old worries. He exhaled a long-held breath and picked at a toenail intently. "She never cared about any of that, not immigrant morality, not anyone's. The city was everything to her. The rest—just bodies. One body, two. Mine, hers. She showed me her leg—god, it was so long ago! She took me into the store-room and the cookie dough was flattened out into all these long, gold runners on the counters, and piles of blank fortunes, so many, like confetti. She pulled up her dress and I laughed at her, but it shut me right up, that mark on her, like some ghost had punched her as hard as he could. And she kissed me so hard, her little teeth, she kissed me so hard and bit at me and I bled in her mouth, and she just didn't care. She never did. It was only once, only ever once with her. An experiment, I think. To see if she could go that far. She pushed me onto the fortunes and I came so fast and hard it blinded me for a minute, like a flashbulb bursting. I could say I gave in, that it was all her, but that would be a bigger lie than I can fit my mouth around." He sniffed sharply, waiting for her disapproval, hurrying to head it off. "You do things, when you've been there, you do things you could never even have thought up before. I mean, it's not ex-actly *safe*, is it, what we do? You could end up churned up inside with disease, pregnant a dozen times over, dead. But it doesn't matter. We'd take all that and more besides if it means *getting there*. Incest hardly ranks."

November considered him coldly, and the creases of his eye seemed to speak of debauch and torment, but more of love and longing and blind stumbling in the dark. She doubted he had ever worn his rings turned outward in his life. She doubted he had thought of anything when he had cried out like a falling sparrow within her but Xiaohui. Certainly she had not.

He cupped his hand against her cheek. "I'm sorry it was your face. That's . . . unlucky. No one gets to choose."

*Things that cannot long be kept secret: death in the family, the loss of a ring, corruption of the spirit, boredom, illicit love. Sickness. Addiction. Pregnancy.*

Within the pure white wimple of her beekeeping suit, wrapped in buzzing, worried voices panicked that their mistress had strayed from them, November told herself that Xiaohui's brother was the last, that she would stop this here. She would stay in her home; she would travel for cacti twice a year; she would send her crates of honey through the hands of others. Plenty of takers, plenty of drivers. The bees did not care whether she was disfigured. She would be a nun of the hive, a soul in the sisterhood of summer.

It would be all right—she had touched a secret thing, but a touch was enough. She had no brothers with which to debase herself, but she did not need or want them. She would not move down the path. If it meant so many strange lovers, if it meant allowing so many people into the small space of her, she could give up Palimpsest. She would refuse it. It was easy; it would be easy. She had enough here—had that not been the purpose of this house, these hives, this place so near to her moss-blanketed father? To have enough, to grow precisely large enough for this place and no larger? The gigantism that the city and those telescoping lovers promised with such vigor was no friend to her.

But this did not save her from her dreams. No nun has ever

been saved by virtue from ecstatic visions of demons and angels breaking the stalks of one another's wings. She called out to the brassy city in her sleep, she touched the Memorial, the ostrich-orphan in the center of the road. She felt within her those three strange folk who moved and ate and sang so far away from her. She felt the bees on her breast. She stood thirty nights in the shop of Aloysius, who shook his white-wigged head at her in such disappointment it pierced her true as his needles. Once he had even wept at her feet, his face pressed to her stomach.

*Why? Why will you not do as the rest have done? Why do you haunt me like this? Is it because of what I said? Because I was rude? I apologize. A hundred times I apologize. When will you yield to us, you awful girl, you who saw me so clearly and purely that my heart broke in your hands?*

Yet when she tried to run from his pleading or his admonitions, when she tried to flee with her lavender-suited homunculus, when she tried to go, not to the shop of Aloysius at all, but down the long planks of another street entirely, she was turned back. Walls of amber shadow coalesced in her path, or barricades of impassably tangled streetlamps like briars sprang up, or else the street simply vanished into a void she could not cross. The world of her allowable presence was limited to two avenues and no more. Her city was constant, faithful, every night her own, but she could not pass beyond the places she had touched that first night she dreamt against the shorn neck of Xiaohui's brother.

In the mornings, she woke weeping. She would snatch her notebooks and cover them with furious scrawls: *Things I Will Not Do, Things Beyond My Abilities, Women I Am Not, Places I Will Not Go, Things Which Are Not Real, Things Which Will Surely Destroy Me.*

She flung the notebooks against the wall. They left marks in the perfect whiteness, and she listed those too. She shut her eyes against her own self, her own need for that place as though it were a person she had not seen in years and missed terribly.

————

"Everything has its place," her father had once said to her when she was young, showing her the long cedar drawers of a card catalogue in the great library where he worked, the brass brackets on its face shining like a policeman's buttons. "But more important, everything's place is *labeled*. Order is transitive: order one precious thing and order the universe."

"Do I have a place in there?" November had asked, peeking over the rim of the long boxes.

"Of course, baby," he had said, and with his big brown hand, cuffed in plaid and smelling of lemon rinds from her mother's morning tea, riffled through a drawer and pulled a card from the stack:

006.332. *The Girl Who Circumnavigated Fairyland in a Ship of Her Own Making*. H. F. Weckweet, 1923. Gleiss & Schafandre: New York.

She had taken it seriously. Even then she had not known another method of doing things. The book was on the seventh floor and she had walked the steps, every one, knowing that this was the only proper way to proceed to her place in the universe—an elevator is cheating. The book was small, in a brown leather cover embossed faintly with a little girl standing naked on a raft, straight as a mast, her stance determined, holding up her dress as a sail. It was, at the time, the oldest thing she had ever seen.

November had read it exactly two hundred and seventeen

times, not counting unfinished perusals, since that day. It was, in fact, a long series of novels for children, but November did not care for the others: her father had not pulled them from the great catalogue and called them hers. She had not climbed seven flights of stairs for them. She had spent her birthday this year, her thirty-first, reading it cover to cover, dawn to dawn. The girl in the book was named September, and she had known that this was meant for her, a message from Hortense Francis Weckweet and her father. Perhaps if the girl had not been called September, November would not have read it two hundred and seventeen times.

Behind her eyelids the image of her father with his hands full of catalogue cards like a poker player warred with the image of Aloysius weeping, begging her: *Leave me alone, I cannot bear it, I cannot bear you.*

November sunk her head in her hands. *I cannot bear it, either, but the alternative is too big for me. I have nothing. I am not a brave girl.*

The bay fog slid over the hills like tea steeping. *I am not brave,* she thought, *but I do have a dress. I have that. A dress like a sail.*

She dried her eyes and pulled a cough of orange silk from her closet. She brushed back her hair into a librarian's bun so that no one would miss her face. Alleyways burned triumphant on her cheek. She turned all her rings firmly outward. They glittered like a knight's glove.

———

It took nine nights in the city. She drank foully sweet things and waited. Hard-angled, fashionable people stared nakedly at her. Her skin flared hot with shame and determination. *I will stand upon my raft until the Green Wind comes for me,* she thought, quoting Weckweet, quoting the book of her childhood. *My dress; my sail.*

And the Green Wind did come, slowly, gently, though in no chrome-walled bar or library annex. November was tired, heading home, walking through the thronging battalion of pigeons in Union Square, back to her car, back to the bridge and the bees and home, to Hortense Weckweet and a thousand unfinished lists.

The woman looked like she must have come from the North Pole: frizzy pale red hair blossoming around broad red cheeks whipped flush by the cold, a great long scarf trailing behind her. She wasn't pretty, but she wasn't plain. She didn't say anything, but her face was so bright and hopeful, so welcoming that November's ribs ached. The woman ran to her and stopped up short, her breath fogging in the evening air, the cutting blue breezes that belong to the Bay at dusk. She unbuttoned her peacoat with shivering gloveless fingers and pulled up her sweater like a child. It was on her belly, just under her left breast, like a patient spider crouching on her skin. The girl glanced at November's rings and grasped her face in delicate fingers, kissing her with the ferocity of a newborn bear suckling at its mother.

# Krasnozlataya and Corundum

Krasnozlataya
and Corundum

A HOUSE SITS SQUARELY ON THE CORNER of Krasnozlataya and Corundum Streets. Over the years it has grown to encompass nearly the whole of both boulevards, up to 19th Street and down to 6th. Through the spaces where its cornerstones do not mark the earth, the gardens of this house spill out onto the street in long emerald swathes. Beggars sleep beneath the pomegranate trees, and the carriage tracks swerve gracefully to avoid the intruding verdancy.

The house itself was planted as a sapling, its roots bound up in muslin and soaked in rose water. Three women brought it in a pine bucket, stroking its bark to keep it calm. They buried it in secret, hidden by a complicit moon, in the soft earth that was then Krasnozlataya Street, before the underground trains and the elevated tracks, before the great spires, before water-spouting, mice-headed gargoyles bred on that broad road with such zeal. The women wore gray veils and crowns of steel gears. They knew how to conduct rites properly—how to dress, how to stand. They came each night thereafter to feed it and whisper to it, they came silently and with sweet things in their pockets: sugar and apples and Spanish tiles and slivers of False Crosses, braids from their own head, ivory buttons, golden sewing needles and the heels of a thousand Sunday roasts, cherries with pits of hard molasses, faucet heads in the shape of men's mouths, frankincense and myrrh, lye and whiskey, long black pokers and swaddling clothes, handbags and haircombs, Christmas cakes, hemlock, lemon tea and glass goblets, a slaughtered blue sheep, and, lastly but most important, the sad gray form of one of their sons, who had strangled in his umbilical cord.

Whose child it was none of us may tell.

All of the women were named Casimira. They did not find it confusing.

The house, well-fed beyond all dreams of cornice and window hinge, began to grow so quickly and with such vigor that the houses on either side of it were forced to pick up their prodigious suitcases and, with much pointed sniffing, homestead elsewhere. The house threw up radiant cedar walls and windows of smoky glass. Bronze roof tiles clattered out from the chimneys like dominoes falling. Palisades and sweeping stairs twisted up from the earth, and long hallways stretched their arms for children to hide in. It opened room after room like blossoms, each furnished in a single color, for it was an orderly house and liked things just so. It sent up eight floors to begin with, and more sprouted with the harvest each year. It peaked and gabled its tiled roof, and threw towers into the air. At night passersby heard the house singing little nonsense songs to itself as it dressed up, a girl waiting with breathless hope for a festival to begin.

Finally, the house opened a room in its topmost tower, the largest of all the rooms it had ever grown before, and this room it colored in every shade of scarlet so that to stand within it was to stand within a beating, bleeding heart. This done, the house locked itself and waited, growing only as a tree will grow, one ring for each year.

It became the habit of the Casimiras in subsequent years to bring each heiress to the door of the wonderful house and press her little hand against the knocker, a lovely thing in the shape of a lion's paw. For many years, the house remained quiet and inert, no matter the charms of the young visitors. When the current Casimira turned eight years old, she was brought to the house. Her mother took her steady hand in hers and lay it against the door.

Perhaps you have already guessed it, for you are no doubt very clever. I certainly knew it must happen this way, but then, anticipation is one of my great hobbies.

———

The lion-knocker sounded clear and long, and the door opened without the smallest creak. It closed sharply behind the child, however, and kept her parents in the snow.

Little Casimira stood in the great hallway, at the foot of a staircase like a tier on the wedding cake of a giant. After a long while, she fell asleep on a plush lavender chair for lack of anything better to do.

When night came spooling blackly through the tall windows, a little boy came tiptoeing down the stairs and held Casimira's hand. He had a thick blue ribbon around his neck, like a girl's necklace, but wider, and it was very tight, but the boy was lovely all the same, with a high flush on his pale cheeks and extremely proper slippers on his small feet. He shook her awake, but very gently, with solicitude.

"Wake up, Casimira," the boy said. "Wake up." The boy smiled at her very perfectly, an expression of pristine technical accuracy, as though he had practiced the smile in a round mirror for eight years. "I do not have a name," the boy demurred, "so I cannot introduce

myself to you, but I would have been your grandfather, if I had not
been so clumsy and tripped over my mother when I meant to come
into the world."

Casimira did not answer.

"I have kept a room for you," the house said, and blushed perhaps more deeply than it is correct for boys to blush.

————

The sky is needled with stars, and November breathes in the green
cardamom and laurel of the Palimpsest winds. She wears the vio-
lently blue dress of Aloysius, and her belly prickles in the breeze.
Peacock feathers graze her shoulder. The buildings of Krasnozlataya
Street spindle tall and thin around her, so tall that long scarves of
clouds obscure their peaks, and she wants to shiver, but she cannot
manage it. From every terrace and corner grin gargoyles through
which old rainwater spurts in sprays and splashes, only to be caught
in long pools at the base of each tower. The little faces are mice and
hedgehogs and opossums, foxes and rats and blind, nosing moles.
Their faces contort as all gargoyles do, peering from within curling
stone leaves, licking sharp teeth, but their faces seem so sweet and
dear to her, she laughs in the middle of the street, and they grin
wider on their heights.

*Yes,* she thinks, *it is all right. I am here. I am here and it was
worth the price. It was worth a stranger with red hair, worth a boy
who loves his sister, and his sister, too. Worth all of them.*

But the bees are impatient with her gladness. They pull her to a
door so great she does not right away realize that it is attached to a
single house. An enormous lion's paw marks its center, and she puts
her hand upon it, as if greeting tenderly the beast whose foot it
must be. The bees scream, and the screams of bees are joy or rage;

there is room in them for only two kinds of cries. The lavender-suited manikin circles her waist with its buzzing arms; the door opens with a grand sweep, as though it had practiced just such a sweep for a decade and more.

Framed by thick ferns and far too many umbrella-stands, a woman stands just inside in the hall. She wears a severe dress, just the sort of thing a governess might wear, green-black from throat to floor, clasped by an enormous copper wasp at her collarbone and a long, ornate belt, copper too, a shining chain of tiny boxes that circle her compressed waist and trail to the floor in line like a monk's knotted rope. Her curly hair is piled high, an artful, decorous shade of green, deeper than emeralds or water, a sedate and proper color. It is the exact shade of her eyes. She holds a child by the hand, a boy with a blue ribbon around his neck, dressed like a little dauphin, and he hides behind the woman's voluminous skirts, peeking out at the newcomer.

The bee-manikin strides jubliantly to the woman and tips her chin towards itself. She kisses the bee-crowded face warmly, tilting her head in the classical pose of the seduced woman. The manikin gestures emphatically toward November and promptly dissolves into a swarm which dissipates through the house, leaving Aloysius's beautiful suit in a ripped, wrinkled pile on the immaculate floor.

"I like your dress," the woman says coyly. The boy hides his face in her bustle.

"Aloysius made it," November says, unable to think of anything better, more clever, more deserving of the woman before her. Her throat constricts.

"Oh, I know! I have several of his. There's no mistaking his work, really."

The two women are silent for a long while. A far-off clock whispers the hour.

"I also know," the green-haired woman says finally, "because I bought it for you. It's a present." Her blush is so furious that November can feel the heat of it just inside the great door.

"What have I done to deserve such a present?"

"Well." The woman looks determinedly at the floor. "My bees became very excited some time ago. They danced and sang a name, over and over, and I could not sleep for their chanting of it. The queen asked for an audience, and I let her sit upon my earlobe. She rubbed her legs together and said that they had fallen in love with an immigrant woman. They said she smelled like gorse and hibiscus pollen. They said she knew how to love them back, they were sure of it. And they were sure, as children are always sure, that their mother would also love the object of their apiary affection."

"Are you their mother, then?"

"I am Casimira, and that is as good as saying: yes."

"I am glad that I fought so hard against coming back to this place, Casimira, or I might not have found the girl with your house on her belly."

Casimira's eyes move appraisingly over November, who feels very much like a child in her lavish clothes.

"The dress will do, I think. Next time I will know better what suits you."

"Do for what?"

"I am taking you to the opera. How else shall we get to know one another? That is why you needed a dress. I do not care much for fashion, but a dress is like a sail, it must be held before one, colossal and dazzling, if one is to get anywhere at all."

November's eyes blur with tears. *My dress; my sail.*

Casimira crosses the quartz-veined floor, takes November's slender hands in hers, and leans forward to press cheeks, two absurd Victorian ladies, too proper for kisses. They stand thus for a long while, and only after that while whittles away does the boy timidly, carefully, place his small hand on November's long blue skirt.

Casimira breaks the embrace and pulls up the length of her belt like a fishwife pulling in her line. She opens the third box from the bottom and withdraws a small ring with a delicate moldovite honeybee in its gem-cage. She slips it onto November's chapped hand and, hesitantly, holding her breath with an excitement she cannot even begin to contain, turns the stone inward. Casimira blushes again with a heat like a broken furnace.

————

Casimira allows her smallest fingers to graze November's as their carriage clatters along the slick bronze tracks. There is no mount—heron-grooms and clip-tail leopards are for those too poor to afford the track tariffs, Casimira explains. But the reins extend stiffly from the jade-trimmed carriage nevertheless, a nod to tradition. The fiery streetlamps blur in November's vision as they pass away from the great house, past Krasnozlataya Street entirely, avoiding the amber shadows that demarcate November's allowable space in Palimpsest. They careen down to the bubbling mouth of a thick white river, and the ramshackle houses crowding the banks. The carriage stops at a tottering edifice. Eleven windows are broken; eleven windows are whole. There are no lights within.

Casimira's gloves are the color of her hair—a size too small, so that her fingers cup delicately toward her palm. With her curled hands she guides November past the great splintered door, down a long hall lined with threadbare rugs, and into a tiny room, hardly big enough for both of them. They crouch together in the dark, knees touching, scalps against the ceiling. Casimira's skin smells like the musk of a striped cat.

"I have brought you here specially," she whispers. "This is Thulium House, the opera house, which you will not have heard of, I know. But it is the best thing I know."

"How long have you lived here, that you know such places, that you have such a house as the one I saw, that you have a child?"

Casimira laughs, looks quizzically at her, and November has a curious moment of double vision, this quizzical woman and another, in a different dress spangled with silver stars, standing by a white river.

"I was born here," she says. "I'm not at all like you. And he is not my child."

"People are born here? How?" November asks, so new at this, the dullest child in class!

"In the usual way, I should imagine. Is there some exciting new method where you come from?"

"No . . . but if you've never been to my world, how did you know about the ring?"

"I listen. I have a billion ears, and they whisper to me of a trillion small things. They tell me all your little protocols—bees are particularly attracted to exotic systems of manners. *They* are my children—it would be more accurate to say I am the daughter of that boy holding on to my skirts! Perhaps if you are patient, I will show you the factory where my ears are made."

"Casimira, what is this place? If your ears say so much, you must know."

"I don't understand the question, my dear. It is the world."

"But it's not. I go to sleep, I wake up here. I take nothing back with me. It may be real, for some values of real, but it is not the world. *I* live in the world. I know its shape and its smell."

There is a small rapping at the door of their room, and Casimira shakes her head. "Later. It's time."

She holds up a long blindfold, and November recoils from it, untrusting.

"Nothing is going to hurt you, November. I promise. I will not allow it. I would never allow it."

Unsure, her jaw tight and quivering, November accepts the fold. When the matriarch bends to her, she sees that the back of Casimira's severe dress is entirely cut away, so that her smooth skin shows past her tailbone. Casimira tightens the ribbons at the back of November's head, and guides the hands of her compatriot to return the favor. It is an oddly ritualistic thing. They breathe together, blinded.

"I have listened to so many of you move through the city," Casimira says mildly. "The beetles know you, and also the ants. You crush them beneath your feet because you are ignorant. I feel their infinitesimal deaths in my smallest finger. I have seen so many proceed as you proceed now, your silly pilgrim's progress through a place which is my home, which is no more strange to me than milk at breakfast. You are all so confused, so young. I feel as though I have heard your dullard's questions so often my stomach is sick of them, though no one has ever gotten close enough to me to ask lip to ear, as you do. They ask it of the heavens, and the dark, and icons, and the stars, and beggars, and the moon. The spiders hear it all and laugh at them. It is *unutterably boring*, the multitudes in progression from innocence to inkling to knowledge to the inevitable apotheosis of desperation. It is wearisome in the extreme; it never varies. No one ever succeeds, they either give up or abandon themselves to nihilism or kill themselves. No one ever solves the equation, no one can ever steal more than a few scattered nights in Palimpsest. You are all so alike you might as well be family."

A hushing, sliding sound interrupts politely, and a draft tells November that one of their walls had been drawn up like a curtain. The skin on her cheek pricks up in gooseflesh. Her pulse throbs.

The voice begins quietly, a low, cheerless note held terribly long. A tremor passes through her—she can feel the singer's breath on her neck, the electric brush of lips at her ear. And the song goes on, the ballad, the aria, so close she knows each motion of the invisible mouth. A woman sings of a child with the head of a frog who fought in the war, who in the center of the battlefield sang dirges to all she killed with her small pistols. The child loved a boy with wolf's hands, and to her song he always came, faithful, to dwell in the peculiar grace of those who have just escaped a great, black thing. But the generals heard her song, too, and came with their tall surgeons to cut out the child's larynx, so that she could no longer give away their position to the enemy. She stood in the center of the battlefield and sang until she cried and her face was red with the effort of it, but she was silent, and without her song the boy with wolf's hands was lost, caught searching for her behind the lines, and gleefully executed by the frog-girl's fellow soldiers.

The song is complex and awful and so beautiful November's stomach twists in fear that it might end. But end it will and end it does, and the singer's tears have fallen into her ear. She puts up her hand in the dark, and it falls upon a wet face, as near to her as kissing, and then it is gone. The unseen soprano retreats; the wall slides back. Casimira takes her blindfold away; November takes hers.

"She will go to the next room, now, and the next, and the next," Casimira sighs. "The opera is an austere and intimate thing, it cannot bear very much light. She will sing in a hundred ears before the night is done. She will sing of the war, and the miserable remnants of it, and of love in the days when Hieratica Street was an inferno." Casimira puts her small hand on November's sternum. "This *is* the world," she says sternly, "just the world," she says, her eyes half-glowing in the shadows. "Terrible things happen here, to children, to the grown. We have a history the same as you do. When you are in your own home and ask where you have found yourself, what do you answer? You say to yourself: *I am home, in such and such city, in such and such province, in a country, in the world.* You are in Palimpsest. It is just a city. I am not a magical thing. I am not a beast or a sylph. I just live; we all just live. We eat and starve, we hoard and we fling open our stores. We fall from grace, we lose faith." Casimira circles November's waist with her gloved arms. "We become obsessed over things against good advice."

"If all that is true, why must I wake up? Why must I sleep with strangers to get here at all?"

"Do you not have borders in your country? And guards? And passports and papers of identification?"

"Of course."

Casimira smiles softly. Her teeth shine. She puts her hand on November's ruined cheek.

"Of course you do. And so do we."

From beneath her dress Casimira draws something that sings as it leaves her side. November can see, even in the murky shadows, a long knife, so pure and silver it is nearly white.

"This is the world, November. It's a difficult thing for someone like you to remember, but I am a helpful woman if I am nothing else. I want to help you. I want you to come back. To promise me you will come back, that you will not make me wait again."

"I'll . . . I'll try . . ." November's eyes open wide in the dark, trying to see where the knife has gone. Her voice trembles.

"I am going to help you see the way of things. To see more quickly than the other lost, bumbling fools who plague my rats in this place. To see as clearly as my bees see. It will go easier for you. There will be no boring existential crises. When you come to my house again, things between us will have progressed very far."

Casimira pulls her right glove off finger by finger and lays it around her neck like a stole. She grasps November's wrist resolutely and spreads her fingers against the smooth cold floor, pushing her first two fingers together into a blessing. November almost falls with the force of the woman dragging her hand downward. But she catches herself: it is a dream and she will be all right, she is sure of it. Almost sure. She closes her eyes and calms her body, sinking into the other woman's grip.

"I've kept a room for you," Casimira whispers, so faintly November barely snatches it from the air before the patroness of Palimpsest swings the long knife down and severs two of her fingers in one long slice.

Three people cry out and fall to their knees, clutching their fingers in anguish—and then it is gone, and they shake their heads, and they walk on through the night, understanding nothing.

# SIMPLE DECLARATIONS

O leg swam up toward waking, unwilling, fighting the current of consciousness. Gabriel's voice sliced through his sleep.

"There's coffee. Drink it. Or don't."

The wadded up weight of Oleg's jeans tossed casually at him brought him fully into the world. Gabriel frowned at him over the rim of a mug that proudly announced the indomitable strength of Denham Steel.

"Please leave as soon as possible, either way," he said flatly.

"What's wrong?"

Gabriel's look turned withering and he tossed the remainder of an ugly, thick black brew into the sink. "Nothing. I don't like company in the morning. Just, please go."

Oleg dressed without hurry. Mila often watched him dress, out of a vague anthropological curiosity, and it felt much like that now, with Gabriel's cold eyes on him. He buckled his jeans with a grimace. His hands smelled vaguely of condoms and lubricant, a smell he associated with things he probably shouldn't have done. That seemed to be about where he was at.

This was stupid. They liked each other, they had been happy, he had seen it in Gabriel's face afterward, sinking into sleep with his head on Oleg's chest. They could have been less lonely in the presence of the other. What had he done?

Oleg collected his tools and stood with finality before the architect, whose eyes were red and slightly wild, shaken.

"Just a dream, right?" Gabriel said, like an accusation, like certainty of guilt.

Yes, just a dream, a dream they shared, a dream that made itself manifest on his stomach. *Livid, like a bruise.* He took a deep breath, a last effort. "Even if it were real, Gabriel, what's the difference between punching a clock here and punching it there? Are you better off, serving elephant to rich people who won't let you look them in the eye?"

Gabriel's broken eyes welled up. "Oh, Oleg," he said, "you don't understand. Here, nothing means anything. It's all just ... *random.* Men and women and buildings and holidays and dinners and streets. It's all flat. It's like it's missing a dimension, deeper than depth. The dimension of *ritual.* There, *everything means something.* Even dinner. Even a time clock." He laughed, and then coughed harshly, as if hacking back a sob.

Gabriel collected himself. Dark circles bruised the skin under his eyes, and he was so thin, as if he hadn't eaten in this world for days. "Get out," he said quietly, picking at something invisible on the plastic counter. "Please just get out."

---

Oleg locked the door behind him, conscientious of the propriety of keys, and stepped into the snow.

---

His apartment was empty.

Lyudmila was often out, on whatever business ghosts might have, and for this reason Oleg did not worry about it when she did not greet him or watch him pour tea or wet the table with her bare feet, except that he felt the errant and ugly need to cry, and had long passed the point where he could cry without her. She would come back. He buttered cold bread and boiled an egg. The back of his neck shivered; Gabriel had not seen the second half of Oleg's dream, could not know it or guess it. How real she had been, how dry, how flesh.

Oleg understood the dead, or believed he did. He had been well brought up by them, well schooled. He knew their vespers and their matins. He walked in their city, rode their trains. He saw Manhattan for what it was because his sister had long ago taught him to recognize the signs, signs that rode on the moribund world like burn marks on an old lightbulb.

But dreams were not his to own as death was. He rarely remembered dreams, rarely cared for them. They were thin and small compared to her, compared to his city. He simply didn't care. And the other city, Gabriel's city—well, it didn't matter. Lyudmila was there; Lyudmila was here. Why wouldn't she be? Nothing else shone as brightly as her. What difference did it make if he fixed locks in a city of glass and stone or walked among mad bankers along a river of cream? At least he didn't have to wait tables here. Lyudmila was a constant. The only constant. The backdrop didn't matter. Gabriel couldn't understand that, could never consider that it didn't matter if the city was real or not.

But Lyudmila did not come back. Weeks passed, a month. She had never stayed away so long, even when he had fallen in love with a Polish girl from Brooklyn and ordered his sister, finally, away. *It was time to let her go,* he had thought. He wanted to marry this one. She wouldn't understand a dead girl living with them. Mila hadn't cried or yelled or broken anything. She had just slipped out a window. And stayed away for exactly seventeen days, each of which he had marked with a small cut on the inside of his calf.

She returned when he stopped eating and the Polish girl began a cozy acquaintance with his doctor.

"Why did you come back?" Oleg had asked.

"You needed bandaging," Lyudmila had said, and buried her head in his shoulder.

The Polish girl had left him for a social worker who brought her orange blossoms every day until she forgot all about him. He hadn't resented it. He had learned the lesson he needed and never sent Lyudmila away again.

But it had been twenty-seven days now, and he had begun to mark them as before, with a razor on the skin of his leg, not out of compulsion, but hoping to call her back through sympathetic magic. If he needed bandaging enough, she would come home. But she did not come. He thought of Gabriel occasionally, but his failure there seemed too big to move.

Oleg bent to his work. He had neglected them, his locks and his keys, in the madness of two such quick and strange lovers. These things happened. They forgave him. He removed the heavy front-door mechanism from a condemned hospital up the Hudson a ways and brought it back to the little bedroom that housed his collection. It shone with dull malevolence, the newcomer among the natives. He brought it a succession of keys to become devoted to, all of which it rejected with an upturned knob. He finally abandoned that. He listened as carefully as he could to each lock he repaired, for its secret cry, for the clicking and turning of its wishes. But most of all he listened for a small, cold voice calling him from further and further doors. He heard silence, and the distant Atlantic. Mila had never tormented him before; it was not her way.

Oleg began to leave the house in disarray. She would never scold him, but she had always been driven to comment upon it. *The egg has gone cold, the tea is acrid. The plate is dusty.* Simple declarations, without accusation or advice. Where could she have gone?

But he did know where she was, he supposed. He had seen her there, by a white river, wearing a blue dress. If she was not here she must be there—perhaps that was where she went when she could not bear any more of the living. Perhaps she fished a coat from the street and walked under palms with that strange snow in her hair. Perhaps she had a lover there.

And Oleg had been there, too, with his sister. He had held her cold hand on an iron bench. He had seen the curvature of her ear. He had been there, he had been there every night since, among the banks and drenched in the white river. And every night she looked up at him through snowy hair and shook her head in disappointment. She turned from him under dozens of moons and strode past the brick walls of the tunnel, and he could not follow her, somehow, could not pass into the places where she walked. Amber shadows gathered to block the way. It was like a puzzle, and he could not solve it. Could not follow.

But Oleg was not so dense that he did not surmise how the thing was done. He had held a lover's body in his mouth twice, and twice he had slept into that place. But he did not know how to find anyone but the other Lyudmila with her liony long hair and wide mouth and thin, brittle Gabriel himself. There were others, there must be. A virus loves company. But he did not know how he could possibly find them. It had been an accident, like an unwanted child. He didn't even know how to talk about it. He had practiced not talking about the things he knew until no man could be called his equal. Manhattan, Lyudmila, the furtive longings of locks and the shrill keening of their destined keys. It calmed him to collect the things he knew and did not speak of. A city on the other side of sleep. That had to be added to the tally, now. Behind the gate of horn—it was horn, right? He remembered that from a long-ago book his mother had loved. Virgil, he thought. A book about long journeys and the sea. *The gates of sleep are two, a gate of ivory and a gate of horn.* He had been horrified as a child, picturing a great door of tangled antlers and tusks.

Surely that was the gate of Palimpsest.

He swallowed the name of the city. It was hard in his throat, like a piece of candy lodged in the wet pinkness there. It was difficult, absurd, to say the word here, in his apartment, under all those other apartments with their individual lives wheeling inside. Hard to say how he knew it, just as he could not remember a time when he did not know that this place was New York, Manhattan. It just *was*. It just existed. It was just called that. But what the Holland Tunnel or the George Washington Bridge of Palimpsest was, he could not say. It had always seemed significant to him, whether one entered the city by bridge or tunnel. Ascending or descending, down to the underworld of violet shadows and civilized bowls of blood or up through the fog and into streets of silver and sheen.

But that place, that other city, Gabriel's city, it was not clearly marked. Inconsiderate. Which way was intended? He was mired to the knees in the river muck, looking up at the lights.

———

*The easiest way,* Oleg thought, sitting at a public computer terminal in the great be-lioned library. Green study lamps bulged at every desk like guardian turtles. He should have thought of it before. People naturally form networks, spangled, spidery hoops of light lying over the world. People wanted to be found.

He logged in to the three or four social sites where he maintained mostly inactive accounts, as well as a handful of classified listings and held his breath while he typed into the empty, inviting, assuring text box:

*Seeking travelers to the borough of Palimpsest. Unexplained spontaneous tattoos? Bad dreams? Find me. Please, find me.*

*There,* Oleg thought. Obscure enough—no one would contact him who did not know what he meant, but plain enough to those who couldn't ignore the black mark on their skin. Some flair. He posted it to all his accounts and classifieds and walked to the corner restaurant for half a Greek chicken, which he devoured. He chewed at the bones for a while.

*If Mila were here,* Oleg thought, *she'd have helped me write it. It wouldn't sound quite so much like an advertisement for skin cream. If she had been here, the chicken would have tasted sweeter.* He would not have chewed the bones—it's not a nice habit. But he would find her soon, and she would tell him to clean the apartment in a very stern tone.

When he returned to his terminal and turtle lamp a few hours later, Oleg found a long series of e-mails in his in-box, all the same. He stared.

```
This post has been deleted by an administrator.
This post has been deleted by an administrator.
This post has been deleted by an administrator.
This post has been deleted by an administrator.
This post has been deleted by an administrator.
This post has been deleted by an administrator.
This post has been deleted by an administrator.
This post has been deleted by an administrator.
```

At the bottom of each notice, someone had typed, in a tiny font:

*Sorry, brother.*

Oleg sat back in his squeaky leather chair, his eyes full of frustrated, angry tears.

———

It is not easy to go without clothing in December. Not in New York. Not through brief, fitful snow blowing down streets like old dreams. The cold was so much keener than he imagined it would be. It tore at him with small cat-teeth, and the blood sped away from his skin, inward, away from the wind. But he was staunch, steadfast. A little tin soldier. Every morning Oleg took off his shirt and walked through the square through which half the world walked. Every night he would sit in a steaming bath until it turned as cold as his shoulders.

By each day's toll of ten in the morning, his chest had already gone clam-white. On his stomach the black mark screamed its dark lines, seething against that frozen flesh. He was ridiculous, terrible in such a throng. He had chosen the most obvious place. Times Square, where the raucous lights were brightest and all the tourists were certain to come, sooner or later. Sooner or later. It was the most dead of all the places the dead loved on this monochrome island, its putrescence beautifully bright against the long gray cadaver, like mushrooms and moths. Everything here had halos. It made him want to die, too, just to stand here, with snow and light on his eyelashes, with the gray daytime sky laughing at all that neon and strobe, all those things whose proper province is the night.

He was preposterous here, obscene. But it was all he could manage. It was all he knew how to do, now, to lay himself at the mercy of his sister, of chance. Whoever the offended administrator was, he was against Oleg, clearly, and cleverer. What could he do but walk through the city, walk among the living who stamped upon the streets of the dead, and let his flesh plead silently for him, to all who watched—administrators, ghosts. An advertisement amid all the advertisements of Times Square, screaming as loudly, flashing as brightly: *I'm here, take me, I am willing to go.* He was good at this. He knew how to walk straight ahead and allow some wraith he could not now see to come to him. He had never sought a thing out in all his days if it was not a key or a lock. That sort of thing was for other men, other temperaments. Mila had crouched upon *his* bed, he had called her by no fell rite, sprinkled no blood in a circle, bought nothing at great price.

Yet Oleg walked through the snow, and the wind chapped his skin, and the pain was a wrangling, thorough thing.

"I miss you, Mila. I'm coming as fast as I can," he whispered, and a woman with her hands stuffed deep in brown pockets flinched away from him: a mad, half-naked thing whispering to himself. Oleg did not look at her. He was proving himself worthy. This was how it was done: you bare your belly to a great beast and endure trials and it all works itself out. There is a treasure or a sword. Or a woman. And that thing is yours not because you defeated anything, or because your flesh was hard and unyielding, but because you were worthy of it, worthy all along. The trials and the beast were just a way of telling the world you wanted it, and the world asking in her hard way, hard as bones and hollow mountains, if you really and truly did.

And Oleg did. And he watched the people around him, how their gazes flickered to his stained stomach, to the jack-knifing streets there, and back to his eyes, how full of fear they were, how close many of them came to calling the police. But he walked on. He was worthy, a worthy knight, and he would enter the city by low ways. Sooner or later, someone would see him who hid matching cartography under the pad of their foot or beneath their hair, and they would fall together as he and

Gabriel had, as he and Lyudmila had, and the world would nod sagely.

Oleg practiced this flagellation for fifteen days.

He had imagined a warm hand pressing against his back a thousand times before it occurred, imagined it so often and so fiercely he hardly felt it when it did happen. Such a small hand, and he was so cold. He looked down at her, a woman with short brown hair whipping around her face like a storm. She was androgynous, unnoticeable, small, her eyes angled upward slightly, a silver fur ruff framing her high cheeks, blistered red by the wind.

"You don't have to do this," she said, her eyes searching him earnestly, with a kindness like saints kissing. She bent her head before him and smoothed over her hair: on the back of her neck, it was there, black, bright, prickled with gooseflesh.

"I'm here," she said. "I came."

Oleg's knees buckled and he dropped to his knees. The tears came faster than he wanted them to, unstopped and messy, chasing breath he could not catch, hitching, heaving gulps of the winter air as he pressed his spinning head into her within a crush of people so great it became a wall and they were alone.

"I watched you," she said. "I've watched for ten days now, until evening, from that window just there. That's my office. I wanted to know how long you'd do it. I drank about a thousand cups of tea. I ran out of sugar. You just kept coming back and I just couldn't interrupt you, it was so beautiful, so awful. I saw your lips split open. I saw the sore on your temple grow." She put her hand in his hair. "It was like watching someone be born.

You were an angel, a real one, with a terrible name, like in the Bible. No feathers or light, just hardness and falling into the dark. My hands shook on my teacups for ten days. I didn't dare interrupt. But I decided I wanted you, after all. I wanted to stop it for you, to stop the wind and the snow and hold my arms over your head. So I'm here, I came. My name is Hester and I came for you."

Oleg clawed his way up her height as though she were a craggy hill and his kiss was like biting into her warmth. Under his teeth the blood of her lip welled up, a hot red thing between their mouths.

"I'm here," he choked, "take me, I'm willing to go. Anywhere. Away. Please."

And Hester took him like a beggar onto the train, which he would not remember, far to the north end of the island, and into an apartment he barely saw through the film of his cold and his grief and his need. He was so hungry for her he thought for a moment his body would simply leap out of itself and into her, a second body, compressed and crimson and screaming within the freezing shell of his elbows and knees. He kissed her neck where it was black as frostbite, bit it, shut his eyes against her and grabbed at her hips, just to pull her closer than anatomy allows, just to swallow her warmth, her sweet breath like milky tea.

"Wait," she gasped, her shirt already wrinkled up over her belly, her jeans unbuttoned. "It's been so long . . . just *wait*." She put her palm against her cheek, her eyes wild, glistening. "It's been so long since I did this."

"What? I thought you'd be . . . I don't know. Old hat. A veteran."

"I didn't want it," Hester snapped, slumping onto her threadbare brown couch. "I *don't*. I said no—remember that word? I turned away from it. All of it." She pulled out a drawer on a small blue table; it was filled with dusky orange bottles the color of dead suns, bottles not unlike his own at home. "I have six prescriptions to make sure I sleep black and deep. Dreamless. Get it? *I didn't want it*. I didn't want to see that place, ever again. I grew my hair just long enough to cover the mark and I ate pills till the city went away. It's been years. I stopped. It *is* possible to stop. Until a ghastly, frozen angel comes walking down the street and you think: *No more. He's not my responsibility. Someone else take this one, someone else come with a long coat and wrap him up, someone else kiss him until he's warm again! Why won't they come? Why won't they come?* But they don't come. No one else is coming, and he's freezing and so beautiful you think the wind might take him just to ease its loneliness. And you're lonely, too. And you tell yourself he's worthy, if anyone ever was."

Hester was up on her knees on the couch cushions, bent over the torn arm of the sofa, her nails digging into the upholstery, staring at the floor, her voice thick and ragged. Oleg stroked her arm timidly, not knowing how to help her, until she grabbed his hand and dug her nails into it instead. She tilted her face to be kissed again, such a terribly deliberate act, slow and resigned, that he simply slumped into her, awkwardly, falling together in a heap onto the couch, their tongues hard and hostile. Her breasts were small and cold beneath her shirt;

she did not stop him when he pushed her jeans down, or when he turned her around so that she held the edges of the unraveled upholstery to keep herself kneeling as he moved her knees apart and pushed into her, still frozen and shaking. It was not easy—she was dry and unyielding, her teeth clenched, her breath sucking thin and sharp at the air. That she did not stop him was all she seemed to be able to contribute, and the pills rattled in her drawer as he buried his face into her neck. His body leapt out of itself; she held his arm around her waist.

"I don't want to go back," she whispered helplessly.

# Coriander
and Ultramarine

Coriander
and Ultramarine

A GROVE OF BAMBOO SPRINGS up near the southern barrens of Palimpsest, just before the city slides away into desolate desert. It is very green and very tall, so tall that the fibrous crowns get lost in the deep blue clouds. Between the willow-bright trunks grow scarlet tulips, each as sedately filled with rainwater as a cup with tea at the finest of houses. The stalks stand like a portcullis against the desert, and no man may say where they end. Certainly not I. Certainly not you. But we may come here and look out on the waste, for it is a singular pleasure to be warm and safe while one watches horrors unfold, is it not?

The dead come here; the dead sleep fitful and dreaming.

If only there were a funeral tonight, then we might see such things—but there! Is that not a fine baroness shrouded in stoat fur, her fingers and toes ringed with tourmaline, tied to her golden stake and hoisted up by her weeping catamites? Is her spider-waist bound up in daisies? It is! Surely, you can see it, just there!

They will dig her grave screaming, her boys. Straight down into the earth, a pit of black and dust, in such an abandonment of grief that one or two may eat dirt until he follows her into the bath-houses of the dead. They will sink her down, standing tall and proud as she always did, as they remember her, calling for a tureen of rosemary broth and a favored one to ply his tongue beneath her gracefully uplifted gown. They will tilt her head toward the crescent moon, and as they shovel in the seedful earth around her, they will shriek, oh how they will shriek, until the owls shrink from them and hide their heads. It is possible that they will spill their seed after her in shuddering, lurching convulsions of anguish. And they will set her bamboo pole in place, small amid the great giants, and all her jewels will feed its roots.

The dead of Palimpsest are thin and tall. The process will not begin until the bamboo grave-marker reaches past the cloudline, when the vapors of the stars seep down through the impossibly long green whistle-stalk. Only then will the scalps of the deceased break the soil like babies crowning. Without noise, without opening putrescent eyes, the dead will stretch toward the scent of the stars, mute, atavistic, slow as mushrooms. Their limbs will elongate, their softened skulls compress, their hips fold in like suitcases closing, and slowly as they stretch, they will grow long and lean as their stalk of bamboo. In a thousand years the peaks of their heads may peek out of the leafy terminal end of the trees, and they may breathe the exhalations of the stars.

So they say, and so I hope.

There are some who believe that the stellar winds will blow through the ears of the dead and carry their souls back down to the city on a palanquin of light.

———

Leonide tends the grounds here. He has a great belly, and used to joke to children that he ate the moon when there was nothing left in his cupboard. He has an enormous manicured mustache and thick hair he keeps in a bun like an old woman. His legs are those of a shaggy zebra, and he keeps them covered in stained rags and shoes made painstakingly to appear as though he still had human feet. He spades the bamboo beds and, in the honored manner of grave-keepers, long ago learned to converse with the dead. It is a happy tradition, requiring no long rituals of indoctrination or apprenticeship; the dead teach their own and in their own time.

The house of Leonide is also thin and tall. It is made of marble. He was thinking of another place when he built it, a frightening, fairy-tale world his grandmother told him about, where they bury the dead lying down, and erect marble angels over them to watch and make sure they do not reach up toward the vaporous stars. The angels are diligent there. Thus the house reaches high, but not so very far up along the length of the bamboo is stark and white, and there is an angel crouching at the door, half hidden by ferns and bougainvillea, to watch over Leonide as he comes and goes. This angel is also diligent.

Once in a very long while, during the autumn when no one can bear to die and miss the fiery trees or the coming of hoarfrost to Palimpsest, he feels himself grow forlorn and longs for conversation among the chestnut smoke and apple-heavy wind. Men are like that. It cannot be helped. On these occasions Leonide removes a pocketknife from his prodigious trousers and cuts into the side of a stalk of bamboo. He is very careful. He cuts only a small piece, a rectangle, a fortune-teller's card, and removes it like a plaque from a high wall.

Within, a gray hand moves slightly, sluggishly. Leonide takes it in his. He holds it gently, strokes the old knuckles.

The hand squeezes back, softly, hardly a motion at all. Only a grave-keeper of the highest order would feel it, but Leonide is of such an order and such a rank, and he kisses its fingernails.

———

Oleg places his hand upon the cool skin of a bamboo stalk. His fingers still throb, and he can feel cold, hard skin on his, though nothing touches him, and taste a red tea on his lips. He crawls with the sensation of it, with the other senses he carries with him like satchels. But they are less now, they fade. All things do, he thinks.

He looks between the trunks of this great forest; half-formed mist noses at the leaves. It is perhaps inevitable that he notices, as a locksmith must notice, the small rectangles carved into the sides of the great trees. They are so very like doors, you see. And if he finds the little doors, then he must find the long fingers, the pinched hips with sprays of birthmarks, the kneecaps like burls. And he must understand it, he must, for the dead have taught their own, in their own time, and Oleg Sadakov knows their vernacular, their diphthongs and phonemes.

"Oh," he says. "Oh. You were here. You came here, and you saw inside the bamboo. Poor Hester—that's why you didn't want to come back."

"I remember her," comes a voice by his ear, a voice familiar and low, like hushed singing. "She screamed and screamed. And I had such things planned for her sake."

Oleg turns, and she is there, she is there, beyond hope, she stands in her star-spangled dress, its blue train wet and sopping. Snow threads her hair. She holds a parasol that shades her sweetly, though when he looks closely at it he sees that three white foxes are sleeping on its surface, so pure and pale they seem no different from the diffident silk beneath their paws. Her face is whole and stern, Lyudmila's face, her lips rosy and full, not burst and drowned, her eyes gently gray, her skin flushed and alive. She is warm and real and young.

Oleg feels he ought to genuflect before her as he did before the woman in the freezing streets of his waking life. But he cannot; his legs will not show her weakness.

"Where have you been?" he cries instead, and shakes her by the shoulders. The foxes stir and yawn, their pink tongues unrolling. "Why did you leave me?"

Lyudmila looks puzzled, her fine eyebrows knitting, and she puts her cold hand to his face. "I've been just here. I was waiting. You took so *long*. I was beginning to despair."

"Well, it's hard, Mila! It's not exactly like hopping a train uptown. I never had to go to such lengths to see you before."

Lyudmila purses her lips. She looks so very like their mother in that moment, her elfin face drawn in concern.

"Sometimes I worry about you, Olezhka. Really, I do."

Oleg puts his arms around her, as needy as a young bear snuffling for friendly paws in the wintry dark. She allows herself to be held, even lifted slightly off her feet; she pets his head tenderly. Her weight is real and solid in his grasp—she is so alive, and her skin beneath his palms is hot.

"I missed you, Mila. I missed you so."

"You were not relieved to have an apartment to yourself? To let your tea go cold if you pleased, to kiss pretty things on your couch without dark eyes burning behind the curtains?"

"No." Oleg shakes his head fiercely. "No, never."

"Well." Lyudmila disentangles herself, smoothing her skirt with a blue-gloved hand. "Well, then. That's settled." She catches his wrist suddenly, sharply, her even nails cutting into him, her grip bony and rigid. "Don't make me wait again," she hisses, and looses him as suddenly, as sharply.

She leads him away through the forest, and he can hear, as if from far away, winds whistling through the stalks: it is almost a song they make together, but it cannot hold, and falls into scattering storm-whirls before the first verse is done.

———

There is a small boat tied with a length of leather to a tarnished silver pier. It is not Gabriel's gondola, but it sweeps in slender fashion from end to end in same general manner, and there are garlands on it, of seaweed and of marigolds. Lyudmila holds out her hand, intending in some genteel forgotten way to communicate that he ought to help her aboard, and Oleg hurries to her.

The river is milky and thick as before, the cream in it a long golden ribbon. Lyudmila sits primly at the head of their craft and it drifts tranquilly downstream. She neither steers nor rows, but they keep their course. She gives him a smile like a present wrapped in red.

"I will take you anywhere you wish to go," she says brightly.

Oleg touches her foot with his foot. Her color is high in the honey-sweet wind, he has never seen her like this. *She is beautiful,* he realizes, *she grew up to be beautiful.*

"Take me to a place where you and I may lie on a long bed with our knees tucked together. Take me to a place where I can make smoky tea that you will love to drink, where lemons grow and also where plovers sing at dusk. Take me to a place with a little mirror where I can shave, and a basin full of water where you can wash your hair. I could be happy in a place like that, I think. I could watch you sleep there. I could boil eggs for us, and bake bread for you."

"You want so little."

"Not so little."

They pass an hour in silence. The parasol-foxes chew at fleas and snap at passing mayflies, the jeweled bodies crunching between their vulpine teeth. Palimpsest yawns enormous on one side of the river, towers and leviathan flying buttresses ablaze with hanging lanterns, falcons screeching down the long canyons between them. On the other side, small towns stretch lazily along the greening mud, the clotted river thickening in the shallows, the polished logs of underwater nets floating sleepily on the yellowish currents.

"Look to the banks, Olezhka," Lyudmila says finally. "And the moon falling there, on the spires and houses." The knotted white buildings sleeping on the right-hand bank are warped like gnarled bones, many of them half-crushed, their dust feeding the river. There is a cathedral of a sort, and on its roof a lonely monk blows a long black trumpet. The moonlight is brighter than day there, and only there. The river remains in shadow. Men and women crawl out of the ruined houses and hold great glass jam jars above their heads, their long hair spilling back to the earth. The moonlight pours into the jars; the women screw on brass lids with muscled arms, piling their shelves with them, jar upon jar.

"There was a war once," Mila murmurs. "It began here. In this very spot. It was not a very long time ago."

"How can there be war in this place?"

Lyudmila shrugs, her eyes downcast. "War likes best those towns that have grass growing on their roofs and apples on their trees, and especially those with industrious women who have lovers with strong brown backs. This was a town like that on the shores of the Albumen River, whose yolk was once rich and young.

Before Casimira and her chariots, before the fires, before the moths with their awful wings and poisons. The cider was so fierce here it would take you off your feet in a swallow."

"Who is Casimira? What happened? How did it end?"

But Lyudmila's face is shadowed, as if she grapples with some private grief he cannot touch. Instead, like a good brother and a dear one, he lays his head in her lap and wraps his arms around her knees. The boat wavers, but rights itself and passes the mournful town in utter silence. The last jar is screwed tight, and the moon goes out. It is very dark on the river now, and the stars shiver. Lyudmila smoothes his hair absently.

"In the land of the dead," she says finally, her voice clear and cold across the water, "a boy who died of a fever wished to make his fortune in the munitions factories of that unfortunate land. And so he went to the districts of those who had died in battle, and begged from each of them the bullets that had pierced them, which they each carried in their tin lunchboxes. There was one girl only who would not give over her bullet—"

"Lyudmila," Oleg interrupts softly, "why don't you drip water from your mouth when you speak anymore?"

She is quiet; her hand freezes on his temple.

"Do not ask me that, Olezhka. Let it be just a little while longer."

"All right, Mila."

Clouds sweep over the stars, and there is no light left on the long, white river.

# FOUR

# PEREGRINATIONS

Nerezza cradled Ludovico's head in her arms. She did it awkwardly, not being by nature a nurturing dove of any breed, unused to ailing men in her bed, in her kitchen, in need of her coffee grinder's shrill whirring and her boiling water, in need of her. But she tried, gamely, as another woman might try to swallow fiery spices out of politeness.

"Ludo, drink. You have to."

He turned his head from her, for a moment thinking he might throw up.

"Lucia," he groaned.

Nerezza rolled her eyes. "Yes, Lucia. I know. It doesn't mean you don't need to drink when I tell you to."

Ludo drank. It was bitter and thick and duskily sweet. Lucia had often ordered him about—he required it, flourished under it, as he could never remember that eating remained vital even when a book was overdue and so beautiful it cracked his sternum with the force of it. She had had to curl his fingers around a spoon once, when a new American translation of the *Bucolics* was on the press and unconscionably late. Ludo had not tasted the carroty soup or the bread, but she had tasted for both of them.

"If you cry in my house," Nerezza said, "I shall call security."

"I don't understand." Ludo opened his eyes to a room flooded with sunlight, all the brighter for her sparse belongings. The sunlight seemed to be unsure of what to do in the absence of a couch to fade or curtains to shine through, and so had gone helplessly nova in the center of Nerezza's living room. He groaned again, his head throbbing like a struck bell.

"Don't you? I know it's hard to keep in your head, a hard wrestle, like Jacob and that angel. But she's there, you must see that. You saw her. She's there and safe and you don't have to worry about her anymore."

"Where the fuck is *there*?" Ludo did not often swear, but he felt he had placed the word perfectly, squarely.

Nerezza looked at her shoes. She was dressed already, in cream and camel, impeccable, and Ludo thought she probably didn't know how to be anything less than that.

"Palimpsest," she whispered. "Don't make me . . . I don't like saying it. Here. I don't like saying it here."

Ludovico extricated himself clumsily from her and stalked into the small kitchen, buttering bread and slicing cheese for himself without speaking to her. He could feel her watching him fumble with her knives, knew his cheeks blazed with little points of blush that could not quite spread.

Nerezza folded and unfolded her hands. "I know—"

"I am not discussing this," he snapped.

"You were there, Ludo! You saw the horses. You ate a snail with a silver shell. You saw her, you saw Paola—that's her lover's name, Paola. Did you know her?" Nerezza hurried on. "You sat next to me and I tasted your tears."

"I had a bad fucking dream." He felt satisfied having used that word again, as though it were a badge he could wear and polish.

"Dreams don't work like that. Two people don't dream identical dreams."

*"I am not discussing it."*

Nerezza shrugged. "It's not that I feel responsible for you. I feel..." She stared at the precise moons of her cuticles. Strands of dark hair had begun to work loose from the meticulously messy knot at the nape of her neck. "I feel that Lucia left her life untidy, and as her friend it is my duty to order it. If not for her, I would never have seen the things I've seen. It is the least I can do to..." She looked sidelong at him through her lashes. Ludo could not tell whether she meant the expression to look kittenish or morbid. "Feed her animals while she's gone."

Ludo gripped the edges of the cream-colored countertop. He shut his eyes; the sunlight turned his eyelids to a ruby smear. Had she been here? Had she eaten this brown bread with crystals of coppery sugar in the crust? Had she let a cigarette sigh into ash on that light-scoured terrace? He tasted the snail still on his lips; there were such screams in his ears, ringing, ringing! But it was a mad thing, an impossible thing. Leave it to Lucia to find a madness so big she could vanish into it and drag him with her, far behind, weeping for her, like a penitent on a chain, stumbling behind the priest's cart.

"If you want to see her again," Nerezza said quietly, "you have to accept this. It's fairly simple, in the end."

"If she wanted to leave me, there might have been a divorce.

I've always liked legal documents. They feel so real. That would have been easier. Quicker. More final."

"This is very final. Or will be, when she's finished."

"You don't know her. You don't know us. She will find a way back to me, if the world is as you say and all this is real."

Nerezza laughed, a bark, a snap of an eel's electric tail. "She's *gone*, Ludo. And if she's lucky, she'll soon be in Palimpsest forever, and you'll only see her if you fuck the right shopgirl."

"But she's not there yet? Not completely? She's somewhere here, too, in Italy, in Europe? America?"

Nerezza threw up her hands in disgust. "Oh, for Christ's sake. *No one* has gotten there yet, completely, permanently. But yes. I drove her to the airport. So that she could try. I helped her get a passport. You have no idea what she and I have been through together—I was *there*, I watched her go, toward Paola and Palimpsest and all of it. I helped her. She would have bled through her eyes for it. So would I. God," she raised her eyes to the impassive ceiling, "if only the toll were as cheaply paid as that. If only I could bleed and that would be enough."

Helpless in the face of his idiocy, she lifted her slim shoulders and let them fall. He tired her, he could see it. An animal who made a mess all over her house. His tears and his semen on her sheets, the endless laundry of him, the endless water he required and gave back uglier, saltier, than he had received it.

A small knock came at the door, like a polite cough. Nerezza's face did a curious thing; it flushed, and she smiled, a smile which seemed to come out of her marrow, raw and livid. Her dark eyes dazzled and Ludo quailed from her a little, from this woman, the mark of whose mouth still blazed on his cheek.

A man and a woman stood at the door, clutching each other's hands fiercely. Nerezza took them both in her arms and the three of them stood for a moment, their heads pressed together, their arms hanging limp around each other's waists. Ludo bit his lip, bearing within him the awful feeling of stalking in the cold just outside the warm glow of a fire, unable to draw closer. The man kissed the top of Nerezza's head with a rough tenderness; the woman laid her head in the crook of her shoulder. When they finally broke ranks, Nerezza led them both by the hand to the kitchen, where Ludo shrank against the wall, trying not to appear as though he shrank at all. They were strangers, their eyes full of tears, and they advanced on him like assassins. He longed to flee.

"I asked them to come, Ludo," Nerezza said. Her voice was rough and harsh, an eel-voice, from the deeps, and he found in that moment that he hated it. "So that we could explain to you, so that they could. It's a hard progress we make, and lonely, frightening—but it doesn't have to be like that. This is Anoud, and this is Agostino. They are my lovers." She paused for a moment, as if to make space for Ludo's disapproval to have its little fit. "But that's not why they're here." The two of them nodded eagerly. Anoud was dark, Moroccan maybe, her skin the color of old dust. Agostino was tall and ascetic, with an ungainly nose and a distantly grieving expression. He looked to Ludo like a man who wept often. The trio guided him to the long chaises of Nerezza's minimal living room, and he allowed himself to be seated, his limbs arranged like a doll's. They stared at each other for a long time, unwilling to be the first to speak, but Anoud and Agostino did not let go of Nerezza's hands, clutching them so tightly that the tips of her thumbs had gone purple. Nerezza began, her voice soft, buoyed by her lovers' presence.

"Do you remember, Ludovico, the first night? Do you remember the house with the frog-woman in it?"

He did not want to admit to this. It was like admitting to syringes in the refrigerator or being unable to read. He did not like to be pried open at the hinges and stared into, murmured about in disapproving tones. Why couldn't Lucia just stay with him, in their little home, with their books and their roasted chickens? Why must this horrid scene now play out?

"Yes," he said gruffly, biting the word in two.

"Her name is Orlande," said Agostino. His words echoed loudly, too loud in this place.

"Do you remember that you were not alone?" asked Anoud sweetly, looking tenderly at Nerezza, and a flood of jealousy released bile into Ludo's heart.

"You must think very hard, Ludo," said Nerezza. "You must try to remember. There were others, with you. Then, and now. When you sat in the stands with me, you felt them, you felt someone else eating when you had no plate before you. Someone else kissing when you were not."

He struggled—it is never easy to remember a dream. A fleeting vision of long, blue hair swept through him, and he shuddered with it. *St. Isidore, you never imagined this thing,* Ludo implored silently. *In what column would you have placed it?*

"There were three of them," Ludo said slowly, and he felt the weight of that memory lift from him. "One had blue hair. She was very young. Another, I think, another had a bee sting on her face. And there was a man with keys hanging from his belt."

"Yes," breathed Nerezza. "Anoud and Agostino, you understand, were there when I sat in Orlande's shop, when I put my feet into the ink."

"Only two?"

Nerezza pressed her lips together until they went white, and her companions would not look at him. They seemed to sag into each other, their breath stolen.

"About three years ago," Nerezza said, "our friend Radoslav was killed. He was the other one, in Orlande's shop with us. It's . . . so hard to stay careful *there*. It is easy to become involved in unsavory things, and easier still to find oneself without shelter in dark alleys. There are people in Palimpsest—they call themselves Dvorniki . . . it means 'street-cleaners.' They're veterans, you remember? Like I showed you, at the races. Their leader, or priestess, or whatever, has a shark's head. They hold sabbats in doorways, any doorway, but they have a great, huge one built in the basement of the big train station . . . you haven't been there yet, though. Anyway, it's just an empty, carved doorframe, all black. No door, no hinge. And they . . . well, it's wonderful there, in Palimpsest, but sometimes it's not very nice."

Anoud took up when Nerezza's voice faltered—Ludo did not even know such a thing could happen! "Radoslav cheated a Dvornik at *Valorous,*" she continued. "That's a game, with little copper stars you move around a board covered in white silk. He couldn't have known the man was political. Radya was just . . . like that. Reckless. They came for him while he was drinking licorice wine in a hotel—the most civilized thing you can imagine, and the Dvorniki just grabbed him, with crab claws and donkey jaws.... They dragged him to the train station, to that big black doorframe, and they cut his throat on the lintel, praying that no immigrants should ever find their way to Palimpsest, that his blood would seal all the ways and roads."

"It's so stupid." Agostino sighed. "Brutal, idiotic, Neolithic rituals, and they don't work anyway. If they worked there would never have been a war."

Ludo shook his head. "I'm sorry he died, but—"

"You don't understand," Nerezza snapped, her eel-tail back, her blue sparks crackling. "We wrote letters to him. We talked on the phone, for hours and hours. We had found him working in a provincial post office in Isaszey, in Hungary, of all absurd places. We had planned to meet that summer, we had rooms at the Sofitel in Budapest, we had planned it like a picnic. We needed time, you see, time to tidy things. And to delay the pleasure of it was natural to us."

Again, Nerezza lifted her shoulders—not a shrug, but her only gesture of helplessness, of submission to the constellations and the turning of invisible clocks. The grief on their faces was so naked that Ludo turned away from it with the same propriety he would have shown to a girl caught undressing.

"But didn't he just wake up? I mean, if it happened there, shouldn't he be all right here? Isn't that how it works?"

Anoud began to cry softly, little wrinkled noises he could hardly hear. Agostino caressed her face with two curled fingers. Nerezza stared stonily at him and shook her head.

"Do you remember how often Lucia traveled out of Italy before she disappeared?" Nerezza continued, abandoning his question. She did not weep, even a little.

No, of course he didn't remember. Lucia left; she came home. He did not try to track her, what would be the use, with that great tail, that determined erasure? Where had she gotten the money for such things? Impossible that this could have occurred while he looked the other way, that Lucia could have been so consumed by something not him. He wanted Nerezza to stop talking, to just *shut up* and leave him alone.

"She was looking for her . . . Quarto. That's what it's called. What *immigrants* call it."

Anoud laughed through her tears, a squeaky, mouselike sound. "That's us," she said. "Immigrants. Saying these words is always so hard! They sound so ridiculous in the daylight, with coffee in the pot and cats crying to be let in. They sound poor and small. But we did know her, Ludovico. We all did. There are not so many of us that we do not find ways to know each other. She was looking for them, and she found two of them. Their names are Alastair and Paola. We never met them. Paola was Canadian; that's so far away."

"But Hal," Agostino cut in, his gangly arms still draped around both women, "Hal lives in—" Nerezza shushed him, and he hurried on without naming a city. Ludo wanted to throttle him. "Well, he wasn't so far. They met just a little while ago. They found each other, like we did. And they went to find the others together. We think . . . we think that's how it's done. How you get to Palimpsest permanently. How you . . . *emigrate*. We think you have to find your Quarto here, in this world."

Ludo felt his blood beat against his face. The great unsaid thing floated heavy and choleric in the room. "Am I correct," he said, "in assuming that there is no one in this room who has not slept with my wife?"

He had been prepared for silence and took it for his answer. Ludo was, he knew, deep in the book of beasts, crushed between their many pages, growling all around. Anoud slid out of the grasp of her lovers' hands and alighted by him. She had a pinched nose, small eyes—an ungenerous face, he thought. A mouse, certainly, if ever a woman had been a mouse. Hay-child, impossible generation, and such plagues. He was distracted by her hands, so slender he could not imagine there was flesh between skin and bone, and on her smallest finger was a carnelian ring, a smear of red on gold, the tiniest of stones.

Ludo had bought it in Ostia that long-ago summer, the summer of the yellow dress, when he and Lucia sought out that wonderful pecan-red shade on everything: rings, couches. When they bought wildly things to build a house around them, certain that nothing they laid their hands on would ever need altering, replacing.

Ludovico reached for Anoud's hand and she gave it warmly, stroking his cheek with the other, a kind attention, as if soothing a child whose knee has been skinned. But he did not want her hand. He tugged at the little ring; it would not come. Anoud tried to draw her hand away, but he seized her wrist and scrabbled at the ring with his fingernails. His tears came as quickly as her little well of blood beneath the band, and between their fluids he wrested it from her, his breath hitching with panicked cries. Anoud held her finger to her lips and glared at him, wounded, bereft. Her gaze flickered to Nerezza and back to him. She inched closer, carefully, a little mouse seeking the owl's audience, with one round ear lost already. She held her scratched hand to his mouth; he knew this gesture, as every Catholic child knows it, and he kissed the signet of her blood.

"I'm sorry," Anoud whispered. "I loved her, if that matters. It's easy for me to fall in love. You could say I'm a prodigy. I loved her, and I can love you. I can see a day not so very far distant when you bring me tea before dawn and kiss the hair from my forehead. My capacities are not less than hers."

She kissed him truly, her tongue small and hesitant, her curly hair brushing his cheeks. She tasted strange, foreign in his mouth, like a red spice. Ludovico's bones groaned in him. She was sweeter and smaller than Nerezza. Softer. More tamed, gentler, eager to be loved.

"Don't you want to *see* it?" Anoud breathed. "Just see the races and the feasts and the ocean? Just taste the air? Don't you remember how sweet the wind is there? Does the city hold nothing you desire?"

Ludovico did remember, after all. Not just Lucia. He remembered the snail-seller, and the sea wind. *Fine*, he thought. *I give in. I give in to this, if that is what is asked. If I must pay in women for the city, for all it contains. I can bend under it as under God. As I bent under Lucia, my star of the sea, my endless storm.*

And so Ludo returned Anoud's kiss. He pulled her white shirt from dark shoulders and pressed his face to her breasts, fuller than Lucia's, with nipples like coffee beans. He cried out into her skin and she accepted his cry with a merciful quiet, letting his cry fall all the way down to her heart. She guided him onto her, moved Nerezza's spare bathrobe aside to bring him into her, arching her back to show him the hidden smallnesses of her mouse-body, pressing her knees to his hips. Ludovico looked past her as he rocked back and forth with her motion, providing little of his own. She was so slight he hardly felt her beneath him, just the wet warmth of her around him, clutching gently. Ludo was silent, aghast in his submission, the little ring still clutched tight in his fist. He looked to Nerezza—shameless thing!—her head thrown back in Agostino's arms as he thrust his angular body into her over and over, his braying bull-voice muffled in her neck. Her mouth was open, her face streaked with tears.

# Quiescence and Rapine

**PALIMPSEST POSSESSES TWO CHURCHES.** They are identical in every way. They stand together, wrapping the street corner like a hinge. Seven white columns each, wound around with black characters that are not Cyrillic, but to the idle glance might seem so. Two peaked roofs of red lacquer and two stone horses with the heads of fork-tongued lizards stand guard on either side of each door. The ancient faithful built them with stones from the same quarry on the far eastern border of the city, pale green and dusty, each round and perfect as a ball. There is more mortar in the edifices than stones, mortar crushed from Casimira dragonflies donated by the vat, tufa dust, and mackerel tails. The pews are scrubbed and polished with lime oil, and each Thursday, parishioners share a communion of slivers of whale meat and cinnamon wine. The only difference between the two is in the basement—two great mausoleums with alabaster coffins lining the walls, calligraphed with infinite care and delicacy in the blood of the departed beloved contained within. In the far north corners are raised platforms covered in offerings of cornskin, chocolate, tobacco.

In one church, the coffin contains a blind man. In the other, it contains a deaf woman. Both have narwhal's horns extending from their foreheads; both died young. The modern faithful visit these basement-saints and leave what they can at the feet of the one they love best.

Giustizia has been a devotee of the Unhearing since she was a girl—her yellow veil and turquoise-ringed thumbs are familiar to all in the Left-Hand Church; she brings the cornskins, regular as sunrise. When she dies, they will bury her here, in a coffin of her own.

She will plug your ears with wax when you enter and demand silence with a grand sweep of her forefinger. You may notice the long rattlesnake tail peeking from under her skirt and clattering on the mosaic floor, but it is not polite to mention it—when she says silence, you listen. It is the worst word she knows.

———

Ludovico chooses the Left-Hand Church. He cannot say why. It does not seem like much of a choice, but he makes it, with determination. If there is anything a Roman man knows, it is how to associate with a church, how to choose one in a city of churches and become loyal to it, to know its clerestory and its finials like the breasts of a wife. To predict the exact tone into which it will weave your voice with all its heights and rafters and soaring galleries.

The congregation is silent, though the pews are crowded with parishoners. Ludovico treads softly on the aisle, which is covered in chrysanthemums planted deep in the soil of the church's most secret parts. Far above, ravens line the clerestory, and between them some few folk with long black wings, dangling their feet in the air. He stares at them in horror and enthrallment: there are no humans here. Each of the faithful is in part another thing: men with the heads of great serpents, women with shells like tortoises upon their backs. Children with long, hairy orangutan arms fidget and bent, scolding crones' legs end in elephantine feet, or cheetah feet, or musk-ox soles, warted and blackened. A man with a giraffe neck grafted to his shoulders sits politely in the rear row, so as not to block anyone's view. Not a few have fins protruding painfully from their backs which their aunts and uncles keep solicitously wet with the help of small and sacred cups.

At the altar, a priest with the head of an ancient, worried lion holds out her arms in mute supplication, her mouth gaping, her feline face red with the effort of her silence, tears streaming through her whiskers. A few worshippers are crying, too, and nodding as though she spoke. A little girl in the front row holds out her long, mottled arms to the priest, an octopus's tentacles, their suckers opening and closing in mute pleas. The child opens her mouth and wails as children will do when they are grieved, but only a throttled gurgling emerges. Her parents gather her in and she buries her face in their scaly breasts.

Ludovico sinks to his knees in the flowers, overcome. Why should he care for these wretched animals? Perhaps because they are in church? He trembles—this is not like the Troposphere with its pounding mechanical horses. It is so quiet here.

*Here begins the book of the nature of beasts,* Ludo thinks. *All the best bestiaries begin that way. If I were to write of this place, I could make a book longer than Isidore's, greater than the Etymologiae. Here there are creatures beyond any Spaniard's fever-dream and more, they are real. I have seen them. I will be able to write truly that I knelt among them, I prayed with them and saw them weep as though they were possessed of souls. No Pope will ever believe me, or beatify me, or sanctify my encyclopedia, but I will know it was true.*

The silence lays hands on him and Ludovico is moved beyond

himself. For this church of invalids he will bear mouse-women and eel-women and anything else. He will bear Lucia's abandonment, for this is the land of St. Isidore. Bee-crowned Isidore, who wrote the great compendium of wisdom and Christian magic, human behavior and the names of monsters that medievalists still pore over with glee—he must have seen this place. He only reported what he saw. Ludo's hands fly to his St. Isidore's medal. The vision of the octopus-child compels him to his knees. In his life, Ludovico has never loved a thing that did not destroy him, and he goes gladly to this third thing in his small catalogue of loves which before now was comprised of a book and a woman alone.

He stretches out his arms, his skinny, human arms to the lion-priest and calls out to her, his voice ghastly in the echoing cathedral, a thing made for shattering.

*"Ave Maria, gratia plena!"* he cries. It is all he knows how to say, the most sacred thing. *"Dominus tecum, benedicta tu in mulieribus, et benedictus fructus ventris tui!"*

He is laughing and weeping, and all stare at him. The octopus-girl pulls away from her parents as he begins again:

*"Ave Maria!"*

She walks toward him like a little bride, serious in her white dress, hair the color of a bruise hanging in two long, straight planks to her knees. Her pace is slow and she does not try to run—Ludo is sure she has been told not to run in church. She puts her cold, wet tentacles around his neck; they coil heavily on his shoulders. She fixes him with a solemn expression. Slowly, she kisses his cheek.

*"Ave Maria!"* he sobs, and the congregation, as if released by the child's gestures, descends upon him, straining to put their paws and their hands on him, their fur and their slime.

*"Ave! Ave! Ave!"* he howls, and the ravens recoil, wheeling in the rarified air of the upper balconies, screaming in alarm and ecstasy.

A hundred hands and more cover his mouth, gently, like aunts tasked with the care of an unruly boy. He bellows grief into their embraces, and the Left-Hand Church is filled with the sound of him as he is rocked in the arms of the wretched and the plagued, rocked until he is quiet, and can bear their kind eyes and their grotesque kisses.

# PART III:

## The Princess of Parallelograms

# In Transit,
# Westbound: 8:17

SIX EXPRESS TRACKS and twelve locals pass through Palimpsest. The six Greater Lines are: Stylus, Sgraffito, Decretal, Foolscap, Bookhand, and Missal. Collectively, in the prayers of those gathered prostrate in the brass turnstiles of its hidden, voluptuous shrines, these are referred to as the Marginalia Line. They do not run on time: rather, the commuters of Palimpsest have learned their habits, the times of day and night when they prefer to eat and drink, their mating seasons, their gathering places. In days of old, great safaris were held to catch the great trains in their inexorable passage from place to place, and women grappled with them with hooks and tridents in order to arrive punctually at a desk in the depths of the city.

As if to impress a distracted parent on their birthday, the folk of Palimpsest built great edifices where the trains liked to congregate to drink oil from the earth and exchange gossip. They laid black track along the carriages' migratory patterns. Trains are creatures of routine, though they are also peevish and curmudgeonly. Thus the transit system of Palimpsest was raised up around the huffing behemoths that traversed its heart, and the trains have not yet expressed displeasure.

To ride them is still an exercise in hunterly passion and exactitude, for they are unpredictable, and must be observed for many weeks before patterns can be discerned. The sport of commuting is attempted by only the bravest and the wildest of Palimpsest. Many have achieved such a level of aptitude that they are able to catch a train more mornings than they do not.

The wise arrive early with a neat coil of hooked rope at their waist, so that if a train is in a very great hurry, they may catch it still, and ride behind on the pauper's terrace with the rest of those who were not favored, or fast enough, or precise in their calculations. Woe betide them in the infrequent mating seasons! No train may be asked to make its regular stops when she is in heat! A man was once caught on board when an express caught the scent of a local. The poor banker was released to a platform only eight months later, when the two white leviathans had relinquished each other with regret and tears.

A great number of commuters witnessed the girl with blue hair and her now-famous leap into the waiting doors of the Marginalia. Their coats flapped in the hot wind of the station-bowels. Their lips went suddenly dry; their pulses quickened as one stream of blood through one heart. A few smiled, and all noted in their observances that a woman was taken from the platform on this date, at that time. It is important to know these things. They have happened before. Rarer than mating season is this one, and they must know when it begins and when it ends, in order to compare notes with their fellow enthusiasts so that they may predict when the contents of their prayers must change, and when they will shift to the Secondary Prime Schedule, which conforms to both the phases of the moon and the retrograde orbit of Mercury.

Three men were crushed beneath the trains in order to prove the Second Prime, and their names are holy writ.

———————

The space between carriages is a rollicking, noisy, dank place, nothing like the chrome interstices of the Shinkansen. Sei thinks briefly of Sato Kenji, and wishes for the fourth or fifth time that she had known when she held him shaking against her what manner of creature he was, possessed of what secrets. Her heart would have beat faster, would have leapt into him fully.

The Third Rail regards her solemnly. The two of them are pressed close together, and Sei does not think the red-faced woman's long cheeks and slitted eyes are entirely flesh, not entirely. They seem always wet and hard, like a lacquered mask. But it is so dark; the light is fitful and unkind. Sei does not think she hears her breathing. The Third Rail grazes her collarbone with long white fingers, hesitant and slow, as if unsure of permission to do so. Sei takes her hand and kisses her palm—the skin burns her, like medicine, like ice, but she does not flinch, and the Third Rail shivers in pleasure.

"We are so very eager for you to see us," she says, and her scarlet face tilts towards the clattering carriage door. "We have dressed ourselves specially: we have had to guess the things you like."

Sei smiles uncertainly, and presses her hand to a black square to release the door. The wet smell of weedy swamps waft out; her nose wrinkles. But the Third Rail sweeps Sei into the next carriage, childlike in her delight, stroking her cobalt hair with a possessive affection.

Sei can make out seats and railings, handholds looping down, certainly, though from no visible ceiling. But the walls are wider than they ought to be, and a broad yellow sun beams where fluorescent lamps should shine. The seats terrace up the sides of the wall, and what Sei at first takes to be brilliant blue cushions are glimmering rice paddies, rippling water combed by raw green shoots. Folk tend them in wide red hats trimmed in a fringe of tiny hanging pocketwatches, golden as her grandmother's, golden as a temple. They pluck the rice and savor it, all the way up, past Sei's vision, like a mountainside dwindling to nothing. She is dizzy with the sudden space. A child, his red hat jangling, holds out a green stalk to her, his little face happy and new.

"Thank you," Sei says, and the child hugs her.

"Thank you, thank you!" he cries into her hips. "We thought you would never come!"

Sei chews the thick, unprocessed rice. She knows she ought not to do it. She remembers clearly a day when her mother was not well and not strong enough for the room of the grass-mats. She had fallen, shaking, to the floor of their little kitchen, and screamed as she pulled Sei's hair painfully: *Do not eat the food of the dead! They will try anything to make you eat, but no child of mine would do it!* She had burned all their *mikon* oranges in a great fire that night, insisting that the moon had filled them up with poison, that the poor, unassuming fruit would kill them all. Usagi shuddered and wept beside the flames, holding her elbows and rocking back and forth as the air filled with the acrid smell of boiling orange-flesh.

Sei knew she ought not to, but she had come this far, and already drank their bitter tea, and she could not imagine a version of herself which did not swallow this thing in her palm.

"It is the rice of grief," the boy said brightly. "I have harvested it all my life. Every fortnight, the flowers of the rice of grief weep and must be comforted with a glass bell and soothing hymns concerning incense and virtuous fathers with black beards. I have soothed them in your name, Sei! And they were comforted! With my own fingers I cleared the mud from them, and with my mouth I plucked them from the water. I would like you to become proud of me, because I have done this thing. If you do not believe I have enacted a sufficient virtue, I will ask my overseer to send me to the rice of martial prowess, but the application process is long, and I have heard that the rice is bitter."

Sei pinches the boy's chin lightly and grins at him. He blushes deeply and is too overcome to speak. She bends to him and lifts his hat to gently kiss his forehead, the rice of grief heady on her breath. The child's eyes well with tears and he squeezes them shut, leaning close to her for the smallest and longest of moments. He runs to his friends to boast and preen, and Sei laughs.

"How kind you are," the Third Rail says. "I did not expect you to be kind. It is not a trait we select for."

"What do you select for? And for what are you selecting?"

The Third Rail looked coy. "Loneliness. Old grief. World-weariness. Stamina. Mechanical aptitude. But if I were to tell you the rest it would spoil the surprise."

"Does that boy live here? All the time?"

"Of course. Where else should he live? If you had sent him to the rice of martial prowess, he would have brought you a red sword in one year, and begged you to bless it. If you had not, he would have sought the rice of the intellect, and become as clear to look upon as glass, and begged you to breathe the fog of a soul upon him. He has waited his whole life to know which rice is best. It was kind of you to give him such a short journey."

The other rice-pickers wave and shout from their high terraces, and as one offer her a copper ladle full of water from their sacred wells.

"I am satisfied!" she calls out. "I do not need to drink!"

A ripple of fear and despair moves through the rice paddies, and Sei sees one girl with long braids fling herself from a great height, only to be caught up by a solicitous handhold. She hangs there by the waist, in misery, weeping.

The Third Rail offers no comment, but shakes her head in untouchable sorrow. She guides Sei through the fields, the glowing green grain which is so bright she suffers sunspots in her vision.

"I'm sorry," she says to the villagers with their long-handled ladles. "Please forgive me, please slake my thirst." She reaches out for their water and they lean toward her, keen and terrible hope like welts on their faces. She sips; they collapse in relief, and as the carriage door closes behind her she can hear the beginnings of a festival, music like water spilling, and a boy's high, reedy voice singing a psalm above the pounding of drums. She knows she will refuse nothing else. She drinks and she can hardly feel them anymore, the phantom others, who drink wine like tiger's blood when she drinks water. They are so far from her.

———

Again, there is a moment like a hyphen in the space between cars. Sei can see the track rushing by beneath them, in the spaces, in the joining, in the iron grate below her feet.

"Why do you look down?" the Third Rail demands. "Do you wish to see me more naked than I am? Am I not more pleasant to you in this shape than deep in mire and grease?"

"You are beautiful. In grease. In mire. In flesh. Why is it so important that I think you're beautiful?"

"Because if you do not, you will never love us, and if you do not love us, you will not help us, and we need your help, or we shall never get where we are going."

"I already said I would help you."

"You can't say that yet! I would like to believe you, Sei, but I am wicked, and I have hidden things from you, and you will not tell the truth about us until you know them all, and you will not know them all until we get to the last carriage. We have to hurry—you don't have all night."

She pulls Sei into the third carriage with the eager stumbling of a child on the morning of their birthday. The seats are lined with great pale cabbage plants, deeply veined in violet and green. The walls are silver leaf, untarnished, gleaming like water. Women hang in harnesses, polishing it with their impossibly long hair. The cabbages cover floor and cushion, even the ceiling, extending far into the distance, though the walls are closer here, and there are windows which show a coppery rush of city flashing by outside, the beginnings of frost at the frames.

They walk sedately, two queens surveying an empire. Sei looks for Yumiko among the polishing women, and yes, she is there, of course she is there, a jade pendant hanging between her breasts, her bare feet tucked up like a ballet dancer's. Their eyes nearly meet. But the Third Rail flushes a furious black and moves between Sei and her lover, shaking her prodigious head. There is a pleading in her small eyes, and Sei acquiesces, still shaken by the keening of the villagers with their long ladles. She will see Yumiko in the morning, and her girl will forgive this one minute, small slight.

"Is there such a need for cabbages in the world?" Sei asks,

wondering, trailing her hand across the leaves which are thick and hoary as chilblained flesh.

"Of course not. These are not for eating." The Third Rail lifts the leaf of one, and within, couched in vegetable, wet and black, wrinkled and quivering like a newborn butterfly, is a character, a slightly wobbly kanji, signifying "plenitude." It murmurs softly, and stretches up like a baby seeking a nipple. Sei strokes it with her knuckle, and it writhes beneath her hand.

"They have to be born, you know," the Third Rail says. "They don't come from nowhere! When a child sits in her chair with a clean *suzuri* and her long brush, she believes she is writing, but she is simply calling to these poor lambs, calling them to attend her, to pass through her. We can hardly keep up with demand; the pollination season is intense. And yet, they learn fewer and fewer kanji as the years go by, and more and more English, more katakana, more foreign things. The graveyard is on another train, where turtles set incense on the stones of words no one learns in your world anymore, words passed out of the reach of any mouth. It is important work we do. We hope you agree, of course, but we are willing to admit it is foolish if you call it so."

Plenitude crawls up Sei's arm like a caterpillar, and perches just inside her elbow, fluttering its strokes.

"Of course it is not foolish," Sei says, wondering. "I had no idea."

"It is not widely known, or else we might be subject to poachers."

"Does that mean there are . . . spaces to pass between this city and the child at her desk in my world? Tunnels? Bridges?"

The Third Rail slides her eyes sidelong at Sei. "Did you not pass through such a place?"

"I suppose, but kanji are . . . ill-equipped to come by the path I took."

"How many roads are there into Tokyo?"

"I don't know ... dozens."

The scarlet woman shrugs and smiles secretively. "Palimpsest is the same. Only one, though, is big enough for people to squeeze through. But a character is small, small as a thought. She does not need such a great highway."

Sei considered, and tried to shake off Plenitude. The little kanji clung to her, making tiny gurgling sounds, like ink bubbling.

"They get attached so easily. Insoluble little dears," the Third Rail coos.

"How much longer does this night last, Rail?"

"One more car, Sei. It pains me that you cannot stay longer. Perhaps one day you will allow us to become dear enough to you that you will do what is necessary to stay."

Sei grips the Rail's arm, hard and hot beneath her hand. "What is necessary? I don't know! Tell me how."

"I do not know either," the crimson woman says, dropping her chin in shame. "I am too big to pass by that path. I must stay here, there is no road wide enough to bear me. But I hope one is wide enough for you."

———

A rich and mushroomy loam covers the floor of the fourth car, toadstools fulminating beneath benches. Pine trees sprout everywhere they can grasp hold, growing sideways, diagonally, crawling across the aisle. Between them nestle parcels, wrapped with brown paper, tied with twine, dozens upon dozens. The contorted, warty pine-roots splay over cushion and wall, sucking tentatively at windows. Their needles shine dark and glossy and thick, and from their boughs hang great orange-gold lanterns, globes ablaze with light. Some few folk in severe black clothes clutch the handholds and stare into the lanterns. Their faces are marked with white lines like smears of chalk. Sei looks up—the ceiling is far too distant, far too high, and there seem to be stars there, behind green-gray clouds.

At the far end of the great carriage there is a fox. He is also red, and his nose black, in the manner of foxes.

"I know you," he says dispassionately.

"I don't think you could," Sei replies.

"Imagine a book at the bottom of a lake." The fox yawns. He paws the soil and lies down to sleep.

"Fish," the Third Rail whispers tenderly, "read it. We read it."

Sei shuts her eyes against sudden tears. The room seems to tilt, and the great peace of the rice and the cabbages drains from her like rain. Plenitude quivers in distress on her shoulder. "I can't," she gasps. "I couldn't ... I don't want to. This is too much. You talk like a dream. Nothing matters in dreams."

"We talk like your mother talked." The Third Rail scratches her elongated cheek fretfully. "We thought you would like it."

"I don't!" Sei cries, half a scream, the other half squeezed off by her suddenly aching throat.

The scarlet woman hangs her head in shame and pulls her kimono around her breast to hide herself. "We are not infallible," she whispers.

"What's in the packages?" Sei feels ill. The shaking of the carriages tips her into the arms of a seated pine, which wriggles with pleasure and cradles her in its branches. It allows one ecstatic drop of sap to fall onto her hand.

The Third Rail looks toward the sleeping fox in agony. "If you don't like it we shall take them away! We promise!"

Sei shrugs off the purring pine tree and pulls frantically at the twine of the package nearest to her. It comes open cleanly in her hands, like origami falling away from itself. Inside is a red mask, longer than a human face, its eyes and mouth hard black slits. One of the men in his black tunic reaches in and pulls it onto his face. He sighs resignedly, as if he knew all along that it would come to this. Sei gapes, hides her face in the pine tree. She does not want to look at the Rail again, at her hard, red, long face.

But the Third Rail kneels in submission at Sei's feet, imploring her in silence, her face a broken panic.

"*These trains speed past each other,*" she says, "*utterly silent, carrying each a complement of ghosts who clutch the branches like leather handholds, and pluck the green rice to eat raw, and fall back into the laps of women whose faces are painted red from brow to chin…*"

Plenitude caresses her cheek with a bold stroke.

Sei moans and falls into the Rail's arms. The long-faced woman wraps her kimono around the girl and holds her tenderly, sweetly, with infinite care.

# ONE

# THE RABBIT IN THE MOON

Sei woke sobbing in a strange apartment, her hair plastered to her face, clawing at her shoulder. Yumiko did not hold her. She just watched, calm as a teacher watching a slow student struggle through a simple passage.

"It's always hard to wake up," she said.

Sei clutched her, her eyes rolling and wild as a dog's. "I need—"

"To go back? Yes. I know. Do you think I'm different than you?"

Sei could not breathe. Her body ached, her joints, her lungs. "Take me back, take me to someone, anyone, I don't care, just … the train, I can't leave them, they want me there, I have to go back!" She groaned. "God, let me go back to sleep!"

"You have to wait. The Floor of Heaven opens at dusk. I sympathize, I really do, but I've been where you are now, and I had to wait, too." She put her arm around Sei's naked waist. "There's a tenor there, at a place called Thulium House. He gives me sapphires every night; he pierces my arms with a long needle and hangs me with jewels until I cannot move for the weight. He puts opals on my eyelids, and kisses on my lips until I am bruised with him, and all over blue. Do you think I don't miss him?"

"There is a train, full of strange fields and forests . . ."

"I envy you."

"They need me!"

Yumiko put her head to one side. "Have they said what for?"

"No . . ."

"Then it can't be good. Don't be in such a rush."

Yumiko rose and began the rustling, habitual motion of making tea. Sei realized that this must be Yumiko's place. The walls were bare; she had a bed and a table and nothing else. The apartment looked like someone has just moved in, or expected to move out soon.

"My mother told me once," said Sei softly, to Yumiko's back, "when I was little, she told me that dreams are small tigers that live behind your ears, and they wait until you're sleeping to leap out and tear at your soul, to eat it up at very civilized suppers to which no other cats are invited."

Yumiko quirked an eyebrow. "Was your mother, if it's not impolite, totally crazy? I mean, that's not really a working theory of the subconscious."

Sei shrugged. "Back then, I just thought she was wild and beautiful, like a goose, and like a goose she flew at me in a rage sometimes, and bit my toes. And sometimes when I came to see her in our tatami room her kimono would be torn to pieces, and she'd be naked and bleeding on the floor, her own skin under her nails. She was bleeding like that when she told me about the tigers. So I guess she was crazy, when I think about it now, but when I was a kid I believed her because she was my mother and mothers know everything."

Yumiko set a thin green tea down on the floor. She ran a hand through Sei's hair.

"But you aren't, you know. Crazy. I know what you know. We're not like your mother. There are no tigers for us, just a city, waiting, and it loves us, in whatever ways a city can love."

"Maybe the tigers are there. Maybe they're just better at hiding than trains and tenors."

———

*The Floor of Heaven.*

The little brass plaque said nothing it did not say before. Sei stood in front of it, motionless, while Yumiko straightened her plaid skirt.

"Ready?" said the faux-schoolgirl, her eager smile a little too manic and stretched for Sei to find it comforting. Sei closed her fists at her sides, suddenly not very brave. She could see that night plainly in her mind, how it would play out in that dark, furtive club, how every other night would unfold, too.

So many people would crawl inside her.

Sei knew she would search them out like a fox, the ones whose maps linked together to create a route, a route to keep her on the train, on course. She would find them in the shadows of the Floor of Heaven, in the offices of that place with tall silver cabinets, in the bathrooms with Asahi posters glued to the walls.

Sei could see it all happen, the whole tawdry parade:

A man with a silver tooth would want her to get on her knees in the black-tiled bathroom. She could see herself kissing the depth-chart etched on his toes, his wrinkled knees, his ex-hausted cock.

A woman with two children sleeping at home and a mole on her left thigh would slip her fingers into Sei's cunt right on the dance floor, in front of everyone. Sei could see herself writhe, impaled, embarrassed and abandoned.

There would be a sweet boy with a thin little beard—his thumb nearly black with gridlock and unplanned alleys, as though he had been fingerprinted in an unnamable jail. Sei saw herself straddling him on one of the long leather couches that lay between the club-lights, grinding against him until he came so hard he started to hiccup, and she found him so ridiculous she wanted to cry. That one would run after the train in her dreams, trying to catch it, trying to catch her, too poor in skill to manage either feat.

Sei knew she would seek out the dream-city on all those skins. She would seek out passage on her train, and all these fleshly tickets would fall to her feet, used and pale. She knew she would refuse to return to Tokyo, where it would not be so easy to find them, to snarl at them: *Take me, take me, why are you waiting?*

Sei would never want to drink, or dance, only to grip them between her thighs and then sleep like a dead thing. She would become naked and raw and without guile; she would seek as truly as a knight.

Sei could see it all so clearly, a path through the woods: touch no one who does not carry the map—she and Yumiko would certainly agree between themselves that this was wrong, risky, that the secret was theirs and those of their tribe, and not to be squandered.

But perhaps once, after the snow melts, Sei thought she could imagine a version of herself that would make an exception for a young man with cedar-colored skin and a nose ring like a bull's, or a minotaur's. No one special. Someone who came to the club and was, of course, turned away. By then he would seem so alien and strange to Sei, so blank and empty. Pristine. Possessed of purity.

Sei knew her weaknesses—she would plead with Yumiko: *I am weak. Sometimes it is still about love, and need.*

When she wakes with him, in that not-very-distant future, that Sei watched blankly in the reflection of a brass plaque, the grid will brachiate out from his footpad, its angles dark and bright, and she will envy him, for wherever he walks now he walks in Palimpsest, and it will be all new for him, all new. Before he stirs, she will leave his house without tea or farewell.

Standing before the door to the Floor of Heaven, the train hurtled so fast into the future. She could hardly bear the speed, the inevitable, unavoidable sequence of stops and passengers, the toll, never to be paid in full. Tears pricked behind her eyes.

It all stood in front of her, behind a black featureless door, ready to swallow her whole.

"Yes," Sei said. "I'm ready."

# Inamorata

Inamorata

**INAMORATA STREET ENDS** in silver sand and a great craggy finger of stone, stretching out into the sea. The glittering water flows out to the horizon and over it, a great dark expanse, whitecaps glistening in the moonlight. Foam shatters into seaglass on the beach, and couples walk arm in arm along a strand of shards, glittering and wet. Striped tents dot the beach head: red and yellow, green and white, rose and powdery blue. Women change into bathing uniforms with flared waists and broad hats to keep out the moonlight; tuba players march back and forth, blaring out nocturnes.

The infirm of Palimpsest come here to recover, to collect seaglass on their bedside tables and write novels on the nature of the solitary soul. Mustached men sell bottles of seawater in the inland markets for the price of kingdoms, and false phials abound. The air blows fresh and sweet; it smells of tangerines and salt and white sage, and charlatans bottle this too and sell the empty glasses to immigrants for the price of a parliament seat.

Each evening the hopelessly ill are brought in gauzy palanquins to view the moonrise, and all applaud the appearance of its white disc over the water. The wind is considered to have such restorative power that surgery is performed on the beach, anesthesia administered by waifish women with hair like spun sugar, who close their mouths over the ailing and breathe the vapors of their crystalline hearts into weakened lungs.

Ermenegilde has been a patient here since the war ended. She is a charity case; her reassignment went poorly and she was rendered useless for the field. She has bled from her wounds every day for twelve years. Bluebells drape her palanquin: the veteran-flower. Medical gauze swathes her face in long bridal veils. All agree that if not for her mouth, she would be now a great dowager-beauty. But there is her mouth, it remains, and cannot be denied.

Once, in a field hospital set up for such amputations, surgeons removed her jaw, her teeth and the better part of her nose. In its place, they inexpertly sewed a panther's muzzle. The practice was new then, though it was to become the single great symbol of the war—there were no experts in those days. Ermenegilde's graft did not take, it would not heal, and stitches are still required to keep her two faces joined together. The wiry knots are black with blood. And though her new teeth are sharp and vicious, as they were intended to be, though her whiskers can detect the smallest drop in barometric pressure, she suffers infections and fevers.

And of course, of course she cannot speak. None of them can.

Ermenegilde is always the first to be carried to the shore for moonrise. She took up photography many years past, and her nurses help her each evening to set her daguerreotype in place so that she may print her plates of the great full face she still hopes will mend her. She breathes deep, and prays the moon will hold still for her portrait. Ermenegilde knows, however, that it is difficult to do, and does not blame the heavenly body for her restlessness. She, too, has had to sit for pamphleteers and medical historians alike. She is possessed, after all these years, of immense empathy.

———

November cradles her left hand gingerly in her right. She does not want to think about it, not now, that morning three days past when she had woken up with that poor girl's pale hair covered in blood and her own fingers gone. Her blessing fingers. It's almost funny. There was no wound, the stumps as smooth and tan as if some hand had simply plucked off her fingers like fruit. But there was blood, blood everywhere, though it came from nowhere, and they had scrubbed and scrubbed to get it clean.

But Casimira was right. Things are clearer now. There would be no more of this "it's only a dream" business. What happens here happens there. November is not a slow student. In her way she appreciates the act. It's like cheating on a test—so much easier when you have the answers written on your hand.

"My house misses you," comes Casimira's brandywine voice beside her.

November turns, and the green-haired woman is there, her curls loose to the backs of her knees, in a bathing dress that reveals no skin at all, billowing and green. November puts her hand over the place in Aloysius's dress where her own belly shows through. "He weeps dust all night long and has turned all the calendars to fall. It is extremely tiresome. If you do not visit I shall have no peace at all."

"How did you know I would be here?"

"When will you learn that if a fly, if a bee, if the smallest worm witnesses a thing, I witness it also? I have tried so hard to explain matters clearly. Will it take another finger to impress this upon you?"

"No," says November hurriedly.

"If the fingers are a very great loss, I can arrange for replacements here. In that, you are lucky to have come to this place above others. The sea is so good for one's health. Also the surgeons gather here to beg for work. The debauched and the desperate are always drawn to water, is that not strange?"

Casimira kisses November's broken hand like a mother kissing her child's ills away. "I can purchase a whole paw, I think, though they are not very dexterous. Tiger, perhaps, or lion? Cougar? Or maybe just the fingers, in which case it will have to be an ape of some flavor. Please do not think of the cost."

"What about human?"

Casimira laughs. "Don't worry, they're quite skilled at it by now. War is such a marvelous instructor."

"If the options are ape or cat, I think I'll have to decline."

"No fun at all." Casimira smirks.

———

The two women stride arm in arm along the beach. Casimira shoos away the beggar-surgeons with her umbrella, and saves a piece of seaglass for November to keep on a bedside table, should she ever acquire one. They talk about the air and the water, and how November's father might have benefited, in the days when he vomited blood and had to be carried to his tiny downstairs bathroom to do it.

"We do not exist, however sad your father's case may have been," Casimira says primly, "for the benefit of all."

November does not want to discuss it, not really. She knows her place in the universe, knows its label, and none of it can help her father now. There are mushrooms in his skull, and that is all.

"What is wrong with them?" she asks instead. "The ones on the long beds, the woman with the muzzle sewn onto her face."

"There was a war. I told you that. It was not a very long time ago, not very long at all. I was a child when it began."

"What happened?"

Casimira's mouth curls into a feline grin. She looks up, sidelong, at November. "I won, is that not apparent?"

November starts, a lock of faded brown hair pulling free of her knot. "What, you against everyone?"

"Not quite so simple, no, but it ended that way, certainly." Casimira turns sharply to November, and though she is quite short, manages to look precisely like a stern schoolteacher. "List for me, November, the reasons one may start a war."

November blushes, frightened, unwilling to speak her lists aloud, into the sea, into the surf. Not when ordered to. They aren't soldiers, they don't come when called. They're *private*, they're hers, Casimira has everything in the world. She can't have them, too.

"Now," the matriarch orders, "or it's orangutan fingers for you." Nearby, a bent old man in a white laboratory coat shoots them a hungry glance.

"Religion," November whispers, her stomach knotted, her heart seizing itself in shame, as though she had just opened her dress and shown herself naked to the matriarch of Palimpsest. "Territory. Vengeance, historical enmity, alliances." She starts to hitch and sob, losing her list to the air, to the wind and the sea, lost to her notebooks, to herself. "Resources—food, fuel, water, labor, expansionist government, I don't know . . . I'm sorry, I can't think . . ."

November's face burns. She wants to cry again but will not allow it. She will not humiliate herself, and she is sure she has not hit upon the cause Casimira wants to hear.

"Can war, do you think, be a tool of policy?" she says with a gentle didacticism, as their walk takes them around a bend in the surf that throws up glimmering, half-translucent urchin shells onto the beach.

"I don't…I'm a beekeeper…you can start a war however you like…"

"Well, thank you, but, in your opinion."

"Of course…"

Casimira looks November up and down, her dark eyes glittering with amusement. "Immigration policy, perhaps?"

November wrings her hands, closing her right hand over the place where her left fingers have been. She is still not used to the wretched stumps and recoils from herself as though burned.

"Casimira, I don't know!"

The older woman's face softens and she stops, taking November's cheeks into her hands. "Am I being very dreadful to you? It is hard for me to remember, sometimes, that others live alone, and do not have a billion children to whom lullabies simply *must* be sung. Come, let us get you a drink, it will do you good. And then we must go home, for my house is threatening to tear down the haberdashery next door if I do not bring you as soon as I am able."

As they walk toward a gleaming black pier, something like obsidian strung with white lanterns, folk they pass, ill and well, shrink back from Casimira, cross themselves or sink to their knees in reverence. One or two doctors spit at her. She holds her head high, until the spit splatters on the hem of her bathing dress. She casually flicks her fingers in the direction from which it had come, a gesture like removing dust from a collar. Three wasps fly from her sleeve with a high, rageful, indignant screech, and defend their mistress with keen stingers of brass. The doctors fall to the shore, their arms raised over their heads.

On the black pier, Casimira takes a great wooden pitcher from a wire rack and dips it into the sea. She offers it to November, who still trembles and rubs her elbows. She drinks; it tastes of tangerines, and salt, and white sage. It tastes nothing like the sea she knows, nothing like her Pacific with its long gray arms—it is sweeter, and thicker. The midnight tide crashes diamond wave against stony shore, sending spray into the thready silver clouds that collar the moon.

*Did I ever think San Francisco was beautiful?* marvels November. *I was a fool.*

———

"We must take a circuitous route." Casimira sighs. "You are too new to have forged any reasonable path through the city."

"I'm sorry, I tried … you know, on the other side, there are people who try to keep you from finding too many people."

Casimira snorts. "There are people like that here, too, I assure you. But of course you tried, my dear. One cannot really be so fortunate as to choose adjacent lovers. No one blames you."

An emerald carriage rolls onto the sand, spraying white granules, and opens a silent, solicitous door. November all but collapses into it. She lays her head in Casimira's lap, exhausted. She has grown too big for herself, that is all. Terrible things occur when you outgrow the space allotted to you. You cannot really circumnavigate Fairyland like September did, not really. It's too big for you.

A few forlorn bees crawl over her hands, their tiny clockwork wings whirring. November gives them a halfhearted smile and strokes them gently.

"I have three secrets I want to give to you, November. Like in a fairy story. They are very big things, and I have had them wrapped specially. But you must be good for me, if you want it. Do you understand?"

Suddenly she is alert. Three gifts—that is something. She knows how to behave, if this is the sort of story where an imperious woman offers her three gifts. "Yes," November says, sitting up straight. Casimira pats her head.

"Good girl. My bees want a thing from you, and I would like to ask you to give them what they crave. It is not mine to give."

"Aren't we going to your house?"

Casimira laughs like a glissando of bells. "You have caused such a commotion in my districts! Everyone bawls and throws tantrums for you. You are the star of all their fever-dreams. I suppose all mothers must prepare for the day when their children fall in love and no longer need her, but it pierces me so! My heart is not so efficient as theirs! We are going to the factory, my love. Then home, where your present awaits, if you are a good girl and a pliable one."

"*I will stand upon my raft until the Green Wind comes for me,*" November says gravely. "*My dress; my sail.*"

"That's lovely. Scripture?"

"Yes," November answers with fervency: clasped hands, wet eyes. "Hortense Weckweet."

"How marvelous! Her daughter Lydia was such a fine sculptor."

November gapes as the carriage clatters on, and Casimira offers nothing more.

————

The factory is a mass of green-white spires, and the song of the shift change spills from it as though they are the pipes of a church organ. Casimira strides boldly through the front gate: it is her place, nowhere is her power so piquant as here. In a mother-of-pearl lockerroom where the third watch has left their helmets, she changes into no more than a wage-slave's dress: white and green scales, laid one over the other, little pearly discs glittering in the spirelight. She provides one for November, and it is not very unlike being naked: every curve and wrinkle is visible, and the scent of the scales is like crushed mint stalks.

They ascend past great vats and printing presses so old the wood-worms in them have written three full encyclopediae of the contents of their empire. The whirr and buzz of insects fills every inch of air, but also the chirruping of squirrels and heated mating of rabbits newly molded. Mice learn from a great machine how to wash their whiskers, and as Casimira passes, they scream a hymn of joy to her name. But the bees are kept high, high in the towers, and still they climb.

"My grandmother built this place," Casimira says, her voice neither quickened nor stuttered by the endless stairs. "Not really my grandmother, of course, but the number of greats involved is so many it is considered impolite to use the actual number. Outside the family, she is a legend of legends—impossible that she truly lived! Preposterous! Yet still. She is the blood of my blood of my blood, and I know her sorrows like my own bones."

The stairs become steep—November is winded, panting, but

Casimira continues as though they are strolling across a meadow. "She dreamed of a butterfly once, and upon waking was seized with grief that she could not possess it. On three hundred subsequent nights she dreamed of vermin, of cockroaches with shells that shimmered in her heart, of grasshoppers and mantises and centipedes, beetles and mosquitoes and wood lice like tiny pearls. Starlings and ravens flapped darkling in her mind, and chipmunks with livid stripes like war-paint. She was tortured with these visions of beauty, and her family could not heal her, though she was taken to just the seashore where you drank the brine, and she drank, too, but was not calmed. She dug the foundations of this building with her hands, clawed the soil to her will. I am a great admirer of my grandmother. I, too, have my claws. I, too, have my soil. Little must be said of my will. But the day that the first fly opened its wings in her hand, the first worm nosed blindly at her cheek—she knew such sharp and secret satisfactions on that day! I know them now, yes, I know them, I know them as old friends and lovers, but time dims all things. Here."

They duck into a great room, further up the spires than November would have thought bees would prefer. The chamber is all of wax the color of fine butter, arching like a cathedral dome, hexagonal holes yawning black and thrumming, and more bees than November could have imagined swarm over it, excited, palpitating, expectant. Casimira spins slowly in the center of the room, her eyes shut, her emerald hair coiling around her like seaweed. She reaches out her hands to November as though inviting her to a stately dance, and under a million black-bellied bees, November shyly steps into the strange woman's arms.

"Do you know why it is that I have done so much for you?"

Casimira says fiercely, drawing November too close, too tight. "You would agree that I have done much, and promised more?"

"Y...yes." November's stomach turns over. She begins to think that Casimira was never taught the word "no." The matriarch is beautiful, and terrible, and she takes everything in the world for her own. November has been taken, she knows this, and one does not argue with the one who takes. No one whose father was a librarian is ignorant of their Greek myth: when Hades hauls you into his chariot, you do not argue that he has been rude not to ask if you really wanted to go.

"It is because you are my proof," Casimira breathes. "You are proof of all I have done, all I have done in service of my city. Proof of my rectitude, of my virtue. You stand in my halls and I know that I was right, I was not a fiend that tore into my home as though...well, as though I had the mouth of a lion. I am a creature of complex geometries, General of Grotesqueries, Princess of Parallelograms. But I am not a queen, and never shall be. No matter what they say I did not want to be. I have committed my crimes, and horrors have flown from me into the world, but you look at me in your blue dress, in Aloysius's dress, and in your innocence say: *Casimira, all is forgiven, for I am here.* My bees scream: *Casimira, all is forgiven, for she is here.*"

"What do you want from me now, Casimira? There are..." November's lip trembles, her eyelids slide shut in a half-swoon. She does not want to do this, but she feels she must give something in return for the seawater, and the dress, and this golden room. "There...there are...nine sorts of people..." She swallows hard, marshaling her nouns into columns, her heart into steadiness. "There are nine sorts of people deserving of absolution: wives, saints, children, adulterers, debtors, students, those thwarted in love, melancholics, and those seized by occasional angers." *This is my gift to you,* November thinks, as loudly as she can, *I have wrapped it specially, a list, for you and only you.* "Nowhere are there listed beekeepers or generals. We find comfort only in each other. There is no grace waiting at the end of a long journey, not for us. Tell me what you want from me."

Casimira sniffs slightly, her eyes reflected crystalline in a rim of hard tears. "I thought you would have guessed it. They want you, they want you as their own, forever. They have not made a queen in all their lives, they have no jelly, being all wire and glass and infinitesimal engines. I have always been enough. Perhaps this is my punishment. It is certainly keen. Secret, and sharp. But I am willing to give them what they want. A mother must be willing."

November shakes her head, laughs a little, ruefully. "What will that mean?"

"I don't know, exactly. They won't tell me." Casimira frowns. "I am...jealous. Yes. I am jealous. But it is all right."

An arrow of aspic life tears from one of the combs and arcs toward them, landing before November in the shape of her bee-manikin, her suitor of the second night, the night of her dress and the memorial on Seraphim Street. It bows to her, and when it rises its buzzing hands are full of golden liquid. It holds out its palms to her, imploring, beseeching.

"I thought they hadn't any jelly."

"I made it for them, as I make all things in this palace of industry. How could I do else? I clawed the soil to my will. In a vat of red clay I stirred so many of their poor bodies, golden oils to lubricate the invisible gears of their hearts, their honey, which is a secretion under the thorax and has a peculiar flavor of pine pitch, and my own blood, which is all of a queen they have known. It is their first jelly, and they are very proud of it."

The manikin opens its mouth as if to speak, and the buzz that issues from it is like a strangling. November rushes to it as to a crying child and hushes it, crooning in her way, the way she has always used to calm her bees, and though she has no flowers for them, no heather or heartsease, no basil or orange, she supposes she is enough, and if you put enough bees together they become more than bees, just as nouns become more than nouns, and she cannot turn that away.

*My dress; my sail.*

"This is not, of course, your present," says Casimira casually.

November hushes the manikin, strokes its buzzing forelock gently. "Oh . . . I thought—"

"Yes, well, being a queen may sound nice, but it is not much of a present in the end. You must earn that." Casimira gestures at the mewling bee-manikin. "Thrust your fist into his heart, and you will find it. They brought it for you, from their comb. The manikin will fall to pieces and, without its heart, will never rise again. But you will have your present."

November looks at the prone bee-golem. It smiles at her, full of black, thrumming trust. She feels the tiny fur of the bee-bodies under her fingers.

"I don't want to hurt him," she protests.

"This is Palimpsest, November. This is the real world. Nothing comes without pain and death." Casimira kneels by November's side and kisses her, her mouth soft and open, but tongueless, half-chaste. "I chose you," she whispers. "The difference between myself and my bees is very small, in the end. I chose you because they chose you. They love you because I love you. If you want to stay with me, and drink from the ocean, and rule over the bees, you must do as I say, and be a good girl. It's not a sin to cause death if by doing it"—Casimira swallows hard—"if by doing it you make something new."

November shakes her head—she doesn't know what Casimira is talking about, but it doesn't matter. If she wants to stay. If she wants to stay. If she wants to circumnavigate Fairyland. It's not so hard. She just has to kill a few thousand bees. Bees who danced with her, and protected her, and walked down avenues with her like a gentleman suitor. That's all. And then she can stay, in a place so big she can never outgrow it. She can *stay*.

November closes her eyes and puts her palm to the manikin's chest. It begins to cry, an awful, humming, droning, broken sound. November's eyes flood in sympathy, and she turns her head away as her palm curls into a fist and punches through the thin bee-sternum, ignoring the crushed wings and thoraxes, the scream of agony from the manikin's gaping mouth, searching, grappling in the mass of bees—and she finds it, wet and slimy and hard, the heart of the bees.

November pulls it out, her hand stung and swollen, a tiny golden thing, like an egg, covered in jelly. She scoops the jelly off into her palm and swallows it—it tastes like honey, nothing more. Perhaps there is an undertaste of motor grease, of metal, but it is fleeting. It does not taste like red lilies, or heather. There is no patina of the heart with which November has always layered her own honeys. It is pure, an essence, distilled past tasting of anything but itself. It is the emptiest thing she has ever tasted.

The manikin, in its last motion, clutches her head with a desperate, outflung arm, dragging her face down toward it, embracing her, clamping its mouth over hers in a husband's kiss. Suddenly

November knows what is coming, and yet cannot steel herself, cannot be prepared for it. Their stingers pierce her in a thousand places, everywhere they can reach her. She is penetrated by all of them, their venom in her sweet and sour and sharp and secret. She is rigid with it, and they are dying all around her, their one great sting spent and finished, falling from the body of the manikin as others fly to join it, and she pulls away before the hive can obliterate itself in its frenetic, desperate desire for her.

She falls, of course she falls. She is only a woman, and her flesh runs with poison and honey, it spills from her pores like golden sweat. She shudders and seizes on the floor of the great honeycomb, her back arching and spasming, her legs jackknifing beneath her. The egg clatters out of her hand. She is so full, and the venom pours from her mouth, the honey and the blood.

Casimira watches, without expression.

———

Far away, two men fall, spasming, to the floor of a boat and a church, and a woman falls to the floor of a train car. Their mouths fill with honey, and their vision goes white, and black, and white again.

———

"Wake up, November," the boy says. "Wake up." November slits her eyes open, as cats will do, unwilling to commit fully to waking. The boy smiles at her very perfectly, an expression of pristine technical accuracy, as though he had practiced the smile in a round mirror for twelve years. "I have kept a room for you," the house says, and blushes perhaps more deeply than it is correct for boys to blush.

She opens her eyes fully, and in the boy's hands is a golden egg, shiny as a beetle's back. It is carved over with long streets that intersect each other at wild angles, cut deep into the metal of it. The boy can hardly contain himself, it is as though the present is for him. She fits her fingernails into an equatorial street, and with no strength in her, flicks at it until it creaks open, sticky with jelly.

Inside is nothing more than a scrap of paper, finely cut, thick as a violet-leaf. On it is written in a flowing hand which can only be Casimira's:

*Oleg Sadakov*
*Amaya Sei*
*Ludovico Conti*

November thinks of a girl with blue hair, a man with stained fingernails, a man with keys jangling his belt. She does not know if the images come from her or the bees. She cannot tell the difference, anymore. Her mind leapfrogs over itself, seeking logic, seeking a reason.

The bees flow out from November, propelled by her will, and their buzzing in the dark streets sounds like names, whispered over and over.

# YES

*Things that are unsightly: birthmarks, infidelity, strangers in one's kitchen. Too much sunlight. Stitches. Missing teeth. Overlong guests.*

Her name was Clara. November stayed in her apartment for four days. They made love again on the fifth, a small and cheerless farewell. After everything, it wouldn't really be fair to call it anything more. Clara had kept her eyes shut when November kissed her, fiercely shut, her lids wrinkling with the effort.

November was too much for most of them, she understood. Too much now, with her ruined face and her severed fingers. No one else was mutilated like that. It had never cost any of them so much. She was hard to look at. *I can't even look at you*, Clara had said, after they had gotten the blood out of her hair. November thought it better to leave when the sky was still a cutting blue, and Clara lightly snoring. She did not have to see again the disappointed, pitying look on that pleasant face. She ran from the house with her hooded coat drawn up around her face like a leper.

But Clara had been kind, and possessed a strange and tiny tea service of solid blue agate, brought home from Iran by a lover of hers. A lover from *before*. Clara poured blueberry tea into the palm-sized cups and rubbed vitamin E oil into November's fingers, though that did not seem to be strictly necessary. She made chicken sandwiches and brought oranges from the winter market. After the second day, she managed to stop looking at November's mauled hand while they drank and ate and spoke softly, as if the apartment might overhear them.

"Clara, do you know who Casimira is?" November had whispered on the third day, over that blueberry tea and frosted gingerbread. She was in a fever, her mind slamming pistons into place, full of Casimira, full of the house. She had hardly remembered to make her list that morning, she was so prickled with high blood and the ghostly soprano in her ear. "Have you heard her name, you know, *There*?" November disliked how she had begun to capitalize the indistinct "there" in her mind, but the name of that secret city remained a thin knife in her mouth.

Clara tapped her cup with sparkling fingernails and averted her eyes. She hated to talk about it, November had learned. Wordless communion was Clara's way. She preferred unspoken understandings and the meeting of knowing eyes across vast spaces.

"She's the one with the bugs, right?" Clara clicked a tongue piercing against her front teeth nervously.

"Yes."

"I don't know, I've heard the name. I've never met her, if that's what you mean. Nobody likes her. I think she had something to do with the war everyone's always going on about."

November raised her eyebrow, rubbing her fingers absently.

"I don't know," snapped Clara defensively. "It's over, the war is over. There's enough of that shit here. It's supposed to be different there, nicer, prettier."

"Prettier, anyway."

"You only say that because of your face, and your hands." Clara's voice pitched upward, like a vase about to fall. Her gray eyes narrowed. "It's *better* for the rest of us. Easier. It's the most beautiful place in the world. Nothing but flowers and perfume and jewels. Once I went to a ball where everyone wore masks made of bones—so many skulls—waltzing to violins played by little girls with no faces. The chandelier dripped crystals—everyone rushed to catch them when they fell! It was good luck, you know? My mask was a roc's skull with a hundred moonstones set into it—do you know what a roc is?"

"Sure. A huge white bird that eats elephants." The children of librarians are rarely faced with an obscurity they cannot name. November smiled a little, proud of herself.

"Well, *I* didn't know. I had to ask the man in the alligator skull mask, and while he told me about the elephants he undid the ribbons of my dress and let it fall to the floor. He ground his teeth against my beak and called me *Corazon* and kissed me until I couldn't breathe. I danced naked with all those men in jeweled skulls, and they lifted me up into the air, fed me chocolates, poured blue champagne into my mouth..." Clara was transported by the memory, her hands on her throat, her eyes wide and shining. She looked at November for confirmation; her savaged face brought Clara back to the little table and the tea. "I'm sorry it's so bad for you," she hissed. "I'm sorry it took your face. I'm sorry she took your fingers. But don't ruin it for me."

216 Catherynne M. Valente

November smiled weakly. Would she go there, someday, and wear a mask of bone? Would Casimira take her, and dance with her under that dripping chandelier? Would she take a thumb as payment for that?

"Do you know what you carry on your skin? What part of the city?" November asked, eager to talk about anything but her face.

"No, of course not. No one does, unless you're lucky enough to get into a neighborhood next to it. What are the chances, though?"

"It's her house, Clara. Casimira's. On your stomach, right there. And it's huge, and alive, and she took me inside—"

"I don't want to hear about this! Casimira is way beyond the circles I move in, and the circles I move in don't want anything to do with her."

November waved her hand apologetically, the one that was whole and unmarred and easy to look at. She took a deep breath—this was the big question. The only question. She let it fall between them like a little meteorite, smoking on the table, spoiling the tea.

"Is there a way to go there in the daytime, do you think? Like emigration. Permanent."

Clara grinned, her elfish beauty returning in a rush from hidden, angry furrows. She leaned in, taking up November's meteorite and letting it glow. "There are some theories. You know, no one really knows. It's not like there's a manual. A couple of times, I heard that someone wanted to write one, publish it as fiction—but *we* would know. *We* would see right through all those made-up characters and silly little narrative twists. *We* would know what it was: a primer."

"What happened?"

Clara giggled—a wild, uncanny sound, not a feminine laugh or a trivial one, but a panicky, animal thing.

"Well, you know, they'd cheerfully burn down any warehouse that carried it. Letters got written, stock changed hands. No one would publish it, not ever, not anything that even mentioned the city. Not me, but . . . there's this Chinese guy, glasses. Has a sister. It's really kind of funny, if you take a step back. Like freaking *West Side Story*. She wants to let everyone in; he'd be the first in line to torch any book that smacked of the place."

November sipped her tea, overwhelmed for a moment by the *blueness* of its taste. She thought of Xiaohui's brother, endlessly crawling through the Internet and low-circulation magazines to erase a single notice. "I think I know him," she said.

Clara shrugged. "Probably. There's not too many of us on the West Coast. No one knows where it started, though once, there was this guy, maybe the fourth or fifth one I had, you know, the fourth or fifth one with the tattoo, and he told me this horrible story. We were lying around naked in his house, eating leftover pad thai and drinking bourbon, and he looked at me all funny and said he'd heard there was a woman in Cambodia or something, I think it was Cambodia, anyway it was a really long time ago, way before the war—"

"Which war?"

"Either one. Before, like, white people or anything. Anyway there was this woman. She fell in the Mekong River when she was pregnant, and these mynah birds came flying in from everywhere and fished her out, and they bit her a lot doing it and she almost bled to death after almost drowning. The river mud got all into her, and she had fevers and infections for weeks and weeks. Everyone prayed over her. And then, after ages, she just got up and walked again one day. Talking and making soup and things like that. But she was crazy afterwards, and she went to every village and got their shamans to tattoo her with secret, obscene things, ugly things, and she couldn't stop until she was completely black, all over, and no one could tell anymore what her tattoos looked like, and that was a relief.

"But she had her baby and named it Chanthou—I think it was Chanthou—and after that no one would feed her or let her sleep in their huts. Because the baby was tattooed all over, too, not as much as her mother, but still pretty bad, even the whites of her eyes. And the baby never learned to talk, even when she grew up, so they thought she was a devil. But she was still beautiful. The men in the village paid her to let them fuck her, and so she got to eat, still. Probably her mother, too. Not a lot of work in a village like that. But it was the daughter they paid the most for. And every time one of them slept with her, they'd wake up with one of her tattoos, and one space on her body would be clean and blank again, just skin. The men had to hide it, but the daughter was so beautiful and so quiet and so *good* that they couldn't leave her alone. But that kind of stuff is pretty hard to hide."

Clara looked nervously away from November's blackened face and cleared her throat. "So finally, the wives in the village got together and snuck up on her at the well and beat her until they thought she was dead. They just left her there. And that was it, right? Except that no one buried her, since she was a witch and all. But the body disappeared. After that, the men who had slept with her kept on seeing her in the jungle, without any tattoos, smooth and brown, just standing there, all quiet and creepy, with a tiger sitting on either side of her. She would hiss at them, like a cat, and disappear.

"But then the mother disappeared too. And after a while no one saw the girl or her tigers anymore. But just when everything was normal again, the men started to disappear, one by one, and the women, too. There was no one to take care of the farms or keep the well clean or keep the roofs sewn up. And when the shamans from other villages came to see what had happened to the village, to see why no one came to trade rice or shrimp or ask for wives, there was no one left in the village at all, and they put bones and stuff at all the corners and threw salt everywhere and said it was cursed. And supposedly no one lives there even now, it's just a blank space in the jungle. A big circle."

"Sounds kind of familiar."

"Yeah. I admit, I always kind of keep my eyes open for a girl with tigers, but even if it were true, it would've happened so long ago that I suppose that's pretty stupid."

November shrugged. "But you don't know how to get there any other way? Or how to stay?"

"Nope. Nobody does. Nobody here. I don't think there, either, though. But come on. Just . . . enjoy it. Isn't it *nice* to know a secret?"

The tea had gone cold. "But the thing is, Clara, I don't think I can get there that way, anymore. My face and my hand . . . it's hard enough for you, and you've lived with me for three days."

Clara flushed with embarrassment. She seemed so young, built up out of snow and ice cream. "November," she said angrily, "it doesn't work like that. It's not just pretty people. You can't hide what you are, now, and I'm sorry. But it's not the end of anything."

"I was lucky even to find you."

"Oh, that?" Clara gestured away a world of concern. "I'll give you a number. You'll be fine." She closed her hand over November's maimed hand. "It gets easier. Really."

---

November had not been able to bear her bees when she got home from Clara's tea and wide hips. She knew it was wrong, neglectful, that the honey might suffer from their distress, but she could not make herself cross her little wheat-tufted field to the hives. Instead she sat in her bare, angular bedroom and pulled a single brown book from the endless rows of brown books. The one with the naked child on the cover, holding up her dress to catch the wind. She opened it to a well-thumbed first page. When her father finally bought the book for her, instead of letting her drip honey and milk all over the library copy, she often used to just read the first page, for comfort, like covering herself in a favorite blanket.

*Once upon a time, a girl named September grew very tired indeed of her father's house, where she washed the same pink and yellow teacups and gravy boats every day, slept on the same embroidered pillow, and played with the same small and amiable dog. Because she had been born in May, and because she had a mole on her left cheek, and because her feet were very large and ungainly, the Green Wind took pity on her, and flew to her window one evening just after her birthday. He was dressed in a green dinner jacket, and a green carriage-driver's cloak, and green jodhpurs, and green snowshoes. It is very cold above the clouds, in the shantytowns where the Six Winds live.*

*"You seem an ill-tempered and irascible enough child," said the Green Wind. "How would you like to come away with me and ride upon the Leopard of Little Breezes, and be delivered to the great sea which borders Fairyland? I am afraid I cannot go in, as Harsh Airs are not allowed, but I should be happy to deposit you upon the Perverse and Perilous Sea."*

*"Oh, yes!" breathed September, who, as it has been said, disapproved deeply of pink and yellow teacups, and also of small and amiable dogs.*

November wiped the tears from her eyes with the back of her mangled hand. September had said *yes*. More than the name, that had been what had struck November, then, in her father's house, swinging her legs under a huge chair. She had said yes, without hesitation, without worry or fear, without a moment's thought for her mother or her father. September had said yes, with all her heart, and so she had gotten to go to Fairyland, where other children had to stay in Omaha and wash dishes.

In the margins of Hortense Weckweet's novel, November had written long ago in a tiny, uncertain hand: *Things I Will Try to Say More Often: Why? I love you. I'm sorry. May I have chocolate? Yes. yes. yes.*

November picked up her telephone and dialed the number Clara had given her. It rang twice: precisely correct. He would be here in two hours.

*It is a long drive from the city, you understand.*
*Of course, yes.*

———

When he arrived, November was surprised just how little she felt about the whole business. He was nothing to her, a conduit, a door. When she closed her eyes, she could not picture his face, even though his lips moved over her shoulders. He was just a door, a tall, broad door in a long green coat, which made her smile so brightly and with such a keen joy that despite her face and her missing fingers he swept her up into his arms as though they were in a movie. November let herself warm to him. She touched his face, a thin dark beard, sweet green eyes that seemed tired—*from the drive,* she thinks. *We all get plenty of sleep, after all.*

But his arms were huge around her, slabs of flesh closing her in, keeping her safe. November had never been with a man so much bigger than she was. He dwarfed her, protected her with his mass, sheltered her in his coat. He tried to take it off, but November insisted, delighted with its rough wool against her heavy breasts. Her legs seemed so small around his waist, a doll's limbs—but she didn't want that, she decided. Didn't want to make room for him inside her. November clambered up onto her knees and tucked her hair behind her, leaning down to take him in her mouth, a thing she rarely did and did not enjoy. But he wore a green coat, and he came to her door to take her to Fairyland.

*Yes,* she thought. *Oh, yes.* She wanted to thank him for ignoring her disfigurement, for behaving as though she were utterly whole, and the taste of him was neither sweet nor sour, but simply skin, clean and hard, so big she felt her jaw pop as he groaned and moved the shaft of his cock in and out of her throat. November closed her eyes and pictured herself on the velvet seat of the Green Wind's carriage—or was it Casimira's? While the huge man in her bed swelled towards his private, wordless orgasm, she was a thousand miles away, in the clouds above Omaha, pushing open the coat of the Green Wind and sitting astride him, taking his—surely green—flesh into hers, rocking back and forth while the Wind moaned and groaned and dug his emerald hands into her buttocks.

But there, in Benicia, November closed her hand over the black mark on the strange man's huge bare calf. He thatched fingers through her hair, and his cries echoed in her house like a list of things a man can want: *god, god, god.*

# Oblation and Legerdemain

Oblation and Legerdemain

**TENEMENTS LINE THE ALBUMEN RIVER**, raised on stilts over the wash. It is difficult to say in this late age how they were built, for the stilts are little more than spider silk, and they waver in the wind. But the houses are borne up nonetheless, and it is rumored in the wealthier neighborhoods that the poor have discovered a tree—possibly some sort of pygmy birch—which longs to fly. Logically, then, the riverside slums are collectively referred to as the Aviary.

For obvious reasons, the manufacture of ladders is a highly prized skill in this part of Palimpsest. It is a holy profession, and each rung is possessed of spiritual significance. The first is the Rung of Honest Labor, and the last is the Rung of the Salt of Heaven. Between, each ladderer may stack his own path. If a rung should break, then bad luck infects the household, and at least one child must be adopted out to avert disaster. These are called Little Rungs, and tend to be swapped from house to house in a rough circle through the Aviary, as the quality of local laddery is never so great that they will not eventually return home.

When they are old enough, the young girls of the Aviary greet each morning on the banks of the Albumen. They braid their extraordinarily long hair together to make a great net, and hand in hand, float upon their backs on the gentle currents. Great golden koi live in the shallows of the river, and the poor beasts are obsessed with the taste of curls. They become tangled in the net, and by noon the girls drag themselves back to shore and gut their catch with small bone knives strapped to their calves. The koi perish in a rapture of braids and young girls' savage laughter. Their meat tastes of coconuts and birdfat, and the girls have the rest of the long day for their lessons.

Nhean lives in one of the floating houses, an aged man with a paunch and the head of a snarling, split-lipped tiger. He has a livid, purple scar where stripes meet skin. He makes a yellow goulash of the unfortunate koi, and in it is a sweetness coveted by all his neighbors. But he does not like to share, even though he would not have any koi at all if the girls did not make their rounds and share their catch with the elderly who cannot fish for themselves. He eats by himself every afternoon, tearing his meat with fangs savage and rotting.

He is mute, as all of his kind are.

Even the babies of the Aviary know that veterans usually end up here, in the river muck. Children learn better than to chatter at them. A woman with hyena's feet in the third ward lets some of the fishing girls watch her while she cleans her cassia-wood shunt and peer with held breaths into the place where her larynx once was. Nhean would never allow this. His family has lived in Palimpsest for longer than trees have longed to fly, and he understands the necessity of certain dignities.

Though he has a kind of sign language of his own invention, the local children can only guess correctly the gestures for *mother, southeast,* and *sleep.* They would have given up long before now if his goulash was not so wonderful, if it did not have green onions floating in it, and also flowing orange fishtails.

Nhean is also a ladderer, and the rungs between Honest Labor and the Salt of Heaven he names strange things: Phirun, Who Loved Betel Nuts; Sovann, Who Did Not Like His Wife but Never Let Her Know; Veasna, Who Was a Drunk and No Good to Anyone.

Samnang Who Loved Her; Vibol Who Loved Her; Munny Who Loved Her.

Chanthou Who Loved No One.

No one understands this nomenclature, and he does not have the voice explain it. *It must be the war,* they say. *Those must have been the people in his battalion. In his squad. Maybe people he killed.* They are wrong, but it is a reasonable story, and he lets it lie.

Nhean, for many years now, has made two of his rungs weak. They will splinter, eventually, and sooner than the rest. That is how it should be, how it happened in a village long ago, in a green country whose name he cannot even remember anymore.

I remember it, of course. I could tell him. I don't think it would comfort him. Shall we spoil his day completely? Lean in to his big, striped ear and tell him a single word, a word from another world, which will bring back all the terrible memories he ever wept to forget?

I cannot do it. He is so old. It doesn't matter now.

———

Secretly, Nhean keeps a hope in his heart, and at least that is still whole. He hopes that enough rungs break that someday a child will come 'round to him, and he can love it and teach it to make a yellow goulash, and sleep with his tail curled around it at night.

It hasn't happened yet.

The rungs which are weak are the rung of Chanthou Who Loved No One, and the rung of Mealea, Who Fell in the River.

———————

"Do you remember when mother let us eat caviar for the first time?" Lyudmila asks. "I remember how red the little eggs were, and how they burst on my tongue, and all that fishy golden oil ran down my throat. I loved it, there was so much salt in it, as though they were little sacs filled with salmon tears."

Oleg frowns. "That was before I was born. I could not have been there, if you were there."

"Oh," she says, her fine forehead creasing in confusion. "Of course. I forget, sometimes."

"I know."

The river curdles by, and Oleg thinks he can see eyes open in the pale, dark, piscine eyes.

"I remember when you told me the story about the land of the dead," he says, trying to cheer her up. "I told it to mother and she took my books away for a month. And I remember when I asked that girl, the Polish girl, to marry me. You whispered in my ear that she did not have a yellow rainslicker, and it would end badly."

Lyudmila bobs her head. "Didn't it?"

Snow still spatters her hair. He does not think it is meant to melt.

"Will we get there tonight?" he asks. "Where we're going?"

"I think so. I hope you do not mind heights." She is quiet for a long while, and Oleg strokes her knee gently, chastely. "It is a strange and pleasant thing to play the game of 'Do You Remember?'" Mila sighs. "The only answer possible is *yes*. A *no* stops the game cold. Do you remember when I went away? From the Brooklyn girl, and also from you."

"Yes, I'm sorry for that. I've said I'm sorry."

"Didn't you wonder where I went? Did you think perhaps there was a Prince of Cholera?"

"You didn't die of cholera," he points out.

"A Prince of Drowning, then. With a blue umbrella. Maybe he kissed me, and maybe his lips were cold."

Oleg considers this. It had not occurred to him before, but he is not really upset by it. The dead keep their counsel, and he never expected to be told of his sister's love affairs.

"Is that what happened?" he asks.

"No." She shrugs.

"I miss you, Mila," Oleg says, his throat thick. "Your strange little ways of saying things. I can't see the world the right way up without you."

Lyudmila shakes her head, as if to clear it, to make it empty of all that disturbs calm water. "This is . . . difficult for me," she says.

"It is hardly easy for me! This is such a crazy place. It's . . . pretty, but it's not right in the head. But I had to come back! You're here, and not at home anymore. It's cold there, now, and I sleep on the floor. I can't bear our bed. Hester—I guess you don't know her, but she's the one who didn't want to come back, the one with short hair like a boy. She brings me orange juice and cold hamburgers, sometimes, when I don't have the energy to go out, and that sounds bad, it sounds like things are bad, but I'm okay. I don't mind. I don't mind coming to you these days. It's like I'm your ghost, now. I can be as faithful as you were. I can."

"Yes, fidelity is important. I select for it."

"What?"

"It's so strange," she murmurs, "that the village of the moon-drinkers was destroyed and yet these spindly little houses on their stalks survived. How can that be? The bombardments were astonishing, wasp-cannons firing fusillades like golden clouds, pale green rockets that sent burrowing weevils into the foundations of every house. I cried. I remember crying. But it was for fidelity, all of it. I understood that, even then. The whole war, just for that. And because of it I learned so many things." Lyudmila turns her face up to him, her fine, high cheeks streaked in tears. "I believe that you are faithful. That is why I bring you to my boat and stay beside you, because the war said with bombs like beetles that faithfulness must be answered with faithfulness, and that is a harder lesson than it may sound." Lyudmila cocks her head, as if seriously considering a snarled problem. Her tears stop very suddenly. "And so I am trying to decide," she says dreamily, "how long I ought to let this go on. It is pleasant to be held by you, after all, and pleasant on a late winter evening to be called Mila, and pleasant to smile at you and receive your smile in return. I am enjoying it."

"Mila, what are you talking about?"

"A little longer? Just a little? I think I would like to be your sister, for a little while more." Oleg's grip tightens on the edge of a broken, useless oar. "But I see I have handled it badly, because I have become bored with saying some things and not others, with wearing masks. I should not be blamed. It is my nature. And I must pay the price for that. I am not your sister, Olezhka. Perhaps it was wrong of me to dress myself so that you would think so, but I am not a very nice creature, not really."

"Please, Mila, don't talk about this. I can't bear it."

"But it is cruel to let you think she is here! I did not realize you would not know the difference. It's not a very good game if you don't know we're playing. It was cruel to let Hester see the hands of the dead with no one to dry her tears. I learned my lesson; I won't do that again. I am capable of learning."

"I don't want to hear this. I've only just gotten here. Let me lay my head on your lap again. Tell me stories about the municipal parks of the dead."

"I am worried about you, Olezhka. I do not think you are very well at all, and I love you. I want you to be well."

"No," he moans. She grips her parasol tightly. Her snowy hair hangs all around her.

"Look at me, Olezhka! Listen to me. I am ... something else. The thing I am is called a Pecia. I am ... like a machine. You would think of me like a machine. I am made of snow, and of silver, and of the bones of river fish. I am covered in the patina of cupolas. Made out of all the things you remember about your childhood, out of Novgorod and the Volkhov, out of a little girl in a red dress, out of wintertime. *I was made for you;* there is a place where people like me are made. Inside me are not bones as you would think of them, nor blood, yet the things inside me are also red, and also white, as you know bones and blood to be."

"This is insane. You're real, I can feel you."

"Yes, I am real. And I am alive, and warm, and therefore I cannot be Lyudmila. But," and Mila leans her parasol against the rail, the foxes snoring lightly. She crawls to him along the floor of the boat, her long hair dragging below her. "But I remember Lyudmila. I remember what you remember of her. I know the story of the Princess of Cholera, and I can tell it to you, as many times as you want. I remember the girl in Brooklyn who you wanted to be your wife, and I remember her orange blossoms, how sickening their perfume was in our house. I was built to remember. I was built out of remembering."

"Who built you?" Oleg is numb, his hand trailing in the pale river, his throat tight as a fist. She smiles and wraps her arms around his knees.

"Palimpsest. Olezhka, did you think it did not love you and pity you? Do you think I did not? For I am as much this place as I am Lyudmila. I remember when you were fourteen, how bitterly you wept in my arms when that little brown-haired girl mocked you. I remember carriages on my skin and a war in my belly. But for all that I can smile at you with Mila's lips and tell you Mila's stories and even smell like Mila, all for your sake, to answer the terrible things you cry out for during the night."

Oleg's palms sweat. He does not want to know the answer. *Do not ask*, he thinks, and tries to clench his throat around it. But the question is a lock and it seeks the key of her and he cannot stop himself, even though the taste of it is like the Volkhov, muddy and reedy and cold, and he doesn't want to, doesn't want to know, doesn't want to think or be, just bury himself, in her, in what looks enough like her to pass, in what is good enough. But it flops out of him anyway, and he stares at it, how ugly and pathetic, how himself, how shameful.

"Why," he whispers, "if you, here, in Palimpsest, are not my Mila, if you are a robot or whatever you say you are, why has she stopped coming to me in the real world?"

Lyudmila looks up at him, and her face is so like his: elongated, made more graceful by high cheeks and fuller lips, by long hair and a finer jaw than his own. But it is his face, his mother's face, a thing shared privately, jealously, among family. And it is so full of pity and sorrow, love and helplessness, and such *disdain*. He wants to claw at it with his nails until this well-dressed, lying thing dies and his own Mila is left, until she comes back, his girl, his, and she will remember everything, and apologize for leaving him like a poor dog, and they will be happy, and this will all end.

He grabs her face, his own face, and tilts it to him, pushing his nails into her cheek. Drops of blood show, real and red, red as dreams, and she does not seem very much at all like a machine. He doesn't want her to speak. He doesn't want her to say what she knows. But she is close and she does smell like Mila, like dead, wet Mila tangled up in his bedsheets. He kisses her; her mouth opens underneath his, pliable and cool. Oleg does not want to admit that he has wanted this. He claws deeper, and she does not cry out. She tastes like new paint and he wants to vomit, to die on the river rather than face this thing which looks so much like his sister. He shoves her away.

"Get out," he hisses. "Leave me alone."

"Am I for this, then? I am to understand that this is what I was built for, to bleed and be kissed? Would you take this whole city thus into your mouth, to bleed her and kiss her?"

"Just go! Mila! I didn't ask you to be built! It's not my fault."

"No one asks to be made. I happen. We just *happen*. Look at my hand. This not a hand. It is a street winding to you, asking you to love it, asking not to bleed, asking to be walked and adored. You can kiss me if you want to, but not like that, please, I'm so tired, so tired of bleeding for the love of you, of everyone, of all the madmen clawing to get into me."

Oleg shrinks away from her, his eyes rolling, his fists bunched against his knees. He begins, slowly, to hit his head against the side of the boat. It calms him. He ignores the others' sensations within him, whose hands he has felt on women, on cabbages, on snail-shells. They are so faint, now, anyway. He has allowed himself to bloody his head only once or twice before. He has not wanted to violate the act, for fear that it would lose its potency with familiarity. *Thunk, thunk, thunk.* It is as though his poor, battered head can fit within the lock of the world, and turn tumblers to some semblance of symmetry and grace, some kind of rightness, of evenness. *Thunk, thunk, thunk.* It doesn't hurt, not really. It is rhythmic, like a heartbeat. His heart is not enough, it needs this to keep the time.

———————

Lyudmila stares at him. She presses down the front of her dress, fretful, unsure. She does not think he means to stop. She wore the snow for him, and the stars, but he does not mean to stop. She wants to touch him—it is in her to want that, she remembers wanting that, and wants it herself, all at once. She is in sync, as she was meant to be, the model of her and she herself in perfect alignment. She feels her components sing with the pleasure of it, but still he does not stop. He will not stop. Slowly, Mila turns and dives into the river, leaving him, her bustle bobbing up like the fin of a great fish, and begins to swim for shore.

# THREE

## Now. Now.

Hester came to visit Oleg, most days. She was always prettier when she had come in from the cold. The blood in her face was whipped up, her hair full of snowflakes that barely melted in the air of his apartment. She brought him a little bottle of orange juice, which he somehow remembered being sweeter than this, tasting more of sunshine, of mad and green places with Spanish names. It was acidy instead, thin. Hester could not keep food warm on the long walk to him: gray hamburgers arrived with gluey ketchup, street hot dogs with sauerkraut frozen at the edges. Oleg wolfed it down, every afternoon. He did not care.

One day, Hester arrived to find him shivering, an empty paint bucket in his hands. Oleg had filled it in the industrial sink down by the boiler and lugged it up five flights to dump it onto his bed with a dull splash. He stared at it until it started to freeze—he had stopped paying the heat a week before. But *she* hadn't come, not *her*, not Lyudmila, the one he wanted, not his sister in her squeezing, tiny red dress who would hold him until all his memories which were not of her fled, and she was the only thing left in him.

But only Hester came. "Well, fuck," she had said succinctly, and he had curled up on the floor.

But Hester had recognized it all, all of him, all of his acts. She knew him, somehow. She sat up with him and talked about the night she had woken up in the graveyard and all those gray fingers had reached out of the bamboo to her, and all she could smell was death. He didn't understand why this could upset her so, but he listened. He was good at hearing, at receiving. She had known that there must be others, but had not sought them out. Could not bear the smell. Once in a while one of them found her, and she hated them for it, for their eagerness, for the beauty of the city they told her about, when she knew it was not so, that it was a cold, grim thing crawling with worms, still reaching out for her. Hester could never see the burnished, gleaming thing they saw, and she reviled them.

"What did you see after me?" he asked her.

Hester quavered, and a tear fell past her chin to the sodden floor. "I couldn't," she hissed. "I took my pills. I took *eight* of them. I needed to be sure I wouldn't dream. I took enough that it couldn't get through, it couldn't touch me. It stayed in its tree."

———

That sort of thing happened when he spoke to her. He often did not. She left the juice and food near his prostrate body and locked the door behind her. He had made her a key on a particularly good day when the sun was out and she had brought bisque from a far-off, surely mythical, deli. He had felt warmly toward the little brass thing. It was hot in her hand. But the days were not always so kind. He stared at his bed for a good and honest shift of nine hours, and willed Mila to appear there.

*In a moment, she will come,* he thought. *Now. Now.* But she was not, and would not.

He slept as often as he could, until his body was so weary of sleep it tasted like ash settling over him when he could manage it at all. He wanted Hester's pills, but they would take his dreams, and that he would not allow. He hadn't taken his own pills in weeks. It didn't help—Lyudmila would not shiver into being on the footboard of his bed.

Oleg called her sleeping and waking, letting that horrid little boat float up and down the river of cream, calling her name. She did not appear there, either. He had lost her utterly, a more profound loss than the day she drowned. The girls with their braided nets stopped their fishing to stare at him as he screamed for her, screamed until his voice was gone and he could only whisper her name to the stars.

His hipbones had begun to bother him—he could not sleep on his stomach any longer, as they lay against the floor like sharp prongs holding him up. Oleg didn't think about it much, just rolled to his back and murmured her name again, like a koan. His shoulder blades protruded like wings, and that hurt too, but not as badly. Hester brought ointment for his sores and he did not know why, did not know why it would matter to her.

"It hurts you," she had said, finally, her face a mask of distress. "The city. It hurts you like it hurts me. It's *not* just me. It's not kind to everyone else and cruel to me. It's cruel to you, too. On the outside, and to me on the inside."

"I just want Mila to be there when I go back. For her to be somewhere, anywhere. I did a bad thing to her. I scared her, the way the graveyard scared you. And now she won't come back. But I want to, I want to . . ."

Hester had cried with him and eaten the rest of his lunch. She did not come back for two days, and he mildly wondered what might happen if she left him, if she decided that he was not kin to her after all. He supposed he would starve. Mila would come then, wouldn't she? She'd have to, to get him. To pack his bags for the country of death.

But Hester returned, wearing two scarves against the cold, and set a great, swollen address book beside him on the graying floor. Business cards stuck out of it like porcupine quills. It bristled.

"I told you they always tried to find me," she said. "It used to happen so often. Nightclubs and bus stops and grocery stores, they'd just come up to me and grab me, like they had the *right*. I spat at them, especially when they sat there, all fat and in love, and tried to tell me all the wonderful things they'd seen. But I keep everything, really, everything."

There were numbers, so many, and addresses. Organized, if not neatly. He looked up at her, imploring. How could he choose?

"Fine, fine," she snapped. "Boy or girl?"

He laughed hollowly. "I'm not . . . in fighting shape. I think it'll have to be a boy."

Hester wrinkled her nose, though he could not tell if her distaste was for his choice or that he meant to do this at all. But there was a boy, by dinnertime—hardly a boy, a bookish-looking man with a thin beard that ran around his jawline and a long coat with its collar turned up. He kissed Hester and she let him, but when his hand strayed to her breast she bit him, hard, and shoved him toward Oleg in the sodden bedroom. He tripped a little on the doorframe. Hester stood in the doorway, shaking, rubbing her fingertips and keeping her mouth so tightly closed a soul could not have slipped through the space.

The bookish man did not seem to mind Oleg's thinness, or that he was too weak with hunger and too much sleep to do much of anything but let himself be kissed, his legs plied open. But the man had a gentleness in his mouth, held there like a sliver of candy, a sliver of sweetness. He looked with understanding and pity on Oleg, and held him so very close.

"I know," he whispered in his ear, "I know."

And there had been some heat, some pain, some desire in his dull, depleted body when Oleg felt himself suddenly full of the bookish man, suddenly weeping with need for this, for this living thing within him, for the leaping, bright, and blood-rich life that was abruptly in him where only sleep and Mila had been before. The man held his sharp hips firmly and tenderly, so as not to bruise him, and came quickly as though he knew Oleg could not take very much of this. He called a name as he did, and Oleg wished him well of that stranger, wherever they were, wherever he could find them.

Hester watched, and wept, and clutched her book to her chest.

# Seriatim and Deshabille

**ONE MUST CRAWL TO ENTER A TEAHOUSE.** Those who do not know this are too prideful ever to approach. There is a door in the side, big enough for shoulders, for a head bent in humility. The roof is thatched from the fingernails of hermits who send small black boxes full of translucent clippings every winter. They are never yellow, or else the true connoisseur would know that the tea brewed there is inferior, brewed by those of dubious skill and biography.

Darkness confronts you when you enter; there is so little light to be found when you are on your knees. The dim shadows clear as your feeble eyes adjust, and you see the golden walls, like skin, like the inside of a saint's body. There are pillows for your penitent knees. A painting on the wall shows, in the quick, sure brushstrokes of a certain school of art, a city whose buildings are nearly as tall and spired as those of Palimpsest. But it is not Palimpsest, and you know it. It is just a landscape, like a mountain, or a flower; it was the great fashion some years past to sketch cities of the mind, places remembered or hoped for, with the same reverence given to a peony or a plover.

A man and a woman move through a ceremony which will be inexplicable to you, ignorant and foreign as you are. Rosalie will draw her tongs of mother-of-pearl from her dress and pull new cups from a kiln of great beauty and delicate construction, whose gaping red mouth is the only light in the teahouse. Scamander will draw his tongs of black pearl from an ice bath, and pluck a disc of frozen tea from an icebox of great beauty and delicate construction whose gaping blue mouth is all you are able to see. There are tea leaves suspended in the greenish ice. He places the disc within the glowing cup, and the cup is cooled by it as the tea is heated, and the steam which unfolds is as rare and sweet as a ghost of sugarcane long perished. They will hold your head as you drink, exactly as parents teaching their child to drink will do. And when you have had your fill, they will smash the cups against the wall and wail in grief for their passing, and you will be brought low by their pure and piercing cries.

I taught them how to do this, when all of us were young. I do hope you enjoy our little local customs.

Scamander and Rosalie have spent their lives in service of this ritual, and they believe wholly in the symmetrical thinness of the edge of a teacup on the potter's wheel and the edge of the tea as it freezes. These things are full of meaning for them, and they wrote a monograph on the subject when they were in the fullness of their faith. Their teahouse is situated in a small park between Seriatim Boulevard and Deshabille Street, a trapezoidal space with seven white stones in a pleasing arrangement under a larch tree, which was confused in its profligate youth and now drops chestnuts each spring. In order to reach it, one must dodge the traffic rails, which are well-greased and smooth here, and leap into the park before one is crushed by a carriage, motorized or muscle-drawn.

This, too, is pregnant with significance in the eyes of Rosalie and her husband, for grace may only be found briefly, and always in the midst of madness.

———

Ludovico does not know he is meant to crawl, but it has become his natural locomotion, like a rabbit jumping. It is dark inside, as it should be, and he lifts his eyes to the crowded house only to see what he has so long wished to: a blond woman with a green scarf sitting calmly cross-legged as a deva. She holds the naked hand of another woman in hers, a woman with mad black hair and a stare like a lion flicking its tail.

———

I have saved this for him. For us to watch, and for him to suffer. But I could not hold her back from him any longer. Perhaps I am over-eager. I know you will forgive me.

———

It is Lucia, of course it is Lucia, why should it not be Lucia? Why should this not be granted to him, this chance and this grace? If he would but ask Scamander about the coincidence of it, the old man would explain about discs of ice, and how they thin as the edge approaches. The place where air meets ice is fraught with possibility, and it is not for mortal men to inhabit.

Ludovico whispers to his wife.

"Lucia. Oh, Lucia. You're here. You're here."

Her eyes constrict. She stiffens as if to run, but the ceiling is too low and it would be an impoliteness beyond bearing.

The blond woman beside her, who can only be Paola, coughs apologetically and Lucia nods to him exactly as a stranger just introduced might: meaningless kisses on the cheeks, a cold countenance, but she is shaking. As her lips graze the still-hot rim of her cup, her chimera mouth pleads without sound:

*Please go. Let me have this.*

But Ludo does not know the protocols. He is too full of tears and hope for that. He cries out, loudly, and the room freezes, the drinkers sneer, their lips curling back from sharp teeth. "Lucia," he brays, "where have you been? What do you mean?"

Her eyes are liquid, enormous, a child caught out. "This is mine," she whispers, mortified by him, his appearance, his disrespect. It will reflect poorly on her. "You can't have it. Please."

Ludo is beyond comprehension. He crawls to her on his knees, in humility, in shame, penitent. Begging to enter again his severe and monstrous idol.

"I didn't want you here," she hisses.

Paola snorts a little. She is too familiar with Lucia, behaving as if she is in full possession of the situation, and how dare she presume to know a thing about them? Ludo hates her immediately, sorts her past eel and mouse and into insect, devouring, soulless ant.

"He couldn't have gotten here in the first place if not for you, my love," she says gently, "so don't be too angry. If you didn't want him here you should have shut up your bedroom like a mosque. I did. I thought you would."

Lucia rolls her eyes. "I was sure he wouldn't figure it out—no one does from the first night, and what were the chances he'd find another one of us? He never leaves that apartment."

"Figure what out?" Ludo is conscious of a great many eyes on him, but he cannot make himself move from his wife. She looks at him pityingly.

"This place, Ludo. Palimpsest. This city. How to get here, how to live here."

At that, the patrons scramble to the tiny exit, a sudden riot of velvet hats and gold-soled shoes, shoving and squeezing through the little door, crawling desperately over each other to get out. They do not like it, they do not want to hear it, to know it.

"Lucia," he says when the room has cleared. For him it is so simple. "Come home, please, I have missed you so much."

She puts her hand on his head, an old gesture, not yet leeched of tenderness. Her hand and her voice are cold. "But it couldn't have been only me. He's here now, and this is very far from where I would have taken him. Who was it, Ludo? Who let you crawl into her like you come crawling to me now? Did you even know that's how it works?" She stares spitefully at him, her hair piled up and strung through with tiny bronze feathers.

"Nerezza. And Anoud, later. It didn't *mean* anything. It was a way to you. She said it was. The only way."

Lucia hoots haughty laughter. "That's impressive. Nerezza's like a sphinx. Awfully hard to pry open. Is that what you liked about her?"

"It wasn't about liking."

"But you do, I can tell. I was married to you. Was it eight years? I stopped counting."

"What difference does it make? *You left me.* You could not have run further away from me. How can you be jealous?"

She looks at him blankly. "Do as you like," she spits.

"I'd *like* you to come with me. Give me your hand, come home. It can be easy. I won't reproach you, not ever. I swear it. It will be as it always was. You will lie on the couch the color of pecan shells and I will kiss your shoulder blades. It will all be forgotten."

Paola puts a firm hand on his shoulder. "Save it. It's over."

"Who the hell do you think you are?" he shouts furiously. Scamander flinches in the corner of the teahouse and Rosalie clutches her tongs in the event of hysteria. "Who the hell are you to talk to us? You have no *right.*" He strikes the floor with his palm, and it is wrong, a tantrum, a childish thing, but he cannot help it.

"I'm hers," she says simply. Her eyes slide into him, appraising, searching, and withdraw, finding him lacking, surely, small, an animal. "She lives with me in the real world. In a little flat overlooking a river. We have geraniums and a cat. We belong to each other, and soon we'll find the last one of our Quarto, and then we'll be able to live here forever. And you will only ever visit."

"I met someone, Ludo, a long time ago." Lucia sighs. She is trying to be kind and he recognizes that this is a trial for her. She can barely contain her scorn. She holds it before her like a shield. "A man with a funny birthmark. You know it by now. You have it. I'm sorry for that. Fucking him seemed harmless, an act performed outside our walls, and therefore unreal. You taught me that, that nothing outside us could be real. I believed it, I think. I believed it in Ostia. I believed it until him. And it *was* harmless, it was. You were so busy with that book, that Japanese thing. You didn't need me. And to have a thing I didn't have to share with you was rich and sweet. I was spread out under you so far and so thin, nothing of me was my own." Lucia looks at her empty cup. "It is so beautiful and awful here, so much more real . . . well, more real than you. Than the story you told about us. This is my place, now, it's not yours, it's *not*. You have the world, this is *mine*." Her voice had grown high and panicked, as if he were preparing to steal something from her. "You have Isidore and your glue and you have your brothers in Umbria and I had nothing, nothing but you and those stupid walls, and I was *lonely* living inside you, Ludo. You are not big enough for me."

"I . . . I thought we contained each other. I thought you were happy, as happy as you could be."

"No, Ludo, *you* were happy. Now listen to me, please." She leaned close to him, her breast brushed his arm. "Get out."

"No! I won't leave you. I can do as well as you, I can crawl through Rome on my belly like a worm and find all the secret ways in."

"You can't follow me. I'm inhuman, remember, a monster, a *chimera*." She spat their private word between them and he recoiled from the lump of it. "You are just a man, you cannot go where monsters go."

"I'll find my Quarto first. I'll beat you to it. I'll take this place from you."

Lucia laughs, loudly and cruelly, a braying, mocking laugh he had only rarely heard. The blond woman all in green draws to her feet, pulling his wife with her.

"Ludo, you're a fool," Lucia hisses at him. "You might as well be wearing a hat with bells and drool on yourself for the amusement of your betters. You'll never manage it. They fought a *war* over this, Ludo. People died, for real, in the real world and here. They bled and they had their hearts eaten by . . . by people like me. Death, real death, not some dancing skeleton on vellum. The price of it, the price of the tea I drink, the races I watch, the slices of chestnut I will eat, the wines I will drink, the price of all that would break you in two. It nearly broke me. No. Rot in the real world, Ludo. That's where saints live, under the sun, under the open sky. Their holiness means something there. *I don't want you here.*"

Ludo reaches out for her, grabbing at her feet, pathetic, knowing he is pathetic, unable to stop himself. "I love you, I love you, stop it, please. Just come with me. It doesn't have to be home. I will stay here with you, and we'll be a world within each other again." He is wretched, yes, and he knows it. He is crying, and kisses her knees. She rolls her eyes.

"Give me back eight years of huddling for warmth in a cave of your making. Give me the dress I wore in Ostia, and my cigarette case with the cockatrice on it. Give me everything in me that was stamped out by everything in you. Give me back a girl who had never heard of a chimera, who had never read that stupid encyclopedia, who had never had to hear herself called an animal. Then I'll come home."

Paola strokes Lucia's cheek with the back of her hand and pulls her like a doll, extricating her from Ludovico. He does not trip her, but he wants to; he knows her ankles and they are his, forever, always. But she crawls past him, weeping so bitterly that her back arches and heaves with it, as though she is trying to expel something from deep within her. They disappear out the tiny door, and Ludo lies slack-mouthed on the floor, his heart livid and black, his throat cracked like an old book.

———

Rosalie pulls an incandescent cup from her kiln, and Scamander pats her hand warmly, the dirt and blisters of decades in the fingers he puts on hers, the witness of themselves in Lucia, in Ludo, in all the times when the children were a trial and the money was scarce, when tea and cups were too thin, far too thin, to separate them from the empty, sterile air. Rosalie cradles Ludo in her lap, and Scamander steams the tea. He holds it to the poor man's chapped mouth, and the bookbinder drinks mechanically.

"It's all in how you swirl the tea in the cup, son," he says gently. "Clockwise, four times, not a bit less. That's the secret."

———

Ludo crawls again from the teahouse. The grass is cold and wet. The tips of the blades are beginning to freeze, stiff as quills crackling under his clumsy palms. He stands up beneath the baffled larch, and traffic sings by, little different than Roman traffic, carriages and motorcars more ornate, more frilled and flared, but a bustle and shout he knows, that comforts him. In no city can he imagine the traffic as anything other than this exercise in martial prowess and disdain of death.

Ludo looks down to see that a bee has alighted on his hand. It perches on one of his protruding veins, that ropy road traveling up his arms and out of sight. He always wore his blood too bright, too close to the surface. Blood was the trouble. All that worry about the Phlegmatic tissues and it was always the dark, red, splattering blood that would be his plague.

The bee does not leave him, but instead rubs its legs together impatiently, as though irritated to find no pollen on this sanguineous flower. A second joins it, and a third. Ludo thinks he ought to panic, but, after all, Isidore had his bees, in every icon, in every fresco. If he could bear them, Ludo can—but of course, Isidore's bees were representative, metaphorical, the spiritual manifestation of his remarkable intellect. These are quite real, and they seem to be whispering to each other.

There are five now. They ignore the larch and flutter their wings with indefinable emotion. Ludo turns his palm over and they eagerly gather in the little valley of flesh near the pad of his thumb. Their fellows are coming thick and fast now, a black veil with flashes of gold like lightning glittering within. Their buzzing is a long shriek, and he knows it, he knows the sound, for she knew it, that other woman, with a bee sting on her cheek, and he knows her, for he has tasted with her and danced with her, far from each other. Ludovico closes his eyes, letting them settle onto him, praying to his saint, his patron, his last guardian ghost.

"Let them bite me, Isidore," Ludo whispers. A prayer. A plea. "Your small and industrious lovers of virtue. Let them taste me, who has no virtue, and carry me away to become honey in the mouth of a king with a diadem I shall never wish to see."

# FOUR

# ACTS OF VESTA

L udovico had told himself a thousand times over the
years that it was stupid to come to the Forum to think.
Tourists indulge themselves because they think it makes
their thoughts more magnificent, eternal. A man who had lived
here all his life should have been beyond such childish acts.
Ludo approached forty years of age with an utterly accurate in-
ternal map of Rome laid out over his heart, so that his ventricles corresponded precisely to a history of epochal lust and
clam-dye and death by poisoning. He should have been above
a place so well trampled by the tiresome and well-meaning that
it could possess no molecule of its original self, only the cells of
their bored and time-strapped bodies, squinting in centuries of
suns.

But he liked it there. He couldn't help it. Ruins were calming to the scholarly soul. He liked to think about the Vestals
in their great round house, which always looked to him like a
salt mill, tending their little fires and writing diaries forever
lost, diaries of quiet lives spooled out into virginity and the
contemplation of a goddess of whom no stories were told
at all.

Ludovico liked to think that, in the long years of their

seclusion, the sisters wrote amongst themselves a secret Encyclopedia of the Acts of Vesta, stories of the hearth in which Vesta was a great and beautiful thing, her long hair dropping embers wherever she walked, striving in knightly fashion—of course she would have a furnace-grate for her shield, and a curling black poker as her lance—against demons of the everyday, against unfaithful wives and the winds of winter, against cruel merchants out to cheat her and against those many-headed ogres who seek the death of children: sleeping sickness, starvation, military service. Against the death of love.

Ludo liked to contemplate how their virginity was meant to keep the city whole, and as he sat in the shade of Byronic cypresses, he suspected it wholly true: that the inviolability of one soul can keep the whole of hell outside the gates of the city she chooses as her own.

Ludo thought, that day as they sat together on a low rise of crumbled stones far from the center of things, that Nerezza should have been a Vestal. In her utter impenetrability, she could have held the whole of Rome within her, red brick and *tufa* and aqueducts and catacombs, within the borders of her womb, and they would have been safe within her, safe forever, for no Goth or Gaul could broach that barrier.

"They didn't sting me, at all, not even once." Ludo sighed.

"I'm not surprised. Insect life is a funny thing there." Nerezza squinted herself in the broad, brazen sun, the molten light which poured like splashing wine over every shattered plinth and capital.

Ludo cleared his throat a little. "The *Etymologiae* says that bees are virtuous because they are much loved by all, and sought after with great longing by everyone, because their honey tastes as sweet in the mouths of paupers as in the mouths of kings. Do you think that's logical? That a creature can be virtuous just because it is loved and sought after, that the act of *being loved*, of being *sought after*, even if it is passive, is equal to an act of martyrdom or great piety, which is active? That it can confer grace to a whole species?"

"I think any encyclopedia is bound to have a great number of lies and fancied-up stories in it, Ludo."

Ludo shut his eyes against the light; he saw the pinkness of his eyelids swim before him. "But what does it mean, then, if a man is sought out by those virtuous bees? Sought out with great longing by creatures whose very souls are defined by the fact that they are greatly longed for?"

"I don't know."

"I wanted them to sting me. It was like the church, with all the silent people and their awful limbs, animal limbs. I wanted to be covered by other souls until mine was pressed to death, like a witch. Why do I feel that so much, when I'm there? Why do I want to be drowned in other people? I never want that here."

"It's different, for everyone. I can't answer any of these things, Ludo. I'm glad you saw Lucia, that it . . . gave her up to you. Because you can't really think that by chance you stumbled onto her Sunday tea. But I have no grace, nothing to add to any encyclopedia of that place, I am not sought after and I have no virtue."

He wanted to say: *I seek you.* He wanted to say: *You are not my wife, but you are my Virgil, leading me through circle after circle of Purgatory. How can a man not love the body that brings him so close to God?* But in the face of her inviolable mood, her frowns and her stares, he could not make himself drag her into Dante.

"Oh, Ludo," she whispered, "if you want to be happy, just let it be."

"Before the teahouse, I would have clawed through the earth for fifty years to find Lucia on the other side, an old woman, bald and tired, leaning on a cane. Maybe she'll still be there, with arthritis and absolution. But even if I never see her again, I have to go, I have to keep going to Palimpsest. I have to try. It is a world without an *Etymologiae*. Without an etymology, without origin. I'll go, and I'll lay a map of that place over my heart instead of Rome. I'll rent a small shop, an accountant's office, and write columns upon columns, everything that people know in that city. I will *write*, do you understand? I'll bind books, too, I'll bind them, as I have always done, and there will be pages like raw cream and the finest glues, the strangest glues, made from every kind of rendered beast, but I will bind only what *I* have written. Perhaps in fifty years, an old woman, bald and tired, leaning on a cane, will pass my shop and ask herself what strange old man is looking for his glasses in the display window, and we shall have a great deal to talk about. We will have coffees. I will save a chair for her. I am capable of that. Of waiting, of faithfulness. I am capable of service, of holding a city in my inviolable belly."

Nerezza watched him with murky eyes, shaded by pity and loathing and envy. Ludo did not understand it, but the nature of eel-kind is beyond the comprehension of land-dwellers, and he let her invisible body, black as rope, circle him, circle him, crackling, sere.

"How can you talk about it as if you've already managed everything, merrily planning your little life in Palimpsest? Such a selfish little boy you are, Ludovico! You've borrowed a toy, and you think it's yours forever. If Lucia had shoved you off her that night you would never have known about any of this." Hard, friable tears moved in her eyes. "Do you understand anything? Radoslav is dead. If we have it right, if what Agostino told you is true, if we've guessed the way, *I can never go*. Not ever. And I won't watch you gaily traipse into my country because your wife thought it was easier to just lie there and let you fuck her."

Ludovico chewed his lip. *Mine, mine and not yours.* For as often as he heard it, there might as well have been a sign reading thus hanging over the city.

"I suppose a knight cannot always expect the monsters he meets in the wood to kindly point the way."

Nerezza narrowed her dark eyes. "Are you the only human in the world then? And all of the rest of us monsters?"

She stood and strode away over the broad ruin, leaving him to chase after her, to seek her, to follow her meandering path home.

But Nerezza lost him in the close streets, and when Ludo finally came to her door she was not there. Clever bee, sought out after all. Agostino answered the bell, and sat with him on the couch while he warmed his hands around a mug of coffee—Ludovico found he could not bear the thought of tea, after the wonderful cups and discs of ice. Tea on this side of the world was too quotidian, too bitter, too thin.

"They've gone for the night, Anoud and Nerezza," Agostino

said, rubbing the bridge of his enormous nose. "You must have upset her."

"Probably." Ludo sighed. "I seem to do that rather more often than I mean to."

The two men sat on Nerezza's long, hard chaise. "How did you find her?" Ludo finally said, trying to keep his voice from sounding too eager. He had no jealousy in him anymore with regards to his eel-girl, anyway. Not too much. Impossible to pull such a feeling up and into the sunlit world. She was unpossessable, a Vestal with a terrible gaze.

"She found me." Agostino shrugged. "I don't know how she managed it. I was living in Madrid, my company's satellite offices are there. I was in sales." He laughed a little, rueful, amazed, at who he used to be. "We made pencils. I used to smell of nothing but graphite. One morning my phone rang and a woman told me very matter-of-factly that I would need to come to Rome immediately, that she knew me and needed me and loved me, and even her voice was like someone reaching through the line to kiss me and strangle me at the same time. I couldn't even say no to her *voice*. She's . . . like that. You can't say no. And, you know, we had a lot to talk about. She introduced me to Lucia," Agostino hurried forward nervously, "and we found Anoud together, brought her up from Rabat. She was working in an olive oil plant, can you imagine that? She was always shiny, like she couldn't get it out of her skin, even after we kissed her and kissed her. And Radoslav . . ." But there he trailed off, his voice grew husked and tight, and he passed a broad hand over his eyes.

Ludo put his arm around the young man, and a single

wracked sob escaped his skinny chest as he let himself be held. After a long while Agostino turned his face to Ludo's neck and kissed him gently, hesitantly, and again on his jaw, his ear. Ludovico stiffened and sucked in his breath. It was not that he had not expected something like this—surely his wife had not been prudish, and had as many women as men. But he was not Lucia, not a great serpent-lion with long and indiscriminate teeth. He did not have a different body for everyone. He did not look at men the way he looked at women. Ludo tried. He tried to decide where Agostino might fit in the menagerie of his recent lovers—the Bull, he thought, testing it against the heft of his heart. Evangelist, earth-tiller, labyrinth-tenant. Could he take such a thing within himself? If his body refused such an inversion of the usual order, would Agostino be hurt, angry? How could women do this, how could Lucia have done this? How could they bear so many other bodies within their own?

But it was not, in the end, necessary. Agostino seized his face and the kiss between them was rough and ungainly, slouching, mismatched, but Ludo found his hands knotted in his short hair, found his tongue sweet, found himself hard, after all, wrestling the bull into service. They struggled with clothes in the manner of new lovers, but Ludo was afraid, still afraid, to touch the rigid, unavoidable penis that rose to meet his own, could not be so abandoned. But when Agostino lay beneath him, tears shed for the vanished Radoslav dried on his cheeks, Ludo could see the mark, flared black and deep on his hip, and he was overcome, as surely as he had ever been overcome by the twisting bodies of the three wild creatures before this one. He hooked his fingers into Agostino's scrawny hips and shut his eyes again, against the light, against the world outside. He let his soft stomach cover Agostino's hardness, and the young man moaned, cried out as Lucia had refused to, as Narezza had refused, under him. He could think of nothing but spit to ease the passage, and when Agostino winced, his heart gave way for him, hardly more than a kid, hardly ready for any of this. And it was not so alien a thing as he had imagined to move within the tall, ungraceful boy whose cries were, in the end, so very like the lowing of a great bull.

# PART IV:

## CHARON

# In Transit,
# Westbound: 9:23

It became apparent to enthusiasts of locomotive travel that there was at least one unscheduled train on the tracks of Palimpsest. It did not stop at any of the stations, for one thing. Astrologers and geologists were consulted; they are much the same folk in this part of the world. The astrologer gazes upward and scries out shapes in the sky, and to do this he builds great towers so as to be closest to the element of his choice. The geologist is an astrologer who once, just once, happened to look down. From such great heights she glimpses the enormous shapes stamped on the earth, the long polygons made by the borders of farms and rivers and mill towns, littoral masses and city walls, a reflection of the celestial mosaic. In these loamy constellations Palimpsest is but a decorative flourish; they are so vast and complex that in her lifetime the geologist may chart but the tiniest part of the conterration which contains her tower. It is a long and lonely life to which few are called.

The great transportation system is of some mild interest to the geologist, as it comprises a small and only half-organic Constellation of Utility. However, a famed scholar of the fundament consented to turn her moss-clogged oikeioscopes onto the commune of the trains and discover the origins of this stubborn and unyielding train that escapes all their attempts to tame it.

The calculations involved for even such a small terrestrial chart are immense, and it took a full year for the geologist to return her findings, and another year's delay in presenting them, for the oceanic currents were trined with the annual snowfall, and this surely portended disaster in the revealing of great works. But at last she drew her colleagues and interested parties to the grand convocation chamber of Colophon Station, and announced that the 3:17 northbound Decretal had had a somewhat unhappy affair with the 12:22 eastbound Foolscap. The mysterious train was their child, and like any child whose parents no longer love each other, it runs wild and does what it likes and there is little at all to be done about it.

———————

Sei does not know quite what to do with herself. She feels as though she has been struck in the head with a branch wrapped up in flowers. She doesn't think she ought to smile, as it is certainly not at all funny, but she cannot stop herself, and her head feels thick and drunk as she shakes it.

There is a rabbit on the train. He has a silver mallet, and is standing in a very large barrel of rice looking quite determined.

He is not really a rabbit. But he is not a man in a suit either. He is more like a very sad-looking man who has had bits of rabbit attached to him by someone who was not particularly good at it. Wild black hair tumbles over long, limp ears, fuzzy and gray, the skin within white as crushed pearl. He has long, droopy whiskers like hoary old man's hair, and she supposes he has a tail, though if she went looking for it she would be sure to burst into uncontainable giggles, and he seems like a very serious rabbit.

He wears a black farmer's *yukata* with white chrysanthemums on it and does not look well in it for it is extremely threadbare and dirty.

Plenitude yawns on her shoulder and stretches its strokes; the Third Rail smiles quietly to herself and watches Sei, waiting for her approval or disapproval. That is becoming a great trial, if Sei can be honest. She cannot love everything wholly with all of herself, and it is such a great shame to all of them when she wrinkles her nose or coughs or looks bored. They wait to drink her reactions like beer, and it makes her tense.

But there is a rabbit on the train. And the long seats of this new carriage are quite pale, covered in crusted rock like barnacles. From a high ceiling, so high it has its own clouds—though at least she can see the ceiling this time, its silver bands hard and true behind the mist—hang silver lanterns. Terns circle them mournfully, crying out their dirges. The handholds are a green, rough rope of reeds. The rabbit does not look at her, but with a weary sigh heaves his mallet over his head and brings it down hard on the wet rice. Glops of the stuff splatter out onto Sei's shoes.

"I know you!" Sei cries. "Usagi!" And not her mother, the real rabbit, the rabbit on the moon, speeding through the world in a locomotive that contains all the lunar landscape. Sei wants to laugh again.

"Everyone knows me. That is why I am going to visit relatives by the sea, who will make me very expensive tea and not bother me with silly questions about where I get rice on the moon, and why I do not take up a respectable profession such as television repair, and who would consent to eat sweets prepared by a rabbit, even if he does it with great care and by hand. So to speak."

He holds up his right arm; it ends in a withered, oversized gray paw, a bumpy violet-blue scar ripping through his skin where the fur fades into a man's arm.

"My mother was named Usagi," Sei says shyly. "When I was little

I thought she had a secret life, making *mochi* when I wasn't looking and refusing to share them with me."

"Oh, she did," the rabbit says casually. He seems so young, too young to have been at the rabbit business for long. "All people named Usagi are members of my guild. The broom closet is a common hiding place for the hammers. I suspect if you were to return to your house in Tokyo and look in the storage bins beneath your kitchen floor, you would find several black-and-gold boxes full of sweets she did not deliver on schedule. Your mother was not a good worker, I'm sorry to say. Unreliable."

"I'm sorry. She was . . . unhappy. It was part of her, you could not separate her from it. She was sad the way a horse is strong or a bird flies. I do not think *mochi* would have helped."

"Why should they? They do not help me, but everyone must have a vocation."

Sei bites her lip and looks down at her toes, a strangely childlike pose, but she cannot help it, with a rabbit-man so near. "Have you . . . seen my mother? Since she stopped working for you."

The rabbit stares at her incredulously and looks to the Third Rail for help. The red-faced woman shrugs, and Plenitude shakes its strokes apologetically. "Wrong train, girl," he finally says, laughing. "I think it's my relations you want to talk to."

"And who are they?"

"Mine is not the only moon, child. My cousin the mole lives on Triton, and Phobos has a fine fox. Ganymede has a whole family of turtles. The Horse in the Sun is chewing her oats a few cars down. She is not talkative, though. If you brush her, you may feel that you hear a kind of low chant in the basement of your heart, like nuns singing through a cloud of incense. There are other horses in the stable car, too. We have such a large family. The blue Arabians of

Vega, the two-headed Appaloosas of Sirius, the monochrome Bay of Arcturus. But you'll want the snow monkeys on Charon, who while away their long orbits in hot springs and ice huts. No candies for them, joyless lot. They hammer out souls. Perhaps she is there, pounded flat into a paste."

Sei grimaces, but tries to turn it into a smile, and hands the rabbit a shovelful of sugar to cover her embarrassment.

"And this train is going there?"

"Of course not. What funny ideas you have! Didn't you hear me? We are all going to the seashore—you might call it a family reunion."

Sei does not know how to proceed past him. She wants to hug him, to stroke his ears and his mangled paws and ask how he came to be so wretched. But she feels it would shame him, and she will not do it.

"My name is not Usagi," she says, "but I would like to help you."

"There is only one way you can help us, Sei."

"Tell me."

"I have not been authorized to give you that information." His voice sounds oddly automated, like a telephone operator. "But you can take your mother's place, if you like."

The rabbit holds out his hammer to her, and it is surprisingly light, like a huge feather in her hand. She steps into the rice barrel as though she means to crush wine grapes with her toes, and he stands behind her to help her with her stance. She thinks of the men in exclusive Tokyo golf courses with their bored instructors holding them just so. Plenitude winces and holds its breath, sure it will be dislodged and crushed into rice-candy. Sei lifts the mallet and he corrects her grip quickly before she brings it down with a shout of joy and glops of sticky rice fly against the sides of the barrel.

The rabbit in the moon kisses her on the temple, sweetly, tenderly, like an uncle proud of his blood.

The Third Rail watches them as Sei gleefully sets about smashing sugared rice to paste. She says nothing, but her eyes are full of red and viscous tears.

# ONE

# EIGHT THOUSAND DOORS

S ei held Sato Kenji's book before her like a lantern meant to illuminate her path. She consulted it as frequently as an address book, and followed it, believing in his accuracy.

The book led her to this: Sei stood on the main platform with Sato Kenji's book clutched to her chest. She wore black, her best effort at a suit, her silver-black shirt of that first journey south with Kenji at her back rendered respectable by a business jacket. She thrust her face into the wind whipping down the empty tracks.

*I have been told of a secret society in Tokyo that requires its members to take shifts monitoring certain platforms. It is easy to believe that the men in black suits who stand beside you or me waiting for the train are held to the same standards and schedules as we are, that they have appointments to keep, meetings to attend, supervisors who do not tolerate truancy. But it would seem that some of them are not, but instead are sentinels of a sort, and the blank looks on their faces are careful masks of religious significance.*

*The society believes that a train platform is a nexus, a crossroads that connects many cities that do not otherwise touch border to border.*

*They believe that in the beginning of the world, the first gods stood not upon a bridge of light, but on a high train platform buffeted by winds, and from this place they thrust their jeweled spear into the ocean and created all land and mountain and shore.*

*Thus, they reason, this primal platform must exist yet in some part of Japan, though surely fallen from its greatest height in the heavens, and they have many warring theories about which it is. So, upon almost every plat-form on the Japanese Isles members of this society stand watch, ready to alert their brothers of the arrival of the Train of Eight Thousand Doors, whose engine was fashioned from that very jeweled spear which dwelt for millennia beneath the sea until it was unearthed by devoted monks, at least according to the majority faction. The minority argument goes that Japan Railways desired it greatly and funded recovery operations.*

*In any event, the Train of Eight Thousand Doors is believed to tra-verse the known world, its doors opening onto London one moment, Ulan Bator the next, Tokyo, Montreal, São Paulo, and so forth. One must only attend to the station callings within the great train and one may enter or exit at any platform in the world. To be possessed by this train is the desire of every black-suited initiate, and he would give his soul for such a ticket.*

*I have myself stood watch with them, and they are pleasant enough gentlemen, if single-minded. I am sorry to report that only the neigh-borhood local and the express to Asakusa arrived during my vigil.*

*Both were punctual.*

Kenji would not tell her a thing was possible if it was not. If such a train existed, it would take her there. Sei was sure of it. Sure of him. There had to be another way in.

*I'm so tired*, she thought.

*I'm so tired.* Her mother had said this, more often than anything else. *Why am I always so tired?*

*Because you have all those tigers to fight, Mama,* she had said. *And you have to swim all the way to the bottom of a lake to read my book for me.*

*What a clever girl I have!* Usagi slept on the floor like a cat, her hair in her face, her nails chewed ragged. And Sei had waited, she always waited, as patiently and quietly as she could, for her mother to wake up and smile at her and make tea for them, with sweets.

But Sei was so tired now. As tired, perhaps, as her mother had always been. Her legs were sore and her lips were swollen with kisses and she was sick to screaming of people floundering on top of her as though she were a ship that would take them to safety. But she could not stop—how could she stop? How could she go home, where there was no place called the Floor of Heaven, no easy way, no quick path? The train needed her. She had to keep up. Had to go faster. Had to have more, always more, had to run twice as fast to stay in place. She felt as though the train crouched by her even in the daytime, hiding behind clouds and temples, waiting as patiently and quietly as it could for her to wake up and smile at it and make tea, with sweets.

Sei did not want to be an Usagi-mother to the train. She did not want to disappoint it. She shuddered on the platform.

There was a man with a black suit and an attaché case standing a polite distance from her, stone-still, his profile cutting the breezes of the Shinkansen platform—why were they all so high up? The nature of a train is to fly underground, beneath cities. It is a clay bird, its natural element is earth. But the Shinkansen loves the air, confuses the sparrows, and it is so white the wind must feel filthy to touch it. The high platforms were another world, a glimpse into a cosmos without fundament.

The man glanced at her out of the corner of his eye. He held his hand flat out at his hip, rigid, palm down. She was meant to understand this, clearly, but she didn't.

Usagi had whispered in her ear once, twice, that men in plain suits were servants of the Spider-Kami, who had not eight legs but eight thousand, and they did not sleep in beds, but schemed in empty storefronts where they slept close together on a rack, hangers protruding from their collars. *You must never approach one*, she said tremulously, *or he will take you away from your mother and she will be at the mercy of everything in the world.* And that Sei particularly believed, for her father worked in the city and often did not come home at night, and it was easy to think of him hung up in a store like a blazer for sale.

Sei could not quite help how frightened she was to speak to this stranger, who was not a safe stranger in the Floor of Heaven with a long glass of vodka in his hand and a friendly face and a black mark like a map at the bottom of it all.

"Is it coming?" she whispered. "Is there a better way? Will it really take me to any city, any city at all?"

The man in the suit looked puzzled and not a little alarmed.

The shame of it was like a slap to Sei's face. He was just a man. Kenji did make some things up, and more fool her for believing so much of it. Just because they were true *there* did not mean they were true *here*. But the man's jaw unclenched slowly and he spoke as though unused to it:

"My calculations suggest today, the 4:10 southbound. But I have been wrong before."

Sei's belly lifted in relief, and her fingers fluttered to the neckline of her shirt. She pulled it toward her shoulders like theater curtains, and the mark smirked there, between her breasts, as though she had spilled the water of death as she drank it. This revelation of skin had become as easy as speaking to her—easier, it communicated more with less. She smiled beatifically, eager, sure.

The man stared dumbly. His mouth opened and closed; his throat bobbed ridiculously up and down. He covered his mouth with one hand, aghast.

"What happened to you?" he gaped. "Do you need a doctor?"

Sei blinked, and then she laughed. What a long time since anyone had looked at her chest and not immediately taken her into their arms. What a long time since speech was necessary or even pleasant. Hard to imagine that her codes were not valid in any dark-filthy corner of the world. *Enough secrets for all of us to have our own*, she thought. She rearranged her clothes to hide it again, and waited silently, a vigil, a sentinel, for the 4:10 southbound. The man would not come near her, neither to breathe her air nor risk physical contact. She watched his chest sag as the 4:10 arrived and expelled a noisy crowd of children at his feet. It accepted him apologetically in return, with sheepish doors, bound for Nara and nothing more.

———

Back, always back. To the brass plaque and the dance floor and the long, thin glasses. The Floor of Heaven, which was dark and empty. *This is my tatami room now*, Sei thought in the slow blue evening, when the persimmon trees seemed to bear only black fists. *I close myself up; I tell stories to open faces and the stories make no sense to anyone but me. But they are always believed, I am always believed. Oh, Usagi, I pound the rice after all. After all.*

She pressed her sternum with two of her fingers, though it was not her mark she sought. The doors were open to her, she no longer needed to show her pass. In her suit she would not draw so many as usual, but it wouldn't matter, not really. She would find someone. Two, three. She had to have more than the rest, to stay on the train, to speed through so much city so fast, so very fast. She would drag their hands to her if she had to. She would bear the old and foreign and maimed; she had done it before.

Yumiko was so often late now, wandering into the club past midnight, drinking mechanically, the colors of her cocktails a shifting spectrum, red to ultraviolet. Sei thought she might be able to manage her first lover before Yumiko even arrived, in her uniform, looking disappointed, looking desperate. A mirror in a blue skirt, and Sei could not bear very much of mirrors anymore.

But Yumiko was not late, not that night. She was drinking already, throwing glasses of sake into her mouth. She teetered on her heels and embraced Sei with relief, the two of them squeezing the other's thin ribs together. They couldn't let go, either of them.

"What do you say?" Yumiko whispered in her ear, her breath like rotted plums. "Nothing tonight. No one. Just you and I. I'll take you to meet my parents. We'll eat noodles. It'll be just like we're normal."

"I'm pregnant," Sei answered.

# 121st and Hagiography

**THE WEALTHY OF PALIMPSEST** send their children to finishing school at St. Folquet's, whose brick and marble and long, sloping peasant's roof of wild grass and violet sprigs nestles between two defunct fountains. Groping bladderwrack and redolent poppies have reclaimed the hydra's nine dry mouths and the bronze bull's regal horns. Feral cats sleep in the coils of the serpent and in the twisted, gaping mouth of the bull. The serpent and the bull are beloved of the students, and many exercises have been composed as to their symbology, though the faculty know that it is a happy accident of urban planning that the school was established there and not between, say, a golden lion and a silver stag. It keeps the little ones busy.

The prosperous keep this great secret: their children require this charming institution, require it as surely as water and milk. They would prefer it were not so; they have prayed at the Right-Hand Church in earnest, fur-wrapped cabals for surcease of it. They watch the children of immigrants and the poor grow sharp-featured and brash-voiced, they watch the wastrels play in the river and their hearts fill up with bile. St. Folquet's is a blessing beyond blessing, a curative of highest worth, but the process is long and severe, as are all things in Palimpsest, and they miss their small ones so.

Where does it begin? What may one hoard and yet avoid this congenital plague? How many silos of barley, how many vineyards, how many horses with buttery flanks, how many houses with crisp Weckweet finials may they acquire before this gentle disaster settles down upon the wombs and seed of those who love sealskin and rubies? Accountants from Zarzaparrilla Street have been fed with chocolate and songbirds' livers, tobacco like corn silk rolled into linen for their pleasure, yet none have been able to locate the tipping point, at what decimal doom descends.

If we have passes, we may be able to look within the ponderous pearwood doors and glimpse classes in session. Let us say we have, let us treat ourselves to the costly jewel of a hall pass. Nightfall courses have just begun, the children are all in their rows, hands folded slackly before them. The teacher has not yet arrived, indolent wretch! Yet why do they not move, you ask? Why do they not pelt each other with erasers or crack jokes about the stock market, as the spoiled offspring of the affluent are wont to do?

Because they are not finished.

The children of Palimpsest's aristocracy are born with a terrifying blankness: they are receptive, they respond to stimuli, they learn to walk and they learn to sit very quietly, but they do not speak, they do not run and play, and they have no faces, no hair, no genitalia at all. For this reason, in whispers they are called Brauria, a word from a language the fashionable cannot be concerned with remembering, signifying "little bears." For bears in epochs long dead were said to be born formless, shapeless, and licked into bearform by their mothers.

The Brauria are small dolls, posable, pliant, but they are unfinished, unreal, and the day a lady of rank gives birth, wrapped up in her lionskin with purple rings on her fingers, she prays she has not earned enough to earn this. She listens for the cry of her child; it does not come. And she knows it is St. Folquet's for this one, and all its brothers and sisters to come. When she rises from childbed, she will begin to give away her dresses one by one, her houses, her lovers, hoping to descend once more into grace.

But, lady, weep not! At St. Folquet's is hope, at least! When you leave your jewel-studded basket at their doorstep, it is not an orphan, not *exactly* an orphan, you abandon to their care.

For the children do hear, they do receive, and their lessons are easy for all that. For fifteen years the students are calm and even-tempered, motionless. They must be washed and fed intravenously, and this is delicate work to be sure, but they grow, as all children do. And they are taught as though they could recite, do sums, and debate with vigor the concerns of the day. Their clumsy feet are taught to dance, their soft spines shaped to posture with dread machines.

And when they are fifteen, they are finished.

It is a ritual of intense secrecy—at least, the wealthy believe it to be a secret. In a dark room the congenial little bear is seated, and another child enters, a true child, no older than her subject, with sparkling eyes and wicked jokes on her lips. Great goblets of water are provided for her comfort. Slowly, with infinite care and diligence, the child begins to lick the skin of the Braurion, just as a mother bear might before the bears decided collectively upon the inefficiency of this method. Every inch of skin is subject to her tongue, and she is merciless, though her own mouth becomes sore and tired, and though the process takes five days and nights—she has immeasurable endurance; she is strong.

And beneath the blankness a grown person emerges, with an aquiline nose and a mole on the left cheek, with red hair or skin like coffee, with graceful hands or full breasts, with excellent posture and a fine, clear brow. On the fifth day the Braurion is no more, and in his or her place sits an exceptional soul, tempered by so many years of forced silence, of reliance on the utterly rarified spirits at St. Folquet's, a soul who knows his Latin and her calculus, his rolls of kings and her ecclesiastical history. They are proficient in the composition of poetry and have extraordinary memories, trapped as they have been within themselves. They are soft-spoken, sweet-natured, and have a remarkable felicity for dancing.

They are not returned to their families—how could they be returned? No one has a name or a face until he or she is finished, and to determine who belongs to whom is a tedious enterprise the responsibility of which no man is willing to take. From St. Folquet's the little bears, now bears entire, go into the city and make their fortunes. It is extremely common for them to marry the child who licked them into being. The bond does not easily break.

But where do they come from, the boys and girls who minister to the Brauria for five days and nights? How are they convinced to do such a thing?

They are brought from the Aviary, of course. From the poorest of places, the Folquetters come to find those peculiar, clever, outcast children who are born into every part of Palimpsest, whether stews of goose or cat bubble over the hearth. The faculty bring in harvests of children, one for each of their poor charges, and until the young paupers are fifteen, they sleep well in their own soft barracks, the walls trimmed with garlands of wintergreen. They are taught no less than the Latin and calculus and ecclesiastical history of the Braurion, and more, for they are keen and quick and boisterous, and the faculty adores them after the maddening silence of the rest of the student body. They compose the essays on the nature of the serpent and the bull, and debate it merrily. They are doted upon, and fed sweetmeats on beds of beet and coconut. And they do not return to their families, either.

Years hence, the ladies with their lionskins may come across a lovely young woman with a fiercely inquisitive young man on her arm, and she may notice that they never cease to touch one another in small ways, even as she chooses oranges and he squeezes quinces in the market. And she may ask: *Is this my child?* But it is not for her to know, and in such a manner no one family rules Palimpsest for long.

———

Save Casimira, always save her.

———

There is a cat asleep in the bull's bronze mouth. Its paws flop over the hoop of the ring thrust through his flaring nostrils. November scratches its ears; it yawns. Her fingers still tingle with the bees' exhalations; she wonders if she will ever get used to the feeling of it, of being possessed of a million arms which may reach out to anything. She pauses and listens within herself—but the bees are still in drunken celebration of her coronation and have nothing useful for her. A girl is dancing Cossack-style for coins on Zarzaparrilla Street. An old man has died of drink in the doorway of a bookshop on Vituperation and 9th. Nothing she cares for or can use. Instead, November considers the names: *Oleg Sadakov. Amaya Sei. Ludovico Conti.* She whispers them, like little rosaries. She almost thinks she knows what to do.

November holds up her hand; her skin is a mass of stings and welts, little ropes of hardened skin where venom flew fast through her veins. But she smiles—the wounds make a kind of map of her known world, circumnavigated by pain and need, an echo of the black lines on her face. She will never be clean again, or walk without wincing, but the joy of the bees of Palimpsest shrieks in her.

St. Folquet, presumably, stares at her from the face of his building—a tall statue of polished red wood, its features half-eaten by wood lice, the thin, imperious saint holding in one hand a divining rod and in the other a cello bow. At his feet infant bears rock on their haunches, regarding him with ursine awe and adoration.

Though deep in the city, the street is empty—November can see nothing but the long canyons made by buildings stretching up into the heavens, so far, so high that the moon is hidden. The sky seems to have given up a silent battle against the city and surrendered its heights to concrete and marble. But yes, there it is, she had known it would come for her: a carriage sliding up its slick tracks and small, surely green-shod feet stepping toward her, a hand slipping into hers. She knows the weight of Casimira's hand by now and enjoys it. It is familiar, kind, like sinking into warm water, to be held thus.

"Would you like to go in?" Casimira says brightly. "I donate a great deal toward the upkeep of St. Folquet's; I am sure we would be welcome. The new graduates will be having their last meal."

"Did you graduate from this place?"

Casimira smiles in her secret way. "Don't be ridiculous. Though," she pauses thoughtfully, "Aloysius did, you know."

"Then why donate so much?"

"It can only benefit the city to have endless waves of exceptionally capable, even brilliant, folk unfettered by class and family connections. They change the world once a generation. That is certainly worth something."

The two women pass under the knowing gaze of St. Folquet and into a grand hall filled with tables, which are draped in black linen and spattered with empty plates, starkly white against the table-cloths. The professors, when they finally sight Casimira, draw up to their full height and smooth the wrinkles from their stern and byzantine clothing, which to November is a blur of suit tails, high boots, corsetry, epaulettes, and dashing capes. The women have partridge feathers in their hair, the men have crow. They encourage the students to stand, and though the Brauria are awkward, shy of their new faces, their new voices, they rise as one and applaud Casimira, their benefactress, their mistress.

She demurs, too far above them to need their praise, and leads November to a long bench like one found at a monk's mess hall. A young man moves aside to allow her access, blushing beneath exquisite features. He clutches the arm of a radiant young woman, whose gaze is appraising and steady. She does not blush at all.

"Casimira," November says quietly, so that they will not be overheard as the suddenly loquacious children laugh and tell old jokes which are for them raw and new. "When will I feel like myself again? I feel all the time as though I am about to fall into a great depth, and my blood is always singing, singing as though the world is ending. So many voices, all those bees—I know all their names! How can I know all their names?"

Casimira turns to her in frank joy, and her face in that moment is so full of surprise and sisterly recognition, of relief in the presence of a compatriot, that November does not suppress the need to touch her: she presses her cheek to the matriarch's and kisses her roughly, a savagery which may only exist between queens. The children around them exchange grins and stare—they have not yet learned not to stare.

"Never, poor girl," Casimira says when they part, and her eyes are full of tears. "You are like me now, the only one like me. It will never stop, and you will know all their children's names, too. And the names of everyone they touch, everyone they sting, for they will not be able to wait to tell you, to report to you all they know, to make you proud of them. You must be gentle, for they are tender-hearted as you and I cannot be. You have their stewardship, and it is a great task." She squeezes November's hand. "But you have me, and I have you, now. And we shall not either of us be alone again."

A great bell sounds and supper arrives—a tiny roasted finch placed on each plate, its head and beak and body intact, overflowing fig and breadcrumbs from its unfortunate mouth. The faculty and graduates draw great black napkins from beside their plates, and Casimira follows suit, smirking slyly as she lifts it and drapes it over her head. As one creature, the hall plucks the tiny birds from their plates and slips them beneath the napkin whole. November stares as two hundred people eat draped in black, as though they were witches, heads bent in prayer to worlds below their feet.

The meal goes on and on—there is no other dish, and November can hear the crunching of avian bones. She does not wish to shame them; November veils herself and takes the finch by its roasted beak, pushing it into her mouth with two fingers, her remaining blessings. It is sweet, at first, the burnished skin and meat, glazed in something like brandy and something like plum wine. But as she chews—methodically, for it fills her mouth to bursting—the organs rupture, bitter and bilious, a taste like despair, like the loss of love. And deeper, the bones shiver and crack and cut her—the taste of her blood flows in, salty as tears shed over a ruined body, mingling with the marrow, and it is sweet again, sweet as herself, herself remaining at the end of all trials.

And November can see why the veil is needed. No god should bear witness to a woman devouring a meal of herself.

She swallows what is left, finally, and lifts the veil from her face, wiping a smear of blood from her lips. Across the city, three souls clutch their bleeding mouths in shock and agony. The hall is empty; they have all gone, and only Casimira remains at her side.

"Are you ready to go home?" she says. And November is.

———

The house is hiding behind a column when they arrive, dressed as beautifully as November can imagine a boy dressing, in turquoise silk with a wide white collar and pink satin slippers, his belt buckle ivory, his hair combed to brilliance. He has made himself special for them, but he is bashful now, and November kneels, holding her arms out to the boy. In her, the bees dance: *Mother, oh, Mother and Wife, stay with us, this is your home!*

She holds tightly to herself—she is so spread out now, there must be a list of all the things she is that are not herself. But at the bottom of her heart, she is still November, still the child of a librarian and a woman who caught a shark when she meant to catch a little fish, and she smiles at the boy encouragingly.

*My dress; my sail.*

He flies to her, his arms small and tight around her neck. Casimira watches them like a satisfied brood hen.

"I have another gift for you, November. A secret in a story. Not so important as the first. Yet it is my hope that in time it will become as vital that you know it." Casimira sits down on the floor in the center of her hall, and the house climbs up into her lap, kissing her cheek with a loud smack.

"I was born as the children of St. Folquet are born, you must have guessed. It is not possible that I should be otherwise, as our family has within it more wealth than Palimpsest can imagine. We have long thrived on adoption, but my mother could not give me up. The brothers and sisters of that school are not alone in their skill.

"The story they tell of how I came to be in possession of my house is ridiculous—when I was eight years old I was blank as a page, and my mother had to lift my hand to the door knocker, as I could not even do that of my own will. I stood dumbly and mutely in this very hall for a week, neither eating nor moving, so stupid are the unmolded Brauria. Finally the house overcame his shyness and cared for me, as best he knew. He taught me all the languages a house can know, and all the calculations required for its construction, and all the dancing performed and poetry recited upon its floors. It was a good education. And though I cannot think how he came to imagine such a thing, one day he set about licking me into shape, with the smallest tongue and the greatest patience."

"I talked to the other houses," the boy says shyly, hiding his face in Casimira's arm. "They knew where the rich little boys and girls went, and St. Folquet's School, the school itself, you know, the building, she knows how to wake them up."

Casimira strokes his hair like a fond cat's. "I woke up under his mouth, and we have never separated since. That is often the way of it, I understand. And so I alone of my family was able to be both born and live as Casimira, to take my place at the center of the factory and open my ears to all of the small things made in my vats and presses. I daresay I am better at it than any Casimira before me, for I was educated by a house, and this has taught me to think strange enough things to tolerate the secret dreams of the ants in my heart."

November traces circles on the polished cedar floor. "I thank you for the secret, and for . . . for the bees, but I can't think why I should ever need to know this," she said.

Casimira holds her house to her, his fingers tangled up in her long, green hair. Her voice is thick and hard when she speaks, and

November understands by now that this means the great lady does not wish her to know that her words mean worlds to her.

"So that you will know, my love. So that you will know that you can be happy here with me. That you can live. That you can have a child in my house and it will not be taken from you. That I was given grace, and you may have it also. So that you will stay until you are old, and close your eyes with me, listening to all our bees and rats and starlings dream, and you will lose nothing by it."

"Your love is a terrible thing," November says. "It sits heavy. It stings. It cuts."

She shrugs. "I am Casimira."

"I don't know if I can bear it."

"I would not have chosen you if you could not. You will get stronger. You will grow calluses."

The house crawls over to her, his eyes bright blue and as dashing as he can make them. "I will lick your babies alive, I promise," he says. The love of this one, this small thing inside a big thing, that she can bear. November holds him and rocks him, and she can feel in his little body, which is not exactly flesh, and not exactly plaster, that whatever comprises his heart is thundering in exultation.

"There is a man here," he whispers finally, as though he does not wish to admit it, to interrupt his time with this new and wonderful toy he has found. "He is waiting for you."

November starts. She looks at Casimira with alarm—she has had no warning from the bee-minds that hover around hers.

"I think," Casimira laughs, "they wanted to make you a surprise. They can be like that."

The boy frowns. "He cannot come in, mistress. He is not allowed.

The bees brought him as far as they could, but he is . . . stuck. In the back, on Shuttlecock Street."

The trio make their way through the yawning lower floor of the house, and November's heart hammers against her ribs, intent on creating some new chamber for itself. She closes her eyes and tries to feel him, as she has so many times, but the bees drown out his presence with their pleas that she be proud of them. She is proud, so very proud, and she calms them with her heartbeat. They buzz sleepily, content. She is ready. They have done as she asked. She has earned the secret Clara longs for, and Xiaohui, and her nameless brother, and the green-coated stranger. Not from a book or from guessing, but by bearing up under venom like love. Would she tell Clara? Would she open up to that poor redheaded girl, like a friend, like a lover? To Xiaohui?

She would not. November knew she would not. *Because it is a sacred place*, she thinks. *I owe it, I owe it protection. I owe it my soul.* And perhaps she ought to feel guilty for this less than honorable intent, but she does not.

And there is a man, at the great window behind the house. He cannot even quite get to the window, the lineaments of his permitted transience appear to be the borders of the broad avenue behind Casimira's enormous house. He tries to push toward it, but he has not known a girl named Clara with a piercing in her tongue, and the amber shadows push back. He is forty or so, his curly hair thinning lightly, a long, pointed nose holding up old-fashioned spectacles. His clothes are wrinkled and plain, his eyes mild and watery.

November throws open the window.

"You can't!" the house cries. And it is true, the golden half-mist will not let her climb out, resisting gently, even apologetically, but resisting nonetheless. She closes her eyes. The bees trumpet triumph with a million horns. She makes a guess and cries out:

"Ludovico!"

He starts, stares boggle-eyed at her, at her dress, at her ruined, blistered, vaguely glowing skin, so full of poison and honey. A vague expression of recognition crosses his shy face. But November stands in her surety, and she smiles though it hurts so much, blisters stretching and tearing on her face.

"Ludovico," she says calmly, boldly, the deep hum of the hive in her voice. "My name is November Aguilar. I live in Benicia, which is in California. You have to find me."

"What?" he finally sputters. "You're right here."

"Close your eyes and remember, Ludovico. Remember me. In the frog's shop. Remember the bee sting on my face . . . well, yes, I suppose there is more than one sting now. But remember. I was there, with you, that first night. I held your hand."

Ludovico covers his mouth with his hand. "I felt it . . . oh, God, the bees, I felt them when they did that to you . . ."

"I'm sorry. I felt the people in the church, too. I think . . . it's to make it easier to find each other. It doesn't help that much, really."

"No." Ludovico seems to be calculating, weighing something precious in his mind. "You said California?"

"Yes! You have to find me in the real world. You have to find me."

"I know! I mean . . . I know how this works."

November blinks—she is stung. She had thought it was her secret. "Remember this," she says, "don't forget when you wake up, no matter what. Tell me where to meet you. Tell me where you live."

He shakes his head, beset by her own bees, who float lazily, happily, around his hair in a black-gold corona. "Italy, I live in Italy. Rome."

"Okay. Tomorrow, I'm going to call you. Give me your telephone number."

He does, stuttering, and she repeats the numbers to herself over and over until she is sure she can remember.

"There's something else, though. And it's important, please, please remember." She cocks her head, listening to the bees' confused report. "We have to get to them, too. The next time you come, you have to find him, the other one, Oleg Sadakov. He keeps running away from the bees, but he's ... by the river, he's under a black bridge with stone cockerels on either side. The bees will help you get there, it's far, and we're too new to have access to much of anything. That's why you can't come in. Unless you meet a girl with red hair called Clara. Or find Oleg. And I'll find Amaya Sei."

Slowly, as though speaking underwater, Ludovico says: "The one with blue hair?"

"Yes. She's on the train, but I knew that anyway. I smelled it."

"Yes, I did, too!"

"Ludovico, tell me where to meet you. Tell me where to go."

He says nothing for a long time, staring at her. She thinks for a moment that he does not want to come, that he is like Clara, and does not want more than he has.

"The bees sought you out," he says. "I don't know what that means. But I think it means you are virtuous."

November is laughing, her body bright, full of certainty all at once. "There is a list, Ludovico! A list of the things necessary for happiness, and the list is us! Ludovico Conti. Oleg Sadakov. Amaya Sei. November Aguilar."

Ludovico tries to cross the street to her and is quietly repulsed by the amber air.

"Caracalla," he says finally. "Meet me at Caracalla. I'll remember."

# TWO

# THE BUSINESS
# OF HUMAN PURITY

November woke laughing. She put her hand over her mouth, but the laughter would have none of it. Her hand ached—the blisters were still golden and painful, but they were not so swollen. She thought that when they had healed, she would be an entirely different color. She did not pull a brown book from the cabinet, though her hand strayed to it. She breathed deeply. It would wait. It would wait.

*I am an ill-tempered and irascible child. The kind the Green Wind wants,* she told herself.

November pulled her telephone from its cradle instead, and dialed the number still glowing in her head before it could fade, before she could forget. Her heart was her own again—the bees were gone, but she felt their absence lurch and sway in her. She missed them. Her tangled brown hair fell over her face, and her sheets were a disaster of folds and creases, and in the sheets was the disaster of her, fingerless, her face a nightmare, half-healed welts reddening her skin and sure to scar, but she could not feel them, could not care about them. She could not even risk breakfast before this, before this act she could not bear to delay, to risk losing the fire in her to speak through five thousand miles of wire to a sad-looking man with hair like fit-ful sunshine.

The phone rang on the other end, that strange European tone. A man's voice, bleary, tired, slurry, answered.

"Ciao?"

"Ludovico, it's me, it's me," she cried, laughing again, unable to stop.

"*Chi e questo?*"

"November, Ludovico, it's November Aguilar. Do you re-member?"

His voice sharpened immediately, tightening into panic. "*Oh, Christo, Christo, non parlo Inglese! Sono un tal sciocco!*"

*Oh, God,* November thought. *Of course it's easy there, of course all those people, from all those places, they have to speak to each other, somehow, it's managed there, but here…*

"Ludovico," she said slowly, sure it wouldn't help, "You said Caracalla. Caracalla. Just tell me when. Just say a day. Monday, Tuesday, Wednesday. Thursday, Friday. Saturday. Sunday. Say one."

There was a long pause, and November thought she could feel him struggle to push himself through the telephone line as she did, under the Atlantic, with all the bony, luminous deep-water fish.

Finally, his tortured voice escaped into the ether: "*Domenica. Domenica.* Sunday. *Mezzogiorno. Mi dispiace.* I am sorry. Sunday. Caracalla."

------

A plane, in the end, was as easy as a raft. November wore a green dress, though she could not decide if she meant it as a gesture aimed at distant Casimira or the nearby Green Wind, bundled against the frozen cities past the clouds. She did not see the shanties of the Six Winds outside her little submarine-small window, no spires of cirrus sunsets or broad pavilions of blue ice, but she allowed herself, considering everything, to think that perhaps they really were there, invisible, bustling, raucous. Like bees, little winds, little breezes in a great pearly hive. After all, Weckweet had been there. Must have been there. Casimira knew the name. Her father had been right. He had pulled out a card from a catalogue and—chance beyond chance—he had been right. Everything in the world had its place. Even November.

She had opened the hives that morning, and the bees had not flown out, but stayed sleepily in their droning, buzzing palaces. They would go when they pleased, they were not hers. Her bees waited for her, and she flew toward them, as fast as she could.

Of course people stared at her. The stewardess was careful not to touch her, and she was questioned as to her communica-bility. She had almost laughed at that, it seemed richly hilarious to her. But she was really and truly demoniac these days, her body scored with healing stings, her fingers gone, her face a swollen black mass. She kept the hood of her jacket up and smiled apologetically at the children who were jealously herded away from her. *Don't worry*, she wanted to say, *it's not catching, not like that, anyway.* But she remained silent.

———

Caracalla was a bathhouse. Or had been. A stately ruin, old brick and long grass now, crumbled arches, stairs fallen into walls and mushroomy hillocks. It was on the outskirts of Rome, a city November had never seen till now, a city full of light that seemed palpable, that seemed flesh. Everything in Rome had taken on the color of that sunlight, everything was half-golden, one half or the other, a pervasive gold quietly conquering all, having learned lessons from the stones. Everything was so old, so old, torn down and rebuilt and renamed a dozen times. She had read on a tourist's plaque that the cold, courteous marble of St. Peter's Basilica was quarried from the old Forum, and it had made her inexplicably sad, that she had looked at the mammoth church the day before and known nothing of where it had come from, what it had been before. Cities built out of cities. All of them, built out of each other. Torn down, etched out, and built over again, without revealing a whisper of their old selves. Palimpsests. Manuscripts scratched away and rewritten, over and over. November smiled to herself, walking through the stony streets.

Sunday, as is its nature, was slow in coming, but it found her eventually, nosed her out with its beatific muzzle, and found her sitting in the seedy grass of Caracalla, waiting, her heart racing itself in circles around nothing. *These walls once had pipes in them, steaming water gurgling up and down,* she thought, *and now they are so dry. In magnanimous retirement from the business of human purity.* But November liked the idea of sitting in a place that was once covered in water. It felt permanent, peaceful. She felt she could still be cleaned here, with the grass and the stone, that they could grind anything away from her and leave her whole.

Ludovico was long in coming, or at least she felt that he was. He came walking around a crumbled red wall, looking just as he had before, an intractable reader's bent posture, a shy man's gait. She felt as though she had met him a thousand times already, had felt that woman's mouth under his, had felt the paws and claws on him at the church, had heard the screams at the races. She wanted to hold her arms out to him. She ached to do it.

But Ludovico was staring. She had known he would stare. She did not look like this there, in her fine dress and her corona of bees. There, November was full of light. The venom of the bees glowed in her. Here she was just a woman in her thirties with a bad dye job and a green winter dress, her nails chewed, her fingers gone, her welts half-healed, leaving tracks across her body like premature wrinkles, like a burn victim. And her face, as though the city had struck her. She tried to smile under that stare, but she knew what she looked like, and though she had planned this so carefully, she did not think now that he would touch her.

"Hello," he said. His accent was gnarled and barbed, and she knew in a moment he had practiced the word in a mirror all week.

He sat next to her, and the sun ringed his thin hair. He looked like a saint to her, with that golden disc behind him, such a serious face, such gentle eyes and gaunt cheeks.

They said nothing. They could not, they had no tongue between them. The air between their mouths thickened and crackled, but neither had the blades to pierce it. They sat thus, beneath the towers of brick, the old, broken city, looking at each other and saying nothing, and November felt it was ridiculous, that she had come so far, and had nothing to offer but her wounds.

And then Ludovico ducked his head a little and sought her mouth, and finding it, would not let it go. He clasped her hand in his, the wounded one, the one Clara could not look at, and he kissed her with a wolfish need, groaning into her with such force she felt she had stolen his breath.

*You felt it*, she thought, *when all these things were done to me. Is that why you do not care?*

But he already had her tight around the waist, and tears wet both their faces, water again flowing in that dried-up place, and he called her name over and over, morphed strangely in his mouth, but her name nonetheless. He suckled at her breasts like a child, and she bit his shoulder lightly, catlike, whispering his name, too, the only words they knew. The only words in the world. He lifted her against the half-wall of the old caldarium, clumsily, for an intractable reader is not a strapping man, and she winced—she had not been ready, but she did not care, and he did not. It was a virgin's hurt; too much too soon, and she did not mind that. November tilted her face to the sky, and the sun washed her bare, washed her clean with its great old hands. His body leapt up into hers, pressing against her core as though it was the skin of a drum that he could break, and let loose such strange songs. She laughed again: *there is a list of things necessary for happiness*.

Ludovico cried out like a maddened sparrow when he came, as though he had broken, vanished, leaving such feathers in her, drifting slowly down to her bones.

# Kausia and Ossification

**As on the banks of many famous rivers,** there is a small, dreary maritime museum on the Albumen, near where the shallows become swamps and those particular folk who own not grand ships but small, sweet boats never meant for fishing, but for flying dearly-bought scarlet sails and hoisting golden-skinned girls into the wind, store their treasured craft in the winter. In addition to the museum's prodigious collection of prehistoric trivia and supplementary material, at least sixteen new varieties of dust were brought into being, catalogued, and annotated within its poor, sagging walls.

No traveling exhibits visit this place; the few glass cases and heavy iron frames have been here since before Oduvaldo, the current curator, began his tenure, and will be here when he passes the keys to his daughter Maud, who with her first giggling, gurgling words admonished her mother into silence. The long and distressing history of the white river is captured, boxed, and made small within this place, made to sit up and do tricks for the half-dozen or so visitors that it is proud to boast each year.

There is a photograph on the north wall—but how can it be a photograph? Yet it is, black and white, faded beyond any reasonable verisimilitude, and certainly someone spilled tea on it one hundred years ago, two hundred. Its frame is lead, hung with fishing weights in a previous curator's attempt at festive decoration. It shows, as if from the air—but how can it? How can this angle ever have been possible in a world without airplanes, how can anyone have photographed this thing?—a broad, flattened circle on a vast, muddy plain full of twisted tamarisk trees and mammoth, antediluvian ferns. High, vicious mountains ring the savannah, and the sun is feeble between their peaks. The circle is enormous, and nothing grows within it. There are faint lines criss-crossing the circle—ah, but they must be creases, accordion folds, some crude soul must have mishandled this fragile thing! Your credulity can be stretched only so far! The lines are no more than spidery streaks where one sort of mud becomes another. But they remind you of something, of marked skin and maps. They spoke from the center of the plain like a wheel, and the center is a black space, like a hole dropping down through the earth and out again, and the tamarisks seem to lean in to peer at nothing at all.

The card beneath it, which was once handwritten, and is now neatly letter-pressed with inhabited initials and other unnecessary flourishes, reads:

*The Plain of Palimpsest, Seen from a Great and Unknown Height.*

There is no date. There could not possibly be a date. It is surely a fake, and not even a clever one, as photography is hardly an ancient art. Of the half-dozen annual visitors, at least four angrily accuse Oduvaldo of playing them for fools. He sits placidly in his great felt chair, crosses his mottled mule-legs, and smokes his churchwarden with satisfaction. He knows nothing of archeophotography and does not care to—the picture was in the museum when his grandfather was young, and that is enough for him.

In the glass cases various items rest on faded velvet—a primitive tattoo needle, coins of indeterminate age and vaguely Asiatic appearance, a street sign from some early local settlement, the word *Thoa* large and still clear, if faded nearly to the color of the wood. And there is a remarkable variety of anchors, one artifact that comes easily to the curdled lowlands of the Albumen. There is a large and colorful mural of the great naval battle of Kausia Shallows—Casimira's green galleons explode with oily abandon, showering the beached and wretched wooden frigates defending this very spot with a vicious rain of glistening spiders. It is garishly colored in a school of art long out of favor, but its very gaudiness lends it gravitas. There are three musket balls and five desiccated spiders, their innards smashed and molten, arranged in an elegant star-shape on a threadbare velvet pedestal below it.

Oduvaldo is content with his life. He served his time in the army, he feels justified in his contentment. Maud has labeled all her toys and the silverware as well with small, hand-printed placards, and he is confident in her inheritance. He has no secrets, save the bits of chocolate he smuggles into every drawer in the museum, so that after lunch, and coffee, and his churchwarden, he can slide a black square into his mouth, close his eyes, and let it melt on his tongue as the sun fades his artifacts with gentle, inexorable affection.

———

Oleg huddles under what he understands, but does not care to know, is the Kausia Bridge. Angry, leviathan cockerels sneer down at him as a diffident rain begins to take an interest. The old man had not liked the look of him, and when he touched one of the musket balls, the old beast had silently, furiously, shoved him out of the door and into the first creamy puddles of the river. He wants to see that photograph again. He knuckles rain out of his eyes and squints at the current, at the towns across the water, at the lanterns on fishing boats still hoping for koi at this hour.

Miserable in one city, miserable in another. Oleg hunches against the gracefully arching underside of the bridge and turns up his collar. He has seen movies with men like him in them, turning up their collars against the rain, made wretched by women, beautiful in their gruff, cigarette-studded despair. He is not beautiful now if he ever was, he knows. He is a ghost, and it is not as pleasant as he had thought. Lyudmila was always so even-tempered, and the land of the dead, when she spoke of it, seemed to him a sensible and well-ordered place, full of all the sorts of things lands and nations ought to have, save that they are populated with people like his sister, with awful, unblinking gazes and unflinching faithfulness. Instead, he is cold and unhappy, and alone. He cannot find Lyudmila no matter how many impossible creatures he confronts. And it rains in the land of the dead, or whatever this place is; it rains and old men kick him out of shabby little shops.

A fish flops in the frothy pale water, its orange tail sweeping up and slapping thickly down again. Oleg scowls at it. He will not find her. She does not want to be found. Mila's river is deep and she is a strong swimmer. She ought to be, by now.

"I'm sorry!" he screams to the river. "Come back!"

But she does not, and he knows, now that his head has cleared itself with small and shameful ritual, that it is because he does not deserve it. He has not made himself worthy, in this place, of this Lyudmila. It was all right that he had kissed her—she was not his sister, not really, and even so ghosts had no morality. But he had hurt her, and whatever the red stuff so like blood had been, he should not have spilled it. If one has the power, he thought, to make ghosts bleed, one must be careful with it, so careful.

He hears footsteps behind him, and whirls, expecting the usual city villainy—a knife, a gap-toothed lunatic. But it is just a sorrowful-looking man with glasses, soaked to the bone, his blue sweater leadened by rain. A carriage glides smoothly away above them, and Oleg blinks, baffled.

"Are you Oleg Sadakov?" the man says.

"Yes, why?"

"My name is Ludovico Conti. I came to find you."

"I don't want to be found," he snaps. But the man looks familiar, instinctively familiar, like one's own hand.

"Don't you remember?" Ludovico says softly, his voice all but blown into the clouds. "The frog-woman. The ink. The girl with blue hair. I know I'm not memorable, but . . ."

Oleg blinks again, his mind scrambling to assemble itself into a shape capable of understanding what he is being offered.

"The one with the bee stings sent me. Her name is November. She . . . she has *access*. To everything, it seems like. Anyway, I'm meant to tell you how to find us, in the real world, or, rather, the other world. I don't think it's any more real, not really . . . I don't suppose you enjoy medieval literature?"

Oleg shakes his head dumbly.

"Well, there's a book, like an encyclopedia. It's called the *Etymologiae*. And it's full of impossible things, really impossible, like griffins and phoenixes, right alongside ants and turtles and cities in Christendom. And I think this is like that. Palimpsest and the real world. An impossible beast sitting next to a possum. Or something like that."

"Why do I need to find you?"

Ludovico looks up from under his lashes, as though he is afraid to give voice to what he knows.

"It would appear that is how we come here. Permanently. Emigration, you understand? The people we came with, if we can find them in the daylight, we can, somehow, be here for good, for all the time."

Oleg reels. His heels slip in the beige mud, rendered impossibly silky and rich by the milky river. He sits down heavily in it, neither knowing nor caring.

"No," he whispers. "I don't want to come here. Permanently. Forever. It's fine for people with *access* and green carriages. But I work in restaurants and hide under bridges. I hurt her and she'll never come back here. But maybe, in the real world—and it is more real, it has to be, it has to be—she'll come home, and forgive me, and it will be all right again."

"Who do you mean?"

"My sister. Lyudmila. Only . . . she's not really my sister here. She's like her, but she isn't. She's a . . . I think she said she's a Pecia."

Ludovico laughs, and it is a nervously genuine thing. He is warm, all of the sudden, in familiar territory. His laugh reverberates against the dark, wet stones, and the cockerels scowl on.

"Pecia? That means . . . well, I mean, it was a thing they used to do, when that book I mentioned was written. Instead of copying out enormous volumes they split it into pieces and sent it out to novices for copying. The originals were exemplars, the copied pieces were *pecia*. So I get it, actually, I get what you're trying to say. She's a copy. Someone made a copy for you."

"Well, I was rude to it. Her. And it left me, it jumped into the river and I don't know how to find it again. I have no interest in this place without her. So you'll have to get on without me."

Ludovico lays his head on his shoulder and contemplates Oleg. Oleg is defiantly self-conscious, he knows he must look horrid, and his sneer of masked desperation has very likely turned his face into a small gargoyle.

"Shall we find her, then, you and I?" Ludovico says simply, as though offering to take him to dinner. "The river is vast, and if she went into it we may find her. If we are stalwart. And worthy."

Ludovico holds out his hand, an oversized and graceless thing, and it is a long moment before Oleg takes it.

"I hope you don't have any qualms about stealing boats," says Ludovico, and they move into the rain, the shallows, the curdling, splashing river. They pull clear the lines of a canopied summer ship with long, upturned ends sporting small wooden lynx-heads on either end. The canopy is probably blue when the sun shines, it is now a sodden, ugly black, its fringe gray instead of spangled. They are quiet; they are unseen. Ludovico gamely oars them onto the high, boisterous current, and Oleg slumps against a long box of frill-skirted children's swimming garments and fishing poles.

The moon shows hesitantly through the clouds and hides again, blushing furiously.

"We're in Rome, Oleg: 50 Via Manin Daniele. Find us. Please come."

# THREE

# THE GIRL BEHIND BRIARS

Hester was gone. It was three days past now. She cried—Oleg remembered, as through a screen, her crying.

"I'm finished with this," she said. "It's too much. I am not a very good person, in the end. I can't watch you–" she had clutched the wall as though it could clutch her back, "—with *them*. I can't watch this thing happen. It is so ugly, so very ugly."

And she had gone. Oleg had thought once or twice in the intervening time that she might have hurt herself, her eyes were so red, so whipped and worn when she left, but he didn't have enough blood in him to fuel worry. He had not known her so very long. She was not a Princess of Cholera. She was not one of his people. There can be no real love between strangers.

Oleg had stumbled, painfully, on feet that had forgotten they were feet, to the grocer's twice now, bereft of Hester and her diffident care. The juice of a real orange was so bright it burned his throat. He tried to eat bread, and a little meat, but it was too much for him. He could stand only cold, fatty soup from the deli which was not, after all, mythical, and water.

His bed had dried, or frozen. It didn't matter which; he slept on it, dead weight, mute, ashen.

And on the fourth day, she came to him.

She sat on the edge of his bed in her little jacket with the fur-lined hood. There were great dark circles under her eyes and her lips had no color at all. There were dried tracks of spittle or vomit on her cheeks, and she stared at him hollowly, her knees drawn up to her chin.

But it was not his Lyudmila. It was Hester, and her tongue was swollen in her mouth, her speech slurred.

"Why are you here?" he asked fearfully, pulling up his sheet to protect himself.

"I don't want to be."

"Then go away. I don't want you."

"I did notice that."

They stared at each other in silence, two wild animals who have caught each other's eye in the wood, and neither sure which is the less frightful.

"Are you okay?" Oleg finally whispered, his voice faint and weak. Hester narrowed her eyes and swallowed.

"I'm not feeling so well."

"Me neither."

Hester smiled then, a leering, half-hinged smile. "I think we could have been lovers, you know, real lovers, the kind that make coffee for each other and read the same books. We have so much in common. Both of us dying of despair. Murdered by a whole city."

Hester crawled into bed with him, pulling his sheets up over her cold shoulder. She put her arms around his neck. "Remember that story you told me?" she whispered, her voice a little slurry and strange. "About the land of the dead? Well, I have one for you. Once upon a time a girl swallowed all of her pills at once because she wanted to stop dreaming, and the angel she thought would save her turned out to be a crazy sack of shit. Do you like this story? I like it. It has a good ending." She kissed his cheek, and ever after he would feel the mark. Her voice softened. "Do you think, if Columbus had stood on the bow of his ship, looked at the New World and understood everything to come, all the disease and death and betrayal, all the ugliness, all the blood—do you think he would have embraced it, called it paradise? Or do you think he would have run home as fast as he could? I just want to go home."

Her eyes were so big in the dark of his bedroom, like locks, opening all the way to the Atlantic, and beyond, to the salt sea of the dead and all the dark islands there.

Hester turned away from Oleg and threw up onto the cold floor. He put his hand on her back and held her hair as it kept coming, all her grief, all her loneliness, everything, and he could not stop it. Her body heaved under his hands, determined to live, determined to expel all that was not living. She sobbed, and bent double over the bedside again, and through her spine something passed between them, more intimate than semen, a communion of agony beyond themselves. Oleg knew in that moment he would remember that about Hester, long after he forgot what it was like to move inside her, he would remember holding back her hair as she retched her heart out onto his floor.

Hester left before he woke up, and Oleg knew that was the last he'd see of her. No one wants witnesses to their failures.

———

That morning Oleg managed an egg and felt triumphant about it. With the help of a second orange and a makeshift umbrella-cane, he managed an entire city block to check his bank accounts. He felt as though he stared into Hester's eyes again, dark and deep, and he leaned against the glassy, clean bank doors, to steady himself.

No one propped him up. His family here was gone. Lyudmila had left him, surely, permanently. His frozen bed was testament now to too many lost women. Only the Lyudmila in Palimpsest was left, alive and warm. A gift. He would find her there, he just had to follow the river—but not at this pace, too few nights strung together like loose beads. It was too slow.

If he didn't pay his rent, he had enough for a ticket to Rome.

If he bought a ticket to Rome, there was a possibility he would not have to be bothered with paying his rent. It seemed fair enough.

Except that he did not feel, at present, that he could make it to the airport. There was a rattle at the bottom of his lungs, like a shard of glass that each breath dislodged. He had slept for so long, such a desperate sleep, that he felt like the girl in the story, the girl behind briars, sleeping until she had throttled all the sleep in her, and waking to an empty castle full of ghosts. No part of him seemed entirely convinced it was awake.

Oleg withdrew his money, all he had, and closed himself into his room of locks and keys. He put the money in a neat stack on an ancient law-office lock with a little Libra sigil embossed in the brass.

He watched the money, to be sure it did not escape. The room smelled thickly of metal, a smell he had often found comforting, strong, impenetrable. Like him in no part. It was not a very large stack of money. But it was enough, he supposed. In the days when the gates of sleep were two, a gate of ivory and a gate of horn, they had put coins into the eyes of the dead to pay their passage across the wide, black river that separated the living from millineries and munitions factories. He had wondered, then, how the coins were translated from living to dead. The books were mum. How did it make the journey, the money of death, how was it expected to disappear here and reappear there? Was there a long road for them, too, down through mountains and up through rills—was it difficult? Was it harrowing? Did some of them give up, did some of them fall?

Lassitude and Languor

# Lassitude and Languor

THE WAR ENDED on the day of First Midwinter twelve years ago. Winter is long in Palimpsest, and summer is longer, and the scholars of calendars are clever and formidable souls. Winter is divided into four seasons—the Winter of First Frost, the Winter of Branches, the Winter of Snow, and the Winter of Mud. The First Midwinter, the Midwinter of Frost, when there are still late and lazy fruits to be had and ciders brewed in diamond tankards, has always been a festival day, the Festival of the White Fox, the Festival of the New Rime, the Festival of the Swept Hearth. Like all things in Palimpsest, its name has been erased and rewritten many times.

The red leaves were encased in ice and silver on the day the treaty was signed, on this very spot, where you stand. It is nowhere in particular. It is nowhere special. There is no commemorative sculpture; there is no marker with helpful information to guide the sightseer. The river pounds the cliffs below the streetside, and there is a quiet bakery where a widow named Klavdia weeps into her dough and produces delicate, frosted cakes of tears and hollyberries. She still makes the winter cider, and her tankards are plain.

Casimira wore mourning red that day, and her face was streaked with tears no one could have expected as she signed the broadsheet. Her ships in the harbor below flew red sails and red flags. General Ululiro, her mottled blue shark's head glaring pitilessly, unbeaten, at Casimira's bent green scalp, stood for the army, signed for the parliamentary forces.

She was so young, obscenely young, she could not be more than twenty. And yet, she had broken Ululiro's spear, the war was done, her single, unassailable desire triumphant.

Do not be cold to her, Ululiro, daughter of a noble lamplighter, who danced at the gaslit balls of her youth with such frenzy! The simple truth is, Casimira wanted it more than you despised it, and I am a wanton thing—I answer the want which is keenest.

The frozen leaves fell one by one onto the dais, shattering silently as they alighted. There was no brass band, and no one spoke. Most present were beyond the capability.

In the treaty were provisions for the hundred thousand veterans left maimed and irrevocably mute throughout the city. As is the way of things, their sacred places and comforts have dwindled to a lonely strip of shoreline and a polite nod whenever they are passed in the street. In the meticulous paragraphs are also concessions as to an area of quarantine, and this is that place, this wooden disc, raised slightly above the street, where once the queen of insects and a shark stood side by side and watched the leaves fall.

———

Though most would prefer not to discuss it, this is where immigrants, permanent residents, once entered the city. When they come again, if they come again, who knows where they may arrive? But long ago they woke here, raw and naked and bleeding, for the ways here were hard, and they exacted their costs with regret and determination.

Klavdia has cakes for them, if they should come again. She fought for their sake, at the loss of an eye and a leg at the knee. Her other leg is a knotted, muscled bear-foot, covered by a time-softened apron. Each morning she sets out cakes and pies to cool on her sill, seeping with red juice. She watches the dais. She is quiet and cradled in her faith that nothing is ever in vain. Casimira told her they would come again.

———

Ludovico steers their boat through the evening. It is bright and cool, the rain passed, the stars like white and open mouths in the sky. He looks to the young man still hunched over by the bench, watching the milky current bubble by. He wants to say to him: *My wife's name is Lucia, and she is here too, and not a copy, she herself. She does not want me. But I cannot stop running after her, as though I am a rabbit and cannot slow down or my little heart will burst. I understand this thing you do. And there is a woman sleeping on Nerezza's hard couch who will understand it too, even if you cannot say a word to her. She is like an ibex, who is clever and wily and strong on the thinnest and highest of peaks. Their fur is like the moon, but if you startle one, they leap with abandon to the earth, where they land gracefully upon their horns, safe and whole, and look never upon you again.*

*But no,* Ludo corrects himself. *She is like a human woman. She is like an anchoress chained to herself. And when I looked on her, despite every bruise, I could not remember the name of my wife.*

But he finds he cannot say these things, he does not know how to say them to a young stranger in such pain his face is a weal, any more than he knew how to tell November that she was like an ibex or an anchoress. So he says nothing, steering south, and it is not difficult. Every hour on the hour, he kneels by Oleg and whispers in his ear:

"50 Via Manin Daniele."

Oleg has begun to nod when he speaks, and Ludovico takes this as a victory. They pass below high bluffs, and he does not begin to guess what has occurred there, upon this harbor or those cliffs. It is pleasant, bucolic to him.

But you and I know, and we may appreciate, as the two men glide by, what has transpired to allow their passage.

———

Lock 19, where the Albumen dips downstream, following a course toward the center of the city, is normally staffed by a bored old mariner, picking his teeth with baleen and writing secret shanties about the beauty of land, the tilling of soil, the baking of bread. A small office houses the more-or-less interchangeable lockmaster—they all keep a potted basil plant, for the scent, and a white cat, for the company. It may well be the same plant and the same cat, from lockmaster to lockmaster. No one can be certain. The lock console gleams—polished, upstanding cherry wood and brass. But today there is no old mariner with a cheerful beard chewing basil leaves. Today there a woman with the head of a shark is waiting, and with her the sort of nameless, faceless men who mean to do nameless, faceless things for the sake of their mistress. Behind them a woman with hair like eelskin is staring at her shoes—she has done what she feels is right, and we ought not to blame her.

———

Ludo pulls a heavy red rope to alert the lockmaster; a long horn sounds low and deep, vibrating in his teeth. Oleg peers over the edge of the boat through heavy rain as the cream of the Albumen drains from the lock, and their little boat descends, slowly, towards the lockhouse.

"Thank you," Oleg says. The rain seems to have wakened him, made him sharper, cleaner. "She's not your sister, I know you don't have to do this." He looks down at his hands. "She's not my sister, either. I know that. Really . . . I know that. But a copy is better than a world that doesn't contain her."

"You may not think so, but I do know what you mean, brother." Ludo smiles wanly; rain drips from the pleasure boat's awning, from his hair, from his glasses.

"Will it really work? If I come to Rome?"

"I think so."

Oleg frowns, staring at the lowering waterline. "And if one person says no, if one person thinks that this place is anything but paradise on a silver platter, no one gets to go. That's it, isn't it? If one person takes pills every night to keep themselves from dreaming, three people lose their tickets. Lose everything they want."

"Please don't say no, Oleg."

"Can you imagine what it would do to a person, to know that they were standing between three people and that marrow-deep, desperate need?" Oleg covers his mouth, shakes his head, but Ludo cannot share his private revelation, cannot know who he means.

A second horn sounds, and the great, scored walls of the lock rise above them, marble and quartz, old as amber. They drift toward the lockhouse, and there is a moment, just a moment, when Ludovico thinks he sees a shadow behind the boisterous green of a potted basil plant, the shadow of a flat, dark head, tossing back and forth behind the window. But it is nothing—of course it is nothing. No harm can come to him here.

The bow of their boat explodes in a shower of splinters.

Ludo and Oleg reel—the blast shattered the glass window of the lockhouse, and in the rain they can see the shark-headed woman and her servants, her gray-slick skin dull and peeling, her teeth yellow with age and neglect, her pupilless eyes exhausted, wild. Her clothes are brown and ragged, a general's uniform long since gone to moths. She points a ridiculous, old-fashioned blunderbuss at them, a shiny thing with a flared bell. One of the muscled young men at her side reloads it for her.

Behind the shark-headed woman stands Nerezza.

Ludo gapes. He cannot understand what is happening.

"Why? Nerezza, what are you doing?"

Nerezza will not look at him. She keeps her gaze on the shark-headed woman, and when she mumbles, the rain tramples her words—but Ludo can see her lips move: *You don't deserve it.*

The two men wade in and drag the boat to the lockhouse, where they lash it to the little dock and haul Ludo and Oleg out. The shark-headed woman is silent, but glances up at the door frame, beaten sea-wood, and seems to judge it fair.

"How can you do this, Nerezza? Are you going to watch them bleed us out? Are you content to make me into Radoslav?"

A fist cracks across Ludo's jaw. "Don't talk to her!" one of the men growls. Ludo's eyes roll—when they focus again he sees a huge face purpled in rage, with a line of freckles across the nose. The other one is missing an ear. "If you have to talk," Freckles growls, "you talk to Ululiro, and show some fucking respect."

"What's happening?" says Oleg, shaking, uncomprehending, looking from Nerezza to Ululiro to Ludo. "What are they doing?"

"They're Dvorniki." Ludo snarls. "Street-cleaners. They are going to cut our throats on the door jamb because we're immigrants."

Oleg opens his mouth and closes it. "Nice word for a mob," he mumbles.

Ludo grunts agreement. "They think it's magic. That it'll keep us all out. Or maybe they don't. Maybe they just think it's fun."

No-Ear doesn't see a difference. He wrestles Oleg to the floor, bashing his head against the door frame and jamming his chin up-ward, exposing his throat. Freckles pulls out a long, curved knife. He looks to Ululiro for confirmation. But Ululiro is watching Ludovico, and she does not move. She does not speak. *She is like the people in the church,* Ludo realizes. *A veteran. She was in the war. On the losing side, from the looks of it. Oh—oh. There is no was. She is in the war. This is the war.*

"Your uniform," Ludovico says gently, knowing his life hangs be-tween them like a thin curtain. "Were you a soldier?"

Ululiro nods.

"Not just a soldier. A general. Even … *the* general. *Generalissima.*"

Ululiro nods.

"You have to know this won't matter. Not really. If it's not us, it'll be someone else. We're coming. Someday, the roads will be full of us, and you'll have to watch us fall to our knees in rapture, in relief, you'll have to watch us grow old and bear children and hang hams in store windows, set our watches by our wives' hearts, drink coffee on sunny afternoons."

"General, let me cut that one's throat first, so he shuts his filthy mouth," Freckles barks.

Ululiro does not move. Ludovico does not stop.

"We're coming. The world is changing. And even if every door frame in Palimpsest runs red, someone will find a way." Ludo chuckles. "Do you know what a palimpsest is, Ululiro? It's vellum, parchment that has been written upon and then scraped clean, so that someone else can write on it. Can't you hear us? The sound of us scraping?"

"Ludo …" Oleg moans, his neck beading scarlet under the taut knife.

But Ludovico ignores him. He thinks of November's broken

hand, her fingers. What she gave up for safe passage. "But, General. If it has to be anyone, why not me? Why not us? Why not someone who is willing to become like you, who is willing to lose a thing he treasures for the sake of this city, for the sake of his friends?"

Ludo slowly extends his tongue. Rain spatters it; he lets it run.

"Take it," he says. "Take my voice as the toll of this lock. Take my tongue, and I will be silent, like you, like all of them. I will be a monument—better than all the rest because I will bear witness to your suffering. Folk will look at me, setting my watch, drinking my coffee, and they will say: *Ululiro snatched victory from her enemies after all. She got to choose. She chose the first one, and marked him as her own.* Everyone will know that you had a battle left in you, and bought one last joy in the name of the silent." Ludo was so close to Ululiro he could smell her fishy, acrid breath, seething between sharp, yellowed teeth. "Mark the frame with my blood, General. I will be silent forever in your name. An immigrant. A veteran. And it will be over."

Ululiro's throat worked beneath a ghastly scar that marked the join of her shark skin with her human body. She burned to speak and could not. Nerezza reached for her elbow, but the general slapped her away, seizing Ludovico's arm and stalking to the door frame, tossing her head from side to side as though swimming through deep ocean. Freckles and No-Ear backed away from her, pulling Oleg with them, spines suddenly straight with fear and love.

Ululiro snatched Freckles's knife and caught Ludo by the throat. She raised the blade, and with a soundless howl slashed through his tongue.

# THE KINGDOM OF HEAVEN

N erezza sat between November and Ludovico. Her face was a mess of flushed skin and tears. Ludovico shook to see her so, and looked to November to steady himself.

"I don't want to," Nerezza hissed in fluid, cultured English.

"You don't have to," November said softly. "But I am asking you."

"Why should this be easy for you? Why? It is not easy for me," she spat at Ludovico in Italian.

Agostino had taken Anoud to his house while the three of them talked—he had at first been delighted with November, and they had played the visitor's game of half-signed, half-remembered phrase-book slivers of the other's language. But Ludo had found himself suddenly jealous, and he did not know who he envied more. None of them were playful and dear with him. When Nerezza had finally returned home, however, and seen the shape of things, she had crumpled to the ground as though the steel strings which had held her all this time were slashed through and dashed against her walls.

"Get her out," Nerezza had begged, over and over. "Get her out. If we cannot have our Radya, he cannot have her. He *can't*."

November had gone to her and taken her in her arms. Ludo could see she was hardly more used to this than Nerezza herself, but she held Nerezza's dark head under her chin and rocked her, and sang softly to her, and Nerezza bore it. She bore it and did not protest, but her jaw clenched, she ground her teeth, nonetheless. They spoke to each other in English, and he did not understand them. But he had asked his eel-girl to translate, and the tears had come again.

Nerezza looked at the newcomer with black and glittering eyes. In the bald apartment light, November was even less impressive-looking than she had been at the baths, her scars deep, her mutilated hand undisguisable. And the mark on her face—what she must have borne, unable to hide herself as they could! She was a ruin of a woman, and as thus he found her calming, like the white-stoned forum.

Slowly, Nerezza began to nod, and he suspected it was because to look at November was to know it had not been easy for her, not in the smallest part, and Nerezza saw her own grief writ in blood and ink and scar tissue on the American woman's body. He saw November take a deep breath, and her hands trembled. Whatever she was saying was intricate, painful for her, and she was afraid of it. He longed to reach out and touch her face—would she, lithe ibex, leap from him to land on her horns and bounce up, bounding off into meadows he could not touch? Nerezza turned to him, not meeting his gaze.

"This is what she says, Ludo. If you can make sense of it, good luck to you. 'These are the folk who may pass into the kingdom of heaven: the grief-stricken, lovers, scholars of a certain obsessive disposition. Brute beasts. Women who have become as men and men who have become as women. Writers of books with long titles. Only those knights who have failed to touch the Grail. Industrious women. You, and I, and a boy named Oleg, and a girl with blue hair.'"

Nerezza was crying again. She turned to November, speaking rapidly, angrily, and all Ludovico could understand was the name Radoslav, repeated and repeated, desperately added to the list. But Ludo hardly heard Nerezza. He stared at November, her wet and hopeful eyes. She thought he would not understand. That he would think her words irrelevant. But he did know, he understood, for he had loved St. Isidore all his life, an encyclopaedist, a man whose intellect was confined in long, precise, radiant columns of text, illuminated lists which placed together circumscribed the world.

Nerezza looked back and forth between them, helpless and livid.

"Another one is coming," she hissed in Italian. "I heard her talking on the telephone. I hate you both, and I curse you, as well as I am able to curse anything. You blithely stumble into this, and in a few weeks you've done what I can never, never do. Do you understand? *Radoslav is dead.* None of us can ever go. Not ever. And it took us *years* to find each other. It took everything from us. Husbands, wives, jobs, children. You're like a rich man's son, who has earned nothing in his life and is given everything. I let you live in my house and you cover it with your shit. I hate you. I hate you." Her voice was even and furious, it did not hitch or break, and he could see the sparks of her eel-flesh grimly blue at her ears.

"Nerezza," November said, "Nerezza. Nerezza."

November kissed her reddened forehead. "I'm sorry," she whispered, over and over. "I'm sorry." And she kissed her mouth, her jaw, her ear, her neck, trying to kiss everything hard of her away, and if he had not felt the bees in her, if he had not heard them sing, he would not have understood how November,

broken and battered as she was, could have the courage to comfort the wildness, the bestial scream of Nerezza.

But Nerezza would not let herself be kissed. She was stiff
and cold, her body held tight and inviolable. She clamped her
eyes onto Ludo, full of bile and bitter loathing.

Then Nerezza's eyes shone, and suddenly she smiled. She
put her arms around November, never taking her gaze from
Ludo, and let herself warm, alight, feign ardor. Ludo shuddered. What had she hatched in that lightless heart?

Nerezza clung to November as the bee-stung woman
pushed the top of her own green dress down to her waist and
held her breasts out like St. Agatha, an offering. November
opened her eyes and caught his gaze over Nerezza's shuddering
body. Ludo could not tell if the shuddering was false or true.
She was whispering in Italian, too ashamed to be understood,
and Ludo knew the beekeeper could not hear it, and vowed to
explain it to her, when he saw her on the other side of night.

"Am I, November?" Nerezza was saying. "Am I among the folk
who are permitted to enter the kingdom of heaven? Tell me.
Tell me."

———

He left them then. He did not want to watch. He did not want
to see.

But he knew November now, he knew her, and she was his
Isidore, his Isidora, and he would tell her everything, everything he knew, everything engraved in his marrow, when all this
was done and they could speak, and drink together wine like
blood, through the starry night and into day.

# PART V:

## THE GREEN WIND

# In Transit,
## Westbound: 11:09

THERE IS A PLACE on the far western edge of Palimpsest where the tracks have fallen into disrepair. It is wild and sunny, furry with green wheat and snarling raspberry vines. An olive tree, some speculate, rooted out the rails, while others are certain that the nearby sheep are the culprits, that they gnawed at the tracks until they broke, and surely their owner ought to be held responsible for damages. No one has volunteered to take up the wig and adjudicate the issue, and so lonely, moth-bothered Oathusk Station has slid slowly and genteelly into disuse. It was not often frequented even in the first heady days of the transit system, and so few consider it a great loss, save, perhaps, for enthusiasts of the particular pastoral style of architecture employed in the station house, whose rosebud windows were once a mild source of pride.

The trains did not discover the breach in the tracks for some time. They were distracted, the season was not right for westbound travel, the Missal Line had gone into heat early for three years running—the life of a train is ever tossed by strange and chthonic tides. But as of late some few of them have begun to nose around Oathusk, sniffing the wind for news of the rosebud windows, of the black-faced sheep, of stationmasters gone to seed and drink. A train or two came quite close to the break, but reared in alarum and proceeded east into the comforting arms of the city once more.

There is concern, in the highest echelons of sport commuters, that a train might one day become bold enough to jump the tracks at Oathusk and escape Palimpsest altogether, into the wilds beyond and the mountains, through the wide farms and pastureland, and from thence who knows? Yet still others deride this idea as the worst sort of fancy: the trains are happy, they are loved, they are well-fed and well-mated. In the midst of debate, the tracks go unrepaired. The wheat bends the wind at Oathusk, and the stars watch the raspberries grow long.

———

The next carriage is empty. It is a long, vast stretch of new tatami mats, redolent and bright green, their ribbons black and gold. Sei cannot begin to count them. There is a slender station map like an ukiyo-e painting on one wall, and the room shakes like a carriage, but there are no benches, no rails. It is a place she knows and does not wish to.

"No," she groans. "I don't want to be here."

"But it is your home," the Third Rail says. Plenitude scratches at her neck encouragingly.

"I don't like it, I don't want it. I told you. I want to go to the next car. The rabbit said there were horses."

The Third Rail shakes her long head. She strides to the center of the room and Sei knows what will happen but she cannot bear it, she cannot bear this. "Why?" she yells at the Third Rail's back. "What purpose could this possibly serve?"

The Third Rail turns and seats herself in the great room, letting her unlined kimono pool out around her and smoothing her long hair into two flat planks. She reaches into her robes and withdraws an enormous book—it is swollen and waterlogged, and reedy bits of kelp and grass peek out from its pages like ribbonmarks. She opens it on her lap; lake-water splashes out. The Rail beckons Sei with sweetness, as if she is luring a cat from under the bed.

"No," Sei moans, but she is going to her, could never have done less than go to her.

"Imagine a book at the bottom of a lake," the Third Rail says.

"I told you not to say that. I don't like it."

"But I have gotten you the book. It was a very deep lake, frozen in places, high at the top of the world. I held my breath for a very long time."

"You're lying. There was never any book. My mother was crazy. She said those things because she was sick."

Yet Sei inches closer. She is watching the space between the Third Rail's breasts, white and smooth. The book is open; its pages are blue. The Third Rail opens her arms to take Sei in and cuddles her against her hip, pointing her long finger to the pages so that Sei can read.

"This is to say: I will hold nothing back from you, with either hand. All things, at the bottom of all lakes."

Sei rubs her throat; it is tight and thin and she wants to run from this, but she is the Sei-fish again, twelve years old, blue and separate from the other fish, and she does not know the piscine joy they find in this volume, but she wants to, so very much.

She peeks at the page. *Just a glance,* she thinks. *And then I will end this. It is obscene, and I can shame her into stopping it.*

The book reads:

*I really was born in a train station, you know. My mother went into labor, and I came so fast. I was always too fast. Too soon. She took me home, and I grew up, just a little girl, my head full of books, my hands full of calligraphy brushes. I had dreams like some children have freckles. And my sisters made fun of my name.*

*I married your father as soon as I could manage it, and he left me so often. I was so alone. I had only books and dreams and brushes then. And often I slept—but it was not like really sleeping. The world went black, and it went light again much later. My head hurt as though there was another baby inside it, pushing with her little hands to get out. The walls seemed so close, so close! The whole house was like a gag in my mouth, I could never breathe, and I could not leave it—your father could come home at any moment, and if I were not there, he would never come home again, I was certain.*

*You do not know that I went away when you were very small. I was not even finished nursing you. I went away to a place in the country where they folded me up into a very white bed and put a piece of wood in my mouth and arced blue electricity through me. I remember that it was blue, like the light at the bottom of a lake. I held it all within me, all of it, all that light, I would not let the smallest bit out of me. I held it as though I was made to hold it, as though I was a third rail and all the world's tracks laid around me—it was mine to move the lightning, mine to bear the white heat and the burning. I am sure they were impressed. They knew they could trust me with it, they gave me more and more, so that I could keep it safe for them, and I know you saw it when I came home, saw how incandescent I was, saw the light sizzling in the roots of my hair.*

Sei looks up, her tears naked and hot as blood. The Third Rail is bleeding, thick trails of it, hot as tears. The space between her breasts is gouged open, and her blood pools on the already sodden book, stains the hems of her kimono.

"Please stop. Please, please."

The Third Rail puts her hand to the bottom of her red mask and lifts it, and of course it is Usagi beneath it, Usagi-mother with such sad eyes, her face wan and worn, her lips shaking.

"*The floor of heaven, Sei, is laced with silver train tracks, and the third rail is solid pearl. And they carry each a complement of ghosts, who clutch the branches like leather handholds, and pluck the green rice to eat raw.*"

"But this is not heaven. It isn't."

"No, Sei. But it is enough. For you. Everything for you."

"*Why?* What do you want?"

"We want to fly. We want to leave the tracks, we want to roam and graze and howl at the mountains. We want to escape the world of our mother and our father, who pretend not to know we live and move and desire under the earth, just as they do. Don't you want to escape your mother?"

Sei stares at the blood on her lap. She is not listening.

"I sat with you for hours, and there was so much blood. It took so long. It took so long."

"It takes a long time to die. Even if it is quick, it takes a long time. It was hard to leave you—I think that is what you want me to say. That I did not want to leave my child. But it takes a long time. Your heart must stop, and your breath, and then the small things that you did not know kept you alive, books and dreams and brushes. And then you must walk a very long way in the dark, through the mountains, and there are pine trees there, and lanterns, and you can see before and behind the long trail of lanterns winding up and down the mountain, before you and behind."

"You're not really my mother. I know you're not."

"I am as good as your mother. I can be your mother, and you can be mine. It will be like a game. I remember your mother. I was built to remember. I was built out of remembering."

Sei looks into eyes that could be Usagi's, that could be her own sad, confused expression, with all those tigers at her ears. She puts her hand to her mother's breast, the ruin of tissue and blood there, the wound like a heart.

"Lie below me," Sei says, remembering her grandmother beneath the weepholes and her mother beneath the earth and she herself so far from the sun. "And I will watch over you."

Beneath her palm the slash of her mother's wound vanishes, as though the skin there had never dreamt of tearing.

Sei sinks into the arms of the red-masked ghost, and the Rail holds the blue-haired girl tightly, with a love like light. The Third Rail rocks her, and Plenitude curls up between her arm and her still-flat belly, and soon enough begins to snore inkily.

"There is not so very far left, not so very much left of the train," the Third Rail says. "Before we open the conductor's cabin and pay our respects, tell me, my Sei, my little fish, my child: is there someone who would come looking for you?" Her red voice is suddenly softly accusing.

"No, of course not. No one knows me here."

"We knew you."

"That's different. There's no one, I promise."

"And yet she is here." The Third Rail kisses Sei on her shoulder and purses her pale lips. "Tell us. Give us a command. Tell us to open our doors to her, or keep them shut as a mouth and leave her gasping on the platform. Guide us, tell us what it is right to do."

If Sei tries—and it is becoming harder and harder—but if she tries to feel the others whose phantom senses float up under her own, under her tongue, under her fingers, under her feet, if she tries to feel them, she can just discern the smell of a train station, of the oily tracks, of the underground.

"Let her come," Sei says, and falls asleep on her mother's lap.

# WISHES TO THE TREES

I t's over," Sei said, folding her hands in her lap. They sat, squinting in the bright sunlight, at a restaurant wedged between two Buddhas.

"What does that mean?" Yumiko said, slurping her mushroom soup. "It's not like you're the first. Get an abortion."

"It means," Sei breathed deeply, ignoring her, "that I think there is no one left in the Floor of Heaven who is new for me. I'm not . . . like you. When I am there, I am always on my train, always with the folk there, and they barrel through under the city at such a speed—I've had to chew through Kyoto at the velocity of a new whore just to keep up. I am tired, and there is no one left. It's time for me to go home. To visit my mother's grave. To see if I still have a job. To figure out what to do about the baby. To find others, if they are there."

Yumiko frowned. "An abortion would be better."

"I'm not saying it wouldn't."

Yumiko shook her head. "You don't understand. I said you weren't the first. Occupational hazard, you know? It happens, kind of a lot. It happened to me. I had a son, about two years ago."

"You never told me this before."

"My father kicked me out. I come from a small town—girls don't turn up pregnant there, except, you know, when they do. But I'd been coming into the city for years by then, and he sent me back there, to sleep with demons and drink myself to death, he said." Yumiko saluted Sei with a glass of yellow wine. "I didn't know how it would be. I had my baby, because I had some misplaced idea about the sanctity of motherhood, and I was young enough that I figured it would be more or less like having a doll. I had it, in the back room of the Floor of Heaven, between the wineglasses and the bar rags. My son was covered in streets, these long black lines from his scalp to his feet—but it wasn't Palimpsest. It was someplace else. I think it was someplace new. I've never heard of a street he had on him, and anyway they didn't look the same. They were long and straight and even, a grid. It was someplace *else*. And he looked at me, just turned his baby head and very clearly said: *I want to go back*. I screamed for a week. He was in me all that time, dreaming and traveling and learning, and I couldn't bear to have him look at me."

"What happened to him?"

"The owner and his wife adopted him. Thank god. I told them never to bring him there, bring him up to be a priest, hope he dies a virgin." Yumiko took a long, shaky drink of her wine. "So, you see, you're not breeding. You're not having a child. *It* is. Palimpsest. An abortion would be better."

Sei swallowed hard. She couldn't answer. Couldn't imagine that child, couldn't imagine her own.

"And I don't want you to go," Yumiko said. "I won't say I love you, I think we're both beyond that. But it's good to have a friend who knows what I know. Peaceful. Who never doubts that there are wonders outside this city. Isn't it peaceful to know what we know, and know it together?"

"Of course it is."

"Then stay. Stay a few days more. Pray for your mother here. There are more shrines and temples than you could count in a lifetime. One of them is good enough for her."

Sei scratched her cheek and stared off into the bustling street. It was peaceful to know, and yet to know meant that the volume, the resolution, the brightness of Kyoto was dimmed and fuzzed, and she could not pick out faces here anymore, because they were not long or red.

"My mother killed herself when I was fourteen," Sei said slowly. "She stabbed herself in the chest with a kitchen knife and crawled into our tatami room to die. I found her when I came home from school. Do you know how long it takes someone to die from a wound like that? Hours and hours. More hours than I could count then or now."

"Sei . . ."

"And I never called a doctor. I'd like to say she begged me not to, but she didn't. She just looked at me, she just waited to die, and didn't pull out the knife, didn't move. She talked about the tigers, when she talked. I held her for hours and I let her die and all I said was: *Go, go, please just go.* Which shrine do you suggest to purge that, Yumiko? What god do you think will forgive me?"

"I don't know. I know you're not her, whatever you think."

"I talk about crazy things and abandon my child."

Yumiko took Sei's hand, laced her fingers through it, shaking her head all the while. "Please: stay, stay, please just stay."

The late afternoon light played in Sei's hair, turning it turquoise and black, like the light at the bottom of a lake, like the light in hidden places.

———

Two women stood on a wide pavilion of crushed white stones and high orange pillars, one with blue hair, and one with a blue skirt. Hand in hand they sought out the row of heavy bronze bells with their ponderous red ropes. They clapped their hands and rang the bells for the soul of Amaya Usagi; they gave their coins to the gods and stood in the shadowy alcoves in contemplation of statues with dead eyes. They tied wishes to the trees, and did not tell each other what they wished for—there was no need.

They drank silver sake and fell asleep in each other's arms, without kisses, without farewells.

# 77th and Ambuscade

**THE ZOO THAT ONCE SPRAWLED** over Ambuscade Street is empty. The cages are still there, and pigeons have found them acceptable housing, being full of slow, fat lizards and flies like blackberries. But the animals have gone. There are kiosks whose awnings were once gaily gold, and sold frozen green apples and phials of crystal honey—but they are empty now, and the spilled seeds have long sprouted so high that each of them is a small grove, and if children ever ventured here any longer, they would find the apples so cold, so cold and sweet.

At night, the moon sweeps through the paths like a tumbleweed. The stars sit on the benches and smoke corncob pipes and throw petrified peanut shells at the ghosts of giraffes.

There is no mynah bird left to tell you what happened here.

But I will tell you, for I feel we have become friends, you and I. Casimira, beloved of my soul, fought with such weapons as she had: vermin, and insects, and scurrying creatures. Her cannon, her artillery, her cavalry were all these things—oh, the days when the rabbits of Casimira were larger than horses! When her elephantine crows soared high, casting their gargantuan shadows over whole districts! Was there ever a general like her, ever a creature who dared more? How could I not love her? How could I not give myself to her?

The opposition could not bear her strength, and her soldiers seemed to be endless, as ants and bees always seem to be. They felt, Ululiro felt, that they must become as she was if they were to save the city from her green hands.

So the Ambuscade Zoo was confiscated, cordoned off, and the animals in it brought to a building like a palace, but not a palace, where they were penned up, frightened, shaking, cats with cats and fish with fish and like with like. Ululiro herself underwent the procedure, as a gesture of loyalty, and I did love her then, too, in that moment. But my heart was given, given already. Ululiro wept as they cut into her, and into the shark, and her blood is yet upon the door frame of that palace which is not a palace, indelible as the stone.

Thus the soldiers of the opposition became as Casimira: innumerable beasts, stronger limbs were sewn in the place of weak human ones, stronger teeth, more vicious heads. And because they were ashamed, because to become what they became was to become inhuman, the surgeons cut out the larynxes of all the poor souls they altered, so that they could not speak of what had been done to them, or what they would do in service of the war. Perhaps they knew, even then, how uncharitable their cause had become. I cannot say—they do not speak of it now.

I know you weep for these things. I weep for them. And more for those brave, gallant souls of Casimira's tribe who underwent such procedures secretly, without glory or fellowship, in order to be trusted by the opposition, in order to fight well, who took mule-legs for her sake, and bear-feet, and frog's heads.

———

Ambuscade Station is a dreary, dank place since there is no zoo to draw the laughing or the moneyed. The shouts of the not-too-distant Troposphere barely penetrate the gloom. The platform is empty, and spiders crawl along the poles, ticking, clicking, and November can almost understand them, they are close to bees in language, but in the end they are beyond her, their paeans to Casimira private and eight-versed.

She stands, and cannot imagine what time the train might come, but she knows the train is the right thing, she knows the girl with blue hair is nearby, and she trusts, she trusts now, that the golden, liquid hymn vibrating within her will call it like a river-lure. *Please*, she thinks, *oh, please*.

The train arrives like an answer, and the doors slide open. She is surprised. It is a long, silver train, bright, new, gleaming like an arrow shot from the moon.

*Would you like to ride upon the Leopard of Little Breezes?* she thinks, and leaps before her stomach can answer.

———

The carriage is lined in silk, red silk, and women in long, glistening masks the color of blood and thick, layered kimonos stand at small tables set with tea services. The tea is red, and there are lumps of black within. A few men and women sit hunched at the tables, and the women look proprietary, caring, possessive of their charges. They glare at her coldly. They offer her nothing.

She walks slowly down the polished floor of the carriage, and as she passes the women with their poised teakettles, they turn their heads as one to regard her with icy disdain. They smell of metal and cherry pits.

"Get out," one of them hisses. "You can't have her."

November runs and steps into the space between carriages, her heart throbbing.

*Where are you, Amaya Sei?*

The next carriage is vast, covered in rice terraces stacking up to a genuine sky, a genuine sun. All along the terraces folk stand in red hats fringed in gold, lined up perfectly along the water's edge, staring down at her with wintry, hurt expressions. She begins to walk under their gaze, but it is very far, the carriage is so long.

"I am thirsty!" she calls out.

A little boy with a jangling hat screams down: "There is nothing for you here! The rice of grief is withered because you have set foot here, where no one wanted you!"

"She wants me!" November cries. "Amaya Sei! I will find her!"

"She is ours! We have made all these things for her! You can't take her away from us!"

And the villagers of the second car let loose long copper ladles from bows of rice roots, and November runs again, she must run, through the pleasant countryside, and even still the ladles strike her and bruise her and the bees within her shriek in terror. A fusillade crashes into the carriage door as she closes it, and November's belly flinches with every blow.

She passes through the carriage of cabbages, and the plants recoil from her. One opens and there is a thing inside it, a word, in black print that wavers like skin crawling: *stranger*. It hisses at her, and ink spatters her already-black cheek. She passes through a carriage of pine trees, and men in long black suits scowl and spit upon her. As she passes them, they reach out to clutch at her coat, her breasts, her hair.

"We do not want you," they slaver.

*Amaya Sei*, she thinks, *is this your kingdom? Amaya Sei, is this your hive?*

November passes through a carriage of crusted white rock and hanging reeds. There is a rabbit-man there, a veteran, she thinks, mashing rice in a barrel with a great hammer. She tries to inch past him, but he blocks her way with a withered paw.

"Please, I am trying to reach Amaya Sei."

"I know, child," he says mildly.

November is surprised again—veterans do not speak.

"Then don't stop me. If you want her so much, let me find her. It is the only way you can have her for good."

"I know that, too."

"Then I'm confused." She touches his long, gray ear; he endures her wounded hand. "Were you in the war?"

"What an interesting question. No, you might say, and yes, you might say. You might say I am embroiled in its final skirmishes even now."

"But you speak."

"I was not in the war, I said. The mochi needed such care in those years, I could not leave it."

"Then why have you such ears, such paws?"

The rabbit looks at November with a chagrined, sorrowing expression. "It is what she expected," he says. "To see a rabbit with a hammer, and rice. I wanted to look right for her. For Amaya Sei. There are still surgeons in the world, and this train has caught a few when they were not looking. As it caught me, on a platform, on a Wednesday morning when the coffee was thick and I was not paying attention. As it caught a war-rabbit, still bound up in its saddle, in the last days of it all, when it bent to snuffle for scraps in the dark. I could not even tell my employers I would not be at my desk. I could not tell my wife or my son that I would be away. I was a candymaker, you know. I like to think the city went sour when I vanished from it, but that is probably not the case."

"In what sense, candymaker, are you fighting the war even now? I am not a warrior, I have not come to fight you."

The rabbit leans in close and brushes her nose with his. It is soft, as a rabbit's ought to be. "Do you not know, even now, what they fought for? There was a time when it was easy to cross the bridges and tunnels into Palimpsest. When you might fall in a river or bleed until you fell through the skin of the earth. When you might dig a hole from China all the way here. But too many came, and the streets were always being renamed, and feral, hungry folk came, with money and polished spears, and they knew words like *empire*, and in killing them half the city was killed, in the ages before ages. All the ways were closed up. Painted over. Barricaded. And there was peace, for so long, so long.

"And then a child named Casimira was born. She should not have been allowed to stay with her family. She was a Braurion. She ought to have been sent out with a new name to haggle with lettuce merchants or bronze-casters. Instead, she grew up in a house that loved her as we love Amaya Sei, and when she was thirteen, she was so lonely that she went to the barricades and began to tear at them with her fingernails. 'It is not right,' she said, 'that all our doors are closed!'

"They stopped her, of course, but Casimira is a creature of will, and she saw in her heart an open city, a city full of the world, full of new people who would love her and new suns in new skies. And she had a billion creatures at her command. Do you know what a thirteen-year-old girl can do when she is alone and frightened and believes she is right? And she wanted it so much. She wanted the immigrants back, and she opened, at last, with a treaty and a pen, under the eye of the shark-general, a single way. And she has waited for twenty years for someone to take it. All we have done and been done to has been for a lonely girl, and there are some of us who say that is enough of grace—that one of us is no longer lonely. We believed that. And now...there is Amaya Sei."

"Are we the first? The first in all that time to come so near to it?"

The rabbit smirks, wiping rice paste from his mallet. "Casimira wanted to choose, of course. She wanted to pick her triumphs by hand."

November swallows that. Half of her is proud; she is worthy, she was chosen. Half of her glowers. "If you want Sei you can have her, rabbit. Casimira may choose all she likes, but she cannot leave Palimpsest, she cannot know us beyond it, how we struggle and suffer. How we choose. I chose. And you cannot have Sei without me," November says.

"I know."

"Then let me pass."

"November Aguilar, help me press the rice for the feast of her. Swing the hammer yourself, and I will let you go. I took ears for her, and paws, and I am delayed in my production, because of love, because of need."

November nods with great solemnity, and steps into the barrel, lifting the hammer over her head and bringing it down hard onto the gluey white masses. It is so heavy, so heavy she can hardly lift it, but she swings and swings until her flesh burns and tears come and she falls back into the paws of the rabbit of the moon, who cleans her with his tongue and sings her the folksongs of the wild glow-worms that live in the Sea of Tranquillity.

———

There is a blue-haired woman sitting in a wide, empty room lined with grass mats. She wears a long, unlined kimono, and her nakedness shines beneath it. Over her face is a long, red mask.

"Amaya Sei?"

"Yes." Her voice is dull, almost drunk.

"My name is November."

"I know. The train told me you were coming."

"What's wrong with you?"

"Partly I drank a great deal of rice wine so that I would not dream, and it did not work. Partly I am afraid."

"Of what?"

"What is in the next car. I . . . I think I know. I think I know. I read a book, and I think it had my future written in it. But I am afraid. And I am so tired. It's so hard, you know . . . to lie down under so many people. It is like taking on passengers. You get so heavy. So bare. And then there is the baby." Sei touches her belly absently.

"What is in the car?"

Sei clears her throat and recites through her mask like a tragedian: "*When new conductors are assigned their first train, they are brought on board on a very cold winter's night when the train is stopped and no one lingers in the cars. The senior engineers gather tightly in the conductor's cabin. They put the earnest young man's hands onto the control console and anoint them with viscous oil from the engine before pulling loose several wires and tying them into knots around the man's fingers. He is then told the secret name of the train, which he may reveal to no one, and his third finger on his left hand is cut, and his blood mingled with the oil, which is then returned to circulation in the engine. In this way the train becomes the beloved of the conductor.*"

"Oh. I see."

"I think this train is lonely, and new. It's like . . . a child. I think its parents left it when they parted ways, and it was . . . looking for me.

Not me, but someone like me, for a long time. For a mother. For a conductor."

"Sei, I have to tell you something important."

"But I don't know if I can bear enough men inside me, enough women in my mouth, to move with this train forever. So many ... it's just so many. It takes so many. My womb aches already. And I think ... I don't think I will really be myself, when I am the conductor. I think I will forget my name. I think my body will open up and flow along the tracks and become metal, become wire. And that means my child will become metal, and wire, and plastic, and never have a name, and never have eyes to open."

"Isn't it what you want? To be a conductor?"

"Yes." Her voice breaks. "But I also want to be Sei."

November breathes deeply; the air of the car is thin and grassy-sweet. "I need to know where you are. Just tell me where you are. In the real world."

There is a long silence, and November can see tears drip from beneath the mask. "Kyoto. I'm in Kyoto."

"Can you come to Rome, do you think? Could you?"

Sei shakes her head. "I don't have any more money, really. I haven't been to work in weeks. I can't."

"Okay, that's okay, Sei. We'll come. Just tell us where to meet you. In Kyoto. You have to tell me now, though, because on the other side I don't speak Japanese, and it's harder."

"Who is *us*?"

"The man with the keys. And the man with glasses. And me, with the bee sting. Who were with you in the frog-woman's shop. Who have gone down into the dark with you. Who have gone into the dark for you. We will come and get you, if you cannot come to us, and carry you into the sun. I promise."

There is another silence, and Sei begins to shake. "There's a shrine," she says finally. "With orange gates, a lot of them. Outside the city. It's called Fushimi Inari. Meet me in the pavilion. I will be there every day at sundown until you come."

November watches as Sei reaches into her kimono and draws out an enormous, waterlogged book. She opens it at a seaweed bookmark and begins to read.

All the pages are blank.

# TWO

# THINGS WHICH ARE
## FULL OF GRACE

The man from New York came on a Tuesday, and Nerezza immediately slammed her bedroom door, refusing to even look at him. He was so thin, November could slip her fingers around his wrist entirely. But his color was high and his eyes gleamed and he had once been a handsome man. She and Ludovico met him at the door and there was a long and awful moment of quiet, knowing that anything she said to Oleg Sadakov would be inexplicable to Ludo. She would not do that to him, would not make him an outsider. Not now, not after he awoke serene, radiant—and without a tongue, blood spattering the immaculate sheets, the muscle gone as though it had never been. Nerezza stared at him for a long time, and he held her gaze. November did not want to know what their silence said.

But if Ludo did not speak, she would not. Her hands, her face, her body, all knew the grief of having been stolen, and she would spare him her old pains. November instead took them both in her arms and the three of them stood for a moment, their heads pressed together, their arms hanging limp around each other's waists. Ludo bit his lip. He kissed the top of November's head with a rough tenderness; she laid her head in the crook of Oleg's shoulder.

*Things which are full of grace*, she thinks. *Mary. Orchids. The sea when it is calm. Frost, ruins, virginity. Us. Us. We are, we are so full of it we shine.*

She was hardly aware she did it, the motion was so inevitable. She led them to the long, hard couch and both men fell against her, full also of exhausted want. Oleg kissed her lightly, hesitant, unsure. Ludo held her, stroking the back of her neck, his need already pressing against her. She kissed Oleg more fervently, as though she could push prayers into him, and a cry of recognition and half-spasmic joy ripped from his lips. Oleg whispered her name, and she could hardly bear his joy in finding, in the sacrament he made of her silly name.

November tried to be the bold one, the brave one. She was not good at it—she fumbled with belts and angles, trying to open herself enough for both of them. She took Oleg in her mouth, his cock thin and hard and earnest as the rest of him, and Ludo entered her from behind as she closed her eyes, rocking back and forth, into and onto and between them. She thought, idly, that this might have been considered ugly, filthy, a slatternly thing to do. Yes, slattern, she enjoyed that word, like a thing hurled. But it felt profound to her, a completed circuit, and she knew without seeing it that Ludo and Oleg found each other's hands over the borders of her body, and there would be time for them, too, in the small rooms of this house, time enough for all of them before Japan and the endless orange gates that waited there.

Oleg called her name again, and Ludo moaned a half-mangled, tongueless version of it, all vowels, and in their coupling and tripling was an orgy of naming, Adamic, atavistic, Edenites with a world of stars and bread and salt to name and label and list in their proper places.

# Signe-de-Renvoi

Signe-de-Renvoi

**THERE IS A HOLE IN THE CENTER OF PALIMPSEST.**

Which is to say, there is a hole in the center of me. Surely you suspected before now who spoke. Who always speaks.

I do not mind the hole. It is like a fontanel, where all the parts of my skull come together, and do not fit exactly, not exactly, but well enough. The Albumen drains into this place, and on the other side of the world, a single stone weeps white. The river is thick and the reeds are recalcitrant enough that it long ago became a great Delta, and in this Delta is a city, a small city, a hidden and secret place within the great and sprawling city which has had so many names.

My boys are so close to it now. The gates can smell them. I have let them cheat. I held back the shadows like curtains so that they could meet before they ought to have, before they met the girl with the riverbanks on her face. I was too eager, too eager to see them together, like characters in a play. I could not wait for the fourth act. Will you forgive me? Even I require absolution, even I.

---

There is a little harbor here, places to tie boats. All creatures need boats who are not fish, and even I am not a fish. I watch them with a dozen eyes as they knot their little ship to the pier. I watch them climb onto the long grass of the Delta. You're here, my boys, it will be all right now, I promise. I will look after you. I always have, haven't I?

———

Ludovico helps Oleg up onto the strand, and there are men and women there watching them, with long, outlandish hair braided up and out like electrical wire, with smooth faces and clothes spangled in stars. They just watch, they do not move. There are houses clustered in patches like mushrooms, with round windows and broad lawns. There are strawberry gardens and cucumbers growing long and fat. It is a pleasant place. Starlight flickers over chimneys puffing sage-smoke. The Albumen crashes into the gaping hole in the center of the city a distance off, a waterfall like snow, and three little mills turn at its crest.

Oleg walks to the nearest man. He is short, mustached, his cheeks round and friendly, a pocketwatch chain dangling absentmindedly from his pocket.

"Where is Lyudmila?"

The affable man's whiskers droop. "Now," he says, "which would you prefer? I can pretend I haven't the foggiest, welcome you to Signe-de-Renvoi, plate you up a nice helping of beet-greens and pan-fried koi, and pour you wine that'll make you believe in God. We'll have a nice evening and you can be on your way, whatever way that is. Or I can tell you that she's just in that house there, and she's been crying for weeks over you, and you'll run off before I finish talking and there'll be no beets for anyone—"

But Oleg is already gone. The man chuckles behind him, and Ludovico tries to keep up, but Oleg does not want him there. She is his sister, and the door of the little house makes a satisfying sound as he slams it in Ludo's poor, baffled face.

Lyudmila is sitting in a large green chair, and indeed she is crying, and there is a kettle on in the rear room, and beet-greens sizzling in a pan with golden, buttery koi. She looks up at him with reddened eyes.

"Tell me why," he says softly.

"Why what?" She sniffles, wiping her nose with her sleeve.

"Why they made you. Why you came to me."

"What do you want, Oleg? You are so difficult! You are why we have to have this place, why we have fought to carve it out of a rushing river and three blades of grass. It is so exhausting to be always *guessing*. I ran away because you wanted something to chase. I did not come back because you knew you did not deserve it. I am only crying because I thought you would want it." Abruptly, she smiles brilliantly, abject joy spilling over her face. "I can be overjoyed to see you, too, or scorn you and make you grovel, I can whip you like a horse to do your penance. Just tell me, just tell me, please."

"Mila, stop it!"

"I came to you, Oleg, *I* came to you, a whole city in one body, because you were so alone, and you missed her so much. I wanted you to love me, *me*, the girl from Novgorod and the city, together, inseparable, the child of their mingling. I wanted you to be happy. I made shoulders and feet and breasts and hair out of the substance of you. I did my best."

"Why me?"

Lyudmila cocks her head to one side, finchlike. "Who said it was just you? I am a Pecia. One manuscript in many pieces, many copies. I am Palimpsest, many pieces in one manuscript. I do it for everyone who weeps and longs and wants. I cannot turn my back on want. It calls me, as though I were a unicorn and it a virgin. It is the least I can do—it is so hard to get here, you know. I wanted you. You wanted your sister. It was easy for me."

"I wanted my real sister, in the real world, as she has always been, in her red dress and her wet hair."

Lyudmila stands and crosses to him. She takes her face in his hands and her eyes are so big, so gentle and sorry, and she kisses him like a sweetheart, like a good woman courting a lost soul. "Oleg," she whispers, "my poor boy. My poor, poor child. There is no Lyudmila in that world. There has never been. Little Mila died before you were born and she never left the cities of the dead. She works in a hat shop there and has a little cat. You take pills to keep your hallucination away, and they do not always work, so she appears to come and go. You, in that place called New York, have seen and heard many things that are not there, and that is what they call madness."

Oleg shudders and sobs without sound or tears against her, and she smells so much like his Mila, of wet reeds and high clouds, and he did not want to hear this, he did not want to hear it on the boat and he does not want to hear it now. He buries his face in her breast, seeking her comfort, blindly, knowing it to be true, unable to turn his heart to look it in the eye.

"We come here, Oleg. The Pecia, when we are not wanted anymore. We plant strawberries and raise goats. We make holiday cakes and marry and have our dances known to no other. We are Pecia; together we are one long book of marvelous things. But I want to be Lyudmila. We all want to be what we were made to be. It is in our nature to want such things. We are set in motion, we cannot be stopped, and we want to fulfill our part. To love the crying, wretched folk who stumble into us, into this city, into the body of Palimpsest which is also streets and avenues and cliffs and a river and a very deep hole. You tell the city so many things, secret things, like lovers curled up in its arms, in my arms. How can I give in return less than my own secret, best things?"

"I am sorry I hurt you."

"You did not hurt me, Oleg. Unless you want to have hurt me. At your word bruises will bloom on my belly and blood will trickle from my cheeks. Or I will kiss you and tell you stories about the Prince of Drowning, who is a dashing fellow with blue boots, and we will eat fish together and plant rhubarb under the moon."

Oleg kisses her sternum, her neck, her cheek, her eyelids. He wants to choose something brighter, shinier. Something doctors would approve of, would judge "progress." But she is so close, and she smells like a river, and he is not a doctor. "Be her. Be my Mila. Forget, forget that you were ever a Pecia, forget everything in you that is Palimpsest and be my sister, be from Novgorod, be a dead girl who loves me. And let me forget, too. When I see you again, let me forget that I knew you were a false Mila. Let me forget that you told me she was never real. Let me believe forever that you are my own girl, who never left me. Let me forget it all. There can be no love between strangers. Be Lyudmila."

The Pecia closes her eyes and tears tremble in her lashes. She smiles and the room quavers from the sadness of it. Oleg kisses her mouth and she returns it, hungrily, as hungrily as the dead ever are for warmth and blood and living, breathing lovers. She clutches the small of his back to her and pulls him onto the great green chair, where he can taste, on her tongue, the Volkhov, flowing muddy and sweet and deep between them.

# THREE

# A House of No Words

Oleg spent half a day helping November decide whether or not a suitcase was strictly necessary. They decided to err on the side of caution, and packed each of them a change of clothes and toothbrushes. She was not what he thought she would be, the thing so full of golden electricity that he could feel in Palimpsest just beyond the borders of himself. She was a ruin to look at, and he supposed he was too. They had all paid so much to cross the river before them. Two coins for each of them, perhaps so that the other one, the Japanese girl they did not yet know, could cross freely, painlessly, and the ferryman never catch her eye.

Ludo had given Oleg a small key, a present—it unlocked nothing, but was beautiful, small and exquisite, silver and old. He wore it around his neck now, and felt in small part that it was meant to fit within him, to slip between his bones somehow and force him open.

He had not seen Lyudmila in Italy. It is so much water for her to cross, he thought. She must have been frightened. It was easier to think of her keeping house in the New York apartment than to consider for even a moment what the woman who was and was not Lyudmila had said to him. *Only a little while longer,* he thought, *and it will not be important.*

Oleg ate ravenously now, eggs and bread and tomatoes and a dozen kinds of cheese, bacon and roasted chicken. He did not know how to speak to the lady of the house, the severe, shield-faced woman named Nerezza who had been there, silent and staring, at the lock, who had watched them bring a knife so close to his throat, who spoke perfect English but refused to speak it to him. Whenever he looked at her, she shrugged as if to say: *I have done what I have done. Eat my food, take my home, you can do no more to me than has already been done.*

Their days, for the moment, were mainly stolen kisses and laughter and long stretches of wrapping themselves around each other. November did not often talk to him, as she could not talk to Ludo, and so the barriers seemed natural to extend. They became not barriers, but a house of no words that sheltered them all. Oleg always brought November tea afterward. He wanted to. He needed to, to serve her, to be her Pecia, to be enough that what she had done to bring them all this far, what she had lost, had been worth it.

Ludo took him walking in the ruins, and though he did not speak, their kisses were frank and unfettered behind cypress and oak and grapevine, and the light, the light in those places was the impossible light of the rafters of heaven, and such lamps showed through, such lamps, and such laughing.

# Signe-de-Renvoi

Signe-de-Renvoi

**THE CITY SQUARE OF SIGNE-DE-RENVOI** looks out onto the great fall of the Albumen into the earth, ringed in both fig trees and pome-granate trees, so that the air is always sharp and rich and sweet. There are dances there, and when the skirts swirl under the high, high moon, there is nothing in the world like the blue lace that shows beneath them. A charming, handsome woman of a certain age keeps everyone's glasses full, a champagne brewed from pears and frozen grapes. Her hair is so long she has braided it all the way around her body, twice, and this serves as enough clothing for her. She has a pet, a stately old tiger with his claws long pulled, his teeth long fallen out. He is a relic of tigerhood, a bygone age when great cats knew calculus and dactylic hexameter and held a court of dreams in the jungle.

She has forgotten her name. I brought her here so very long ago, and when she died I made a copy, and another, and another. She could not speak when she lived, and I have not felt right making her copies speak, and so we have never conversed but in the silent ways of lovers. Sometimes I think that the war struck half my people dumb in her name, in her honor. But that is surely fancy.

The tiger lived, though, and I cannot explain that but I feel close to him, comradely. We have both lived so long, we old cats. We court of dreams.

I do not know why I have done these things. I do not always know why I behave as I do. Does anyone?

But I cannot let her go.

She is there tonight, dancing naked with her braids undone and flying like black serpents. I watch her in the body of an affable man with a loose pocketwatch chain, through his grandfatherly eyes, his age and his wisdom. I dance with her in his feet, and in her perfect ear I whisper the name I know but that she has lost like an earring:

*Chanthou, Chanthou, my love, my wife.*

---

Ludovico watches the village dance. He would like to join in, but he does not feel right about it. He stands by the pier waiting for Oleg, patiently, as only he can be patient.

*Which is not very patient,* he reminds himself. *But for Oleg I can try.*

"And not for me?" comes a voice across the grass, and he knew it would come, he had prepared for it, he had tested its weight on the river and found that he thought he could bear it.

Lucia stands near him in a yellow dress, the dress of Ostia and the pecan-colored couch. Her skin is lion-golden and her hair a riot of loose, dark curls. He says nothing to her—he cannot. The mound of his severed tongue still aches in his mouth.

*You are not Lucia,* he thinks. *Please don't tease me. You're not her.*

"Of course not," Lucia says as though he spoke. "She would never come here. It is not ... within her circuit of fashion."

She steps into his arms with all the natural grace of a long-wed woman, and their kiss is genuine if she is not, deep and long, and he takes great good from it.

"I'm not Calypso, if that's what you're thinking," she says.

He laughs despite himself. It is a broken sound, like a plate falling. Even in this, she is a perfect copy—she presents the classical reference like a gift, a way of explaining herself, and so it is a gift.

"I do not come to offer you immortality and love of me until the riotous death of the magnetic poles in exchange for your humanity. There are no such choices. I am an honest city, I think you can at least grant that."

He nods, and holds her hand as they walk along the little wharf.

"I want to give you what you need, Ludo. It is important to me, as I think you and I will shortly be friends for a very long time. You gave your voice for me, like the mermaid in the fairy tale. I was charmed. I was wooed. I admit it. And you are so close to me now, it is like Christmas Eve. Don't you feel it?"

He nods, helpless to do more. They are quiet, and she skips a stone or two down the cream-churned river.

She stops and stands on her tiptoes to look him in the eye. She is so young and her brow is so clear. There are no frown lines in her.

"Are you ready?" she says, and her voice is strong and steady. "I love you. I have loved you for nine years, and I knew it was nine and not eight. I only said that to hurt you. That summer in Ostia was the core of us, and it was shining and warm and the color of pecan shells. All of this I did in a frenzy, a madness, but it did not touch us, in our walls, our lair. There, I was yours alone, and I was happy. I am your beast, and you are my saint, and I forgive you, for that is what noble beasts do, and I am a noble beast. And beasts forget, too. It is only the sadness of saints that they cannot."

She kisses him, and her breasts are warm and soft against his body. "I love you, and I am your wife, and I forgive you of all the sins of this world, all the sins we invented just to commit within our cave. I love you," and the light of her eyes seems to shift to something darker and cleverer than his Lucia, something vast and old. "I love you, Ludovico. In a world without end. I love you."

She walks away from him, up the low rise toward the dancing and the lights, and she is carrying her sandals by the straps as she did when last he saw that dress, the torchlight on her hair like an absolution.

# THE FAVOR OF VESTA

I will never forgive you," Nerezza said, clutching her wrist in her hand so tightly that it left red crescent moons in her skin. They had gone for coffee, because she could not bear the house.

Ludo tried to smile at her, his eel-girl, lost in the brumey water, circling herself in the dark.

"I have had to listen to the three of you fucking and laughing for days," Nerezza snapped, "and I am sick to death of you."

He was quiet for a long while. Why had he not taken them to his apartment? *Because it is Lucia's place, and it is pleasant to be among people who know the same secrets. Agostino, Anoud. Even Nerezza.*

Ludo took out a pad of paper and a pen. He wrote, in fine, even lines:

*Is that why you gave us up to Ululiro and those men? To be rid of us?*

Nerezza shrugged. She did not look away; she was not ashamed. "Why should you be different? Why should the rest of us be chained to the earth while you go free? I have done what I have done. It is mine to own and pay for. You lived."

He reached for her hand, and she bore that touch, and so he thought perhaps she was not utterly lost to him.

He wrote: *It is not so easy for me after all, you see.*

"I do see," she relented. "But I do not forgive you. And you should not forgive me."

Ludo wrote: *I want to give you what you need, Nerezza. It is important to me.*

"You haven't the first idea what I need, Ludo. How dare you?"

He squeezed her hand and lifted it to his lips, kissed it, held it as though with that hand, all he was allowed, he could hold all of her. Ludovico let her hand fall and wrote furiously:

*Have I ever told you why I go to the Forum? I go to look at the temple of the Vestals. They lived there, secluded, not just virgins, though that was important, but keepers of wills and historical papers. They wore white; they wore their purity like shields. They were the daughters of Vesta, Vesta, who kept the hearth. And as long as they were inviolable, the city was kept safe, kept whole. Forever. And maybe if they had—because they failed, sometimes, because they were young and they could not choose their nunnery, and they were punished for it, even killed—Rome would not have lost the favor of Vesta and fallen into the dark. Because it was the hearth-goddess who left them without light, without fire. Do you understand?*

Nerezza's eyes were full of tears, but they did not fall, they were hard, harder than anything he had within him. Her eyes were sharp and dark, reflected into crystal. She shook her head.

*They could not live in the city, Nerezza. They could not drink at the festivals, or take lovers in alleys, or eat mackerel in the market. But without them, the city fell into the dark and the cold, into a hole in the world. Because they were inviolable, the city lived within the circuit of their skin, and they kept it safe, like a mother, like a goddess.*

She was crying in earnest then, angrily, harshly, without sound, without forgiveness, but she did not let go of his hand.

He kissed her and kissed her again, and slowly, with a small smile, as though it was a joke shared long ago between them, he kissed the tears from her cheek with his round mouth.

———

Ludovico left her in the café, drying her face, composing it again into eelskin and electricity. He stepped into his taxi and sped off through the Roman streets toward the airport, washed with light, past the ruins of ruins, the city built on its own grave, built out of itself, time and again, a world without end.

# VERSO:

## Young-Eyed Cherubins

# ONE

# THE FLAYED HORSE

Amaya Sei sits in the broad open pavilion of the Fushimi Inari shrine. She folds her hands over her stomach, trying, for the hundredth time, to decide. One thousand blaze-orange *torii* gates open up behind her, winding up the mountain like a long tunnel into fire. Spiders of improbable size string their rain-colored webs in the corners of the gates. They are pale green, though that means nothing here, still it makes Sei smile. There are huge circles under her eyes, and she feels ill, sore in every joint, in every part. *I am the Kami of Engines,* she thinks to herself, *and I have come to take the winds of my lovers into my belly, and to burn.*

————

This is the eighth day she has waited at the shrine. The stone foxes—she has heard there are thirty-three thousand of them on the mountain, an exact number, yet infinite, infinitely variable vulpine faces, and they regard her now with familiar acceptance, like a family dog who has come to love a frequent visitor. The evening is crisp, the leaves almost all brown now, the persimmons flaccid and smeared on the stones. There is a belt of pale gold around the horizon, and above it, all is blue, a universe of blue, like the light at the bottom of a lake.

————

But today they do come, walking through the festooned gate of the shrine, three of them, holding hands. *They are so beautiful,* she thinks. *So strong. I have paid such a price for their easy passage,* she thinks. *It was worth it, that they have not suffered as I have.* The woman's skin looks as though it was burned many years ago, but it is healed now, and shining. She is wearing gloves in the cold. One of the men is tall and older, with glasses and poor posture. The other is younger, sad-looking, very thin. But they know her, they know her immediately, and she runs to them, as fast as she can, and despite everything she flings herself into their arms, and kisses the man with glasses as though he is her most desperate wish. He does not give her his tongue, and she does not seek it. And then the woman, whose mouth tastes like the sugar-candies her mother loved, and then the young man, who circles her waist with his arm and lifts her off the ground.

"Come on," she says in Japanese, but they understand her meaning, and Sei leads them into the tunnel of gates, up and up, one thousand of them, into the crystalline blue night, into the infinite foxes, into the green spiders and the flame-colored pillars. Without knowing why, she begins to run ahead of them, and in her belly the first quavering movement comes with the pounding of her feet. *Oh,* she thinks, *oh, you poor thing. I'm so sorry. You are a terrible toll to pay. I don't think it will hurt. Just... imagine a book at the bottom of a lake. Fish read it. It is your book, all your own, and you can find such wonderful things written there...*

And she is filled with terror, and filled with joy, with the brightness of their kisses, with the fluttering of her child, with the light of the first stars, and—

———

And Sei is speeding at the head of the Flyleaf Line, the unpredictable child-train, through the underground and up into the city, the elevated rails, the sassafras-scented air. She cuts her hand with the edge of a steel disc and laughs softly as oil bubbles up from beneath the controls. She presses her palm to it and the shriek of ecstasy that erupts from train and girl shatters three streetlamps as they pass. She sinks into the arms of the Third Rail, and her legs seem to flow into the circuitboard, and her hair seems to flow back over the body of the locomotive, and her arms are pressed back against her sides so that her face, the face of the train, the new train, can feel the wind dancing by.

At Oathusk Station, they will say they saw a train fly. They saw it jump the tracks without the smallest hesitation, jump into the air as though it had waited a lifetime for that jump, and race into the tall grass. The black-faced sheep scattered, and the raspberries exulted as the train that is Sei who is the train moved like light toward the mountains and beyond.

The sound of its whistle, they will say, is like a mother and a child singing together.

# TWO

# THE UNHAPPY ROOK

S ei is so young, and November kisses her like she will
never get a chance again. The *torii* gates stretch up into
the night like one gate echoed over and over, a stutter of
gates, and the fox statues grin down from their pedestals.
When Sei begins to run ahead into the shadows, November
can see them, she is sure she can see them, she would swear it,
the foxes, one by one, turn their stone heads and bow to them,
their little ears flattened against their granite skulls.

She takes Ludovico's hand and begins to run, too, up and up
and up, and the spiders all around, if she could but hear them,
call her name like a rosary, and—

———

And Casimira sweeps her up with a laugh like a war trumpet, and
sets her down again in a vast red room full of brown notebooks and
printing presses and bees crawling the walls. November opens the
books, one of them, two, but they are blank.

"Didn't you notice the street names, my darling girl?" Casimira
beams. "Enough nouns make a verb, and we have made a verb, and
it is us."

The house tugs at November's hand and presses it to his little lips. Hesitantly, with held breath, he extends his pink tongue and licks it gently.

November looks for Ludovico, but he is not there. Her bees fly from her fingertips, into the city, seeking him in her name. She smiles in the arms of Casimira, arms tight and strong and undeniable, arms like victory. They will find him.

———

In years to come the bees of Palimpsest will be utterly changed, and to be stung by one will be to be honored beyond dreams of grace. On their wings will be printed in infinitesimally delicate script an encyclopedia of Palimpsest, written in a high room in a house that practices its smiles, a high room the house kept hidden for all of them, a lair but not a cave. In the encyclopedia are endless lists of the city's wonders, and in those lists are stories upon stories, and to be stung is to know all of them, and weep for the knowing of.

# THREE

# THE THREE OF TENEMENTS

The dark descends so fast it steals Oleg's breath, and when they begin to run ahead he is afraid to be left behind, he cannot be left behind, and through the wafting incense of the shrine below he wills his skinny, weakened legs to carry him, to carry him toward them, after them, into the shadows, into the blue, into the mouths of all those foxes, who seem to have his own face, smiling back at him, and seem to be saying:

*She is waiting for you. She is waiting, Olezhka.* His chest burns as though his heart has been pierced by a spear of flame, and—

————

And Lyudmila is sitting naked on a broad, dry bed piled with quilts of blue and silver stars. His sister, her arms open, her eyes shining. She speaks to him in Russian and he understands her, falls into her, kisses her laughing, and she laughs with him. When he is inside her he will see snow falling through torchlight on the edge of the Volkhov, which never took any child's breath, which never was anything but a band of silver light in the dark.

In days to come the locks of Palimpsest will fall in love. They will refuse the keys made for them and insist that their owners follow the Albumen until they find an enormous river barge with a canopy of bronze silk, where a thin young man and his wife with hair the color of bread beat keys from the most extraordinary substances, from baleen and dried river mud, sodalite and beryl and bird bones, king's crowns and prison bars, hazel branches and willow wands and corset stays and gold and silver and glass.

No lock will settle for less than its most and dearest beloved.

# FOUR

# THE ARCHIPELAGO

*Don't leave me*, Ludovico thinks when November starts to run after Sei. But of course, of course she would not. She is his Isidore, and she will lead him into the world. She grabs his hands and they run like children, as though there is a wonderful game ahead and the whole day to come for its playing. November laughs and he thinks the sound of it might shatter him, so high and so sweet, inviolable. In just another moment she will be able to speak to him, in just another moment she will turn to him and he will understand every syllable in the etymology of her, and—

———

And he wakes on a wooden dais, a huge circle of oak raised slightly above the street. He stares around him, the empty air of an early morning, before anyone is awake, except bakers and postmen. An old woman stands in her doorway, her right leg a huge, twisted bear-limb, holding a tray of steaming, frosted cake. Tears fill up her eyes and roll down her fat cheeks. She drops the cake. Her mouth hangs open.

Klavdia goes inside and snatches another from the window. She comes running to him, finally, finally, after all this time. Casimira promised her, and here he is.

He swallows her cake, drinks her tea.

The war is over.

———

As Ludovico eats and the old woman fusses over him, her fur bristling against his leg, Ludo turns his eyes north, down the long avenues, to a house with high green spires. *It is fitting*, he supposes, *that I arrived here, in the old place. Out of all of them, I am the traditionalist.*

A bee alights softly on his knee. The old bear-woman grins at him. She gives him a little curtsey. A second bee drifts in, and a third.

*November*, he thinks. He lets the bees coax him onto the street as the first traffic of the morning comes screeching, careening in, and walks up the lane, toward his beloved, his ibex, who leapt from such a far height, and landed on her horns.

# Obsolescence and Unutterable

Obsolescence and Unutterable

THE SUBURBS OF PALIMPSEST SPREAD OUT from the edges of the city proper like ladies' fans. First the houses, uniformly red, in even lines like veins, branching off into lanes and courts and cul-de-sacs. There are parks full of grass that smells like oranges and little creeks filled with floating roses, blue and black. Children scratch pictures of antelope-footed girls and sparrow-winged boys on the pavement, hop from one to the other. Their laughter spills from their mouths and turns to autumnal leaves, drifting lazily onto wide lawns. The sun glowers red in the east, leaving scarlet shadows on all their cheeks.

There are parks, of course, between the houses. Suburbs create children out of ether, and they require the space. Carousels of bone and fur mirror the exact musculature of horses and giraffes and three-toed sloths, so that the children will naturally be inclined to ride such creatures when they are grown and such a thing becomes a necessity. There, just there—a little girl with violet ribbons like reins in her hair is telling her brother that mother will be away tonight, and they may sneak into the city to dance with women with the heads of white foxes. Wicked child!

Eventually the houses fade into fields: amaranth, spinach, blueberries. Shaggy cows graze; bell-hung goats bleat. Palimpsest is ever hungry. In the morning, milk will splash white as a river into a hundred pails and more, butter will come creamy and yellow, and bread will rise as thick as a heart. There are orchards, peaches and plums, cherries and apples like garnets. There are ponds full of fish, their eyes black and depthless. The farms go on further than the houses, out and out and out.

But these too fade as they extend like arms outstretched, fade into the empty land not yet colonized by the city, not yet peopled, not yet known. The empty meadows stretch to the horizon, pale and dark, rich and soft.

---

The war is over.

This was the last of it, and I have told you all you need to know of the breaking of the doors. Find me, find me in black and secret places. I am here; I am waiting. I want no more than any city: to thrive.

Come. Come.

Look out, over my outermost fields, my borderless borders—I am vast enough to contain you.

A wind picks up, blowing hot and dusty and salt-scented. Gooseflesh rises over miles and miles of barren skin.

## ACKNOWLEDGMENTS

This book owes debts to many people, books being the profligate creatures they are, forever leaving their authors to pay their bills. And so I must settle the tab.

Thank you to Ekaterina Sedia, who once asked me to write her a story about a city.

To Christopher Barzak, an invaluable friend and resource.

To Juliet Ulman, my benevolent editor.

To the members of the Blue Heaven Writers Workshop, especially Paolo Bacigalupi and Daryl Gregory.

To S. J. Tucker, whose music continually explains to me what I've written.

To everyone who has supported me, offline and online, allowed me into their homes and their hearts, held me up, made me tea, and listened to (and read) my nonsense: we are all of us Palimpsest, a strange and marvelous city created only when we are together.

And finally, ever and always, to Dmitri Zagidulin, who doesn't like to be called a muse.

ABOUT THE AUTHOR

Born in the Pacific Northwest in 1979, Catherynne M. Valente is the author of the Orphan's Tales series, as well as three other novels and five books of poetry. She currently lives in southern Maine with her partner and two dogs.